Fire
on the
Ice

Rose Harvey

BookReality
Helping Writers Become Independent Authors

To all the readers who have been waiting so patiently for
the final instalment of Nina's story.
I hope that you enjoy reading it
as much as I did writing it.

Also by Rose Harvey

The Ice Flame Trilogy
Heir to the Ice Flame
Heart of Ice

Other Titles
Robin

Prologue

I dreamed that I had died.

The throne room was wide and open, with tall windows of stained glass and pale stone walls. The floor was white marble, and at the far end of the room stood a throne of polished ice. Behind the throne, the ice formed a circle of Hoarfrost, which stretched out to the balcony and down the mountainside towards the glacier far below. In my dream, the flaming embers on the Hoarfrost wavered and died, a faint wisp of smoke all that remained.

On the throne, a man dressed in dazzling splendour reclined indolently, flicking through scrolls with disinterest. He had a high forehead and a receding hairline, with close-set eyes and a mouth that was more inclined to frown than smile. When he smelt the smoke he turned, surprised, and then let out a loud cry of victory.

'Guards,' he bellowed, 'Prepare the palace and the kingdom for my coronation. At last, at long last, the Heir to the Ice Flame is dead.'

From my position high above, I noted the cold, furious mixture of joy and success that spread across his features. If I could have felt anything I might have been scared, but instead I was floating away, hearing his words echo out across the throne room and then being shouted from the rooftops.

Dead. The Heir to the Ice Flame is dead.

Part One

Chapter One: Erik

She was gone.

That was all that I could get through my head in the days and weeks that followed the Trackers' attack on the Underdark. In my mind I relived it, feeling her hand pull away and the desperation of searching, ducking between blade and arrow, calling and calling for her. One of the Tracker's blades caught my side and I stumbled, rolling away, kicking out to knock him down. As he fell, I pulled the blade out and swung, the blood splattering against the ground. He gave a low moan and lay there, jerking slightly. But there was no time to stand around, another Tracker came towards me, grinning with maniacal energy.

'Erik!' Jesse called, 'duck!' She had taken one of the crossbows from a fallen Tracker and was aiming over my shoulder. I dropped down, wincing as the cut in my side twinged, and she fired, piercing the Tracker through the neck. I watched as he tumbled, frozen. I had not seen death like this before.

'Where's Nina?' Jesse asked, loading another bolt into the crossbow. 'She was with you last.'

'I don't know,' I replied, slashing out at a passing Tracker and catching his leg. 'I think she got pulled away.'

Stupid, stupid, stupid, the voice in my head railed again and again. *You lost her. It was your job to stay with her.*

'We need to find her,' Jesse said, as she aimed and fired into the crowd. Together we began to make our way to the edge of the fighting, watching each other's backs as the Dark Elves and Trackers fought around us.

'Look,' I said suddenly, pointing at a tunnel up ahead. There was a flickering light coming from deep inside.

'Erik, Jesse,' Rakael was leaning over a Tracker's body nearby, 'where's Nina?'

'We were looking for her,' Jesse said, 'have you seen her?'

Rakael shook her head, and then paused, her expression going blank as she pointed at the tunnel, 'I saw a Tracker coming out from there. Maybe...'

I didn't wait for her to finish, but raced towards the tunnel mouth, grabbing a lantern from the wall and leaping over several bodies. The smell of burning was growing stronger and I covered my mouth, coughing.

If I hadn't had the lantern, I would have missed her. She was leaning against the tunnel wall, one hand clasped over a wound in her stomach. Her red dress was stained a deeper crimson, and her skin was deathly pale. Beside her lay a curved blade, similar to the one I held. The kind the Trackers used.

I dropped to the ground beside her, a wordless, primal scream ripping out of me. Her eyes stared past me, seeing something beyond our world and I knew deep down that she had gone somewhere I could not follow. But I couldn't accept it.

'No, no, no,' I didn't care that I was crying. I slapped her cheek, pressed down repeatedly on her chest as Stefan had taught me to do, tried to breathe for her, blowing air into her lungs. 'No, no, no. Wake up, Gods, Nina, *wake up*. Come back. *Please* come back.'

But she didn't answer. Ever since she walked into that godforsaken kitchen at Mister MacMillan's inn and had given me a new name and a new identity, she had been there. She hadn't always been perfect– she nagged and argued sometimes, and she clearly didn't understand the importance of having a protector– but she *had* been a sister. Nina had always stuck with me, but now she had left, and by the Gods it *hurt*. It was like losing Ma and Pa all those winters ago, but somehow worse.

'We were supposed to protect each other,' I whispered brokenly, '*don't go.*'

Some of those annoying white butterflies that thrived in the Underdark were fluttering down onto her head, her arms, the jagged wound in her stomach, stepping over her with their horrible little feet. I waved them away angrily.

'Get off her, get off!'

'Erik?' Jesse called, 'What…'

'By the Gods,' Rakael gasped as she and Jesse reached us, 'no.'

Jesse let out a choked sound, 'Nina.'

'Where's that smell coming from?' Rakael asked, covering her nose with a hand and peering down the tunnel towards the flickering light.

'Erik,' Jesse murmured as Rakael moved away to investigate the source of the burning, 'Erik, you have to let her go.'

'No,' I retorted, 'She's not…she can't be…'

'She's gone, Erik,' Jesse was crying now too. 'She's d…'

'*No!*' I shouted, refusing to acknowledge it, hating Jesse for not even trying to save her. She tried to pull me back and I fought her away, holding Nina tighter, her lifeless body heavy and cold.

'Jesse,' Rakael's voice came to us from further down the tunnel, 'I need you to come here. *Now.*' Her tone brooked no argument and so Jesse left, wiping away her own tears with the back of a hand.

I don't know how long they were gone for. I didn't take much notice of what happened around me. I could hear the faint sounds of fighting coming to an end and people running back and forth behind me. I didn't care. All that mattered was that I kept her safe. Albeit too late.

Some knight you're going to be.

Sometimes, when I felt small, I heard Mister MacMillan's voice in my head, reminding me that my dreams were pointless.

What would a useless whelp like you know about being a knight? You couldn't protect someone if you tried. Look at what happened to her – you failed.

I clasped her hand tightly, sobs racking through me. She was so cold, her blood stained my fingers but I didn't care. I continued to hold on until stronger hands came to pull me away.

'You can't do anything for her, Erik,' Leif said, 'Let us take her somewhere fitting.'

I watched as Tobias and Christoff lifted her onto a stretcher and followed them out to the cavern where not an hour ago we had been dancing.

A silent hush fell over the cavern as we emerged from the tunnel, and then more cries began to fill the air. But the Dark Elves weren't just looking at Nina. Their masks were turned to look behind us, at the figure on the next stretcher. Lying there, in a pile of twisted, burned metal, was King Lysander.

'The Trackers used some of that powder and set it alight,' Jesse was telling one of the guards, 'by the time we got there, he was gone. It took a long time to put the flames out.'

The bodies of the Trackers were scattered around the ground, mostly ignored for the moment, as the Dark Elves had been focussing on tending to their own dead and wounded first. On seeing the king's body however, a mournful dirge filled the air.

'The king is dead,' the Chief Counsel was intoning, 'King Lysander is dead.'

'Erik,' Tobias said over his shoulder, breaking my attention away from the Dark Elves, 'you should go and break the news to her. It's best coming from you.'

I felt a heavy weight settle around my shoulders. 'You should bring Nina back to her room. She will want to…'

I couldn't finish.

'Go, boy,' Christoff said gruffly, 'Go and make sure that she knows.' I nodded and navigated my way around the wailing Dark Elves and crying wounded, running towards the boats.

Lisette was mending one of Nina's gowns when I entered their room. She glanced up at me, surprised as I abruptly pushed the door open. It took a moment for her to take in the blood stains, the dripping wound on my side and the tear tracks on my cheeks. She rose shakily, putting the mending down on the bedside table, next to a vase of orchids.

'Lisette,' I didn't know how to begin, how to put the unthinkable into words. She reached out and grasped my hands, turning them over and inspecting them closely. Then she looked at me, her eyes large and questioning.

'I tried,' I stammered, 'I was with her and then she was gone. Nina, she's...'

There was the sound of footsteps outside and Lisette rushed to the door, pushing me aside in her haste. The mad hope in her eyes was painful to see, the desperate longing to prove me wrong.

Tobias and Leif laid Nina down on her bed, while Christoff held Lisette as the body was arranged. When the men had stepped back, she thrust Christoff's hands away and fell beside Nina, pulling her into a tight embrace and rocking her back and forth. A high-pitched mewling filled the air and tore into me, as Lisette's tears fell in an uncontrollable rush. Her hands hovered over the wound, as if she had the power to wipe it away, to bring life back into Nina's cheeks. I noticed one of the white butterflies had nestled itself amongst Nina's hair, trying to hide in the thick streak of white.

'Get away,' I said harshly, stepping closer and trying to brush it off. Lisette reached out and grabbed my arm, halting the movement, eyes wide and frantic. She shook her head, and then returned to cradling Nina, shoulders wrenching with sobs. I knelt beside her, holding one of Nina's hands and wishing that I could wake up, that this was just a bad dream.

When she had regained some of her composure, Lisette ushered the others out and gathered the wash basin and cloth. I averted my eyes as Nina's dress was removed and Lisette began to clean the wound, her hands trembling. She noticed my discomfort and thrust a hand in the direction of the trunks, and I gratefully turned my back and began to search through the clothing.

I didn't know much about clothes. A dress was a dress. Some looked nice, others didn't. As I peered through the trunk, I saw a range of outfits that Nina had never worn and never would wear, many of them highly ornamental and extravagant. They were courtly and regal, but they didn't reflect the woman who had become my sister.

There were some things I knew she would want to have with her: her mother's dagger, her father's cloak. The dark leather soled boots that laced up to the ankle. As I found these items, I pulled them out and laid them to the side, studiously keeping my eyes away from the bed. I finally chose a dress of soft blue. It reminded me of her eyes after they had changed colour at King Aegis' court. There were other shades of blue in the dress as well, with delicate embroidery around the skirt and bodice. It looked like the sort of thing she would have worn on a summer day.

Lisette had tossed the bloodied remnants of Nina's clothes into the corner of the room, and I collected them, folding them. Deep down I wanted to cast them into the fire, to not have to see the deep stain that stretched across the red fabric. There was a curious gasp behind me and Lisette tugged my sleeve impatiently.

'What?' I didn't want to look at the bed, but she wouldn't stop. Reluctantly I turned and saw what Lisette was trying to show me.

There was a dark ooze around the edge of Nina's wound, not the colour of ordinary blood but something else.

'What is it?' I asked. Lisette seemed to know more about potions than anyone else but at my question she seemed stumped. She shook her head bewildered, making a small gesture of protection across her chest. 'Poison?' I pressed, my insides twisting. Lisette nodded, face pale. With a fluttering of wings, the white butterfly landed on the wound and rested there for a while, flickering with soft light.

I made to wave it away again, but Lisette stopped me like before and my side twinged. She heard my intake of breath and paused, assessing me worriedly and starting to fuss.

'I'm fine,' I muttered, 'It's just a flesh wound. It'll heal on its own.'

I hated when Lisette fussed over me. It made me feel like a small child again, and while some people might enjoy that feeling from time to time, I didn't. I'd been working hard to put the boy who was scared of the dark and loud voices as far into the past as possible. I needed to be someone strong, someone fearless, like the Scardian knights Ma had told me about before bed. Knights didn't show weakness and wouldn't let small things like flesh wounds interfere with their lives.

Lisette made me sit still while she dabbed some foul-smelling ointment across the cut and it stung terribly. I gritted my teeth and remembered that this wasn't as bad as when the Tracker had left the scar across my face. I had learned a while ago that when Lisette was in a mothering mood, it was best to just sit and wait until she was done. She was usually efficient when she tended to cuts and bruises, but today she was distracted, the figure on the bed kept drawing our eyes, the unspoken heaviness weighing us down.

There was a knock at the door and Rakael entered, face drawn and pinched.

'The Dark Elves are going to the Lake of Tears to pay their respects to the fallen,' she said tightly, and for the first time I wondered if she was on the verge of crying herself. 'We should accompany them. With the king dead, we need to ensure that we can still maintain the Dark Elves' support for the cause. It's what Nina would have wanted.'

I didn't argue, although I was tempted to. Nina had cared about Scardia, more than perhaps she realised. It was clear though in the way her eyes would flare up either with passion or anger when someone mentioned it, or in the soft loving way she would recount its old tales and history. It was impossible to deny that she had felt a stronger connection than most to her country, definitely more than I did. But I wasn't sure that staying in the Dark Elves' favour for their army would have been foremost in her mind. Nina would have wanted to pay respects to honour the fallen and their loss. She would have been more focussed on asking the Gods for a blessing for the departed souls.

Lisette nodded and together we followed Rakael and the other members of our party, joining the Dark Elves who were moving towards the Lake of Tears in a solemn procession. I had never been there before, and the dark, still water was slightly eerie. The Dark Elves were standing around the shore, lanterns flickering in their hands. The Chief Counsel held the king's misshapen silver helmet, and knelt, placing it on a small raft decorated with glowing flowers and candles, before pushing it adrift.

'Erthor, Creator of Night, guide our fallen to your kingdom eternal,' he intoned, the raspy voice spreading to every corner of the cave. 'Give us strength as we rebuild and grant us vengeance as we strike against those who harmed your Chosen.'

'Erthor, Lord of the Moon, guide our fallen to the Dark Beyond.' Another voice rose in a mournful dirge and was followed soon by others.

'Lionus, Lord of the Death, grant them peace in your kingdom.'

'Lady Sybilla, may they find comfort in your light.'

As one, the Dark Elves approached the lake and sent their lanterns out, bobbing like small boats into the lake's centre. Their voices merged and became uniform, repeating the same phrases over and over. And then there was a sudden hush as a wave of deep shadow fell across the lake's surface, swallowing up all the lights. When it had faded, there was nothing left, save for an uncanny hush and then a flurry of white butterflies swarming out of a hole in the ceiling, filling the space with a flickering glow.

The Dark Elves remained kneeling, their heads bent in silent prayer. Around me the others knelt too, and I followed suit, resting against the damp earth. I closed my eyes, picturing Nina's cold figure lying against the tunnel wall. She had believed in the Gods— more so than I did. I couldn't deny that they existed, but I had always felt like they blessed some and overlooked others— like me. Nina had been blessed, I had been one of the outliers— those who believed but were not acknowledged by the celestial beings as one of their chosen few.

It felt hypocritical praying to them, when I knew from years of experience that they did not answer the prayers of someone like me. I had asked for help so many times in the past, begged for it when Ma and Pa fell ill that fateful winter, and then after they had died and I was stuck with Mister MacMillan. Yet the Gods had never helped me. But I knew that Nina would have wanted it.

Please, I thought, hands clasped together. *Help me to avenge her. Bring her back.*

I thought, for an instant, that I felt a breath of wind, the tingle of something cold against my skin, but when I opened my eyes there was nothing there. Unnerved, I stood abruptly and left the cavern, ignoring the scandalised looks that

Christoff and Rakael gave me. What did it matter to them if I left? They didn't understand. They couldn't understand.

The earth crunched under my feet as I broke into a run, blindly racing away from that cursed lake, from the Dark Elves and their creepy masks and from the overwhelming sense that there was something *other* in the darkness, watching us. Someone had to keep vigil over Nina. It should be me. My mouth twisted in self-mockery as Mister MacMillan's voice filled my head again: *Some protector you turned out to be, Olaf. You had one role – one job – and you couldn't even do that.*

I pushed myself faster, trying to escape the words in my mind. *Your fault. All your fault. If you'd been there, she wouldn't be dead.*

The bedchamber door was ajar when I arrived, panting. Instantly I was alert, gripping the dagger at my belt. Carefully, I pushed the door open and entered, ready to strike.

There was a woman inside. Tall and willowy, with long dark hair and pale skin. She had dressed Nina in our absence in the clothes I had laid out. Nina's hair was clean and loose, her father's cloak clasped around her shoulders and her mother's dagger clasped in her hands, which were crossed on her chest. If one had just been passing, they might have been tricked into believing that she was peacefully asleep.

'Yes, I think that would be appropriate,' the strange woman said to one of the white butterflies that was hovering nearby. She stretched out to the bedside table and lifted some of the white orchids from their vase, placing them carefully alongside the blade in Nina's hands.

'What do you think you're doing?' I demanded, 'Who *are* you? Get away from her!'

She didn't turn or acknowledge me, but instead fussed over the orchids in Nina's hands, and then smoothed the folds of the blue gown.

'Didn't you hear me?' I said, the anger that seemed to have been constantly there since I found Nina's body rose up into my throat. 'Get *away*.' I stepped closer to her, holding the dagger up higher.

'Tell me, Erik,' the woman's voice sounded familiar but I was positive that I had never met her before. 'How far would you be willing to go to protect your princess?'

'How do you know my name?' I asked cautiously, 'I don't know you.' My heart was pounding with fear now too, and I stood feet away from her, unmoving.

'But I know *you*, Olaf Henriksson.' She met my eyes and I was pierced with a gaze as cold as the worst of the winter storms. 'I know you more than you think.'

'Who are you?' I asked, shaken that she knew the name I had tried so hard to leave behind.

'You haven't answered my question, boy.' Her tone changed and became icy, and the room swelled with a fey ethereal power, like I had felt by the Lake of Tears. 'How far would you be willing to go to protect your princess, she who claimed you as a brother?'

I couldn't speak.

'She had faith in you,' the woman continued, leaning back over Nina's body and stroking the white blaze in her red hair. 'The last thing she said was about you.'

'Stop it.' My voice was ragged and burst out of me before I could stop it. 'Shut up. The only way you could know that is if you were there, if you let her die, or if you killed her yourself.' I gripped the dagger tighter, 'I'll kill you,' I whispered, 'by the Gods, I will make you pay.'

She threw back her head and laughed, a clear tinkling sound that shook me even more than her anger a few moments ago.

'You are quick to accuse and even quicker to threaten. But your heart is aching and so I will forgive your transgression this time.' I stared at her, confused, as she continued, 'your sister loved you, Erik. So, I ask you for the final time, how far would you be willing to go to protect her?'

'I would have done anything,' I whispered through numb lips. 'But it's too late now, she's gone and I can't bring her back.' The dagger clattered to the floor and I covered my face, ashamed of the sudden tears that burned my eyes.

'You asked for vengeance,' the woman mused, 'and you asked for her to be brought back. You want more than the Gods can provide, Erik. But there is still a way for you to help your sister.'

She had my full attention now and I lowered my hands, rubbing my cheeks roughly. 'What do you mean?'

'The Lord of Summer is angry,' she said, 'his Chosen was taken before her time, before he could see his game play out. And I am angry too, for she was to be my champion as well. But I knew that the Underdark would not be a safe place, there are vipers waiting to strike when your guard is lowered. That was why I protected her.'

'How?' I burst out, 'she's dead.'

'Her heart has paused, yes,' the woman conceded, 'but with your help it might beat again.'

I stared at her uncomprehendingly. 'What do you mean?' I repeated cautiously.

'Can you protect her, Erik?' Her voice had faded to a whisper, as she gazed back at me, unblinking. 'Can you ensure that she returns to her homeland safely?'

I nodded. 'I'll do whatever I can to have her back.'

She breathed out and a soft mist of snowflakes cascaded down onto Nina's face. 'That was the right answer. Take her home. Return her to Scardia's heart and gather the tear of an innocent, the first drop of moonlight, a heart's desire and the blood of a guilty man. Offer them to the Gods before the sun rises on the Winter Solstice, and you might see your sister again.'

Her words confused me, and I gaped. Half of those things sounded impossible to find. She smiled, as though she could read my thoughts. 'Don't knights have to fulfil a quest of some sort to save a fair maiden?' She asked gently, 'succeed in this endeavour, Erik Olaf Henriksson, and there is nothing you will not be able to achieve.'

She waved her hands and the snowflakes ceased to fall. As the last few landed on Nina's features they sank into her skin, sending tendrils of ice out across her face, down her neck and arms to the tips of her shoes. I watched with horrified fascination as it hardened, encasing Nina in a protective shell, making her look like a carved ice statue.

'She will be protected thus,' the lady murmured, brushing Nina's smooth icy cheek, 'caught between life and death until midwinter. Be careful in your quest, Erik. There is a traitor amongst you, one who wishes you ill. Do not share too widely what you must do. And remember that if you cannot achieve your goal by the time the sun rises on the Winter Solstice, your sister will be forever lost in the in-between of worlds, and Scardia will never be free.'

Chapter Two: Erik

I didn't know how to explain to the others what had happened. For ages I just stood rooted to the spot, staring at the place where the dark-haired woman had vanished, and at the ice sculpture on the bed. It was unnerving, and as my brain began to work properly and I reflected on what had just happened, I realised who she had been. Nina had spoken about her and had read to me the story of the daughter of Erthor and Fionne, who could control the powers of winter. I had never expected that I would see the Winter Spirit in person– she both terrified and awed me.

Mostly though, the main things that she had told me lingered in my mind; I had a quest– a proper one– and that someone had betrayed us. It made me automatically suspicious, thinking back over the movements of everyone in our party, trying to figure out which of them I could and couldn't trust. I remembered the way Nina had been uncomfortable on the dance floor, how she had seen someone in the crowd and she had blanched. Could it be that she had known someone amongst us was not to be trusted?

'If only you could tell me who it was,' I sighed, sitting next to her and touching her icy hand. The white butterfly waved its wings and I glared at it. 'I hate bugs.'

There was a gasp from the doorway. Lisette had returned and she wasn't alone.

'What happened to her?' Dylan's voice was filled with a mixture of shock, curiosity and awe. He had awkwardly caught Lisette as she slumped to the ground in a faint. A Dark Elf beside him helped to lift her into the room and then moved closer to Nina's side.

'There is strong magic at work here.' It was Alex, who had taken Dylan to the Archives days ago. They turned to me, 'It seems that you have been given a task by the Gods, Erik. They must have faith if she has been entrusted to your care.'

'What do you mean?' I was thrown by the statement, unwilling to admit that I had been given a quest and confused as to how Alex seemed to know about it.

'Ah, of course,' Dylan said, pulling out his monocle and peering closer. 'It's like a state of chrysalis. Fascinating.'

'What happened, Erik?' Alex asked. 'We heard that there had been an attack.'

'We heard that the Princess was dead,' Dylan murmured, leaning over Nina and inspecting her minutely, 'but it seems that that might not be true.' He glanced up at Alex, 'this is like what I read about in the Archives.' He turned to me and I was shaken by the intensity of his gaze. 'Tell me Erik,' he pressed, 'were you given a series of tasks to accomplish? Is there a way we can get her back?'

Mutely, I nodded. There was a movement from the ground and I knelt down, gripping Lisette's hand as she slowly sat up. Her eyes were wide, and she stared from Dylan to Nina desperately, making some quick gestures. I could almost hear the hope that was starting to fill her eyes. *Can we get her back?*

I glanced around the room at the three of them, remembering what the Winter Spirit had said; there was a traitor in our midst. But I also realised that the likelihood of any of them being behind the Trackers' attack was slight. Lisette adored Nina, as if she were her own mother, and Dylan and Alex had been in the Archives for days, they couldn't have been involved. From all I had observed of Dylan, he was too absorbed in his work to have time to work against us. As for Alex– I barely knew them, but what reason would they have to wish Nina ill? They had been close to Aidyn and, no matter what I felt about him, he had seemed to care about Nina.

'Erik?' Dylan repeated.

I moved to the door and shut it carefully, checking the hallway to ensure that it was empty before heading back into the room. I took my seat next to Nina again, resting a hand on hers, and told them everything about the Winter Spirit's visit; how she had turned Nina to ice, her warning and the quest I had been entrusted with. I was grateful that the others listened while I spoke, holding their questions until the end. When I finished, there was a silence as they absorbed what I had told them.

'It is like one of the old tales,' Dylan mused thoughtfully. 'We will need to make sure that the others are not told about what you need to do, Erik. This will need to be kept secret until you can be sure who is trustworthy.'

'I think that the Resistance will be too fixated on the upcoming fight to assist you,' Alex said gravely. 'Their Leader is determined to rally her army sooner rather than later.'

'How will we be able to keep this a secret, though?' I asked, indicating Nina's icy form.

'Perhaps,' Alex said, 'we can keep her hidden from view. A closed casket, no one will question that.'

'It seems only right that she is taken back to Scardia,' I said, 'Rakael cannot disagree with letting us bury her there.'

Lisette nodded and gripped my arm, squeezing tightly.

'It is incredible,' Dylan had lost focus on the conversation and was inspecting Nina again. 'It looks like she's been turned into Hoarfrost. In the old texts, they detail how the Hoarfrost Glacier was considered the lifeblood of Scardia, and that its source was the heart.'

Return her to Scardia's heart. The words whispered in my ear, and I knew instantly where we were supposed to go.

'Dylan,' I asked, 'do you know where the Hoarfrost Glacier begins?'

But it was Alex who answered, 'if I remember correctly, somewhere in the Northern Ranges.'

'Then that is where we will need to go,' I said quietly. 'Once we reach Scardia and gather the required items. So long as we get there before the Winter Solstice.'

Lisette made an odd movement, shifting to reach out towards Nina and then withdrawing a shaking hand. I looked at her for a moment and realised what she was thinking.

'That's her birthday, isn't it?'

Lisette nodded, her eyes not leaving the figure on the bed.

'We should set about making preparations,' Alex said firmly. 'I will go and organise a casket to be made. You will need to make sure that she is not seen by the others.' They held out a hand and the white butterfly fluttered onto it. 'You will need to send word, my friend,' Alex murmured, 'let him know that all is not lost.'

I watched, confused, as they departed. 'What…?'

'Probably best not to ask,' Dylan said, 'I found that out at the Archives.' He stretched and got to his feet, 'I will need to go and speak to Rakael. She will be awaiting a report on what we found. I'll see if I can convince her to agree to take Nina's body back to Scardia, shall I?'

Lisette gave a swift nod. No more was she the grieving mother, now her jaw was set and firm, and I knew that she, like I, was determined to succeed in our quest.

After that, things seemed to come together smoothly. Nina's body was wrapped in a dark cloth and placed in a casket. Rakael had agreed all too readily to bringing Nina home; it seemed that the Princess' body would serve as a strong incentive to rally the troops and the people of Scardia to support the cause. It made me feel uncomfortable hearing her discuss Nina in such a callous way, and the dislike I had always felt towards her only intensified.

The Dark Elves had become even more withdrawn and ambiguous, and from the anxious glances that Jesse would give Rakael at mealtimes, I knew that there was something wrong. The Chief Counsel had declared that a period of mourning would take place in the Underdark for seven days and nights before the council would choose a new king. I didn't like the way he described it, his raspy voice eager with anticipation for more blood to be spilt between the three Houses, as their chosen members would fight for the position in the arena.

Rakael was insistent that we would remain until a new king was chosen, although I had heard Jesse urging for us to leave sooner rather than later. Leif and Tobias were also keen to depart, they wanted to get back to the Resistance Stronghold to see their families again. Christoff alone supported Rakael's decision to stay, shadowing her every move as she visited the different factions in the Underdark, seeking to rally support for her cause. She called for vengeance, to strike back at those who had cut down their king and comrades, to join the Resistance and be rewarded with blood.

Meanwhile, between sessions of the Dark Elves' rigorous training regime, I was left to ponder the riddle of bringing Nina back. I wanted to turn to Dylan for help, but he was often sequestered away with members of the Resistance, going over the plans he had found in the Archives. He knew far more about the fables and stories than I, and might have some ideas about where we could find some of the requirements that the Winter Spirit had dictated. To my mind, they were strange, how was I supposed to find a drop of moonlight or a heart's desire? Where was I supposed to find a tear?

'It couldn't have just been gathering incense and burning certain herbs,' I muttered to myself as I kicked away one of the stones on the dusty path, 'no, it had to be difficult.'

If only Stefan was here. I was sure that he would have an idea about what the Winter Spirit had meant. But he was miles away, back in King Aegis' court, or even on the way to Scardia by now. Nina had told me about scrying, and I wished that I could have that ability, it would be a relief to know what was happening in the High Elf Court, how our friends were, and whether the reinforcements from Velkra had arrived yet. Unfortunately for me, I had been born human, no drop of fey magic was in my ancestry and so I had no powers, save for the skills I was learning to hone.

I kicked out again at one of the strange glowing plants that were common in the Underdark, feeling a sense of satisfaction as it broke into pieces and scattered on the ground. I was just starting to think about turning back and returning to find Dylan, when a voice pierced the darkness, startling me.

'Erik? Erik, where are you?' Jesse was striding towards me and I could tell immediately that something was wrong.

'Jesse, what…?'

'Thank the Gods, I've been looking everywhere. You need to come quickly,' she said, 'Leif and Tobias are organising the carts to move out. There's been a change of plans.'

'I thought we were staying for the ceremony to decide the next king,' I said, jogging slightly to keep up with her.

'That was before,' she replied, 'Rakael has changed her mind.'

'What's happened?' I pressed. 'Tell me.'

She gripped my arm and led me on as we entered one of the main caverns, where the amphitheatre stood ominously in the distance. We dodged in between Dark Elves who were moving towards the structure, angrily muttering amongst themselves. It sounded like a swarm of hornets buzzing when someone came too close to the nest, and I realised that the main source of the noise came from the amphitheatre.

'What is it, Jesse?' I repeated, as we drew closer to the rising hum.

'There isn't going to be a ceremony for the next king,' she murmured, 'The Chief Counsel, he…' Her voice trailed off and she pulled me on. 'We need to go, Erik. The Underdark is no longer safe for us.'

Jesse led me towards a wide tunnel where the others were standing, waiting anxiously. Alex was starting to lead one of the carts- laden with Nina's casket and multiple trunks- away up a steep track. Dylan and Lisette were in the other cart, and their faces relaxed when they saw us approaching.

'Hurry up,' Rakael hissed, glancing behind us to see if we were being followed. 'We have to get moving.'

I scrambled into Dolce's saddle, Jesse mounting alongside me, and we began to follow Alex's cart.

'Can someone please tell me what is going on?'

Rakael's mouth pinched the way it always did when she was annoyed that I had asked a question. Jesse answered, 'the council are dead, Erik. The Chief Counsel's men killed them while they slept. He is trying to claim the throne for himself. The other Houses are in an uproar, from what Alex said, there will be fighting amongst them for weeks now until a decision is made.'

'We need to move out now,' Rakael said harshly. 'We'll need to make do with the soldiers we have got. The last thing we want is to get stuck here while the Dark Elves are fighting amongst themselves, especially as we cannot be guaranteed who will be standing at the end.'

I wasn't sad to leave the Underdark behind. I'd found it eerie from the moment we had arrived and couldn't wait to feel sunshine again. Dolce paused to paw the ground, twisting to look behind us, unwilling to leave without Nina.

'Come on, girl,' I whispered, 'it's time for us to go home.' And with a gentle nudge, the horse moved on after the others, heading back towards the surface.

Chapter Three: Aidyn

The moon was starting to rise. An owl hooted in the distance, the sound breaking through the silence. I raised a hand and then lowered it, indicating for the figures behind me to keep moving stealthily from tree to tree.

We had been travelling for weeks, cutting through the Ombre Mountains to the Western Coast, where we set sail. For centuries our people had kept large ships hidden in one of the coves, out of sight from any passing traveller, though most sailors avoided the Western Coast as the waters were dangerous and rocky, with sinkholes waiting to tear unwary travellers down. I was sure that Rakael would be sending groups of soldiers after us, directing them to meet the Resistance in their Scardian Stronghold. I had been determined to get a decent head start, it would be noticeable if multiple ships travelled across the Meridian within a short time and we wanted to avoid as much attention as possible.

Our vessel wasn't particularly large, and if Sybilla and Erthor hadn't been watching over us, we would not have made the crossing successfully. It helped that Beck could call on some of the creatures of the deep to speed us along, and Fain could summon the wind to fill our sails, thus ensuring that our passage across the Meridian was short, swift and uneventful. The larger creatures who dwelled within the waves were calmed by Beck's low voice and posed no danger as we traversed their waters.

I had assembled a small group of the few I trusted to help me infiltrate Icevale Keep. In my experience, having a smaller team made it easier to do what needed to be done, and it made me feel safer. Beck and Fain were the two brothers I was closest to. They were older than I, already with half-grown sons of their own, but had volunteered to assist before I could ask. Gawain had insisted on coming along, marching up to me not long after I made the announcement and telling me point blank that he would join me. I hadn't been surprised: Gaelen had been Gawain's twin brother. We had grown up together, and now that Gaelen was gone, we both wanted vengeance, to find the Tracker who had killed him and make him feel the pain he had inflicted threefold.

It had been midmorning when we had first sighted Scardian shores. We had taken to sleeping in shifts, snatching a few hours at a time while the others focussed on keeping our vessel both afloat and on course. I missed Alex, who still hadn't returned from the Archives when we left, and I felt their absence. The rest of us were able to read maps well enough, but Alex had an uncanny ability to track and navigate without the need for constantly checking a scroll of parchment. They knew which stars to follow and how to find the hidden paths through a forest which would ensure we reached our destination in good time.

'Aidyn, look!' Gawain shook me roughly awake and I sat up, blinking. He pointed at the horizon, where white cliffs were coming into view. 'We've arrived.'

'We'll need to remain at sea for a few more days though,' Fain said as he held up a map of Scardia. 'According to what Rakael and the other Resistance soldiers told us, Icevale Keep is further around the coast. Here,' he tapped a point on the map, 'the Meridian spans the Eastern coast of Scardia. The Resistance Stronghold is to the west – near Tarheim.'

I noted the marked town, near a mountain range and a good way in from the coast. The Capital was more central, with the Hoarfrost Glacier alongside it stretching all the way from the Northern mountain ranges down to the sea. 'Icevale Keep should be around here,' Fain added, indicating the point where the glacier met the sea. 'It looks like we could moor in one of these coves along this coastline and make our approach overland.'

I nodded. 'The Keep will be under heavy guard. We will need to scout the area before deciding on how we should proceed.'

'We'll need to find a safe location to set up camp once we get ashore,' Beck added, 'if you can scry then you will have a better idea about where the captain is being held. Once we get in, we don't want to spend so much time there that we find ourselves trapped.'

I looked back at the distant cliffs, grateful for the mask that hid the distaste I felt when the captain was mentioned. But I had volunteered to retrieve him, had signed and agreed to it under Father's watchful gaze and I wouldn't back out of the task, not when I knew that the prize was worth the cost. If I brought Markus and Keely to the Resistance Stronghold alive, I would no longer be confined to the Underdark. I could leave, escape the fate that my brothers had accepted without question, and experience something new. Furthermore, I would have my heart's desire at my side, a shocking revelation that had struck me from the first time I danced with her. Before then I had considered the political proposal an efficient means to an end, a way to escape the Underdark and my father's court, but then I had met her, and I realised why the Elders spoke so harshly about the dangers of loving another.

She hadn't reached out to me via the scrying pool since my departure which I found disconcerting, I had thought that she would try at least to keep abreast of our efforts to reclaim Markus and Keely. And, a small voice whispered, I had hoped that she would also want to see me. She was always there on the edge of my thoughts. Even now, I could almost see her reaction as we drew nearer and nearer to her homeland; her blue eyes sparkling with excitement, her red and white hair slapping against her cheeks in the brisk sea air, her warm smile.

'Aidyn,' Beck had rolled up the map and was stowing it away. Fain and Gawain were looking at me, clearly waiting for me to say something. 'How long do you think you will need to find a way into the Keep?'

I shrugged. 'Perhaps a few days. It's hard to tell.' Reaching out, I made sure that my bags were secured nearby, sensing the beating of wings from within.

We will arrive soon, I thought, stretching the tendrils of my mind out to the creatures within the bag.

Wet. Cold. Dark. A flurry of soft voices answered, each one tumbling over the other. *Want home. Warm.*

I drew my hand away and the voices quietened. 'Once we have found a safe place to camp, I will get to work.'

And so, we had tacked around the Scardian coast, noting the towns that stretched along the cliffs and seaside, their lights twinkling as night fell. On the third night, we pulled into a small cove with a pebbled beach. We unloaded the boat, bringing ashore our packs, and kept it moored out of sight. Even if it was found, no one would be able to trace our destination or our origin from what we had left behind. Next, we had to go overland, scaling the side of the rocky cliff which stretched around the cove until we got to the headland and determined the easiest way to cross the terrain.

'We could use your father's powers right about now,' Gawain muttered as we climbed up the rock face, gripping into niches with our toes and fingers. I grunted in response, too busy trying to locate the next handhold. Above me, Fain was nearly at the top. Unlike the rest of us, he was a gifted climber and was used to scaling the rocky walls back in the Underdark. I saw him pull himself up and over the edge, and then moments later a rope was falling down towards us.

'Thought you might want some assistance,' he called down, 'otherwise at the rate you're going, we'll be here all night.'

Beck choked out a laugh and grabbed onto the rope, pulling himself up first, Gawain next. I waited until the others had scaled the cliff face before grasping the rope and heaving myself up, hand over hand, keeping my eyes fixed on the moon instead of the watery grave below. Hands gripped mine and pulled, helping me climb firmly onto the clifftop. Fain began coiling the rope up again, reattaching it to his pack and we looked around, taking quick note of our surroundings.

Before us, rocky, frostbitten land stretched away, speckled with dark swaying trees and lights from a distant town. It was achingly cold and I was grateful to have the mask on my face. The wind cut through to my bones, making my breath catch at the sudden pain. From up above, the moon lit the clifftops, showing the crags that jutted out into the ocean, as the coastline continued as far as the eye could see. I shivered, acutely aware that summer had long passed, and winter was rapidly approaching.

'There,' Beck said, pointing at a faint patch light in the distance. 'That must be it.'

'There's only one way to find out,' Gawain said grimly, and hitching his pack further onto his shoulders, together we moved out.

It took a couple of days of travelling overland until we could see Icevale Keep more clearly. Now that we were no longer at sea, we had to pause during the day, hiding either in caves or snatching moments of rest under some of the gnarled trees, bent and crooked from the wind. It became harder to think clearly as we slept less and our rations dwindled, and it was a relief when we reached a small pine forest, slightly inland from the coast and within view of the Keep. We moved now from tree to tree as the moon rose, slipping through the darkness as easily as the shadows themselves, looking for a place to set up camp.

Dark. Home. The voices pressed on the edges of my mind; the small creatures beat their wings, desperate to escape from my bag. I gestured for the others to halt, and we paused as I reached into my pack, withdrew one of the moths and held it close to my face, whispering a few key words.

Safe. Find. Follow. The lunar moth fluttered away, a speck of moonlight dancing between the trees as it began its search.

'How long will it take, Aidyn?' Gawain asked, 'we'll need time to forage before daybreak.'

'And to find some fresh water,' Fain muttered, 'there's only so much longer our flasks will last.'

'Be patient,' I replied, listening intently.

'I'll be patient once we've had some food and a decent rest,' Fain said, Beck and Gawain grunting in agreement.

Wet. Close. I held up a hand, silencing them, and strode away following the patch of light. There was a small trickling not far away, and sure enough a small creek wound its way through the trees. It was incredible that the water hadn't yet frozen entirely solid, although segments were covered with a thin layer of ice.

Safe. Here. The white light flickered and went down into the ground by one of the great trees. I approached slowly, carefully, noting the twisting undergrowth waiting to trip an unprepared traveller. There was a glimmer leading down, the light from the moth's wings seeping through the roots. Together, the four of us closed our eyes and made the same gesture, willing the roots to move aside to allow us entry. With a creaking and rustling, an opening was exposed, revealing what could be considered a small cave.

'Perfect,' Beck said, 'I'm going to find us something to eat. I'll be back by morning.'

'I'll join you,' Gawain said, dropping his pack by my feet and slipping off into the darkness. I picked it up and approached the opening, sliding down the dirt into the space under the tree. Fain followed me, laid down his pack and curled up along one of the walls, falling asleep almost instantly. I was tempted to do the same, but the moth landed on my hand, flickering urgently. Something was wrong.

Home. See. Its small mind was awash with images, and it was too difficult to sort through them. Carefully, I left the packs on the earth and climbed back out, moving the roots back into place to hide Fain from view.

Home. See. It was becoming insistent, darting back and forth in front of my eyes, unable to remain still.

'Slow down, little one,' I murmured as I sat beside the creek. 'Come here.' I held out a hand and it settled down onto the black leather. The moon was now at its peak, shining down on us, and I sent out a prayer to Erthor asking for his guidance. My breathing slowed and I felt myself slipping away into a trance, half focussed on the moth on my hand, half on the reflection of the moon in the water.

'Show me, little one,' I breathed, 'show me what troubles you.'

The moth flickered and when I closed my eyes, the connection strengthened. Erthor had gifted me with this ability long ago and I had honed it since, reaching the point where I could use the moths' hive mind to my advantage. Under his light, their minds all came together, forming images that fluctuated and spun in front of my eyes showing me scenes back home in the Underdark. Sometimes it allowed me to see things in the moment, other times past events. I blinked and focussed, urging the lights to solidify.

Home. Danger. Lost. A chill of trepidation filled me as the voice spoke into my mind and I felt my breathing hitch.

'Where is she?' I whispered into the mist of flickering lights, 'show her to me.' Please, Erthor, let her be safe.

The image before me became clearer and I froze. White light flashed off silver armour which was faintly glowing red, the heat shining in the darkness of the tunnel. The figure inside it moaned and cried, an awful, heart-wrenching sound.

Father. The moth drew closer to him, noting the heat and the smell of burning. There was a commotion from further down the tunnel, startling it back into flight. It followed the direction of the noises and clung to the tunnel wall as a figure rushed past. I noted ferocious eyes in a pale face twisted with scars. Rakael. She strode past the moth, heading towards Father's body.

There was a gasping, choking sound from the darkness and the moth approached cautiously. The light revealed her gradually and reflected off a blade that lay at her feet. She was clutching onto her side, face scrunched in pain, muttering something under her breath.

No, no, no. The moth landed on the hand clasping the wound, pressing to the crimson fabric that was stained darker from her blood. Nina's eyes were turning hazy, struggling to focus on the world around her, they landed on the moth and I could sense her making a supreme effort.

'Find him,' she whispered, 'keep him safe.'

It was like she knew. Like she could sense me there with her in that moment, powerless to do anything, powerless to help. There was a tearing in my chest, a pain greater than any I had known before. I watched as she struggled for breath, the moth lifting away from her hand, and then the emptiness that was filling me entered her eyes, leaving them blank and unseeing.

I broke out of the trance and stared up at the moon, understanding for the first time how Erthor had felt when his Sybilla died. I understood how he had filled lakes and oceans with his tears; I sat there for a long time, wanting to cry, wanting to scream and beg the Gods to not be so cruel. But I couldn't allow myself to.

'Guide me, Erthor,' I murmured, 'Sybilla, help me to see clearly. Show me what I must do.' Deep inside I was cursing myself, hating that I was so far away from the Underdark, so far away from being able to help her. Hollowness spread through me bringing with it the realisation as to why she hadn't tried to scry once. What I had seen had not been in the moment, it must have happened days, perhaps weeks ago. She had been gone for who knew how long and I hadn't known. Perhaps that was what hurt the most.

A cloud moved across the moon, casting a brief shadow over me. The lunar moth on my hand lifted towards the sky, disappearing into the blackness, and I understood what the Gods were telling me.

Shaking, I gripped my hands together, bending my head in prayer. 'Lionus, guide my beloved to your realm. Lady Sybilla, let her join you in your fiery dance across the sky. Erthor, help me to avenge her. Give me the strength to fulfil her wishes and then to strike down the one who took her away.'

My mouth twisted with cold resolve as I thought about the last person who had seen Nina alive. The person who had used that curved blade to cut her life short. Once I had brought Markus and Keely to safety, as Nina had requested, and helped Gawain to avenge Gaelen, I knew what I needed to do.

Rakael was going to pay for what she had done, and I would be only too happy to be the one to inflict her punishment.

Chapter Four: Erik

I learned quickly that the trip out of the Underdark was to be long, tedious and very dusty. I almost wished to be drugged for the departure as we had been for our arrival, but Alex explained that with the Trackers in their midst, the rule about keeping the entrance to the Underdark a secret no longer applied. They doubted that any of us would ever return, which I privately agreed with, and so they didn't have an issue with showing us the exit.

The first patch of sunlight burned our eyes and blinded us, and as we emerged from the mountainside we were assaulted by the staggering heat of the midday sun. Alex led the cart down a nearby track, navigating us through the mountains until we reached a cove where a couple of boats were moored.

'We will need to sail ourselves,' Alex grunted as they began to unload the trunks and carry them to the larger of the two vessels. Tobias and Leif followed suit, while I dismounted from Dolce's back, clasping her bridle in suddenly sweaty hands.

'What about the horses?' I asked, not wanting to leave Dolce behind. Nina had loved her, she would want her horse if she woke up. However on inspecting the boat that Alex and the others were loading up, there would barely be enough room for us all to be on board with the trunks and Nina's casket, let alone the horses.

'Leave them behind,' Rakael snapped, 'we can get new horses when we get to Scardia.'

'I'm not leaving Dolce,' I said resolutely. 'Nina would…'

'Nina is dead, Erik.' Rakael's tone was final. 'All that matters is that we reclaim Scardia in her name. That was her wish. She would not feel the need to keep a horse close. There are hundreds like it.'

I remembered how Nina had bartered for Dolce's passage when we crossed the Meridian, how she had spent hours in the hold, caring for her. I knew that she wouldn't want Dolce to be left behind.

I opened my mouth to argue, but Jesse reached out and touched my shoulder, silencing me.

'There's no use in arguing, Erik,' she said quietly. 'There's not enough room.'

I glared at her mutinously. 'It's what Nina would have wanted,' I bit out.

She looked at me pensively for a while and then glanced at Rakael, who was ordering Christoff and Leif towards the boat. 'Leave her with me,' Jesse said, 'take her saddle with you. I'll take care of the horses. We will meet you at the Stronghold.'

I stared at her, confused. 'How?'

'Don't worry, Erik,' she was striding away now towards Rakael, 'I'll take care of it.'

'Come on, Erik.' Dylan had his satchel of scrolls and books balanced on his shoulder and he stood beside me, gazing unhappily at the boat. 'Let Jesse deal with it.'

I unsaddled Dolce and began to carry that as well as my bag after Jesse. Lisette was overseeing Alex and Tobias, who were lifting the casket down from one of the carts, making sure not to drop it onto the shore.

'Travel safe,' Jesse was saying to Rakael, 'I'll meet you there, someone needs to let King Aegis know what has happened.'

So, she would be travelling overland back to the High Elf court. I didn't envy her being the one to tell King Aegis about what had happened in the Underdark, who knew how he would react when he found out. I was glad that I wouldn't be there to see it. I also didn't want to have to tell anyone else about the Winter Spirit's instructions, particularly because I knew that King Aegis would most likely send out Elves far and wide to search for the different things I needed. It would be impossible to keep it a secret and it would no longer be *my* quest. Even now, I was not quite sure how much of the planning had been taken out of my hands by Alex, Dylan and Lisette, but I felt more comfortable in making my opinions known and heard with them.

'I hope you understand,' Rakael was saying to us now as we hopped aboard, 'that you will be assisting in the crossing.'

'What?' Dylan spluttered, 'but I don't know anything about…I'm a *scholar* not a sailor.'

'You will help with the rest of us, or you'll be left behind,' Rakael said curtly. 'We don't have time to waste on people who are not helpful.'

I thought for a moment that Dylan was going to explode; his face bulged red and his hands clenched, but instead he just pushed past Rakael and went below the deck to the small hold below. Ignoring Rakael's scowl, I followed him, and noted the narrow pallets stacked on top of each other along the sides of the walls. They looked hard and uncomfortable and I dreaded the time night fell, I didn't want to sleep there.

It became apparent, early into the journey, that none of us were sailors. We had all assisted in the past, save for Lisette and Dylan. Alex stayed at the wheel, perhaps the only one on board who was comfortable navigating and steering us through the rocky waters. They called out instructions for the rest of us, but we were a motley crew with varying degrees of skill. The smaller vessel tossed and turned more easily in the waves than Markus' ship had, and most of us got badly seasick at one point or another, barely able to keep anything down before rushing to the side of the boat.

'This is hell,' Dylan groaned one morning, 'absolute hell.'

I couldn't answer, my body was aching from lying on the hard pallet, and I was struggling to adjust the sails for Alex. Dylan was supposed to be helping, but it had become obvious early on that whenever he attempted to help it only made the job take longer. Rakael had begrudgingly assigned him to help Lisette with preparing food for us, although this also proved challenging. Finally, Lisette had sent him to find me, and I understood why.

'If we could only get to dry land, it would be alright,' Dylan muttered, 'the spirits didn't even receive an offering for our safe passage. They'll overturn our boat in the Meridian, that's for sure. Mark my words, Erik, we're going to end in a watery grave.'

I rolled my eyes, yanking tighter on the rope and then tying it the way Karl had taught me. Karl had always been patient while he showed me the different knots, his weather-beaten face spread with a gap-toothed smile. It was surreal to think that he was no longer alive, that he had been cut down by the Trackers when Markus was taken. I remembered Nina recounting the vision to me later, about how Markus and his men had been smuggling something for the Trackers before they had been killed. It reminded me of when I had stowed away in their ship, of how there had been so many crates in the hold that hadn't been unloaded when we left. I wondered what had been in them, weapons? Armour?

'Erik, are you listening?' Dylan's voice cut through my reverie and I glowered at him, hand slipping on the rope.

'What?' My voice came out harsher than I had intended, but I didn't want to apologise.

'There's…there's something in the water.' He had gone pale and was staring overboard at a large, dark shape that was approaching the boat.

'Look out!' Tobias shouted, 'Sea monster!'

'Keep calm!' Rakael cried at the same time, sounding anything but.

Alex was the only one who seemed to be unaffected, holding the helm steady and not saying a word. There was a rushing crash as the creature erupted out of the water, gazing down at us with fourteen beady eyes, seven frilled heads trying to decide who to devour first. It focussed on Christoff, who had rushed to pick up a mace in his hands, preparing to fight.

'Alexia!' I shouted, racing to the edge of the boat, recognising the creature immediately and praying that I was making the right decision. 'Alexia, stop!'

The monster paused for a moment, its heads twisting to face me, bending closer until I could see myself reflected fourteen times. Its tongues flickered in and out, hissing suspiciously as I stood there, paralysed. Its legs stuck out from its sides, almost like a centipede, stretching out like feelers towards me.

'Alexia,' it took everything in me to keep my voice firm and commanding, like I imagined Nina would have done. 'We have King Aegis' granddaughter on board. We need to get back to Scardia and cannot do that if you tear us to shreds.'

The creature stared at me, then glanced up and down the boat searchingly.

'She's below deck,' I managed to get out, sensing what it was looking for.

'She's sleeping,' Rakael interjected quickly, before being silenced by the creature's glare.

'That's right,' I said, 'she's asleep.' It wasn't too far from the truth, not really.

'Ask her to help guide us, Erik.' Alex's steady voice came from the helm, 'she might listen to you.'

'What are you talking about?' Rakael snapped at them, 'it's a monster.'

I reached out a hand to brush against the slimy green scales and the creature swayed, its focus on me unbroken. 'Can you help us get back home?' I whispered, 'Will you help us to bring her back?'

Alexia let out seven piercing shrieks from each head and then twisted and dived backwards, the waves making the boat lurch from side to side so that we had to grip onto the railing for dear life.

'You tried, Erik.' Leif said consolingly, 'but you couldn't expect a monster like that to help us.'

'We should be grateful that it's gone,' Tobias muttered, 'I hope I never see something like that again.'

'There's a reason we are not supposed to cross the Meridian,' Christoff said fearfully, 'the creatures of the Deep don't take kindly to humans crossing back and forth. I knew there would be a price that we had to pay when we first came across. But now, you're wanting a monster to help us? Are you insane? We should be thanking the Gods for it leaving us alone.'

'I wouldn't be so sure,' Alex muttered, ignoring the dirty glances being cast their way. 'That creature belongs to King Aegis– I would be very surprised if it didn't help.'

As if on cue, there was a loud crunching and sucking sound from underneath the boat.

'Gods, it's sinking us,' Christoff whispered, shaking uncontrollably, 'that damned monster's going to take us under.'

'Pull yourself together, Christoff,' Rakael snapped angrily. There was a soft moan and Dylan crumpled to the deck in a dead faint. 'By the Gods,' Rakael growled, moving over to slap him awake, 'how pathetic.'

There was a sudden lurch and the rest of us had to steady ourselves so that we didn't fall as well. The boat began to move faster as hundreds of tiny feet gripped its hull and sped forwards with a powerful flick of Alexia's tail. The wind rushed into my hair and I laughed, exhilarated, as we plunged through the waves edging closer to Scardian shores. We were going home at last, and I would be one step closer to figuring out the Winter Spirit's quest.

Chapter Five: Aidyn

It was nearly dawn when Gawain and Beck returned with a selection of roots and berries scavenged from the forest floor. By then I had pushed down all the emotions that weighed on me. All that mattered was the mission. Once that was done, then, perhaps, I would allow myself time to grieve. But now the desire for blood was in me and Erthor's voice urged me to exact vengeance.

While I waited for them to return, I filled our water flasks from the creek and washed my face in the solitary darkness. Fain was still asleep when I slid back into our small hideaway, noting the shuffling noises of small animals in the undergrowth racing away from the sudden noise. Beck and Gawain closed the roots over the opening when they dropped next to me, their arrival startling Fain awake.

'The forest stretches out for a few miles,' Beck said quietly, 'everything leading up to the Keep is open and flat. They can see anyone approaching easily if the area is well lit.'

'So we approach under the cover of darkness,' I said calmly. 'That's simple enough, Erthor will assist us.'

'The Keep's walls are at least fifty feet high,' Gawain continued, 'with towers on each corner. Two guards patrol at a time, at fifteen-minute intervals.'

'We'll need you to scout out the interior tomorrow night, Aidyn,' Beck said, 'the outside of the Keep at least is well defended, as we expected.'

'We must assume that inside it is similar,' Fain contributed, 'how long were you watching?'

'Maybe an hour or so?' Beck asked Gawain, who gave a nod in response.

'We wanted to have enough time to find something to eat,' he said. 'Tomorrow we can keep watch for longer.'

'Don't forget that we can have someone keeping watch during the day,' I said, 'it'll be easier to determine what we're up against in daylight.'

'But we will have to wait until night has fallen before we can inspect it more closely,' Fain mused. 'I can keep watch when the sun rises.'

'You'd better take something to keep you going through the day, then,' Beck handed over some of the provisions they had scavenged. 'Wash them and they should be alright.'

Fain shrugged, grabbing some of the roots and putting them into a pocket. 'I'll see you at sundown.'

When he had scrambled out of the opening, we covered it up again and lay down to rest. The other two fell asleep quickly, but I lay there, watching the sunlight filter through the roots and undergrowth, feeling empty. When I finally did manage to sleep, it was to be haunted by dreams of her.

Fain shook me awake at sunset, when the last vestiges of the burnt oranges and reds were still stained across the sky. I bit back the resentment at being awoken, having wanted to stay lost in my dreams, where she was within my arms once more.

'It's time, Aidyn.' He helped me to my feet and I grabbed my bag as we climbed up into the clearing. I had a sip of water from my flask and settled myself beside the creek, back straight, legs crossed, listening to the sounds of the forest as nighttime began to settle in.

'I'm heading out,' Gawain said as I passed him my bag, 'I'll report back in a few hours.'

'We'll be here,' Beck replied, waving him away. 'I'll keep watch.'

'I need quiet,' I muttered, and the others stopped talking. Gradually I felt myself slipping into the trance, focussing on the creek and imagining the face of the captain. The image on the water's surface appeared slowly and I leaned closer, careful not to touch it and disrupt the vision.

The captain was in a cell lying on a rough pallet, his face bruised and beaten. On the other side of the small cell lay another man– a large figure with dirty bandages wrapped around his face and hands. Both prisoners had long, matted hair, and looked as though they hadn't eaten properly in days. The walls of the cell were grimy rock, slightly damp and mouldy. An iron door was the only means of entry, apart from a few cracks in the wall which were just large enough to look out onto the glacier and to provide the prisoners with the faintest glimpse of freedom.

'You have to stay strong,' the other prisoner whispered, his voice tired and cracked.

'Like you did, you mean?' Markus replied coolly.

The other man flinched and then groaned in pain. 'If they find out where Milady went, it'll be over. It'll all be over.' Markus condescended to grunt in response, glowering up at the ceiling. The prisoner continued, 'if they know where you took her, they'll kill her they will.'

Markus didn't have time to reply, for there was a scratching from the doorway. It opened to reveal a guard, his armour flashing in the torchlight.

'Get up pig,' he barked, 'time for you to squeal.' He laughed and pulled on a chain that was attached to a nearby ring. Markus was jolted to his feet, the chain clasped around his neck, tugging him forward like a dog.

'Get a move on,' the guard yanked harder, dragging Markus out of the room and down the outside corridor. 'The warden has something special planned for you today.'

'I'm getting tired of the warden's favours,' Markus croaked, and the guard struck him across the face.

'Shut up pig. You've got a special visitor today and everything.'

'I can't wait,' Markus muttered sarcastically, spitting out blood. I was surprised by his attitude– from my experience in the Underdark, prisoners who underwent torture often crumbled within a few days. Markus was more resilient than I had expected. As the guard led him on, I took note of the surroundings– the corridors, the small, cobbled courtyard and the winding stairs that were worn with use. Eventually they reached a room lit with torches, where a range of different implements were displayed along the wall. A brazier burned to one side, which two men were standing over, heating up a poker over the flames. In a corner stood an iron clad box, shaped just large enough for a man to fit inside, while against the opposite wall was a wooden rack. Markus was thrust towards it, the guard removed his chains and tied him to the posts.

'Let's see if you will talk today.'

From beside the brazier, one of the men turned around. His eyes were cold and grey, and his beard was decorated with clay beads. Across his face stretched a burn similar to the scars Rakael had. He was cleaning a selection of sharp knives that he lovingly caressed before replacing on a nearby table.

Beside him was another man, whose blond hair gleamed in the torchlight despite his receding hairline. His thick, wet lips were stretched in a wide smile, his eyes shining with the excitement of a child.

'You'll want to talk, Markus,' the blond man said, clasping his hands together in glee. 'It's going to be painful.'

'You enjoy that pain though, Niall,' Markus grunted, 'don't deny it.' The guard struck him again, the sound echoed across the small chamber.

'You have the gall to speak to your king like that?'

'It's alright, Ethan,' the blond man soothed, stepping closer to Markus. 'Let him have his moment of strength. I do so love seeing the ones with a bit of fighting spirit still left in them. It will be gone soon enough.'

'You sick bastard,' Markus spat, and the Usurper's face went blank and emotionless, rending a drastic change across his features.

'Oh no, Markus,' he said quietly, 'you are the sick one. It is your fault that you are here. You are choosing to prolong this pain, you are inflicting it upon yourself.'

'You're insane,' Markus whispered, 'you're no longer the man I once knew.'

'Ah Markus,' the Usurper breathed as he twisted the handles on the rack, straining out Markus' arms and ignoring his sharp gasp of pain, 'you're right. I am *so* much better now.'

I drew away from the vision and looked up to see Fain and Beck watching me closely. The man on the rack's screams filled my mind and I shut them out, forcing myself to focus on what I had learned.

'I need parchment and some charcoal,' I said and wasn't surprised when Beck handed them over. He had seen me scrying on missions before and knew that the easiest way for me to remember things was to draw them immediately afterwards. I spread the parchment down on my knee and began to sketch an outline of a map, the cell where the two prisoners had been held, the small courtyard and the torture chamber. There were some spaces which I left blank, memory unable to recall the specific twists and turns that the guard had taken through the rabbit warren of corridors.

'I'll need to send scouts in,' I muttered distractedly, 'the moths will help me remember every detail.'

'You'll need to wait a little longer before Gawain is in position,' Fain murmured, glancing up at the sky. Above us the sunset had faded into dusky twilight, and the moon was beginning to rise.

'That'll give me time to prepare,' I said, taking a swig of water and crushing some berries in my mouth, chewing hungrily. The tartness made me cough and then I drank more water. I returned to my drawing, closing my eyes to help with remembering the corridors and entryways, tracing them onto the parchment with short, deft strokes.

When night had fallen, I resumed my position, resting my hands on my knees and sinking back into the trance. This time I reached out, guided by the moonlight, to the lunar moths which clustered together in my bag on Gawain's shoulders.

Night. Free. Fly. The voices urged, demanding their release, and I enfolded them with my mind, filling them with purpose as the bag was opened and Gawain's masked face appeared.

'I'll follow when it's darker,' he whispered, shaking the bag slightly as the moths took flight. 'Find out as much as you can from the inside.'

As one, the moths flew towards Icevale Keep and then spread out around the walls, some perching high on the towers, while others went up and into the courtyard. I focussed on one which followed the wall around to where the Keep rose above the cliff face, looking out towards the Hoarfrost Glacier as it broke up into the sea. I encouraged the moth on, slowly moving up and along the wall, searching for crevices and holes.

In the faint glow from its wings I saw one, just large enough for the moth to crawl into. It squeezed through the hole, navigating the crumbled mortar and jagged stone until it reached a small cell. The man with the bandages lay against one of the pallets, hands clasped over his ears, blocking out the faint screams that resonated through the Keep. I commanded the moth to remain there, watching over the prisoner, while allowing my mind to merge with one of the others, which had found a guard's shoulder to perch on.

The guard had been patrolling the battlements, and then descended one of the staircases in the corner towers. The moth clung on as he turned into the main courtyard, passing wide oak doors which were bolted shut to the outside world. The guard paused briefly at the entrance to a hallway, flinching slightly as the screams from the torture chamber reached him.

'Sounds like the king and the warden are being extra forceful tonight,' one of the other guards on duty muttered as they loitered nearby.

'I heard they might be using the Iron Maiden tomorrow if he doesn't talk tonight,' the guard in the doorway said, 'I hope that I'm not going to be the one to clean up afterwards. She's always messy.'

'Aye, I'm fine staying on the outside,' the other guard said firmly. 'I'd hate to be one of the poor wretches who ends up inside the Iron Maiden.'

Another scream ripped through the hallway and Ethan, the guard who I had seen in my previous vision appeared, looking harassed.

'Bryan, come and help me. It's time to take the pig back to his cell.'

The guard followed reluctantly, moving down the hallway and turning left, descending a flight of stairs and then entering the last room at the end of the corridor. Inside, the warden was placing the hot poker back into the brazier. Markus lay on the rack, unconscious, the burns and abrasions across his chest were red raw. When the guards released his arms from their ties, he was jolted back awake for a moment with a cry of pain.

From his corner, the Usurper watched, a hungry smile on his face. 'Take the prisoner back to his cell, guards. Let him have some time to rest, he has been most helpful this evening. Tomorrow we'll see how much more he is choosing not to share when he embraces the Iron Maiden.'

Bryan glanced towards the iron box in the other corner and then quickly moved to grasp Markus' upper body as he swayed and collapsed.

'Dirty pig,' Ethan growled, grasping Markus' feet and indicating with a jolt of the head for his companion to lead the way out. 'Come on.'

'Give him time to reflect on what he has shared tonight,' the warden said silkily, his flat grey eyes gleaming in satisfaction. 'I like to think we found a way to break his spirit, but only time will tell how much more persuasion we need to use before he is completely broken.'

The Usurper laughed and the sound followed the guards as they carried Markus back to his cell. The moth flew behind, keeping to the roof where it would be out of their eyeline.

Markus watched it through half-closed eyes, as he tried to stifle his groans of agony.

When they arrived back at the cell, Markus was dropped onto his pallet with a crash. The other prisoner cowered away as he was kicked roughly, and then lay still until the guards had left, bolting the door behind them. When the sound of their footsteps had faded away, he looked up cautiously at Markus' body across the room.

'Are you alright?' His voice was a mere whisper, but Markus didn't answer, his body wracked with silent sobs.

The moth fluttered down to perch beside him, wings beating back and forth gently.

'Would you look at that,' the other prisoner breathed, sitting up with difficulty, 'never seen anything like before.'

Markus' eyes squinted open, noticing the pale light before him. His gaze travelled upwards and spotted the other moth in the wall.

'It's not alone Keely,' he grunted.

'So pretty,' Keely murmured as he glimpsed the second moth. 'It's lucky that it can fit through there, I miss being outside.'

Markus covered his eyes again, 'I don't think we'll ever get out of this place, no one knows where we are. We might as well accept it.'

'Just imagine what you would do if you could get out though,' Keely said dreamily, 'sit by a warm fire. Eat a proper meal. Drink a proper tankard of ale. What would you do?'

Markus was silent, either unwilling to answer or too lost in thought to respond. Keely watched him patiently, waiting for him to reply. Finally, Markus said, 'I don't know. Go back to the sea, perhaps.'

Keely grunted. 'I thought you would want to apologise to our princess. From what I've heard, you hurt her pretty bad.'

Markus' face was shuttered, and I felt a simmering anger and bitter resentment rise up in me. 'You don't know what you're talking about,' Markus growled.

'I know that I will be asking for her forgiveness,' Keely said quietly, 'I promised to protect and guard her, but I let her down. But you…sounded to me like you had a lot of unresolved things between you.'

'Shut your mouth.' Markus' tone was harsh, 'you know nothing.'

'Say what you want,' Keely shrugged, 'but you talk in your sleep.'

Markus' face became even paler than it had been before and he turned away, effectively ending the conversation.

I drifted away from the scene, jumping between the different minds and seeing out of a range of eyes until I felt confident in finishing the map of the interior of the Keep.

My hands moved fast over the parchment, half in the trance, half back in the clearing, sketching out the missing gaps. By the end of the night, it was complete and I sat back, Fain, Beck and Gawain around me, plotting out a route for the escape.

'It'll have to be tomorrow night,' Fain muttered, 'We can't run the risk of the warden getting carried away.'

'But we haven't had time to come up with a plan,' Beck argued, 'we've barely begun to scout out the interior.'

'You heard what was said,' Fain replied curtly, 'if they use the Iron Maiden tomorrow you cannot expect Markus to survive.'

I stayed silent as the others proposed ideas and debated the merits and dangers of executing the escape too early. My thoughts were preoccupied, racing through a myriad of possibilities and potential outcomes, trying to decide which one might work best.

'Gawain,' I finally interjected, 'show me where the wall is weakest and the best spot to scale it.' He pointed to two separate locations on the map. 'Alright,' I said, leaning forward, 'This is what we will do.'

Chapter Six: Erik

It took a few more days before we reached the Scardian coastline. Rakael had ordered Alex to navigate us towards the western coast, where it would be easier to reach the Resistance Stronghold in the mountains. According to Dylan- once he had recovered from his fear- being dragged partway across the Meridian had saved us potentially a day or two of travel. I found myself feeling a bit sad as, after several hours, Alexia released the boat and disappeared back towards the heart of the Meridian. Everyone else on board however was pleased to see her go. The other Resistance members believed in the old tales and felt that the appearance of the sea beast had been a warning from the Gods.

As Scardian shores came into view, the others sent out a cheer of relief, and I joined in, grateful to be near dry land again. This crossing had been significantly worse than the one with Markus, and it had made me realise that a life at sea was not something I wanted. Give me a horse, sword and some chain mail instead and I would be content.

Don't forget about the quests, Mister MacMillan's insidious voice pierced my thoughts. *Aren't you supposed to be finding things for one now? How well is that going so far?*

I scowled, not wanting to admit that the inner voice was right. Throughout the sea voyage, I had racked my brains trying to figure out how to find something like a heart's desire, or how to gather an innocent person's tear. As far as I knew, moonlight couldn't be liquified, who knew how I would be able to get a drop of it? The only thing I could guarantee was blood from a guilty man, I felt guilty enough about what had happened that I didn't need to look further afield for anyone else.

The afternoon sun had just started to begin its descent across the sky when I headed over to Dylan in the hopes of distracting myself from my thoughts. He was sitting close to Alex at the helm, neither speaking to the other but coexisting in companionable silence. I leaned against the railing and glanced at Dylan. He was looking out at the horizon, jotting notes into one of his journals. For the first time in a while, he wasn't surrounded by Rakael and her henchmen. With a quick look around the deck, I could see that they were not in earshot of us and I felt like I could finally ask the questions that I had been itching to ask for weeks.

'Dylan,' I began cautiously, aware that he was as prone to being grumpy and reticent as he was to being helpful since Nina's attack.

'Hm?'

It was better than nothing, so I continued, 'you haven't spoken about your trip to the Archives, what was it like? What did you find out? Was it dangerous? Did you find anything there that could help us to save Nina?'

His writing paused and he sighed, putting his notebook down.

'You ask a lot of questions, Erik.' It was Alex who spoke and I jumped, not having realised that they were listening. Alex turned to me, and I couldn't help shivering as I looked at their mask, unable to decipher their expression. I didn't think that I would ever be truly comfortable around the Dark Elves, those masks were too creepy and it was all too easy to remember the Tracker who had almost succeeded at abducting us.

'I suppose the tale is overdue,' Dylan said, 'but I might need your help, Alex.'

'I'm more than happy to assist,' they replied.

Dylan smiled gratefully and then looked out at the waves again, saying, 'you remember that we set out immediately for the Archives after that first welcome meal? I knew that Rakael was eager for me to find new weapon designs, or the recipes for a range of potions and poisons for the war effort. My Karshkan friends from the Larshka's Observatory could only appease her so far. The Dark Elves had been rumoured to have a wide library in the Archives, with designs that dated back centuries and had been untouched for years. I also wanted to see what was stored there that related to my own area of study – the Sigilium stones.'

I nodded, 'I remember you mentioning them.' Not only that, but I recalled being accused of taking one of the many scrolls that seemed to be related to his topic of study.

'I've spent the last decade learning about them,' Dylan continued, and I wondered what it was about these stones that would make any reasonable man give up ten years of his life; just the thought of so much studying made my head pound with a dull ache. 'That was the main reason the Lord of Winterdale sent me to the Eastern Lands in the first place.' Dylan paused as Alex glanced at him sharply, almost as if they were going to speak but decided against it. They held each other's gaze and in Dylan's eyes I realised that there was something else he didn't intend to share. I was tired of secrets, and the realisation that Alex knew something that I didn't rankled.

I scowled and said a touch aggressively, 'so what happened once you left the Dark Elven court?'

Dylan blinked and said, 'well the Archives are a long way from the court. We had to descend many tunnels that led deep into the earth, down into the heart of the Ombre Mountains. It felt like we would never reach it and the methods of getting there,' he shuddered, 'were almost enough to put anyone except the most dedicated scholar off from visiting.' He puffed out his chest, 'needless to say, I was fearless in the descent.'

I snorted disbelievingly. 'You? Fearless of physical exertion? Really?'

Dylan sniffed, offended by my lack of faith. 'I was a model adventurer. Just ask Alex.' I shot Alex a quizzical look, eyebrows raised, waiting expectantly for them to disagree.

'Considering the circumstances,' Alex said, moving the helm slightly, 'the sudden drops, rocky crags and the venomous lizards that were lying in wait, you coped quite well. It's not a journey for the faint-hearted, that's for sure.'

'Don't forget about the duendes,' Dylan added.

'Of course not,' Alex sounded as though they were smiling. 'But they were not a threat to you with me there.'

'What are duendes?' I asked.

'They are some of the other inhabitants of the Underdark,' Alex explained, 'mostly they respect the Dark Elves' authority in the caverns, but sometimes they are disrespectful towards my people. They like to play tricks in the darkness and my kind do not appreciate such impertinence. King Lysander was particularly averse to them; he would use them as jesters or musicians to entertain us in our revels until he tired of them.'

I remembered seeing the small figures wrapped up high above the dining tables in a sort of cage, and wondering what they had done to be put in such a situation. 'It sounds as though they're more often victims than not.'

'Perhaps,' Alex admitted, 'but they need to remember their place in the hierarchy of the Underdark. The Dark Elves reign supreme under the Ombre Mountains, and the other races that share those caverns need to understand that.'

'Anyway,' Dylan interrupted, noticing that I had opened my mouth to argue and probably hoping to avoid a disagreement. 'It took a few days to reach the Archives. They're located on a rocky plateau surrounded by a lake of molten lava. We had to be careful not to antagonise the cherufe.'

'The cherufe?' He had distracted me now.

'It's one of the creatures that dwell in the lava,' Alex said, 'not a kindly beast. We didn't want to alert it to our presence – the cherufe has killed many over the years.'

'It wasn't just the cherufe we wanted to avoid,' Dylan added, 'We also didn't want to provoke the fire elementals.'

'They don't take too kindly to anyone visiting the space near the world's core,' Alex interrupted, 'but we took an offering to appease them.'

'What did you give them?' I asked curiously; I'd never heard of fire elementals before.

'Cedarwood,' Alex said, 'they like any kind of scented wood though.'

'How come?'

Alex chuckled, 'they live in a place where nothing grows and they haven't ventured above the surface. Anything that reminds them of the outside world is welcomed, particularly if it smells strongly. With the cedarwood, the elementals were sated and allowed us to pass through their domain.'

'We had to cross the lava to get to the Archives,' Dylan continued. 'Everything was jagged and rough – obsidian walls that stretched up towards the Underdark. There was strange architecture, like the Dark Elf amphitheatre, but with runic markings. The walls were engraved in the Ancient Tongue, it was truly a marvel.' His eyes glazed over as he got lost in the memory. 'Inside, the Keeper of the Archives was waiting for us.'

'The Keeper is one of the Elders in the Dark Elf society,' Alex said, noting the question in my eyes. 'It is a position that is shared by all three sects on a cycle, as we all are guardians of Erthor's knowledge and secrets. It is a respected position, but a solitary one, it is rare that the Keeper receives visitors, and some go entire lifetimes without meeting another soul. They keep abreast of events in society through the scrying bowl, and our council will check in on the Archives regularly. When one Keeper is nearing the end of their life, the council chooses someone from the next sect in the cycle to journey to the Archives and begin their vigil.'

'It sounds lonely,' I muttered.

'Yes,' Dylan acquiesced, 'but they get to be the guardians of one of the oldest archives of ancient texts known to man.'

'Dylan would have probably been happy to stay there for months,' Alex chuckled, 'but the Keeper could only find so much that could be useful. Without his assistance, we might still be trawling through scrolls in the heart of the earth.'

'How did you know to return, then?' I asked. It struck me as odd that they would have chosen to return when they did – especially since I was all too familiar with how Dylan would become absorbed in his work, to the point where he would forgo meals and sleep.

'I received a message,' Alex replied. 'Aidyn let me know that he was departing the Underdark and alerted us to your potential return to the surface.'

'The trip back was just as bad as the journey there,' Dylan shuddered.

'But you managed it beautifully,' Alex murmured, and Dylan blushed.

'Look there,' Leif's shout cut through the air, and startled, I looked at him. He was pointing at the beach where there was a small group of people waiting to meet us. Dylan rose to his feet and moved away from the helm, and I followed as Alex began to turn the ship towards the shore.

'Ah good,' Rakael sighed. Under her instructions, we brought the vessel into the beach and the waiting group came aboard to help unload our trunks. Dylan and I carried the casket ashore, and as we passed the others a hush spread across the group.

'So, it's true,' one of the newcomers, a man with tied back red hair, said, 'the Princess is dead.'

'How did you know she was dead?' Tobias asked, 'we didn't send word.'

'News travels quickly along the roads,' the man said gravely, 'especially when the Usurper announces it far and wide and begins to prepare a lavish ceremony for his coronation.'

'What?' Rakael said sharply. 'You will need to fill me in about this, Ryan, once we are on the road.'

In a relatively short time, the wagons that our welcome party had brought were loaded, and we were ready to depart.

'I'll take the boat further around the coast,' Alex said calmly, 'we don't want it to be obvious where you arrived if the Trackers come looking.'

'Good idea,' Rakael said brusquely, 'I assume you will meet us at the Stronghold when you've found a safe location to leave it?'

Alex gave a half shrug and nod, 'I'll find you when the time is right.'

It was clear that Rakael did not appreciate the vagueness of their answer, but she didn't complain. Instead, she sniffed and turned away, striding across the sand towards the rest of the party.

Dylan took Alex's hand and shook it. 'Take care,' he said, 'stay safe.'

'I'll do my best,' Alex replied. 'The same goes for you scholar. Remember what the Keeper said – try to avoid getting lost.' Dylan nodded and I watched him depart, slightly confused by their exchange.

'Where will you go?' I asked Alex quietly, not wanting Rakael to overhear.

'I need to find my comrades,' Alex said, 'Erthor sent me a vision last night, telling me that they would need my help. When we have reunited, I will bring them to the Stronghold.'

'Will you tell them about Nina?' I pressed, 'about what I was asked to do?'

Alex regarded me, mask glinting in the light reflecting off the water. 'It is not my story to tell, unless you wish it. I was not the one entrusted with the responsibility of finding a way to cure her, therefore I will not be the one to break the news to my friends.'

Aidyn. I felt a momentary burst of anger and resentment, which I stifled. I didn't want to think about Aidyn, who had come along and taken Markus' place. It hadn't felt right watching him and Nina together, especially after everything she and Markus had been through. I hadn't liked the way she smiled at him, it implied that something else was at work, and when they had signed the betrothal contract, I had wondered what could be done to get her out of it once Markus was freed. I was sure that he would have an idea. He always did.

'I don't think he needs to know about it,' I found myself saying. 'It's not his responsibility and it's none of his business.'

If I could've seen past the mask, I was sure that Alex's eyebrows would have been raised. Their voice was tinged with admonishment and surprise when they replied, 'are you quite sure? They are betrothed.'

'I'm sure,' I said forcefully. 'And they *were* betrothed. But then she was killed. It can hardly still be valid.'

Alex didn't answer and I turned away, suddenly feeling ashamed of myself. It wasn't that I didn't like Aidyn, he was alright. He'd been more than happy to tell me about the Underdark and give advice for developing my skills. He'd even joined me during one of the training sessions, instructing in a way that had been more understandable than the Dark Elf trainers. But no, it was better that he not be told. It was *my* quest, *my* responsibility, as Alex had said. I kicked the sand as I headed towards the others, trying to ignore the slightly sick feeling that had taken root in the depths of my stomach.

'Come on, Erik,' Christoff called from beside the wagons, 'we're heading out.'

I increased my pace, resenting the fact that we had to ride in the wagons instead of riding like the Resistance members who had come to join us. I scrambled into the back of one of the wagons, settling myself beside Lisette and Dylan, and watched as Alex began to navigate the boat away. The wagon jolted and began to move, rocking us back and forth along the bumpy terrain as we began to wind our way up a hill and towards the main road.

'There have been more and more travellers of late,' one of the Resistance members riding nearby told Rakael. She had short dark hair and a wide face, with eyes that bulged slightly, like a frog's. 'The Usurper has been sending riders out all over to announce his upcoming coronation. He's invited foreign dignitaries from Karshka, Velkra and Felshkar to attend. From what the farmers say, it's planned for midwinter.'

'The Winter Solstice?' I asked loudly, interrupting them. The woman looked at me with slightly raised eyebrows.

'Yes,' she said, 'apparently the Usurper wants to conduct the ceremony then. It gives the visiting dignitaries time to arrive, they have a couple of months before then. And knowing some of them— the Velkranian Queen for example— she likes to travel in style. It gives him time to prepare the palace and the Capital, but he wants the whole of Scardia to prepare as well. Farmers are having to pay tithes already but now they are increasing, it's made a lot of people angry. They're starving, Rakael.' She turned back to Rakael who was frowning, deep in thought.

'We will need to support those in the most need,' she said finally, 'and spread the word that we will be fighting. Once the people know, they will join the cause.' She glanced at the trees on either side of the road as we passed, which were dropping leaves tinged with red and brown. 'I thought that summer would last longer.'

'Summer is always short,' the other woman said, 'I think we were surprised that it came at all this past year. But autumn has well and truly begun. There's even been some snowfall in certain parts of the country— Winter will be here sooner than you think.'

I looked at Dylan and Lisette, reading in their expressions the same concern I felt. Time in the Underdark had seemed to be different and it had been hard to tell how long we had actually been there. I could feel the time between now and the Winter Solstice slipping away.

The Winter Spirit's words filled my mind again: *if you cannot achieve your goal by the time the sun rises on the Winter Solstice, your sister will be forever lost in the in-between of worlds.* I shivered and glanced around to make sure that no one had noticed. Dylan was hunched over one of his notebooks, perusing it with single-minded focus, while Lisette was watching the scenery pass worriedly. I reached out and gave her arm a slight pat and she blinked, smiling at me quickly before returning her gaze to stare out at the trees and fields as we trundled on.

'Ryan,' Rakael was saying, 'tell me about the Trackers. Have there been any raids or patrols lately?'

'Since the Usurper's announcement it's been pretty quiet,' Ryan said, pulling up beside us. 'There was a group of them at Tarheim for several weeks, but they moved on once they'd collected the tithes. The Usurper will be swimming in gold by the time his visitors arrive. The townspeople have almost nothing left.'

'They burned Orin's barn,' the woman said sadly, 'he lost some of his livestock, but no one was hurt.'

'Why did they do it?' Rakael asked, 'did they suspect him of being complicit with us?'

'No,' Ryan said, 'Clarisse didn't mean to worry you.' He shot the dark-haired woman a look and she withdrew, urging her horse to ride ahead. 'Orin didn't want it to be spread about,' Ryan continued, 'some of the Trackers had their way with his daughter. She tried to fight, and they took it out on her and the barn. They were punishing Orin for his daughter's disobedience.' His voice was sickened.

'Is the girl alright?' Rakael asked coolly, jaw tight.

'No,' Ryan said quietly. 'She did not survive.'

'Then we can use this to our advantage,' Rakael muttered, 'I assume the villagers know what happened?'

Ryan nodded, 'there have been rumours, but nothing confirmed yet.'

'Make sure they are told,' Rakael said firmly, 'This injustice will help them come around to supporting us.'

'What about Orin's wishes?' Ryan asked nervously, 'he made it clear that...'

'Orin will understand that this is for the greater good,' Rakael said, 'surely, he wants justice for his daughter's death. That is something we can provide him with.'

Lisette reached over and gripped my hand, startling me. I hadn't realised that I was shaking. I forced myself to calm down and control myself; I didn't want her to think that I was weak. But hearing the callous way Rakael spoke made me uncomfortable; it felt as though we were all pawns in her game and she would be willing to dispense with any of us in order to achieve her goal.

'How far away is the Stronghold?' I asked Leif, who was perched on the front seat of the wagon, holding the reins.

He grinned back at me, 'we'll be on the road for several days at least, Erik. Tarheim is many miles from here, and then we need to go through the mountains.'

'Keep your voice down,' Rakael snapped harshly, 'you never know who might be lurking just out of sight.' I rolled my eyes and turned away from her scowl, crossing my arms and glaring out the back of the wagon, glumly watching the ocean disappear from sight.

It took at least a week to reach Tarheim. We had trundled through multiple small towns on our way, to all extents and purposes seeming like simply a large group of travelling farmers, heading to Tarheim for a wedding. No one questioned our story, and it was a nice change to be back amongst normal people again. I didn't miss the endless night, hidden ravines or silver masks that had been constant in the Underdark, and made the most of enjoying the weak sunshine filtering down through trees on my face.

While we were on the road, I got to know the other Resistance members who had come to meet us. Ryan had been Rakael's second in command, and therefore in charge of the Scardian Stronghold while she was in the Eastern Lands, but now that she was back deferred to her judgement on everything. Clarisse- the dark-haired woman with a face like a frog- was his cousin, and had been in the Resistance for only a few years. There was also John, Reggie and Philippe, all of whom were ex-farmers turned Resistance fighters after their lands had been claimed by the Usurper and they had been cast out penniless.

According to John, who told me one night over the campfire with his heavy moustache twitching, the Resistance was less organised than Rakael had made out. She had taken all the strongest fighters with her to the Eastern Lands, leaving the rest to fend for themselves.

'That was why we needed the Elves to give us more men,' John had whispered, taking a long drag on his clay pipe. 'Those of us who joined here don't have the training to stand a chance against Trackers, let alone the Capital.'

As he spoke, I remembered some of the things I had heard Rakael say in the Underdark, about how they had expendable soldiers who would draw the Trackers' fire. I hoped that she hadn't been speaking about men like John, but deep down I realised that she had. I wondered what the Resistance members here would say if they knew that they were going to be part of the first wave of the assault, and that the majority of them would not survive.

I tried to avoid Rakael as much as possible and spent more time with Lisette and Dylan, even though his rambling sometimes drove me crazy. Luckily for me, it seemed that she was happy to ignore my presence, though I sometimes caught her watching me, her mouth pinched in thought. At these times I would awkwardly try to engage Dylan or John in conversation just to avoid her gaze. Dylan was usually caught up in his own studies and would happily monologue about that for hours on end, while John was more of the quiet type, who found too much forced conversation unnerving.

I hoped that once we were in Tarheim it would be easier to avoid Rakael.

We pulled into the stable yard of a tavern whose faded sign decried it as The King's Head. There was a crowd of passers-by milling around the yard, chatting amongst themselves and eyeing the newcomers with interest.

'We're just going to have a meal,' Rakael said brusquely, 'there's another hour or so until nightfall. We can still make some progress before we need to set up camp.'

'Of course, Rakael,' Ryan said promptly, eyeing the rest of us sternly to make sure we didn't argue.

'I'll stay with the horses,' Leif muttered, and Philippe joined him, preferring to stay away from the crowded tavern's dining room. As we entered, the familiar smells from Mister MacMillan's came back and for a moment I was Olaf Henriksson again. But then Lisette took my hand, and Dylan gripped my shoulder, and I was reminded that I was Erik now. And Erik was not afraid.

We sat down at one of the long tables on wooden benches and were served a rich stew that, in my opinion, had too many vegetables and more gristle than meat. Rakael was in cosy discussion with the innkeeper, a rather red-faced man who didn't seem to be thrown by her scars. Meanwhile John, Reggie and Christoff were chatting to a barmaid, who was flashing them with bright smiles. Lisette clicked her fingers at me, trying to draw my attention away from the barmaid and I turned around, slightly embarrassed.

She gave me a reprimanding look and indicated for me to eat, watching me closely to make sure that I did as I was told. I felt my face go hot with annoyance – I was thirteen summers old now, I wasn't a child anymore, and she wasn't my mother. I scowled down at the spoon and shovelled more of the stew into my mouth, forcing myself to chew and swallow. The sound of crying carried across the room and I felt my scowl deepen- the last thing I wanted to hear while I was eating was a small child wailing. The noise intensified and I glanced over my shoulder, glaring at the young infant in its tired mother's arms, as it screamed its displeasure to the world.

'By the Gods,' Dylan suddenly said from next to me, 'Erik, the baby…'

Lisette was slapping my arm excitedly, gesturing for me to stand up and move over. I stared at them both, and then realisation hit.

'The baby,' I muttered jumping up from my seat, napkin still in my hand, and racing over to the mother and child. Once I got there though, I had no idea what to say. Instead, I just stood there until the mother lost her temper with me.

'Yes?' She snapped, 'can I help you?'

I was about to say something when her eyes alit on the napkin in my hand.

'Oh,' she muttered, reaching out and snatching it from my grasp. 'Thank you.' She wiped her baby's face and then glanced back at me and demanded, 'what do you want?'

'Can I… uh… have my napkin back?' I managed, stumped that it had been so easy. She frowned and then returned the soggy cloth into my hands. I heard her mutter something about me to her husband as I walked away but I didn't care. All that mattered to me was the sodden napkin in my hands.

Lisette reached out for it when I sat back down, wrapping it up carefully and storing it in a small bag at her waist. She turned shining eyes to me, and I felt my grin widen as I said, 'that's the tear of an innocent collected.'

'It should be enough,' Dylan said under his breath, 'From everything I've read in the old tales, the Gods are open to interpretations of their instructions. I highly doubt you were needing to bring an actual tear to the Hoarfrost Glacier.'

Lisette nodded and hugged me tightly, and I felt a little weight lift from my shoulders. One down, three more to go. Perhaps, achieving the Winter Spirit's quest would be easier than I had thought. As I glanced around the dining room of the inn, I allowed myself to relax and believe that it was possible.

Chapter Seven: Aidyn

We moved across the open clifftop, encouraging the clouds to cover the moon for slightly longer so that we could reach the side of the Keep undetected. On my signal, Fain and Beck moved off towards the cliff edge, while Gawain and I waited until the guards above had moved past, before throwing a rope up and over one of the ramparts. I tested the rope and nodded to Gawain, who began to scale the wall, pulling himself up, hand over hand. I followed close behind, praying to Erthor to not let the patrolling guards hear us. It felt like an age before we were heaving ourselves over the ramparts, dropping down into the walkway. I pulled up the rope, looping it through my belt and slipped into the shadows beside one of the doorways to the corner tower, Gawain on the other side, waiting patiently.

When the two guards on patrol came past, we made it quick. A short, swift upward jab of the blade and a hand over the mouth ensured that no one heard them. We grabbed hold of their slumping bodies, dragging them into the tower. Once inside, we stripped them out of their armour and donned it, carrying the bodies out along the stretch of wall that overlooked the glacier. To our relief, there were two figures already there, discarding the bodies of two other guards. We watched as the bodies fell down the cliff edge towards the depths of the ocean below. I didn't feel regret or pity for them. From what I had seen, the men who worked here were corrupt and sadistic, I had no qualms in dispatching them.

'Come on,' Fain muttered, pulling one of the guards' helmets on. 'We won't have long.'

Gawain and I led the way, moving down towards the courtyard. The guards' helmets were tight over our balaclavas, but provided us with an effective disguise. We'd left our masks with our packs, hidden in a copse of trees not far away. At the bottom of the stairs our group split again, Beck and Fain heading in the direction of the cell where the prisoners were kept. Gawain and I patrolled the edges of the courtyard, noting the barred doors and the nearby stable. Several other guards were stationed here, talking quietly amongst themselves.

'Thought he would've stayed longer,' one of them was saying, 'but I suppose those high and mighty ones don't have the stomach for too much bloodshed.'

'You're wrong there,' another laughed, 'Lord Niall likes to make them scream, he does. No, from what I heard, he has a special visitor meeting him in the Capital and needed to go back to prepare. Urgent summons, you know. I'm not sorry to see the last of his men though, a nasty bunch the whole lot of them. They had far too much fun with that other prisoner – I can still hear his screams.'

I felt a momentary sense of relief. If the Usurper had left, there would be slightly less opposition to our rescue efforts. And if several guards had gone with him, our job was looking easier by the minute.

'Let's clean up this area,' I muttered, heading towards the sound of horses, and Gawain nodded, moving in the opposite direction. Once we were on either side of the group of guards, I summoned the darkness, bringing it down upon the them, extinguishing the torches and providing the distraction needed to slip in, stab and twist. The guards barely had time to notice the shadows before they were cut down. With only two of us, there wasn't a way to mask the sound of bodies hitting the ground, but luckily no one else was in earshot.

Together, Gawain and I dragged them into the stables, piling them in one of the stalls and covering them with straw. It would buy us some time, perhaps an hour or two, before the alarm was raised. The horses in the adjacent stalls nickered and swished their tails, seemingly not too bothered by our intrusion.

'Aidyn,' Gawain said, 'Let's go.'

I nodded, checking that the courtyard was clear. All was silent as we moved across the cobbles, heading in the same direction that Beck and Fain had taken. When we entered the Keep, we turned left, following the corridors that I had traced on the map. I knew at once that the warden was in the middle of an interrogation session: Markus' screams were ringing through halls at intermittent intervals.

'We'd better hurry,' Gawain muttered, and we increased our pace, taking the steps two at a time. Finally, we were outside the door to the torture chamber, and softly pushed it open.

The warden didn't hear us come in, he was so engrossed with Markus that he didn't notice the door opening and closing. It wasn't until Gawain's blade was pressed to his neck that he registered that he was not alone.

Markus was stretched out on the rack, muscles straining with tension. I stepped around the warden and released the wheel, loosening the hold on Markus' arms and legs, before picking up a length of rope from the nearby table. I ignored Markus' cry of pain, keeping my eyes on the torturer.

'What do you think you're doing?' The warden asked angrily, 'who do you think you are?'

Gawain pressed his blade harder against his neck, until a trickle of blood ran down its edge. Slowly, deliberately, I wrapped the rope around the warden's wrists, tying it with sharp tugs, and then thrust one of the leather gloves in his mouth, silencing him. Gawain pushed him against the wall, ignoring his muffled groans and attempts to break free as he was tied to one of the heavy metal rings.

I untied Markus' wrists and ankles as a knock came from the door. I went over and saw Beck on the other side.

'Any problems so far?' I asked quietly, 'any incidents?'

'So far, so good.' He replied, 'The other one went quietly. He's been injured today though, and pretty badly. Was able to walk with Fain easily enough. Apart from that, all quiet.'

I nodded, 'good. Come and help with this one.'

We moved over to the rack and Beck heaved Markus up until he was half standing, half held up for support. His face was sweaty and red, and he glanced back and forth between us with crazed eyes.

'Who are you?' He whispered, 'where are you taking me?'

'We were sent to get you,' Beck replied, 'be quiet. We don't want to wake anyone up.'

'How…?' Markus' voice drifted away into silence, his confusion evident.

'There will be time to talk later,' I muttered, 'get him out of here, Beck. We'll follow in a while.' Beck nodded and headed off, and I fastened the door behind him. I turned to Gawain and said, 'where do you suggest we start?'

Gawain chuckled, 'I think he deserves some of his own treatment.'

The warden spat out the glove in his mouth and glared around at us, 'who the hell are you?'

'We're here to exact vengeance for our brother,' I said calmly, stepping forward and lifting one of the nearby instruments in my hand.

'Do you remember a Dark Elf in Lowton?' Gawain asked softly.

The warden paused for a moment, his face blanching slightly. The scars on his cheek shone white and his cold grey eyes flickered with recognition. 'Don't tell me,' he said, 'you're some of *them*.' He spat at our feet contemptuously, 'dirty Elves. Like cockroaches, you are. Why don't you crawl back into your hole in the ground, where you belong?'

I felt a cold resolve descend over me and smiled, fully aware that he could not see it. This man had murdered Gaelen in cold blood and then tried to kidnap Nina, harming Erik in the process. It was time for the price to be paid. Erthor demanded retribution for his fallen warrior. It was time for blood.

Gawain and I returned to the stable half an hour later. The warden's muffled screams lingered in my mind, but as I opened the large oaken doors to the Keep, the scar on my hand tingled with Erthor's satisfaction- Gaelen had been avenged and my vow to him was complete. Erthor's desire for vengeance had been temporarily sated, but I knew who would be next on the list to appease him.

'Hurry, Aidyn,' Fain muttered, as his horse shifted uneasily. On the horse beside him were the two prisoners, tied together until we could get out of sight of the Keep. The doors creaked and came to a stop, revealing the dark clifftop and road stretching away. One by one the others passed through the doors and sped away, shielded by the fog that Beck had summoned. Gawain and I shut the doors behind us, mounted and followed the others, as lights flared and shouts began to ring out from the Keep.

'I think they might have found the warden,' I said quietly, and Gawain grunted in response. Neither of us was surprised, but we were grateful that we had evaded detection for the moment.

'Be quiet,' Beck hissed, 'we've got to get away from here.' He pulled up near the copse of trees where we had hidden our bags, leapt down and grabbed them, tossing them up to us and then remounting and pushing on along the road. The prisoners were mostly quiet, although they gasped in pain as we increased the pace, causing them to bounce uncomfortably in the saddle.

'I thought we would've had more time,' Fain growled, glancing over his shoulder in the direction of Icevale Keep. 'What by the Gods did you two do?'

Gawain was silent, so I answered, 'we just wanted to remind the warden that Dark Elves are not to be trifled with.'

'We left him in the Iron Maiden,' Gawain grunted, 'he won't last long. Gaelen's children can rest easy knowing that their father's killer has paid for his crime.'

'Where are you taking us?' The prisoner called Keely asked suddenly, 'who are you?'

'Untie us, Elves.' Markus' voice was faint but still tinged with anger. I felt a flash of astonishment.

'You might want to check your tone, Captain,' I said coldly. 'Don't forget who got you out of that Keep.'

Markus peered around at me, 'we've met before, haven't we?'

I condescended to nod but didn't speak. The moon was coming out again and we were still too close to the Keep for comfort.

'We need to find a place to toss this armour,' Gawain muttered. 'It's weighing us down and it'll attract notice.'

'He's right,' Beck said, 'we should get rid of it sooner rather than later.'

There was a bridge up ahead, stretching out across the ravine where the Hoarfrost Glacier met the sea. I pulled up before it, dismounting quickly and removing the armour which I tossed over the edge. It was a relief to be in our usual black leather, and I helped the others, keeping a lookout behind us as we reattached our masks. Fain cut the rope which held Keely and Markus together so that they could sit more comfortably, but only received a mumbled thanks from Keely.

'I can hear barking,' Beck said suddenly, glancing back. 'Hurry.'

The last piece of armour was thrown away and we continued on, urging the shadowy fog to linger behind us in the hopes of confusing our pursuers. The horses' hooves echoed along the bridge as we pushed them faster, the two prisoners barely clinging on. Gradually, the sound of dogs and shouting faded away and we allowed ourselves to relax slightly. We had taken the last horses in the stables, so we knew that the soldiers following us would not get too far.

We rode on for a few hours, keeping an eye on Keely and Markus, who looked like they would collapse at any moment. Somehow, they managed to stay awake and upright, gripping onto each other and the horse for support. Markus watched us all distrustfully, while Keely's bandages covered his eyes making it hard to tell what he was thinking.

When the faintest trace of dawn began to show across the sky, we began to look for landmarks and signs, anything that could give us an indication of where to go next. I knew we needed to go westward but wanted to avoid as many towns and roads as possible. Under the cover of darkness, we had been lucky and not passed anyone, but that was sure to change with daylight. I was also aware that we were tired, and that the two prisoners needed to rest and have their injuries tended to, we couldn't expect them to travel much further in their current state. I was impressed that they had lasted as long as they had without complaint, although I did not like the way Markus watched us, as though we, instead of the Usurper's minions, were the monsters.

'Look there,' Gawain said, 'Surely we can find some shelter there.' He was pointing at a distant wood.

'It's as good a place as any,' Beck agreed, and we turned our horses in that direction, leaving the road and cutting towards the forest through grassy fields with sighs of relief. There was no sign of human habitation around for which we were grateful- we didn't want to run the risk of being spotted by a shepherd or farmer who could report us to the Trackers.

The trees were closely pressed together, creating a shady refuge from the rising sun and any prying eyes from the road. We moved in deeper until Beck was satisfied that we wouldn't be easily found. I took charge of the horses, tying them to some of the nearby trees, while Fain helped Markus and Keely down to lie in a bed of leaves. Gawain disappeared to find water and food, and Beck began to unpack some blankets from our bags.

Both Markus and Keely were breathing in heavy gasps as Fain bent over them, tending to their injuries. None of us were very skilled in healing magics, but Fain had some experience and was able to ease some of the aches and bruises. Much of the damage caused by the torture he could not mend and would have to wait until we arrived at the Resistance Stronghold before they could be properly tended to. Markus took a deep breath and released it through clenched teeth, as Fain focussed over the strained muscles, reducing some of the tension.

When Fain reached towards Keely to remove some of the bandages, he gripped onto them.

'It's not pretty,' he said, 'I…'

'We have probably seen worse,' I said bluntly, moving over to help Fain unwrap the bandages, 'besides these need to be cleaned. You run the risk of infection if not.'

Keely croaked a small laugh, 'I think it's already too late for that.'

Once the bandages were removed, I couldn't disagree. Clearly, he had been in that place for a long time, judging from the state of his injuries.

'The warden started with my hands,' he said softly, lifting the crushed fingers that were blackened with grime and dried blood. 'Used the screws until I couldn't think of anything else but the pain. I almost talked then, but it was when he did this that I couldn't hold back.' He gestured to his face and I felt a twist of pity. 'It hurt too much, I just wanted to die. I didn't want to tell them about her, but I did.'

'She would forgive you,' I said quietly, resting a comforting hand on his shoulder. He paused, thoughtful for a moment.

'How do you know who I'm talking about?' He asked, 'we've never met before, I'm certain.'

'No, we have not,' I said calmly, 'but we have got mutual friends. One in particular wanted you both to be released from that Keep, it was a request I couldn't disregard.'

'I don't mean to sound ungrateful,' Markus interrupted, sounding exactly that. 'But *why* would you agree to help us? How did you know where we were? I wouldn't have thought that Dark Elves would interest themselves in the likes of *us*.'

'Mind what you say, Captain,' Fain murmured as he drew some clean bandages out of his pack and began to wrap them around Keely's wounds. 'Do not overexert yourself.'

'I just want to know who the bloody hell you lot *are* and why you came for us.' Markus growled, dark eyes blazing with distrust. I glanced at Beck who was leaning against a tree trunk with his arms folded, watching the exchange. He gave a slight nod, indicating that I should be honest. Markus and Keely would find out the truth eventually, so we might as well get it over and done with now, before we arrived at the Stronghold. The only thing I wasn't prepared to share with them was what I had discovered in my visions, which I hadn't even shared with my companions. Let them believe Nina to be alive a while longer.

'You're right in believing that we normally wouldn't interest ourselves in people like you, Captain,' I said coolly, 'If it wasn't for the Princess we wouldn't be here. She sent us after you – she saw your capture and figured out where you were being taken. It was part of our contract that I find you both and bring you to the Resistance's Stronghold.'

'Oh, thank the Gods,' Keely whispered, 'they'll know what to do. I hoped Milady would find them. I hoped she would be safe.'

I bit my tongue, feeling the cold numbness sliding through my veins at his words. Instead, I watched Markus' reaction, the way his eyes flared, before he schooled his emotions into an inscrutable expression.

'She didn't give up on us,' Keely muttered, a wide smile on his broken face. 'It was worth it.'

'What do you mean by a contract?' Markus asked slowly, ignoring Keely's words.

'A betrothal contract,' Fain answered calmly. 'Princess Wilhelmina agreed to wed King Lysander's son and unite the Dark and High Elven kingdoms together. In exchange she would receive support for her cause to reclaim Scardia and you two would be freed.'

Markus' face drained of all colour. He looked suddenly older and I felt a hint of satisfaction.

'She's betrothed to one of your kind?' He asked, strained. Anger flared in me and I scowled.

'Yes,' I said, making sure to keep the emotions out of my voice. 'She is betrothed to me.'

A decidedly awkward silence drew out, as Keely struggled to think about what to say, clearly shocked. Markus just stared at me, partly accusing, partly furious. If he hadn't been so weak, I thought that he would have tried to fight me. But he hadn't laid his claim on Nina, he had missed his chance. Although now, I supposed that it didn't really matter.

'Well,' Keely finally managed, 'that's, well, congratulations to you both.' He coughed slightly and Fain lifted a water flask into his hands.

'Calm yourself,' he murmured, 'drink and rest. You have both gone through much in recent times. We will keep watch and wake you when it is time to move onward.'

Gratefully, Keely drank and settled down under a blanket, falling asleep quickly. Markus however was slower to drift off, eyeing us distrustfully until he finally succumbed to oblivion.

'Well, that could have been handled better,' Fain muttered, 'but I suppose there's nothing we can do about it now.'

I shrugged and moved to sit against one of the nearby trees, but it was Beck who answered, 'it was something that needed to be done.'

'They would've found out when we reached the Stronghold anyway,' I said quietly, 'probably better for them to learn about the contract now before we arrive.' My brothers nodded in silent understanding. 'You two can rest for a while,' I continued, 'I'll keep watch until Gawain returns. I'll wake you if anything happens.'

They grunted and within moments were dozing, leaning against their trees while I gazed around, wondering how long Gawain would take. The sounds of birdsong filled the air, chirping as Sybilla's chariot lifted the sun higher in the sky. I found myself slipping into a daydream, imagining what would have happened when we returned to the Stronghold if Nina was still alive. I saw her smile, her eyes lighting up with admiration and wonder, and my chest tightened as doubts began to crowd my mind. Would she have been happier to see me, or the captain returned alive?

I glanced at him, pondering how much had happened between them. I had my suspicions, of course, but nothing had been confirmed. Perhaps it was better that way; I already disliked the man, partly because of how he spoke about my kind, partly because of the jealousy I felt when Nina had mentioned him.

But she chose to wed you, a small voice reminded me. She agreed. If she had lived, she would have kept her promise. The question then would have been whether she would give her heart to me as well. But the answer to that I'd never know.

Chapter Eight: Erik

When we arrived at the Resistance Stronghold, I was underwhelmed. I had been expecting a vast keep built into the side of the mountains, an indomitable fortress that would withstand any attack, something worthy of an old tale. What met our eyes, though, was a rough camp, spread out through one of the hidden valleys between the mountain ranges. It was not what either Dylan, Lisette or I had anticipated and from their expressions, they were as surprised as I was.

'I thought there would be an actual stronghold,' I muttered to John as we entered the campsite and began to unload the wagons. 'The way Rakael would talk about it made it sound like there was a lot more here.'

He laughed, 'There used to be. It was razed by the Trackers and Usurper's army years ago. Since then, we have tried not to stay too long in one place. Besides, with more soldiers joining us, there's more space in the camp that there would be in a keep. See,' he indicated a group of Dark Elf soldiers who were running a training exercise nearby, barking out commands to each other in a demonstration for the Scardian recruits. There seemed to be several training grounds spread throughout the camp, and I felt excitement trickle through me. It was much bigger here than it had been in King Aegis' court, and I couldn't wait to get back into the routine of training.

'You will be sharing a tent with the other children, Erik,' Rakael said bluntly, handing her horse's reins to a nearby soldier and pointing towards a collection of smaller tents, where a group of younger children were running around, shrieking. I wanted to argue with her – how dare she push me off to the children's camp when I had probably done more than the lot of them put together?

As if she could read my mind, Rakael smiled coldly. 'You don't have the Princess to support you now, Erik. You've tried my patience with your insubordination far too often. You will be staying with the children from now on.' She chose that moment to walk off, heading towards the largest tents on the other side of the camp. I could barely speak through the anger that constricted my throat. I wanted to throw something. How dare she!

'Come on, Erik,' John said, 'I'm sure you'll make some new friends easily enough.' He strode towards the children and I followed reluctantly, trying to catch Lisette or Dylan's eyes, but both of them were too busy unloading the wagon to notice me leave. I stomped after John, scowling at the ground and coming up with ways that I could make Rakael's life hellish.

As we approached the tent, the children noticed John and raced towards him, jumping onto his neck and clinging to him, each one talking incessantly and laughing. John grinned and ruffled their hair, checking in with each child to see how they had been in his absence.

'Jorik, show Erik where he will be sleeping,' he said to one boy who looked several years younger than me. He had big blue eyes and blond hair, and gave me a wide, gap-toothed smile. I managed a small twitching smile in response and let him lead me towards one of the tents. Inside were multiple bedrolls closely packed together, and I felt myself sigh.

'This is where we sleep,' Jorik said, 'But when it gets cold, we huddle.'

I didn't want to even think about that. I couldn't imagine anything worse in that moment than having a group of little kids climbing all over me at nighttime for warmth.

'Thanks for the heads up,' I muttered as Jorik moved back to the group. I dropped my bag and looked around, wanting to slip away before John left and the children trapped me instead. No one was watching as I moved away through the tents, navigating my way around the camp and starting to figure out the lay of the land.

I noticed early on that there were certain areas where each of the allies were located. The Dark Elves had set up their campsite under some of the tall pines, the tents black and foreboding. Next to their area, another group of Elves were set up, their tents in shifting greens and browns, so that they were camouflaged against the undergrowth. Some of them were sitting under the boughs of the pines, fletching arrows and testing the strings on their bows. In contrast, there were several gypsy caravans painted in bright colours near the fire pits. Around them, the gypsies lounged, laughing and playing the pipes or lute, their children dancing to the jaunty tunes. Their cheerfulness lifted the overall mood of the campsite, and soon the group of children I had tried to avoid were dancing around the fire as well.

'Erik!' I glanced around and grinned. It was Stefan, racing towards me from one of the training fields, ducking in between guards and tents to come to a halt in front of me, panting. 'King Aegis said that you would be on your way,' he gasped, 'why didn't you tell me you were going to sneak off to the Underdark? The others were going crazy, they thought that you'd died.'

I felt a momentary lapse of shame and then shrugged. 'The others would have tried to stop me.'

He stared at me, a range of emotions flitting across his expression. Finally, he just laughed and gripped my arm, 'I'm just glad you're here. It's been lonely without you.' I felt a funny lurch at his words, but just hitched a grin on my face.

'Show me the camp?'

'Only if you tell me about the Underdark,' Stefan said, leading me away through the tents. I didn't need to be asked twice, regaling him with the whole story of our trip to the Ombre Mountains, the sea voyage, King Lysander's court, Nina's trial and the Tracker attack. I didn't mention the Winter Spirit's visit or my quest, but told him everything else, happy to answer his questions.

In return I was shown the different mess areas, where a group of women worked at preparing food for the camp. In the centre were the large tents where Rakael had gone, which Stefan told me were off limits to the rest of us. King Aegis, his councillors and the Resistance leaders were staying there, and orders had been given for them to not be disturbed. The best part was the training areas, and we were able to practise archery before the gongs were rung for the midday meal.

It was there that I saw King Aegis and slowly made my way towards him through the crowd. He looked significantly older than when I had last seen him, his face tired and drawn, the wrinkles etched deeper than they had been before. When he saw me, I noticed that his eyes were hollowed, but on seeing me they brightened slightly and he pulled away from the group of councillors he was sitting with. One of them was

Rakael and I saw her expression tighten with disapproval as she watched him approach me.

'Erik,' King Aegis reached out and embraced me, gripping me hard and shaking slightly. 'I heard what happened,' he whispered, 'I'm glad that you were able to get back alive. I only wish…I wish that she…' His voice drifted off and he blinked, regaining his composure and letting me go. 'It's good to see you,' he said, 'you must come and spend some time with me later, I'd like to know more about what happened.'

I nodded wordlessly, suddenly uncertain about my decision not to tell him about the Winter Spirit's quest. Had I made the right choice? Would he be able to forgive me? King Aegis smiled sadly and moved back to his table, leaving me to my conflicted thoughts.

'Come on, Erik,' Stefan said, poking me forward, 'let's get some food.'

We moved closer to the steaming pots and got served a large helping of some sort of steaming mush, which was flavourless but filling. It was worse than the stew from the inn at Tarheim and I had to force myself to swallow.

'What is this?' I finally managed to ask.

Stefan laughed, 'they don't have too much available for us. It's better not to ask, but I think it's some sort of porridge.'

I looked down at the gluggy mess in my bowl and said resolutely, '*that* is not porridge.'

'You get used to it,' Stefan said in between mouthfuls. 'It's not so bad.'

It was significantly better than Rakael's favourite jerky, but a far cry from what we had had on offer in King Aegis' court or the Underdark. I grimaced as I ate, trying to imagine that it was something more appetising, but failing spectacularly.

Thankfully it did fill me up quickly and so I didn't have to eat any more.

'Where are you sleeping?' Stefan asked as we deposited our dirty bowls in large buckets and strode away, towards the side of the valley.

I grimaced. 'Rakael ordered me to stay with the children. It's pathetic.'

'Join us instead,' Stefan said, 'we have plenty of room in our tent. It'll be more fun. Since we arrived everyone's been so focussed on preparing for the march on the Capital that no one's enjoying themselves anymore. It's been so boring.'

'Thanks,' I grinned, 'I'll just get my stuff. Come on.' I set off running and he followed, waving to some of the faces I remembered from the time in King Aegis' court and from the group of Resistance fighters who had come to meet us.

The group of children were gone when we reached the tent and I was glad, pleased that they wouldn't be following me around. I lifted my rucksack and slung it over my shoulder, cutting away from the tent towards where Stefan's uncle and the other High Elves had set up their campsite. The High Elves had tents that billowed in the wind, with light, gauzy fabric which did little to keep out the mid-autumn chill. I didn't mind though; I was far more comfortable here than I had been with the children.

'Put your bag here,' Stefan said, indicating a spot next to an empty bedroll. 'Let's go and join in the training. Elder Haycin will be running through the afternoon sessions, and you know that he hates it if we're late.'

I nodded, and we traced our way back to one of the fields where several lines of recruits were standing, ready to begin. Elder Haycin clapped me on the shoulder and sent me to the back of the group with Stefan, each of us with a staff in our hands.

'Recruits,' he barked, feet planted in the earth and arms behind his back, 'think of your weapon as an extension of yourself. Feel its power resonate through you as you strike and defend. If your weapon is broken, you will also fail. Prepare yourselves. Strike one, two, three…'

It felt good to get back into the routine of training, of going through the familiar motions and pushing myself until my muscles ached and sweat ran down my brow. This was what I enjoyed – it was part of who I was going to be. If Ma and Pa could see me now, I was sure that they would be proud. I gripped the wooden staff tighter and struck out, around and under, Elder Haycin's words ringing through me as I felt myself reach that place of balance, that moment of calm.

'Erik.' As quickly as it had come, the reverie was broken, as Leif approached me from the edge of the training field. 'King Aegis wants to see you.'

The staff dropped from my fingers and clattered to the ground, narrowly missing my foot.

'I'll take care of it,' Stefan said quickly as I began to reach down to get it. 'You don't want to keep the King waiting.'

'Thanks,' I mumbled, as I followed Leif, brushing my sweaty fringe back out of my eyes. He led me up to one of the main tents and left me outside, giving me a moment to compose myself before entering the tent.

King Aegis was sitting cross-legged on a rug on the floor, focussed on a small bowl of water, and did not hear me come in. I coughed, gave a slight bow and then sat down next to him, wondering when he would look up and notice me.

'Erik,' he murmured, 'do join me.'

It was slightly unnerving that he continued to stare at the bowl, ignoring me. I shuffled awkwardly, wondering what to say to fill the silence.

'I have seen some interesting things in this bowl of late, Erik,' King Aegis said quietly, his voice sombre. 'I saw my granddaughter agreeing to a betrothal with our brethren from the mountains. I saw her accept the man who I had given my blessing. I saw her dancing with you on a crowded dance floor. And then…' he paused and lifted his eyes to mine, 'I watched her change. Explain to me why this was not shared with me earlier. How is it that the other members of your party were unaware? Was I too supposed to be deceived about my granddaughter's stasis?'

Something was preventing me from speech. My tongue felt heavy and dry, and I couldn't draw my eyes away from his piercing, reprimanding gaze.

'I took you into my court, Erik,' he continued, 'welcomed you. Firstly, you disobeyed our instructions by sneaking off to the Underdark. Then you keep the truth about Wilhelmina secret? It has been difficult these past weeks, knowing that she is neither dead nor alive, while the world mourns her passing and the Usurper celebrates it. It is like I too have been trapped in time, and it will not resolve itself until she is returned to me. I have lived a long time, Erik, and like you, I have lost many of those whom I loved. I cannot afford to lose my granddaughter as well.'

I swallowed and opened my mouth to speak but no words came out. He watched me passively, waiting for my response.

'I…' My voice was a thin tremor, wavering more than usual, 'I…'

'Explain to me, Erik,' King Aegis said softly. 'Why did you not share this information with the others in your party? Rakael, for instance?'

The story came out slowly, but I stumbled through, explaining about the Winter Spirit and her instructions, about how it needed to be kept secret as she had said there was a traitor in the court and how I had only trusted a few with that information. When I was done, King Aegis regarded me levelly, and I felt myself go red.

'I'm sorry I didn't tell you earlier,' I mumbled, 'But I wasn't sure that you would be able to keep it a secret.'

'Thank you for telling me,' he said, 'I should not have doubted your intentions. Forgive me.'

I didn't know what to say, so I just sat there awkwardly.

'It sounds as though the Gods have chosen to take matters into their own hands, anyway,' he continued, 'you have been entrusted with a gift, Erik. Do not squander it. I will ensure that when you need to leave for the Hoarfrost Glacier, you have enough supplies and transport for the journey.'

'I don't want others to know about it, though,' I interrupted, 'No one can know the real reason why…'

'My men will be discreet,' King Aegis said. 'Only a couple will accompany you; by then we will be marching on the Capital to disrupt the Usurper's coronation ceremony. I will not spread the tale you have told me, if you do not wish for it to be shared then I will respect your wishes. All that I ask in return is that you achieve the task the Winter Spirit set for you.'

I sat up straighter and held his gaze with firm resolve. 'I will do my best not to let you down, King Aegis. I'll do whatever I can to make sure that my sister comes back.'

Chapter Nine: Aidyn

Our progress overland was slow to say the least. After the initial burst of energy on the night we broke Keely and Markus out of Icevale Keep, they began to fade, their need for proper medical care becoming more pressing. Fain did his best, but it was clear that Keely in particular needed a skilled healer. He had started to slip into regular states of near-delirium, which meant one of us needed to ride with him to ensure he wouldn't fall out of the saddle. Markus maintained a distrustful silence towards us and barely spoke, except when he was asleep. While he slept, I learned more than I would have liked, and sometimes needed to walk off to scavenge for food or water to keep a hold on my temper. It became clearer to me that the relationship Nina and Markus had had was passionate and something that still haunted him — and therefore me as well. The others didn't talk about it and for that I was grateful. It was becoming harder to keep calm and to act as though I was unaffected by what Markus said during his dreams.

We travelled by night, and by day we tried to find locations to hide in safety— in an abandoned farmhouse, a small cave, hidden clearings in the pine forests. We kept away from the roads now, passing around the outskirts of towns and avoiding the groups of Trackers who patrolled the streets with burning torches. This meant that our progress took longer, but from checking our map, we gathered that we were almost halfway to our destination.

One day, we found refuge in a rundown windmill, which had fallen into disrepair many seasons ago. As the others rested, I slipped outside, checking on the horses in a small lean-to nearby. Around us fields stretched out, and left untended the grass had grown wild and rose up to my knees, swaying in the cold breeze. Luckily for us, there was a well beside the windmill and I cranked the lever, lifting a bucket of fresh water to replenish our flasks. Something flickered in its reflection and I looked up to see one of my moths flutter down onto my shoulder.

News. Share. See. The voice whispered urgently. I unhooked the bucket from the rope and carried it back into the windmill, trying to ignore the conflicting nervousness and curiosity that were rising in me. With steady hands I refilled the flasks until the bucket was just under half full and then carried it back outside to the lean-to. I didn't want to be watched while I was scrying, especially since Markus had joined us.

My eyes were aching with tiredness, but I couldn't sleep yet. The lunar moth's tiny voice was desperate, demanding that I open my mind and see what it had to show me. I set the bucket down and peered into it, slowing my breathing and allowing myself to relax into the vision that began to solidify before me.

A lunar moth was sitting beside a vase of orchids, watching as a group of people clustered around a still form on a bed. Erik was gesticulating and speaking, while Lisette, Dylan and Alex were listening attentively. There was something strange about the figure on the bed and I leaned closer, trying to see more clearly. I felt my breath catch as I recognised her, though she looked different– she was frozen solid, features serene as though under the icy exterior, she was simply asleep. I shivered– there was deep magic at work here. I tried to focus on what the group around her was saying, but it was hard to distinguish their words.

'We cannot tell anyone,' Erik was saying, 'no one can know. I won't let her down – I won't fail her again. If there's the slightest chance, we have to succeed.'

Master, the moth's voice flickered through my mind, *hope.*

And then I heard Alex's voice, whispering as the moth fluttered into their hands. *Go, my friend. Let him know that hope is not lost.*

The image faded and I sat there for a moment, trying to process what I had seen and to stifle the rush of mad hope that the vision had caused. Slowly, I rose to my feet and took the bucket back to the well, wondering at how in the space of a few minutes, my world had been shaken again.

'Aidyn?' The voice cut through the silence and surprised me, I hadn't expected to hear it for a long time.

'Alex?' I asked, turning to see the familiar figure emerge from behind the lean-to. 'What are you doing here?'

'I found you before they did,' Alex said, relieved. 'There's no time to waste, we need to get out of here.'

'What do you mean?' I was confused, still trying to regain my composure after the vision and thrown by Alex's sudden appearance.

They sighed impatiently, 'I had a vision from Erthor, Aidyn. The Trackers are coming, I saw this windmill aflame as the sun set. We need to get as far away from here as possible.'

I didn't ask any more questions but strode inside, rousing the others quickly. Together we gathered up our packs and carried Markus and Keely outside to the horses.

'Oh by the Gods there's more of you,' Markus muttered as Alex came into view. 'Just my luck.'

'Did you see Trackers on your way here?' I asked Alex, ignoring Markus' words as we mounted and cut away across the fields.

'There was a large group in a town about a mile south,' they replied, 'I'd hazard a guess that news of the escape from Icevale Keep has been spread to all the Tracker towers around.'

'It makes sense that they would be increasing their patrols then,' Fain murmured, gripping onto Keely who was fast asleep.

'We've avoided them so far,' I added, 'they've mostly kept to the towns.'

'I don't think that will happen for much longer,' Alex said gravely.

'Why do they care so much about these prisoners anyway?' Beck asked, glancing at Markus. 'What do you two know that's so important for the Usurper?'

Markus didn't reply, although I noticed that he gripped his horse's reins tighter.

'How did you find us?' Fain asked Alex, 'I thought we were doing a good job of staying hidden.'

Alex chuckled, 'Come on, Fain. You know me better than that. I wanted to find you, so I found you. It's all about reading the tracks and following the signs. If the Trackers lived up to their names, they might have discovered you already, but luckily for us, they seem to be more focussed on terrorising the local villages than finding you.'

'Do you know where we've got to go?' Beck asked, 'Is there a way to get there faster? We need to get to a healer sooner rather than later.' Alex's gaze rested on Keely's slumped form and nodded, urging their mount onwards, leaping over a crumbling stone fence and heading westward.

We rode for a few hours, until we were back in one of the pine forests, hidden from the sunlight and Alex was happy that we had put enough distance between ourselves and the windmill. I dismounted, exhausted, and helped Markus down, ignoring his annoyed grunt as I supported his weight.

'I can do it myself,' he growled, 'I don't need help.'

If he hadn't been so weak, I would have probably left him alone or snapped back. His attitude was grating, and it had been getting on my nerves. I watched Markus lean against one of the trees and then settled down away from him, allowing myself to doze off briefly.

I dreamed of a tall and statuesque woman, who wore golden robes and whose hair gleamed in the sunlight. She smiled at me knowingly and I knelt, recognising her from the murals and images I had seen in books back in the Underdark. Although I had followed her teachings all my life, she had rarely shown herself to me in visions. It had always been Erthor that I saw, who had made me question at times whether I had been raised in the correct sect.

'You have done well,' she said, 'I had high hopes for you, son of Lysander.'

'Lady Sybilla,' I whispered, touching my forehead to the ground, afraid to look upon her brilliance. She glowed, like the sun she pulled across the sky, and it burned my eyes to gaze at her for too long.

'Look up,' she urged, 'my blessed followers do not need to fear my light.' Cautiously I lifted my head, grateful for the mask that shielded some of the brightness.

'Do you have a request of me, my lady?' I asked, 'How can I serve you?'

'I have been watching you from the time you were a boy,' she said gravely, 'I saw the first time my husband gifted you with the ability to commune with the lunar moths. I watched you break free of your bonds when you were sent out to be burned under my sun. I saw the desire in your heart when you met your beloved and the pain when you lost her. Throughout your life you have been tested and have tried multiple times to win the approval of your father. Now that he lies dead, what, I ask, will you make of your life?'

'I seek vengeance,' I whispered, 'I want the woman who killed my betrothed to feel the same pain I felt. And I need to know if there is a way to save the one I love.'

'There might be,' Sybilla mused, 'although that is not something I can control. She has been encased in the unmelting ice of the Hoarfrost itself, trapped in the realm between life and death. Her brother seeks to bring her back. He will need help, although he will not wish it. You must tread carefully if you wish to see her again. It will be important to also be patient with your revenge– the one you seek is protected and will be watching for attack. Wait until the time when her guard drops before striking your blade into her heart.'

I gazed at her, 'tell me what I must do, my lady.'

She smiled and laid a warm hand on my shoulder. 'Remember to be patient, son of Lysander. When the time is right, you will know.'

The dream faded and with it the clarity that I had felt, so when I awoke I felt more confused than before. Markus was watching me, eyes narrowed, which I ignored as I stood and gave Beck and Alex the chance to rest. As they settled down,

Markus continued to stare, assessing me. Finally, I grew tired of it and said, 'is there something you wish to say, Captain?'

His jaw clenched and he tilted his head to the side before saying, 'I'm just trying to figure out what could have made her choose to marry you. So far, I'm struggling to find a reason.'

The anger flared and I felt myself tense, before remembering that I couldn't retaliate.

'You don't like hearing that, do you Elf?' Markus grinned, 'does it make you angry knowing that she was with a real man before you came along?'

It was getting harder to ignore the anger, the crowing for blood that was filling my mind. The slow, calm breathing was becoming more difficult, it was catching in my throat as I longed to strike out.

'Although, if I'm honest,' Markus continued, 'it sounds as though she was being forced into this betrothal. How do you know that she agreed willingly? Who is to say that she wants to marry you? Chances are, she doesn't want to be wed to a Dark Elf. If the stories about your kind are true– and I don't doubt that they are– she would have to have changed a lot from the woman I knew to willingly accept such a proposal.'

'You know what I find interesting,' I said through gritted teeth, 'was that she barely spoke about you at all.' Now was the chance to watch him squirm. His face was an open book and I could read all his emotions – from jealousy to anger to guilt. 'She never mentioned that you were bigoted,' I mused, 'or that you were so unpleasant to be around. My men and I saved your miserable life, and you haven't shown any gratitude.'

'You only got me out of there because *she* asked you to,' Markus hissed, glaring at me, 'if you had had any choice in the matter, you would've left me there to rot.'

'Perhaps,' I murmured, 'but, luckily for you, my betrothed wished for your release. What sort of man would I be to deny her?'

'You're a monster,' Markus spat, 'I heard the warden's screams. I know what your kind does to people.'

'You seem to know a lot about Dark Elves,' I mused, 'in our experiences together we have supported you, paid you well and assisted your crew with some of your less reputable endeavours. We haven't hurt you or your men in any way—the Trackers did that all by themselves. I think that you need to be more careful about who you trust, Captain. It seems that you chose to work with the wrong people and now you and your crew have paid the price.'

He made a movement as if to rush at me, but didn't have the strength to stand. His face had gone red with fury and I watched him dispassionately. Somehow, watching him lose control of his emotions allowed me to have greater control over my own.

'You bastard,' he growled, 'don't you dare make assumptions about me or my crew. They were good men.'

'They seemed to be when we met them,' I conceded, 'it is unfortunate what happened.'

This seemed to placate Markus and his face began to regain its usual colour. 'I guess I just didn't expect her to marry someone like you,' he muttered, 'I thought…I don't know what I thought, but…'

'You expected her to wait?' I tried to keep my tone steady, to hide the disdain.

He shrugged, 'it wasn't like we'd made promises. We said things we regretted. But I still hoped that she would leave all this behind.' He waved at the countryside around us with a self-deprecating smile. 'I suppose she made her choice, she chose her country.'

I bit my tongue to hold back what I wanted to say.

'You underestimate the power of responsibility she has.' The faint voice interrupted our conversation, and we both turned to Keely, who let out a rattling cough. 'You weren't there, Markus, the night the palace was attacked. She was only seven years old and saw things that no child ought to see. For years she ran and hid, until Lisette and I found her. Even then, she tried to get rid of us, to break away. But no matter how hard she tried, the pull of her home– the desire to right the wrongs– was always there.'

Markus opened his mouth as if he were about to speak, but then he cut himself off, his face becoming unreadable and shuttered.

'Were you there when the Usurper took over?' I asked Keely, moving to get him the water flask.

'My father was a blacksmith in the city,' he whispered feebly, 'I was his apprentice. He heard the fighting in the palace and tried to get help from the townspeople. I wanted to help, but he ordered me to stay behind and look after my sisters. He never came home. Most of the men didn't.'

'I'm sorry,' I said quietly. He coughed again.

'That was many years ago now. I moved on when I reached my majority, I wanted revenge and the Resistance seemed the best way to do it. When their Stronghold was razed, I found Rakael. I looked after her and helped her get back on her feet, worked in taverns around the country, scouting out potential members and sending them to her. I thought I was making a difference, and then I met Milady.'

I found myself holding my breath, eager to know more about Nina's life from before; she had rarely spoken about it.

She had mentioned it occasionally, focussing on the brighter memories when we were in the grotto, her head in my lap as I stroked her hair.

'A poor, wasted thing she was then,' Keely remembered as he took a sip of water, 'so thin I was sure she would break if the wind blew too hard. Eyes so large she reminded me of a faun, delicate but strong. She proved herself soon enough, and I realised that she had experienced more than any other seventeen-year-old I had met. Reminded me of my sisters, she did, but always kept herself to herself, afraid to connect with others.'

'She was beautiful,' Markus muttered to himself, 'but then she changed. Became *other*.'

The enjoyment I had been feeling in the moment was instantly gone. Keely was looking in Markus' direction, 'what do you mean, changed?'

'All I know is that she went to stay with the Elves and then she came back different,' Markus growled, glaring up into the trees.

'What does he mean?' Keely asked.

'I think,' I said slowly, 'he means that he did not like how she was different once the magic in her fey blood was activated.'

'Ah,' Keely said, 'I always thought she would be something special, I did. Knew there was more for her, that she could do anything she set her mind to.'

'You don't have a problem with her being half-Elf?' I asked him curiously. Markus sniffed but didn't say anything as Keely shrugged,

'Her mother was an Elf. Makes sense that she would be half-Elf— it doesn't change who she is, deep down.'

'If you are going to talk all day,' Fain's grumpy voice said from under his tree, 'maybe we should get back on the road.'

I smiled and got up, lifting Keely up to ride in front of me, and Alex and Beck stretched as a light drizzle began to fall around us.

'Who needs to sleep anyway?' Beck muttered as we began to head out, plodding through the damp undergrowth and listening to the chirping of the birds as the rain fell.

'Tell me more about your time with her,' I urged Keely as we rode on, following Alex up ahead.

He drew in a raspy breath, and I felt the cough shake through him. 'I thought at first that she was a runaway farm girl,' he murmured, 'she was almost wild at times, you'd see it in her eyes- the fear, I mean. A Tracker would enter the inn and she would turn white as fresh snow. I thought she had left home, perhaps run off to see a bit of the world and gotten lost along the way. It wasn't until Lisette showed me her hair that I realised. I should have figured it out earlier.'

'You've mentioned Lisette before,' I said thoughtfully, and he chuckled.

'A sweet budgerigar. A smart one too. I thought she'd leave like the others, but she stayed after her wing mended. Loved honeyed seeds. Gave her to Milady to look after, right before I was taken.'

I didn't speak immediately, confused by his words. 'I have met Lisette,' I finally said cautiously, 'but she wasn't a budgerigar.'

He froze. 'What do you mean?'

'When I met Nina,' I said, 'She didn't have a budgerigar with her. She did have a handmaiden though– Lisette– she was an Elf.'

'An Elf?' Keely's voice was faint, 'how is that possible?'

I shrugged, 'I'm not sure, perhaps it was magic. The High Elves enjoy practising those kinds of spells.'

'I can't believe it,' Keely whispered, 'what was she like?'

Now I felt slightly awkward. I had never paid her much attention, Nina had been the only one I saw.

'Short,' I finally managed, 'blond curly hair, bright eyes, smiled a lot. Mute.'

'I can't believe it,' he repeated and then his tone turned heavy, 'and I can't believe I'll never see her.'

'You don't know that for sure,' I said, 'Perhaps the healers…'

'There's no need to lie, Lord Aidyn,' Keely said quietly. 'I'm grateful that I have my life, but I don't think I'll be much help to anyone like this. No one wants a blind cripple in their army.'

I didn't know what to say to this. So, instead, I urged the horse on faster and allowed Keely to sink into his own thoughts.

With Alex leading us, we cut across the Scardian countryside faster than I would have expected. Since we only stopped briefly to sleep and rest the horses every few hours, we made good progress. As Beck had grumbled, us Dark Elves knew that sleep was not necessary when under pressure, and so we ate and slept only when necessary, focussing on giving Keely and Markus the primary share of the provisions we scavenged.

It felt like an age had passed when we finally saw the mountain ranges and rode up the dusty track under the cover of moonlight. The guards on watch duty called out to the others in the camp, sending the message that we had arrived. By now, my companions and I were bone weary, starving and just about ready to collapse with exhaustion. Yet we kept control and helped the attendants who rushed towards us with stretchers to lift Keely and Markus into them and watched as they were carried away to the medical tent.

'Lord Aidyn.' I turned to see King Aegis walking towards us, hands raised in welcome. I bowed and felt my companions behind me do the same. 'We were not sure when you would be arriving,' he said warmly, grasping my hand with his and shaking it. 'It is a relief that you have found us safely and without incident. I thank you as well for retrieving the two prisoners from Icevale Keep. I know it cannot have been easy.'

I bowed again, choosing not to reply.

'Come, we will set you up with the other Dark Elves in our encampment,' he said, leading us through the sleeping camp. 'I know you must be tired from your journey, I have asked for refreshments to be prepared for you and then you will be left undisturbed.'

'Thank you, King Aegis,' I said quietly. 'We are grateful.'

'There is much to discuss in the morning,' he said gravely, 'circumstances which you will need to be made aware of and may find troubling, but I will tell you more tomorrow. For now, please know that you are welcome and that you have our thanks.'

I nodded and turned to see some of our brethren beginning to construct a tent for us, working with silent efficiency. It felt good to finally be able to relax and eat a hot meal. When the tent was constructed, I gave a quiet word of thanks and then my companions and I went inside and settled down, unrolling the bedrolls that had been deposited by the Resistance guards while we ate.

I lay down to sleep, and then in what felt like the blink of an eye, I was waking to the sounds of the camp rising and preparing for the day. I glanced at the others, but they slept on, exhausted from the past days of travel. While I too felt the aching tiredness, there was something else that I needed to do before I could rest more.

One of the Dark Elf guards who had been keeping watch outside of our tent led me to King Aegis. He was meditating when I was announced, and he rose to greet me.

'I am glad that you came, Lord Aidyn,' he said, 'there have been some changes since your departure from the Underdark. You may not be aware, but the Trackers attacked shortly after you left. There were many casualties, including your father and my granddaughter.'

I bowed my head, 'I am aware.'

King Aegis hid his shock well. 'You already knew?'

I nodded. 'My companions do not, however. Nor do the prisoners, as far as I am aware. Where is she?'

He was silent for a moment, thrown. 'I beg your pardon?'

'Nina. Where is she?' I tried to keep the sharpness out of my tone. 'I wish to see her.'

'I do not think that would be wise,' King Aegis countered softly, 'she was badly injured in the attack.'

I looked at him closely, noting his stillness. 'I am her betrothed,' I said with quiet dignity. 'I wish to see her.'

He gazed back at me, and I felt that he was debating within himself whether to allow my request. I chose to speak as plainly as I could.

'There may be a way to help her, King Aegis, I need to see her in case there is anything I can do. If she is gone, I need to say goodbye.'

I thought for an instant that I had rendered him speechless, as shock registered in his blue eyes.

'You know?' He finally murmured and I inclined my head slightly. 'Then come.'

He stood and his robes swept around his ankles as we left the tent, waving away the guards who tried to follow us. He led the way through the camp, towards the mountainside where a dark tent had been erected. A guard stood vigil outside its entrance, and King Aegis spoke to him quietly, sending him away while we entered. Inside was a table with a casket spread across it. A sheet was draped over the casket, hiding it from view.

'You know that she has changed?' King Aegis asked, 'she will not be as you remember.'

'I am aware,' I replied, my eyes not leaving the table before us.

'Make sure to replace everything as you find it,' he said, 'Only a select few know about this. The others believe her dead. I will make sure that you are not disturbed.'

I nodded and waited until he departed, closing the tent folds behind him. Then I pulled the sheet away and lifted the lid of the casket, gazing down at the form inside.

It had been as Sybilla said: she was encased in Hoarfrost. Her expression was serene, eyes closed and hands resting across her chest, clasping a cluster of orchids and her dagger. I reached out to touch her cheek and felt the coldness pierce through my glove, numbing the skin underneath. It was colder than anything I had felt before, and I shivered despite myself.

'I am here, dear heart,' I whispered, cradling her face with my hand. 'I did what you asked me to do and have come back, just like I promised.' I smiled softly, 'it seems that I will need to be patient for a while longer, until you come back to me.'

For a moment I thought that I saw something, a rise of the chest, a puff of air under the ice, but then it was gone and I wondered if I had imagined it.

'I will wait for you, dear heart,' I murmured, 'but you must fight to come back.'

There was no answer from the icy corpse, yet I stayed there a while longer, gazing down at her face lost in endless sleep. There was a slight cough from the tent entrance and I glanced around, noticing King Aegis hovering just outside. Reluctantly I covered her up again and left, just as a slight figure rushed up, panting.

'What do you think you were doing?' Erik gasped, face bright with anger, 'you have no right to be in there. Get away.'

Be patient, I reminded myself.

'Erik,' King Aegis said quietly but firmly, 'Lord Aidyn has got a right to be here. He is Nina's betrothed. He has the right to know.'

'You told him?' Erik's voice was scandalised and hurt.

'I knew already that something had happened to her,' I interrupted, as King Aegis' face drained. Erik turned accusing eyes on me, and in them I read his fear, anger and distrust. 'I want to help, Erik.'

'I don't need your help,' he snapped, firing up again, 'If we hadn't been in the Underdark this wouldn't have happened. It's because of you that we were there, it's your fault. Now it's my job to bring her back before midwinter and I don't need you to interfere.'

It was like he had punched me. I felt the blow of his words and forced myself to stop and think, to not respond quickly lest I say something that I would regret. Erik turned and sped off, racing away amongst the tents.

'He is hurting,' King Aegis said softly, 'he speaks out of his own guilt and is all too ready to share blame. I hope that you do not let his thoughtless words cause offense. He will come around in his own time.'

'He needs to recognise who is friend and foe,' I mused, pondering the boy's outburst.

'I think that he feels pressured,' King Aegis murmured as we headed back towards his tent, 'he has been here for almost a month now. Time is running out before midwinter, and he has made little progress in the tasks he needs to accomplish. I have tried to offer help but…' his voice drifted off sadly.

'But you received the same reaction?' I queried.

He nodded, 'It's partly my fault, I put pressure on him to succeed.'

We reached his tent and stepped inside where someone was waiting for us.

'Rakael,' King Aegis smiled, 'you remember Lord Aidyn, I'm sure. He arrived overnight. I'm sure he is eager to learn about the plans.'

It took an immense effort to control my reaction. While all I wanted to do was leap across the room and draw my blade across her neck, I resisted the urge and bowed slightly.

'Mistress Rakael,' I said coolly.

'Lord Aidyn,' She nodded, 'a pleasure to see you again, it is a relief that you made it out of Icevale Keep alive. I owe you a great debt for retrieving Keely.'

I inclined my head and forced my arms to hang loosely at my sides. Lady Sybilla had said to be patient and I would be. I'd learn as much as I could and keep my eyes open, ready and waiting for the perfect time to strike.

Chapter Ten: Erik

One month. One month of training, waiting and racking my brains to try and figure out how I could achieve what the Winter Spirit had asked. Lisette had given me the napkin stained with an innocent's tears, but I was no closer to figuring out the rest of it.

There had been a slight distraction when Jesse had arrived late one afternoon, with several horses in tow laden with heavy bags, trekking their way up the mountain path. She had gone straight to see Rakael and King Aegis, before stepping into Dylan's tent. He had been afforded a full tent to himself, in which he could conduct a range of experiments in relative peace. I followed her to the entrance, listening closely as she had said,

'It worked perfectly, Dylan. Just as you said it would.'

'No side effects?' He had asked curiously, 'they lasted long enough?'

'Just enough,' she had replied. 'I thought at first that they wouldn't for the crossing, but it surprised me. You really are a genius. This will change things for us. Here– I thought you would want them back.'

'Thank you,' he had said, and I heard something exchanging hands.

'I've got more ingredients for you too,' she had added, as she began to head towards the tent entrance and I looked around hastily for a place to hide. Before I could move more than a few paces, she had opened the flaps and seen me. 'Erik,' she smiled warmly, 'how good to see you. Are you here to see Dylan?'

'Yes,' I mumbled, sliding past her, 'good to have you back with us, Jesse.'

She grinned and strode away, Dylan watching her with slightly misty eyes. I coughed, and when that didn't work, snapped my fingers in front of his eyes a few times.

'Come on, Dylan,' I said, 'What was that all about?'

'What?' He blinked several times and then let out a huff, moving to rearrange some books and scrolls.

'What was Jesse wanting to talk to you about?' I probed, perching on one of the unopened trunks.

'Oh,' he said vaguely, lifting open a small box and placing something inside. 'She was returning one of my experiments. Turns out this one worked nicely, in fact. It was a risk but…'

'What was it?' I asked, leaning closer. 'A weapon?'

'Oh no,' Dylan said quickly, 'no, nothing like that. It was one of the formulas I discovered in the Archives and I thought I would see if it would work. Turns out it did, see here.' He waved me over and I jumped up, peering over his shoulder to look into the box he was holding. Inside were some small, distorted shapes that looked like they had been roughly formed out of wax.

'What are they?' I asked cautiously.

'You attach them and drizzle them with some water,' he said excitedly, 'then wait a few hours until they reach full size. Then, so long as it is not too hot and the wax doesn't melt, you can travel across vast distances in less time.'

'What do you mean?'

'They become wings,' Dylan said proudly, 'Jesse tested them out for me. She made a few stops on the way back from the Ombre Mountains and it seems to have all worked perfectly.' He closed the box's lid and leaned back proudly. I was confused and didn't quite know what to say.

'So, she flew across the Meridian?' I finally said, 'but that's at least a week's journey by boat.'

'Oh no,' Dylan said, 'she made shorter trips, I think. Back to the High Elf Court, south to the Northern tip of Karshka and then back to Scardia. She needed to gather my materials after all. Rakael wants me to start developing some more of the formulas I found in the Archives as soon as possible. Ah,' he cut off and moved to the entrance of the tent as a group of men began to carry in a range of bags and boxes, 'place them over here for me.'

I had slipped out in the commotion and had barely seen Dylan since. He had become absorbed in his work, and I had noticed him directing blacksmiths from time to time with a bundle of blueprints in his arms. He was rarely there at mealtimes, Lisette took him his food, supervised by one of Rakael's guards. When I saw them hovering outside Dylan's tent, I chose to stay away, not wanting Rakael to find out and interfere.

Today, the morning air was cold and fresh as I headed through the camp, going on my daily round to check that Nina's tent was left undisturbed. The simple enjoyment of the day was shattered when I saw King Aegis and a Dark Elf exiting her tent. When I recognised Aidyn, I was shaken even more. I didn't want him to be there. He thought he could just come back and expect that he would be able to understand, to help? However, I realised as I ran off, if Aidyn was back then he must have succeeded in his task. It meant that Markus was safe.

I directed my feet to the infirmary tent, which was bustling with movement. Lisette came out, holding a bowl of dirty water and a sodden cloth. She looked tired, as though she hadn't slept all night, and gave me a rather wan smile as she passed.

'Markus?' I cried, racing inside and almost bumping into one of the healers. 'Markus?'

'I should've known you would be here,' his tired voice came from one of the beds at the far end of the tent and I moved to sit beside him. 'Barely been here for a few hours and you come and find me.'

He looked exhausted and drawn, and there was a tightness in his expression that I hadn't seen before.

'Where is your sister?' He asked, 'I thought she would be with you.'

Around us, the healers exchanged swift looks and lowered their eyes, glancing at me surreptitiously.

'The Princess is no longer with us,' the chief healer finally answered, as he hovered his palms over some of Markus' wounds, using magic to accelerate the healing.

'She's gone away?' The man on one of the other beds asked, turning in our direction. His eyes were bandaged, and his body bore the marks of lengthy torture. 'Where is she?'

'Princess Wilhelmina was killed by Trackers,' another healer murmured. Markus' face went white and he stared at me, watching as I confirmed it with a small nod.

'That's not possible,' the other man whispered, his voice breaking, 'it can't have all been for nothing. It can't.'

'It wasn't, Keely.' Rakael had entered the tent and was bending over the man, taking his bandaged hands in hers. 'We will make sure that her sacrifice means something. We will fight back and make the Usurper pay for what he has done.

You will not have suffered in vain.' She glared at me as if I had been the one to break the news. 'Rest now, the healers will make sure that you are back to your old self soon.' She waved over one of the healers and said, 'get him something to help him sleep.'

'No,' the man muttered, trying and failing to push away the glass that was brought over, 'No, no, no. I need to know what happened…' He tried to fight as the drink was poured down his throat, but he was too weak.

'Sleep, Keely,' Rakael said softly, watching as his movements became sluggish and feeble, and he succumbed to unconsciousness. 'And you,' she turned to me, suddenly harsh, 'don't disturb them. They've been through enough horrors without having to be bothered by you.' With that, she turned and stormed away, all gentleness lost in an instant.

'What did you do to get on her bad side?' Markus asked me quietly, 'she seems like a right old prune.'

I bit back a laugh. 'Don't let her hear you say that.'

Lisette bustled back into the tent, shooing some of the healers away from Keely's sleeping form. I watched as she sat down beside him, gripping his hand in hers and gazing at him silently, eyes bright with unshed tears. The expression in them floored me. It was like how Nina had looked at Markus and then Aidyn. It scared me. It implied more change, and I didn't want it.

'Have you been treated alright?' Markus asked, interrupting my thoughts.

I nodded, still watching Lisette. 'They're kind here. I've been working hard, training…'

Not succeeding with that quest though, Mister MacMillan's voice crowed. *Useless, useless boy.*

'Well, I'm glad that you're here and you're safe,' Markus said quietly. 'I think I might try to sleep too, Erik. It's been a long journey.'

I could tell that he wanted to be alone, to process what he had learned in private.

'I'll check back on you later,' I said as I stood, and headed out of the infirmary. Outside, I came to a halt. I thought of Lisette's expression and how it had been so similar to Nina's all those months ago.

'A heart's desire,' I muttered to myself, 'perhaps if I could…'

'What are you talking about a heart for?'

I felt myself reddening as I looked up at Stefan, who had sauntered over to join me.

'What? Nothing.'

He looked at me quizzically and then shrugged. 'Alright. Elder Haycin sent me to find you, we're due to start training in a few minutes.'

'Sounds good,' I said hurriedly, letting him lead the way, as I pondered how Markus would react if I asked him to come with me to the Hoarfrost Glacier.

I didn't manage to see Markus again until a few days later, having been swamped with additional training sessions and packing. From the word around the camp, Rakael was preparing to march any day now, as the Usurper's coronation drew closer. In that time, I had barely seen Lisette, who spent all her time in the infirmary, or Dylan, who was in his tent with his experiments. The Dark Elves kept to themselves, and I would see Aidyn and Alex from across the training field, running through their own routines and then glancing away when they turned in my direction. After losing my temper with Aidyn I felt the stirrings of shame when he was nearby, recognising that what I had said had been out of order but not knowing how to apologise.

While keeping my distance, I kept track of their movements throughout the camp, noticing how King Aegis and Aidyn would spend hours at a time with Rakael and the Resistance leaders in the larger tents. Since his arrival, Aidyn had taken command over the Dark Elf battalions, and they deferred to his authority automatically. I wondered if he knew that his father was no longer King in the Underdark, but no word had been sent since our arrival, which Jesse said was probably a good thing.

'The less we know about their coup, the better,' she said to me while we ate dinner one night, 'I don't think that we should expect any more support from them beyond the soldiers we have received. That Chief Counsel gave me a bad feeling.'

I hadn't liked him either, with his raspy voice and the creepy way he would watch people.

'The way they fight is something though, isn't it?' Stefan said dreamily, 'I thought that Elder Haycin was a good fighter but when he was taken down after a few minutes…'

'It wasn't *that* impressive.' I said, lying through my teeth. I too had watched Aidyn and Elder Haycin fight, had felt the excitement building as they circled each other, striking and deflecting moves as though they could read each other's minds. But then Aidyn had lashed out, dropping and kicking, sending Elder Haycin toppling to the ground. Aidyn had reached down and helped the older man up and they went to King Aegis' tent together, laughing and joking.

'Are you kidding?' Stefan asked, eyebrows raised. 'You couldn't look away either.'

Jesse glanced at me with a knowing smile, and I frowned. 'He's not that bad you know,' she said under her breath.

'I don't know what you mean,' I mumbled grumpily.

'Erik,' she said reasonably, 'just think for a moment. I was in the Underdark as well as you. I know what happened there. There was something about him that won your sister over. She saw something that you clearly are missing. It's time you figured out what that was and move on from this resentment. She wouldn't want you to act this way. Besides, we're moving out within the next day or so, surely it would be better to talk to him before…'

I swore and slammed down my spoon, stalking away from the long table without a backward glance. Who did she think she was anyway? Telling me what Nina would want, as if she *knew* something I didn't. Nina had been upset because of her fight with Markus and Aidyn had come along and messed with her head with his strange Dark Elf magic. It hadn't been love that they had shared, she'd just wanted a distraction. I had thought that was obvious, but now a small voice was whispering that I might have been wrong. I squashed it angrily and strode on, kicking a nearby stone and listening to it roll away.

The infirmary was almost empty when I arrived and I headed straight to Markus' side, still fuming. He was looking much better after a few days of the healers' magic and proper meals, he was almost back to his old self.

'Erik,' he said, sitting up more in bed and smiling, 'I was hoping you would drop in again.' His eyes travelled up to my face and he paused, concerned, 'what's wrong?'

'Nothing.' I grunted. 'How much longer do you need to stay here?'

'Not too long,' he said slowly, still watching me closely. 'Why?'

I shrugged, 'Just wondering. I want to go out on a trip soon and thought you might want to come too.'

He paused for a while, and then nodded. 'Are you going to tell me where we would be going?'

'Not now,' I said brusquely, aware that some of the healers nearby were listening.

'Would anyone else be joining us?' He asked, and I shrugged again.

'Maybe. I don't know.' There was a movement out of the corner of my eye and I turned, seeing Stefan hovering in the entrance to the infirmary, looking confused. 'I've got to go,' I said quickly, 'make sure you're ready to leave soon.'

'Alright,' Markus said uncomprehendingly.

'Good.' I left him almost as soon as I had arrived and brushed past Stefan, who stared after me in shock. My mind was made up as I made my way to King Aegis' tent. If the Resistance was going to start marching on the Capital, I needed to leave sooner rather than later.

'King Aegis,' I entered the tent and froze as Aidyn and the king turned to face me. They were looking down at a map and speaking in quiet whispers.

'Erik,' the older man said, 'do sit and join us.'

Aidyn nodded to me, 'Erik.'

I gave a short spasm that might have been considered a nod and sat down opposite them, feeling suddenly awkward.

'What brings you here, Erik?' King Aegis asked calmly.

'Is it true that Rakael wants the soldiers to move out soon?' The words rushed out before I could stop them. 'Because if that's true then…'

'Some of the men are moving out at dawn,' Aidyn said, 'It'll take several days for everyone to leave. The Velkranian Wood Elves have already begun to leave, I understand that they will be leading the offensive on the nearby Tracking Towers.'

'Then I need to go too,' I said quickly, focussing on King Aegis and avoiding Aidyn's gaze. 'You said that you would help me. I'll need a wagon and horses.'

'You cannot go alone to the Hoarfrost Glacier, Erik,' he said gravely, 'the roads are too dangerous.'

'I won't be,' I said, 'Markus will come with me.'

Aidyn and King Aegis exchanged glances and then the older man coughed and said, 'Markus is still recovering, Erik. I think it would be wiser if another…'

'He's fine,' I insisted, 'he needs to come.'

'I will join them, King Aegis,' Aidyn said, 'if Erik will permit it. I'd be happy to lend my blade to protect them on the road.'

'I don't need you,' I said rudely, instantly regretting it. 'I mean…'

'I would feel better if Aidyn did go with you, Erik,' King Aegis said. 'It would ease some of my concerns.'

'Isn't he needed here?' I asked, 'he's in charge of the Dark Elves after all.'

'My brothers will assist in my absence,' Aidyn said smoothly. 'It won't be a problem.'

I didn't know what to say except to shrug and mumble something like, 'well I guess that's it then.'

'I'll ask Alex to navigate,' Aidyn was saying to King Aegis, 'they will know where to go.'

'Very good,' he replied before turning to me, 'make sure you are ready to leave tomorrow night. We'll take advantage of the movement around the camp to get you out undetected.'

'Thanks,' I muttered. 'I'll be ready.'

Chapter Eleven: Aidyn

I couldn't say that I was enjoying myself. There's nothing quite like going on a trip with the frozen body of your betrothed, her former lover and her younger brother, who for some reason despises you. Thankfully Alex was there. They kept me sane on the first few days, reminding me to stay calm and to not react to the baiting that Markus seemed to enjoy so much.

Everything had gone smoothly the night we left. Rakael had departed earlier with the first few battalions of soldiers, heading towards the Capital. Fain and Beck had agreed to look after our brethren, who I had instructed to not participate in any fighting until I returned. I was going to wait until Erik's mission was complete, because if he didn't succeed, I wanted my men to be where I needed them– close to Rakael so that we could strike.

It hadn't been easy feigning ignorance of what she had done during the past weeks, listening to her going back and forth over plans, describing ideas that I was sure Nina wouldn't have approved of. Now that Dylan was making progress with his formulas, Rakael was making him create more weapons and poisons, which would help to bring down the Usurper's forces. I knew that King Aegis shared my reservations about her new plans– neither of us were keen on spilling innocent blood– but Rakael did not care. Her plans to invade the Capital included a rampage throughout the countryside, striking the Tracking Towers first so that their communications would be disrupted. Personally, I was slightly relieved to not be joining them on the road, from Rakael's expression during those meetings, I knew that the villages in the path to the Capital would either be scorched or damaged beyond repair. Rakael's bloodthirst was similar to our own, except ours was fuelled by the desire for vengeance, whereas hers was tainted with bitterness and hatred.

When it was time for us to leave, the wagon had been covered and left beside Nina's tent, her casket placed in the back and the horses drew away, following the procession of carts and soldiers who were steadily departing from the campsite. Markus and Erik sat in the driver's seat, while Alex and I rode alongside, hooded cloaks covering our masked faces. We barely spoke as we headed off, Alex using the stars to guide us northward. Now though, I was growing tired of Markus and Erik laughing together, acting for all the world like father and son. It rankled that whenever I tried to talk to the boy, he would turn up his nose and scowl. It also irritated me that within an hour of us being on the road, he was telling Markus about what the Winter Spirit had instructed him to do, which I knew he had wanted to keep from me. Markus had listened carefully, supplying praise when it was due and affirming Erik's actions until the boy glowed with pride. When he began talking about Markus being Nina's heart's desire, I urged my mount forwards, gritting my teeth to stop myself from interrupting their tête à tête. From then on, I kept my distance.

We had been travelling for most of the day and night had fallen, when I heard the soft crackle of snow underfoot, coming from behind us. I dismounted and circled around, drawing my blade, ready to strike. The figure following us was slight and gangly, moving from bush to bush in an effort to remain hidden. However, they were clearly not used to walking through snowy terrain and had left obvious tracks. I curled my lip in disdain, the Usurper's Trackers were employing young spies it seemed. Carefully I moved behind him, using the darkness to my advantage as I gripped his arms behind his back, the blade of my knife pressed against his neck.

'Who are you?' I asked forcefully, 'Name yourself.' He whimpered slightly and I gripped him harder. 'Speak, boy.'

'Stefan,' he whispered, 'I'm Erik's friend.'

I loosened my grip slightly, 'why are you following us?'

'I wanted to come along,' he mumbled, 'I didn't want to be left behind again.'

I rolled my eyes and sighed, stowing the knife away. 'Come on then.' I led him after the cart and called out, 'Erik, your friend's here.' I glanced at Stefan and gave a jerk of the head in the direction of the cart. 'You can go and explain to him why you're here.'

He nodded and raced away, scrambling up into the cart and, from the sounds of it, began to answer Erik's angry questions. I mounted my horse and rode up alongside Alex, who was pointedly trying to ignore the argument that was coming from the front of the wagon.

'Let's hope he's the only one to follow us,' they said quietly. 'Probably a good idea to check the perimeter when we stop.' I nodded and gazed ahead, unable to avoid hearing the angry voices which were piercing the silence from behind us.

'I'm not going to just sit by and let you go off by yourself again,' Stefan snapped, 'you're my friend. We should be sticking together.'

'I wasn't alone,' Erik retorted, 'I didn't *ask* you to come along.'

'Like you didn't when you snuck off to the Underdark?' Stefan cried, 'We had no idea where you were and it…'

Another sound reached my ears and I motioned to Alex, who paused, glancing around. I heard it again, a crunch of snow, the faint brush of leaves as they were pushed to the side. I drew my blade again, scanning the trees around us. The wagon came to a grinding halt as Markus pulled on the reins, noticing our exchange.

'There's something there,' I whispered, peering into the shadows. From my bag, a moth flew out and landed on my shoulder before soaring towards the trees, its wings lighting up the darkness. A soft, gentle laugh filled my head, coming from the depths of the shadow, and a figure emerged slowly until they were in the light. I froze, confused and shaken.

'Who are these strangers in our midst, sister?' The figure asked in a lilting voice. She was tall and willowy, with long hair and dark eyes.

'I think they must be the ones we were told about.' Another shape emerged from behind the trees, forming into another woman of abnormal beauty. There was something off about the way they stood too still, how their eyes stared unblinkingly at us. Yet there was something about them that stirred my blood and made my breath catch in my throat.

'Do you think they need some help to find where they're going?' The first woman asked, stepping closer towards us.

'Who are you?' Erik asked, entranced. Stefan too was watching the newcomers, all traces of anger from the argument forgotten. His eyes were slightly glazed, and he leaned towards the women, as if he were a puppet drawn on an invisible string.

'Aidyn,' Alex muttered, 'something isn't right.'

'We came to greet you,' the women said together, drawing in, voices overlapping as if in song. 'You cannot go the rest of the way alone.'

'We're here to help ease your burden,' one added silkily.

An overwhelming sense of sleepiness was filling me, the desire to dismount, lie down and let the strangers take over. It reminded me of the mind games the Chief Counsel used to play on us during training sessions in the Underdark. I blinked, fighting against the sensation, slashing out with my blade as one of the women reached out for my arm.

'Get back,' I snarled. Alex drew their bow, aiming an arrow at the other woman who had paused, feet away from Stefan and Erik.

'Oh Lord Aidyn,' the woman near me said sorrowfully, 'how disappointing. We so hoped that you would be amenable to staying with us awhile, we've always wanted to see underneath a Dark Elf's mask.' I felt my face blanch and tensed, ready to strike again.

'Witch,' Markus muttered, reaching for a knife of his own.

'Oh no, Captain,' the women said laughingly, 'we are so much more than that.'

Under the light of the moon, they began to change, twisting and writhing until they stood up again. This time, their pointed nails were inches long, their eyes flashed red and what had been a mask of beauty was wiped away to reveal the monstrosity underneath. They let out blood curdling shrieks and leaped forward, wings beating and talons slashing without mercy. I struck back, my horse narrowly avoiding the creature's onslaught.

'Markus,' I cried, 'get out of here!'

'No,' he barked, kicking the other creature back.

'Don't argue,' I snapped, ducking under a razor-sharp claw, 'take the boys and get going!'

He grunted and slapped the reins, jolting the startled horses forward, crashing through the trees. The creatures shrieked and began to chase the wagon, leaving Alex and I to race after them. Alex released the arrow, striking one of the women in the shoulder. She screamed and turned, swiping out, nails cutting across their armour. Alex grunted and withdrew a knife, plunging it into the woman's side, twisting the blade as she scrambled to fight back. I rode up alongside and slashed downwards with my dagger, feeling her lifeblood drain away as she collapsed.

The other creature seemed to sense her sister fall and turned back to us, leathery wings tearing through the back of her gown. She rose into the air, looking down on us with diabolical hatred.

'You might want to prepare another arrow, Alex,' I muttered out of the side of my mouth. 'Alex?' But my friend was falling down beside the fallen creature, clasping their hands to their head in agony. I dismounted and took the bow from them, notching an arrow and aiming as the creature dived, claws extended. The horses reared and fled after the wagon as I fired, dropping to my knees and rolling to the side, only just avoiding the slash of talons. The creature laughed, a horrible, gurgling sound, as she turned, the arrow protruding from her chest.

'So brave, little Elf,' she spat, 'but whatever made you think that there were only two of us?'

Something pierced my armour, and the scent of rust and blood filled my nostrils. I gasped, as other figures came out of the trees around us, laughing and crowing. Some wore armour emblazoned with the bull's head, while others were like the woman in front of me, who was rocking back and forth with cold, derisive laughter. My gaze lowered to the blade which had cut through my armour into my side. It hadn't cut in deep, but dizziness was already setting in, which made me think the blade had been poisoned.

'Erthor, help me,' I whispered as dread washed through me, 'Lady Sybilla watch over me.'

'Your Gods cannot help, Elf. Whatever made you think that you could escape?' She crowed as the world around me began to fade, 'we have so many plans for all of you.'

I dreamed that I was sitting beside the pool in the grotto. The waterfall on the other side of the rocks was cascading gently into the Lake of Tears, the glow worms speckled across the roof of the cavern like stars. Nina lay in my lap, her long hair soft beneath my hands. She was gazing up at me steadily.

'I think that I have failed you, dear heart,' I said softly, feeling the tearing in my chest as I looked down at her. 'I wanted to protect you, to protect those close to you, but I think...'

'It's alright,' she whispered, reaching up and cupping my cheek with her palm. 'The Winter Spirit says that everything works according to the Gods' plan. This might just be a minor setback. You cannot give up hope yet, Aidyn. I'm relying on you; I need you to be strong.'

Silent tears were sliding down my cheeks and I blinked them away. 'I don't know if I can.'

'You are not yet in the realm beyond,' she murmured, brushing the wetness from my cheeks, 'watch over my brother, keep him safe. Be patient, Aidyn.'

'I have been patient,' I muttered, and she smiled and raised her lips to mine.

'We will see each other again,' she breathed, lightly brushing me with a kiss, and then she disappeared, along with the grotto and waterfall.

I opened my eyes to a bright, blinding light. There was a pain in my side, and I glanced down, noting that my arms were chained and spread wide along a stone wall. There was a wound which looked several days old. My armour had been removed from my chest, and I noted with dawning horror that my mask and balaclava were placed on the far side of the room, glinting in the light and out of reach.

'Aidyn?' I turned to see glazed, dark eyes staring at me.

'Alex?' I asked, 'where are we?'

We'd never seen each other's faces before and I felt awkward, lost without the familiar mask to hide behind.

'I don't know,' they whispered, 'but the light... Sybilla didn't bless me like she did you.' My eyes widened with shock, taking in red blisters that had spread across Alex's body where the light filled the room.

'How long have we been here?' I asked, disorientated. Alex's wounds suggested they'd been out in the sun for days, not hours. It was nearly winter in Scardia, so there shouldn't be sunlight that was as intense as the tropical heat back home. It didn't make sense.

'I don't know,' they murmured, 'night, day, it all blurs together.'

'Where are the others?'

'So, you're awake,' Markus' voice came from the other side of the room. 'I was wondering when you would come back to the world of the living.'

I blinked through the flare of sunlight and made out his shape against the opposite wall. Like us, he was stretched out and chained, glaring at me from his position.

'What happened?' I repeated. 'Where are the boys?'

He frowned, looked down and said, 'I'm not sure. They weren't put in here with us. We were ambushed, shortly after you told us to run. More of those creatures and Trackers. It was almost as though they knew we would be there, like they anticipated our arrival.'

'What about the wagon?' I pressed, 'the cargo?'

'They took it.' He replied curtly. 'She's gone.'

I felt myself sag against the wall, 'where did they take us?'

'I think we're in the Capital,' Markus said quietly, 'they gave us something that knocked us out for a long time. Forced us to drink it, it made it impossible to fight them.'

'Aidyn,' Alex muttered through cracked lips, 'someone's coming.'

Sure enough, there was the sound of footsteps from outside our cell. The door opened and two figures came in, one who I recognised from my visions of Icevale Keep, the other who I stared at, shocked.

'Ah good,' the Usurper said cheerily, 'they're awake. How wonderful, I've always wanted to see Dark Elves up close. I've heard so many things about your kind.' He moved closer, blocking the light and peering at me, 'what a fine specimen you are. I'll take great pleasure in finding out just how much pain you can withstand.'

I spat, hitting his cheek, and he struck me, his sharp rings stabbing into my cheek.

'Your father clearly taught you no manners, Elf,' he said sharply. 'No matter, we will teach you soon enough.'

'You should control yourself, Aidyn,' his companion said greasily, 'you're disgracing the Sect of Sybilla and your fellow Dark Elves.'

'You're one to talk,' I snarled, glaring at him. 'You've betrayed your own kind. I take it you were the one behind the Trackers infiltrating the Underdark?'

The Chief Counsel fingered a curved blade at his side, 'I might have been persuaded to support Lord Niall. He has got great strength and cunning, and his method of ruling is very appealing. Why have people come to an agreement on who ought to be in charge, or have candidates fight for the privilege of leading, when you can just take that power for yourself? With his support, we could finally leave the Underdark and regain our place, conquer the Eastern Lands and cover them in Erthor's holy night. He has more experience than that Princess of yours did, and once he is crowned King, nothing and no one will be able to stop him. Why should our people support the lamb when the wolf is much stronger?'

'How did you know where to find us?' I asked, clenching my hands into fists.

The Usurper laughed, 'You're not the only one who can scry, or who has been given gifts by the Gods. The Lord of Summer blessed me many years ago with the ability to make men's worst nightmares come to life.' He lifted a hand to the window behind him and clicked his fingers. The sunlight became stronger, burning like a hot summer's day, and I cried out, squeezing my eyes shut. Beside me Alex groaned, trembling with pain.

Master. The tiny voice pricked at the edge of my mind as I struggled to keep control. *Lost. Alone. Help.* I tried to reach out to it, to call to it to come, but the sun's rays became too intense and my connection was lost.

A moment later the light subsided, and I could open my eyes again. I had begun to burn properly, my skin tinged red.

Alex, on the other hand, was gasping for breath, as their skin puckered, red raw, with blood starting to ooze from the wounds.

'Aidyn,' they whispered, 'please.'

The Usurper laughed, 'How pitiful. I expected your kind to last longer, but it seems that they are easily broken.' The Chief Counsel, who had covered his eyes during the demonstration, shifted uncomfortably.

'You were looking for us?' Markus interrupted, 'why?'

The Usurper grinned, turning to him. 'I would have thought that was obvious. I needed the Princess' body to prove her death. I also wanted to make sure that you were somewhere safe, Markus. After your friends here helped you to escape from Icevale Keep,' he tsked, 'there is still so much more pain you need to experience. You know why you must be punished. There are so many years we need to catch up on.'

I looked from the Usurper to Markus, the suspicions I had felt and the questions I had pondered rose again in my mind.

'Shut up, you bastard,' Markus growled.

'I'm hurt,' the Usurper said dramatically, 'are you telling me that your friends don't know?'

'I don't know what you're talking about.' Markus' face was blank, but he was full of tension.

'I think this news might need to be shared,' the Chief Counsel said, touching the Usurper's arm, 'shall I go and bring them in?'

'What a good idea,' the Usurper said, clapping his hands together with unmitigated glee. The Chief Counsel left the room for a few minutes and then returned dragging two smaller bodies. Stefan and Erik had been beaten and were tossed to the floor where they lay in a crumpled heap. Stefan seemed to be unconscious, while Erik looked up hazily, barely seeming to register where he was.

'You monster,' Markus growled, and I gripped onto the chains tighter, pulling them in an effort to break free.

The Usurper laughed and knelt beside Erik, tilting his face upwards and clamping a hand around his chin. 'So young. Such wasted potential. Such a shame.'

'A waif,' the Chief Counsel said dismissively, 'there are hundreds like him, they will never amount to anything more than being a pebble in the shoe of someone greater.'

'He's significantly better than you,' I said harshly, 'and he's still a boy.'

'You know the sad thing?' The Usurper was saying to Erik, his voice soft, 'I knew a boy like you once, many years ago. He too had potential, he too wanted to change the world and he fought for someone he believed in. He had such passion, such drive, but when he followed his hero into battle, guess what happened?'

Erik shook his head slowly, his eyes starting to focus more clearly on the Usurper's face.

'The boy got scared,' the Usurper continued, 'he got the taste for blood and then bolted, ashamed of what he had done. He ran away as far as he could go, until he needed money, so he began to participate in some… illegal activities. Those led to him being caught and brought back home.'

I wasn't watching Erik now. My eyes didn't leave Markus, who looked like a statue carved from stone.

'Isn't it interesting,' the Usurper said, 'how history repeats itself? And just like a circle, my runaway nephew is returned to me, all these years later?'

Erik's eyes widened and he stared at Markus disbelievingly.

'There's nothing quite like a good, old fashioned family reunion,' the Usurper smiled.

Chapter Twelve: Erik

The Usurper's fingers dug into my chin, forcing me to watch Markus, who wasn't speaking; wasn't denying anything. I felt like everything was crumbling around me and I was helpless to respond. It had been bad enough being captured by those monsters in the woods, and waking up in a dingy cell with no idea where we were or how much time had passed. And then the guards had come in, with their sharp iron-clad boots and heavy batons and I'd almost wished to pass out as quickly as Stefan had.

Now I was starting to realise that it was only the beginning. Markus was steadily refusing to meet my eyes. I couldn't comprehend what the Usurper was saying, but from looking at him I knew that it had a ring of truth to it. That meant that Markus…that he…

'We all have pasts we're not proud of,' Aidyn said angrily, 'I don't blame him for wanting nothing to do with the likes of you.'

The Usurper's hand gripped harder and I felt tears prick my eyes. 'Take these two away,' he said coolly, 'I think it's time to reacquaint Lord Aidyn with his nightmares.'

The Chief Counsel led Stefan and I out of the room, half carrying Stefan and only holding onto me with one hand. I took my chance and dropped down, crumpling and rolling out of his grip, kicking his ankles and sprinting away, running blindly through the corridors until I found an alcove in which

I could hide. The Chief Counsel yelled after me, crying out for guards to scour the hallways, and I edged back, pressing into the wall. There was a soft click, and I fell backwards as a door opened, leading into a dusty crawlspace. Barely breathing, I shut the door behind me, just as a group of guards ran past, their armour clanking.

It took a few moments to adjust my eyes to the gloom, and I looked around, noting that the walkway was narrow and stretched away into darkness. It was full of cobwebs and I shivered, recoiling from their cool stickiness. Behind me the door was still slightly open, allowing a strip of light from the hallway to enter. There was a flicker, and then something flew through the crack, landing on my hand.

I jumped, flapping madly to get it off, but it clung on with its tiny legs. Gradually, I recognised the soft pale glow as its wings fluttered back and forth and began to calm down; it was one of those blasted moths from the Underdark. The door behind me had closed properly as I had hit it while trying to dislodge the moth, now the small creature grew brighter, becoming a source of light in the narrow space.

'Alright,' I whispered, 'let's see where this leads.'

Carefully, I began to pick my way down the passageway, trying to avoid the larger spiderwebs and stepping over the debris on the floor. As I walked, I kept my ears alert, listening for any sign of movement from the other side of the walls. Distantly, there was shouting and running, and I knew that the Chief Counsel was sending guards everywhere.

There were occasional cracks in the wall, but nothing to provide a peephole into the rooms I passed. As I moved along, I figured that I must be somewhere in between the walls. One hand gripping the stones on my side, the other lifted in front of me so that the moth could guide my way.

When we reached the end of the passage, it split into two directions and I paused, wondering which way to go. As I stood there, the moth took flight again, leading the way down the left passage, and I followed, unwilling to be left alone in the dark.

There was a breeze coming from up ahead, and I pressed on, wanting to find the source. The moth paused, fluttering up and down against another door which had a grille above it. When I reached it, the moth flew down onto my shoulder, and I caught my breath, gripping the door handle.

'Unbelievable.' A voice cut through the air, travelling through the grille and I froze. It was the Usurper. 'You had one job and now one of the boys is missing?'

'The guards will find him soon, Lord Niall,' the Chief Counsel said waspishly, 'he is nothing to concern yourself with.'

'I should hope not,' the Usurper snapped, 'it's bad enough with the news coming in from the Tracking Towers. Five Towers have been destroyed and the Western towns are in an uproar. I need everything to be perfect for my coronation tomorrow night. I cannot have anything disrupting it.'

'It shall be as you wish,' the Chief Counsel said smoothly, 'never fear.'

The sound of their footsteps drew away and I sank to the ground, clutching my chest to stop the rising panic that was threatening to take over. It couldn't be true. I still had weeks. How was it possible?

'I've failed,' I whispered through numb lips. 'I can't succeed.'

The moth nestled closer, its wings softly brushing against my neck. It was strangely comforting, and I pressed my head onto my knees, clasping them tightly. I rocked back and forth, thinking desperately about what could be done. I didn't realise that I was crying until the moth's wings caught one of the tears. I sniffed, leaning back against the door, listening carefully to check if the room beyond was empty. After a few more moments, I stood and pushed, edging the door open a crack.

The door seemed to open into an alcove, much like the one I had entered through. However this alcove opened onto a wide, airy chamber, full of polished white marble and tall windows of stained glass, catching the first glimpse of sunset. There was a throne carved out of ice that rose in front of an open balcony. Behind it was an empty space, a large circular pit that I knew from the stories should be where the flame of Scardia burned. Something had been placed on a wooden table next to it– a long, covered casket.

I drew in a short breath, recognising it.

Carefully, I stepped backwards, closing the door and retreating into the passageway. I looked down at the moth and said, 'I think we need to explore some more, see where the other passages go.'

It lifted into the air and took off again, and I followed excitedly, a bounce in my step as I began to consider my plan.

Night had fallen and the palace had settled down to sleep. Only a few guards patrolled the hallways, but it seemed that most of them had gone further afield in the hope of finding me. I had walked between the walls for close to an hour before retracing my steps to where I had entered.

The moth's light guided me back along the corridor, leading me towards the cells where the others were being held. I walked stealthily, practising the skills that Jesse had taught me back in King Aegis' court. The corridors were dimly lit, the torches burning low, and I clung to the shadows, stepping behind tapestries or into alcoves when I heard people approaching.

At these times, I held my breath and prayed to the Gods, hoping that I wouldn't be seen. Each time, I let out a sigh of relief as the passers-by moved on, unaware of my presence. The corridor became colder as I drew closer to the cells, the silence deafening as I paused outside the door where Stefan and I had been held. I pushed it open gently and saw Stefan inside, tied to the far wall. He looked like he'd had another beating, and a trickle of blood was sliding down his temple. My chest seized and I forced the feeling down, trying to focus on what needed to be done. When the door shut behind me, he opened his eyes blearily and then registered who had entered the room.

'Erik?' He whispered, 'you came back?'

'Of course I did, you idiot,' I muttered gruffly, rushing to the side of the room where a key was looped over a hook, within sight of the prisoners but just out of reach. I lifted it off and began to unlock his chains, moving as quickly as I could. 'We need to free the others and then get out of here,' I said urgently, 'there's a passageway not far.'

'Lead the way,' he said quietly, swaying slightly as he was released and back on his feet.

'Come on,' I whispered, moving back to the door and listening before creeping out to check the hallway. 'All clear.' I slid out of the door and padded towards the opposite cell. Stefan followed behind me, keeping an eye out for any guards as I opened the heavy door.

The moth left my shoulder immediately when I entered, fluttering over to perch on Aidyn's pale hair, which glittered in the moonlight. It felt strange to see him without his mask on, but it was slightly a relief to know that he wasn't a monster underneath, like those creatures that had attacked us on the road. I took in his features for a moment, wondering if Nina had seen them, or if she had only ever known him with a mask on. Seeing him like this forced me to recognise that he was more human than I had previously thought.

'Erik.' It was Markus who spoke, snapping me out of my thoughts, 'what are you doing?'

'What does it look like?' I muttered sardonically, moving over to unlock the manacles around his hands and feet. When he was free, Markus grimaced and looked towards the doorway where Stefan waited, clearly eager to leave. I moved to Aidyn's side and began to work on his bonds, noticing that he seemed to be half asleep, his eyes unfocussed and almost closed.

'Help me, will you?' I asked Markus, who reluctantly came over to support Aidyn's weight as he was released. It seemed that the shock of his arms being released was enough to startle Aidyn out of his trance, and he blinked, shaking his head and looking around wildly.

'Keep your mouth shut,' Markus grunted, 'We don't want the guards to hear. Can you hold yourself up?'

Aidyn nodded and pulled away, staggering a little as he moved over to retrieve his mask and gear. While he pulled on a dark shirt and his balaclava- wincing in pain as it grazed against his burns- Markus and I unlocked Alex's chains and helped them over to Aidyn. While Aidyn's wounds looked painful but bearable, Alex was almost comatose, unresponsive to our whispers with injuries which were significantly worse.

'We need to get out of here,' Markus whispered urgently as Aidyn began to pull Alex's clothing on and attaching their mask.

'They will draw comfort from being covered,' Aidyn replied softly, 'it will help to heal the mind. Our kind do not cope well with being exposed like we were today.'

Markus rolled his eyes but helped Aidyn to lift Alex up. 'Let's *go*.' He hissed as they followed me out of the door. I pulled it closed behind us and we began to hurry down the hallway. The torches around us flickered and died, a strange darkness filled the space around us and I paused, worried.

'It's fine,' Aidyn said quietly. 'Hold onto each other and follow the moth. It will guide you.'

It felt slightly silly clinging to each other in the dark and creeping forwards, but the darkness provided an effective cover for us to reach the passageway without being detected. The doorway opened and we fell into the narrow walkway, treading carefully through the dust towards the entrance into the throne room.

'Where are we going, Erik?' Markus asked forcefully, 'we should be trying to escape.'

'No.' I replied staunchly, 'we're not leaving without Nina.'

Markus slipped, sucked in a breath and cursed, 'damn stones.' It sounded as though he had grazed himself against the wall. 'We don't know where she is, Erik. Besides, it's more important for us to get away, it's not safe in the palace.'

'No, it isn't safe,' Aidyn murmured, 'but I think we should trust Erik.'

I felt a moment of gratitude and pressed on, painfully aware that the night was starting to slip away. Dawn would be coming soon, time was running out.

'Come *on*,' I muttered after a while, when I noted that the others were falling behind.

'We can't go faster, Erik,' Stefan said quietly.

'Why not?' I snapped, turning back.

'Alex,' he said simply and moved to hover beside Markus and Aidyn, who held Alex between them, trying to keep them up.

'You need to hold on, old friend,' Aidyn was whispering, gripping their arm tighter. 'Once we're out of here, we will get you to a healer, I promise.'

'Erthor showed me a vision of burning,' Alex mumbled, 'I thought it was the windmill, I thought it was a sign.' They crumpled and Aidyn and Markus helped them to lie down. 'I don't think it was a vision of the windmill, Aidyn,' they whispered, 'I think…'

'Don't think like that,' Aidyn said roughly, and I wondered if he was crying. 'We're going to get out of here. You'll be home in time for the Moon Festival; we'll go to the Lake of Tears and climb Devil's Peak, just like we used to.'

Alex let out a small, brittle laugh, 'I don't think you should make promises you can't keep, Aidyn. I can't see a way that I'll be welcomed back home after this, and now I'm slowing you down, I'm a burden to you all. May Lord Lionus see me safely on the next part of my journey.'

'No,' Aidyn said, 'it's not time for that yet.'

Alex grasped his hand. 'Brother of my soul, help me to find peace in Erthor's light.'

'No,' Aidyn was begging now, 'no, Alex. Don't talk like that. We can still get you out, get you a healer.'

'I was glad that I finally got to show someone my face after all these years,' Alex murmured faintly. 'I'm glad that it was you, brother. Please, take me to Erthor's light.'

Aidyn shook his head, shoulders shaking as he gripped onto Alex.

'Please, brother,' Alex repeated, 'help me find peace.' There was a long silence, as the white moth fluttered down and landed on Alex's shoulder. Aidyn took a shaky breath, watching it as though it was giving him a sign.

'As you wish, my friend,' Aidyn whispered brokenly. 'Go and find peace.' He bent over Alex's body, withdrew a blade from inside his boot and we watched in frozen horror as he thrust it into Alex's chest. Alex jolted slightly, let out a gurgling sigh and then stilled. Aidyn withdrew the blade, cleaned it and replaced it in his boot, folding Alex's arms over their body. He knelt there for a moment; head bowed in prayer.

'Erthor, watch over Alex as they journey into your kingdom. Sybilla, grant them peace as they join with the stars above. Lionus, welcome them into your embrace.'

'What the hell did you do?' Markus breathed, aghast. 'You monster.'

Aidyn looked at him and said, 'I granted their request. Now let's go.' He stood and strode away, leaving the rest of us stood around Alex's body, shaken. The moth flew up from Alex's shoulder and lit the path ahead of Aidyn as he moved away. Gradually, I forced myself to move again, catching up to Aidyn and gesturing for the others to hurry.

We reached the entrance to the throne room not long after, and I pushed the door open. The moth had fluttered through the grille and was making its way over to Nina's casket. Our footsteps rang on the marble floor as we followed the faint trace of light across the room.

I glanced out of the window, noting that the moon was halfway through its descent and that our time was nearly up.

Soon it would be dawn and the rest of the palace would awaken. We needed to get out of here before then, although I had no idea where we could go.

The moth flickered back and forth, finally settling down onto her icy forehead. I blinked and stepped closer, realising that the lid of the casket had been removed, as had the sheet that had covered the body.

'What by the Gods...' Stefan began, but I silenced him with a quick jab to the ribs. He winced but held his tongue.

'I didn't quite believe you,' Markus breathed, as he leaned over Nina's body. 'I thought she was...'

'We need to get her out of here,' I muttered feverishly, trying to lift the coffin and failing miserably.

'She would want to be here, Erik,' Aidyn said softly, 'this is the heart of her kingdom, her home; where everything began.'

I stilled, the answers coming all at once.

Of course. The heart.

'Help me get her out of the coffin,' I whispered, 'lift her onto the Hoarfrost.'

Markus gripped my shoulder, 'it's alright Erik. You've done your best, leave her now.'

'No,' I replied, pulling away, 'no, this is Scardia's heart. I thought it was the Glacier, but it's here.' The others just looked at me like I was crazy as I began to push the table to the side, clearing the space. At my urging, they joined in, until the table and coffin had been moved off the circle of ice. 'Help me lift her down,' I begged, gripping Nina's frozen shoulders.

Aidyn reached into the coffin and gripped her feet, while Stefan took one of her sides. Markus hovered for a moment and then reached down to lift her other side. Together, we heaved her out of the coffin and down onto the patch of Hoarfrost Ice, careful to not drop her, though our fingers were numbed within seconds of touching her. It was hard to grip, the Hoarfrost was slippery and heavy, and I was relieved when we had placed her down onto the ground. The lunar moth stayed on Nina's forehead the whole time, its glow brightening as we lowered her. When she touched the circle of Hoarfrost, there was a sudden hush, as if the world around us was watching and waiting for something to happen.

'Give me your knife,' I said to Aidyn. When he handed me the blade, I drew it across my palm, splattering the blood on the ice.

'What are you doing?' Stefan asked, horrified.

'Blood of a guilty man,' I muttered, reaching into my pocket, searching for the napkin that I'd thrust in there before we were taken. 'Tear of an innocent.'

'He's gone mad,' Stefan said, watching me uncomprehendingly.

I reached out and grabbed Markus' hands, bringing them down to rest on Nina's. 'A heart's desire.'

He coughed, and Aidyn made an uncomfortable movement to my side. Awkwardly, Markus moved his hands, leaving traces of blood from his grazes on Nina's body.

'All that remains is the first drop of moonlight,' I whispered, looking up at the stain-glass windows, searching for the moon. The moth flickered and brightened, drawing my eyes.

'Lunar moths are said to have been created from Erthor himself,' Aidyn said quietly, 'they bring the moonlight to all the darkest places.'

I felt myself smile, and then looked down as my hand emerged empty from my pocket. The napkin I'd been searching for wasn't there.

'No,' I breathed, 'no. It can't be gone.'

It wasn't fair, I was too close. Beyond the windows the moon was fading away, the grey light that precedes dawn starting to fill the sky.

'It's alright, Erik,' Stefan said, kneeling beside me and gripping my shoulder. I turned away from him, hot angry tears burning my eyes that I did not want him to see. I scrubbed my cheek with a bloody hand and stared down at Nina.

'Please,' I whispered, sending out a silent prayer to the Gods and Spirits, begging them to make an exception, to recognise that I had done what I could. My tears fell and I wiped them away, feeling ashamed for failing.

'Erik,' Markus said, wiping his own bloodied palms, 'come on. Let's go.'

'Wait.' Aidyn's voice was tight, and I looked around at him, before Markus gasped and pulled me away from Nina's body. I glanced back and felt my breathing seize in my chest.

'Get back,' Markus snapped, holding us roughly. 'Only members of the royal family can touch the Ice Flame and survive.'

The Hoarfrost was glowing, sending blinding blue and white lights out across the throne room, reflecting and bouncing off the windows. There was a loud whoosh as flames encased Nina's body, melting away her frozen exterior in moments. From our distance I could feel it– hot enough to burn away flesh and bone– and I felt a moment's relief that we had moved away. The flames rose higher, up above the throne and towards the ceiling, lifting her up into the air until she hung, suspended in a coil of fiery tendrils. A flaming bird was spreading its wings above her, preparing to strike.

'By the Gods,' Stefan whispered, and I nodded, entranced.

There was a loud crack, like thunder, and a wave of fire flew out from her, shattering the windows. Coloured glass tumbled down like splinters of rain and we covered ourselves to avoid being hit. The firebird dived, vanishing into Nina's chest. The light was fading now and she was sinking back to the ground, still looking like she was asleep.

As she landed on the ice, the flames smouldered down to embers, glowing around her body. We crouched down beside her, torn between wanting to check her pulse and being afraid to touch her.

'Nina?' I asked tentatively.

'Is she alive?' Markus' voice was shaky as he reached out to touch her hand. 'Nina?'

'She doesn't seem to be,' Stefan whispered, peering closer.

'Wake up, Nina,' Aidyn said softly, and in it I heard all the longing in the world. 'Come back.'

In the distance I could hear shouting and people running, and felt my stomach drop. Of course the noises from the throne room would have woken the guard, it was only a matter of time before they came through the doors and found us.

And then I heard an intake of breath and a cough and I turned to see flaming blue eyes staring up at us. I grinned and hugged her, my words spilling out in a rush as I apologised for leaving her in the Underdark, for almost giving up, but that we really had to leave, right now. After a few moments I registered that she was taut beneath me and felt Markus pull me away, staring at her in wonder.

I followed his gaze and felt a faint sense of trepidation as she stood up, lifting her dagger in one hand and cradling a ball of flame in the other. The orchids fell amongst the embers and caught alight, burning at her feet. Her face was tight and distrustful, as she looked at the four of us in turn.

Something was wrong but I wasn't sure what until she finally spoke.

'Who are you?' Nina asked. 'And what makes you think I will go anywhere with you?'

Part Two

Chapter Thirteen

It was cold, the air frigid, and as I breathed out, a puff of warm steam rose like a cloud. I seemed to be on a mountaintop that looked out over a valley of snowfields and a distant village, whose lights flickered. Everything was still and quiet, like the morning's breath of anticipation before the break of dawn. I saw her standing on the edge, where the mountain dropped away to the valley below. She was creating flurries of snowflakes, sending them out into the sky to fall across the land

'You're awake,' she said. 'I was wondering how long you would sleep for.'

'Where am I?' I asked tentatively, 'the last thing I remember was…' My voice drifted off as I struggled to locate the memory. I could feel it on the tip of my tongue, hovering just out of reach. 'I can't remember,' I said slowly.

The Winter Spirit smiled gravely, 'you are in the space between life and death, my dear. Your body is waiting to be awoken again.'

I looked down at myself, prodded my chest experimentally. 'I don't feel dead.'

'That's because of the gift I gave you,' she said. I looked at her quizzically and she smiled, 'I infused your heart with Hoarfrost, my dear. It hardened it, made it more difficult for it to stop beating before its time. Your friends are tasked with bringing you back, but there might be some side effects.'

'Like what?' I asked cautiously.

'That will depend on how soon your brother can fulfil his task,' the Winter Spirit said, 'they will become stronger the longer he takes.'

'That doesn't seem fair,' I mused, watching as the snowflakes tumbled out over the valley and catching one on an outstretched hand.

'It is not up to us to decide the whims of the Gods,' the Winter Spirit replied, 'they will want to test you as well, one cannot return from the world in-between life and death without some consequences.'

I should have felt nervous, but instead was filled with a steady sense of calm. I knew that Erik would fulfil the task, whatever it was. I just needed to be patient. Besides, I had gone through the Trial in the Underdark and survived, so what more could the Gods have in store for me?

I was awoken with a blinding flash and a rush of heat through my chest; I opened my eyes, taking in my surroundings. As I focussed on the world around me, a small boy with a jagged scar down his face lunged at me, clinging to me tightly. He was speaking too fast and his words blurred together. Unable to absorb what he was saying, I gazed at the figures behind him— a tall man with long, dark hair and a tattoo across his chest, another youth who was watching me wide-eyed, and a figure in a mask, dressed all in black. I didn't know any of them.

The boy who was holding me began to talk about leaving and I froze, gripping the silver blade in my hands until my knuckles turned white. The tall man leaned forward and drew the boy away, gazing at me as though I were a miracle.

I got to my feet, dropping the flowers that had been in my hands, and gripped my blade, summoning a flame to burn in my palm. This wasn't right, what was going on?

'Who are you?' I asked, 'and what makes you think that I will go anywhere with you?'

The boy stared at me, eyes bulging with shock. 'Nina…'

'Don't,' I said shakily, raising the knife, 'you haven't been given the right to call me that.'

'But…' the boy was confused, and he tried to step forward, but the man held him back.

'We need to get out of here, Nina,' the man with dark hair said, 'you're not safe here.'

'I beg to differ.' A sweet voice came from the other side of the throne room. A middle-aged man with golden hair and a high forehead crossed the floor, stopping halfway and gazing at me with sharp eyes. Behind him were a number of guards, who had heavy armour emblazoned with a bull's head. It looked vaguely familiar.

'No,' the boy whimpered.

'Who are you?' I asked, moving my blade towards the newcomer.

'Princess Wilhelmina,' the man knelt, 'I have been searching for you for many long years. I've been trying to bring you home.'

I paused, my breath catching. 'Bring me home?'

'Indeed,' the man said, waving a hand at the room around us. 'You have been missing for many years. But now you are returned to us, and I'm afraid I can't let you be taken away by these miscreants. They belong to a group of rebels, those who sought to overthrow your parents' reign and then kidnapped you.'

My blade lowered a fraction as I gazed at him, 'you seem…familiar.'

'Of course I am, my dear,' he said smoothly, 'I was a close friend of your father's and a confidante of your mother's. They entrusted me with your care.'

'Liar,' the boy hissed, 'don't listen to him, Nina.'

I looked back at him, and something in his blazing eyes made me pause. 'I…'

'Come here, Princess Wilhelmina,' the blond man said, holding out a hand, 'you mustn't be swayed by a group of escaped prisoners. You've been through so much, you need to be taken care of.'

I teetered between moving and staying where I was, drawing strength from the embers beneath my feet. There were things that the blond man said which seemed familiar, but the boy's intensity and outrage made me falter. So I remained rooted to the spot, glancing back and forth between the two groups, unable to make a decision about who to trust or believe.

'Markus,' the masked figure said abruptly, 'get the boys and go.'

The blond man laughed, and his men stepped closer. 'You can't escape. My nephew has only just found his way home, Princess Wilhelmina.' He indicated the tall man with the tattoo. 'He was most helpful in assisting us to find you safely, but, as you can see, he is a bit conflicted in his alliances.'

'Now, Markus,' the masked man snapped, and he made a swift gesture with his hand. Deep, impenetrable darkness fell, and someone grabbed my arm, dragging me towards one of the open doors. There were shouts and clamours all around us as I was led blindly on, struggling to break free. The darkness was everywhere, making it impossible to distinguish where I was going or who was gripping my arm so tightly. I struck out with my dagger, trying to be released. There was a stifled gasp and then two arms were wrestling my hands behind my back, the dagger snatched out of my grip.

'Play nice, Princess,' a low voice muttered, and I kicked out, calling on the flames to help me. The darkness pressed closer, extinguishing the flames as quickly as they grew to life. There was another quick intake of breath as my foot collided with a leg and I felt a savage moment of satisfaction.

'Let go of me,' I hissed, twisting my arms in an attempt to break free.

'Not yet,' the voice answered, and a hand was clasped over my mouth, cutting off my cries. I was pushed onward, stumbling slightly through passageways and downstairs. There was a rush of cold air, and I felt icy cobblestones under my feet as we ran, until my captor pulled me behind a wall and paused, panting. I slumped against the rock, and when my hands were released I struck upward, swearing as my hand hit something hard over his face. A mask.

'I told you to let me go,' I cried as I struck again, tearing it away as fire began to shimmer around me. He ducked under my punch and we wrestled, me trying to escape from his grip and he trying to keep me trapped. The darkness was lifting slightly and I saw that we were pressed against one of the palace's outer walls. It was tall and hid us effectively from view, and the frost-covered ground below us slid down a steep hill towards the town below.

'Be patient, Princess,' he gasped, as I hurled a ball of fire which he missed, 'I will explain everything as soon as we get away from here.'

'I am not going *anywhere* with you,' I snarled as I ran to the side and was tackled to the ground. The momentum of him crashing into me knocked us into a downward momentum, slipping and rolling over and over down towards the streets below. The fall felt like it lasted forever, and I tried to cover my head as I hit rocks and grazed myself on the rough, icy earth.

When we reached the bottom of the hill, we lay there for a moment, each of us trying to catch our breath. He stood gingerly and heaved me up, glancing around to check that we hadn't been seen.

'We need to get out of sight, Princess.'

'Then you had better...'

He yanked and I stumbled after him again, the words cut off as we raced through the streets until we reached a shadowed alleyway. He paused, glancing at the doors and checking the numbers.

By now I was angry. Since I had awoken I had been attacked, kidnapped, and fallen down a long, steep hill with absolutely no explanation. I wasn't sure what I had been doing in the throne room, or how long I had been sleeping for, or even why I had been asleep for that matter. Everything before I awoke was a blur, but certain things seemed familiar– the palace, the town around us, the man with the golden hair who had sounded so friendly. The longer I was with this stranger, the more I was starting to believe what the golden-haired man had said. I needed to try and escape and to get back to the palace as soon as possible, where I would be safe.

'This must be it,' the man muttered and pushed on a door which opened with a gentle creak. I was dragged unceremoniously inside and the door shut behind us with a click. I glanced around the dingy space. It was dusty, there were old bowls of dried food on the table and the chairs looked as though they would break as soon as you sat on them. Rickety stairs on the far side of the room led to the floor above and a blackened fireplace took up the space of one wall.

'Is this where you live?' I sniffed.

'Hardly, Princess,' he said gruffly. 'This is a safehouse. There are a few of them dotted throughout the Capital for Resistance members.'

I gave a humph and stepped further into the room. 'Why are we here?'

'We needed a safe place to hide,' he replied, sliding the bar across the door and then, noticing my scandalised expression, said, 'I won't hurt you, Princess.'

'Could've fooled me,' I muttered, wrapping my arms around myself and turning away. 'I suppose you want to get a ransom of some sort,' I continued, 'I think that man back at the palace would pay good money for me to go home.'

He was quiet for a moment and then said, 'you really don't know who I am, do you?'

I turned and saw that he had come closer, to within a foot of me. I jumped back, lifting another ball of flame into the air, 'touch me and I swear I will burn your hand off.'

'Calm down, Princess,' he said softly.

'I don't know who you are,' I snapped. 'Don't come near me.'

'Then I will sit over here,' he said calmly, moving to one of the rickety chairs and settling down in it. 'I think the others should be finding their way here soon.'

I leaned against the wall with the fireplace for a while, watching him closely, desperately scanning my memory for anything familiar. He took off his gloves and pulled off the dark balaclava, wincing slightly. Underneath, his face was roughened and dirty, stained with blood and heavily blistered.

He ran a hand through his pale hair and sighed deeply. His eyes met mine and I pressed back into the stones, suddenly feeling as though he could see more than I wanted him to know.

'Why did you take me away from the palace?' I asked finally, my gaze not leaving his face. 'What do you want with me? Who was that man?'

'You died, Princess.' His voice was quiet, 'that man, the one who tried to convince you to stay, has been running your kingdom for years. He killed your parents and has been wanting to kill you since the night you escaped.'

His words sounded familiar, like he was retelling me a dream that I had once had.

'Who *are* you?' I whispered, moving closer despite myself, until he was within arm's reach. He looked at me, lilac eyes full of something I didn't understand. He held out a hand and I took it tentatively as he stood and slowly moved in front of me, as though I were a wild animal that would lash out at a moment's notice. I held my breath, suddenly unsure about how I would react to his movements, heart beating erratically as fear and curiosity merged together.

'It is perhaps the cruellest thing,' he murmured, as his fingers brushed my knuckles, 'that when you are finally back, you cannot remember me.' I made to pull away, distracted by the rush of sensation where our skin touched, but something kept me still, unwilling to move.

'I…' Time seemed to pause, drawing out each second into an age as his lilac eyes bored into mine. There was something, a faint memory that escaped before I could grasp it. 'I'm sorry,' I finally said, 'I just…'

'I will be patient,' he said quietly, 'I have waited a long time, I can wait a bit longer.'

I tilted my head, puzzled. 'That sounds strangely familiar,' I murmured. His mouth formed a slightly crooked smile.

'You might have heard it before,' he replied softly, one hand rising to my cheek and cupping it gently. I froze for a moment, suddenly unsure, and I saw the realisation fill his eyes. He sighed again, leaning his forehead against mine for a moment, before pulling away, leaving me feeling suddenly cold.

'I'm sorry, Princess,' he said as he stepped back, but something stopped him from moving far. I looked down and realised that my hand was still entwined in his, fingers refusing to break away.

A knocking came from the door and I jumped, retreating to the corner of the room and summoning another ball of flame. The man pulled his gloves and balaclava back on, and then moved to the door.

'Who is it?' He called, drawing a blade from his boot.

'Open the door, Aidyn,' someone grunted from the other side, 'we need to get inside.'

The bolt was lifted and the three strangers from the throne room stumbled inside, shutting the door securely behind them.

'Good to see you made it out alright,' Aidyn said, moving back to sit down on one of the chairs. 'I was starting to worry.'

'We climbed over the balcony,' the boy with the scar said brightly, 'we wouldn't have escaped if you hadn't summoned that darkness when you did, Aidyn. Thanks.'

'Yes,' the other man said, 'thanks.' He stared at me as he sank into the other chair.

'Erik, you might want to show the Princess upstairs,' Aidyn said calmly, 'she may want some privacy.'

The boy with the scar came towards me fearlessly and I shrank back. 'You won't hurt me, Nina,' he said confidently, holding out a bloodied hand. 'Come on.'

There was something in his face, a certain earnestness, that seemed familiar to me. I found myself more ready to trust him, and took his hand carefully, allowing him to lead me up the stairs. The room upstairs was small, with an old bed that covered us in a mist of dust as we sat down on it.

'I'm glad that you and Aidyn got out alright,' Erik said, 'it's not been easy the past few months. I thought you weren't ever going to come back, I thought I'd failed you.'

I let him speak, absorbing some of the things he told me and allowing the rest to flow over me. He was my brother apparently, although I was pretty sure that I was an only child, I didn't say that. We had travelled to the Eastern Lands on Markus' ship months ago to join the Resistance and find my grandfather. Markus and I had been close, apparently, and I blinked, remembering the tattooed man's expression when I first awoke.

'Who is Aidyn?' I finally interrupted, and Erik paused. It was almost like he didn't want to answer the question, but reluctantly did.

'He's one of the Dark Elves,' he said, 'you signed a betrothal contract with him when we were in the Underdark. You wanted to save Markus and Keely. He went to retrieve them for you.'

'So, he rescued them?' I probed thoughtfully, and Erik nodded. 'We got caught by the Usurper's monsters and Trackers and were taken to the palace. He planned to crown himself king tonight, but now that you're no longer dead, he will be unable to do so.'

'But he seemed so nice,' I mused, remembering the blond man's ingratiating smile.

'He's a monster,' Erik muttered. 'I'm just glad we got away.'

I watched him for a while, 'who was the other boy with you?'

'Stefan,' Erik replied, 'my friend.'

I nodded, moving away from him to the small grimy window that overlooked the alleyway. 'I think I would like to be alone now,' I said, 'this is a lot to process.'

'We'll be downstairs,' Erik mumbled, and then gave me a quick hug, startling me. 'It is good to have you back, even if...' He trailed off and darted down the stairs, leaving me in peaceful solitude. As I stood by the window, the voices from below me drifted up through the floor.

'How long do you think she'll not remember?' It was Markus' voice.

'Have there been other cases like it?' Stefan asked.

'I think the Gods will decide if and when she does,' Aidyn said.

'But we need her to remember now,' Erik replied. 'The Resistance have already started to attack some of the towns. The Usurper is getting worried.'

'We need to send word to the Resistance,' Markus said, 'it'll be too dangerous to get out of this city now. The Usurper will have Trackers everywhere looking for us.'

'On the topic of the Usurper,' Erik said coolly, 'is there any particular reason why you didn't share the truth about who you are?'

There was a hard silence. 'A man's past is his own,' Markus finally said gruffly, 'I don't expect you to understand that.'

'You should have told us,' Stefan reinforced, 'Rakael would never have…'

'It's none of her business,' Markus snapped, 'and none of yours. I left my uncle and his machinations behind when I was barely older than you are now. Since then I have become who I wanted to be, and I am happy with that life.'

'You couldn't forgive Nina for not being honest with you about her true identity,' Erik's voice was quiet, 'but you never told her the truth about who you were.'

'Be quiet, Erik,' Markus hissed, 'you don't know anything.'

'I know that she loved you,' Erik retorted, 'and I know what she was like after we crossed the Meridian. Even when you found out who she really was, you…'

'Erik.' It was Aidyn's voice that interrupted now, 'leave it. This is not the time to discuss it.'

'I'll see about finding a carrier pigeon,' Stefan mumbled.

'No, I'll go,' Markus said brusquely, 'I'll not be gone long.'

'But…' Erik began.

'Let him go, Erik,' Aidyn said quietly. 'Let him go.'

The door slammed shut and through the window I saw Markus slipping away down the alleyway. I stood there a while longer, watching the town begin to awaken, tradespeople passed pushing carts of produce, children ran shrieking after a wooden hoop, attacking it with sticks, guards wearing silver armour marched by, the flashing bull's head glinting in the sun.

I drew back then, responding to some instinct, and lay down on the bed. I wasn't tired but I didn't want to go downstairs, to be stared at or talked to or expected to remember something I just couldn't. My breathing evened out and I felt myself drifting away.

Chapter Fourteen

A man with dark eyes was laughing at me, the rubies in his turban sparkling. He held out a hand for me to take, but when I did, he vanished and I was plummeting down into a sandy pit.

'Little Princess,' he crooned, appearing again, 'so good to have you back. I was starting to miss you.'

'Who are you?' I asked, coughing as sand filled my throat.

He flipped over in the air and gazed at me, considering me. 'It is so much more fun when you can remember what you've lost, isn't it?' He said, 'What would you trade for your memories to return? Your eyes? Your sweet voice? Your firstborn child?'

I fought against the sand, struggled to my feet and glared at him. 'If you are one of the Djinnis from the old tales, then you should be able to grant my wishes without needing payment.'

'Assuming a bit much there,' the man laughed, 'I find granting wishes far too ordinary. Although *your* wish, Princess,' he grinned, 'now that was a pleasure to bestow. I can't wait to see how it plays out.'

I felt myself blanch. 'What do you mean?' I croaked.

'Remember, Princess,' he said, 'when I grant a wish, it always comes true.' He laughed again and disappeared into a rising sandstorm. I screamed, covering my face with my hands, striking out to keep the sand at bay.

The sound of a door opening jerked me awake, and I sat up abruptly on the bed, heart pounding.

'Nina?' A voice from the staircase called. I turned and saw Erik standing there, looking worried. 'Are you alright?' He asked cautiously.

I nodded, raising a hand to my temple as an ache filled my head.

'Markus just got back,' Erik said, 'he's got food.'

'And clean clothes,' Stefan piped up from downstairs. 'And water.'

'Do you want anything?' Erik asked. I shook my head and lay back down, massaging the ache behind my eyes. I heard his footsteps fade away as he descended, and the sounds of domestication as the dirty dishes were cleaned and clothing was stripped and changed.

'I got a salve for you, Aidyn,' Markus' voice finally broke the silence, 'it should help with the burns.'

'How did you get all of this stuff?' Stefan asked curiously as Aidyn murmured a quiet thanks.

'I like to think of it as borrowed,' Markus said.

'So you stole it?' Erik stated

'More or less,' Markus admitted, 'we needed to have supplies and essentials, none of us have money. It'll be at least a few days before we hear back from Rakael and the Resistance. We'll need to lie low for that time. Here, Aidyn, let me help you.'

'No, thank you,' Aidyn's voice was cool. 'I will manage by myself, later. I appreciate you bringing it though.'

'There's a well in the square just outside the alley,' Markus continued, 'Stefan, maybe you and I could fill a few buckets for us to wash.'

'Good idea,' Aidyn said. 'Then you might want to rest. It has been a long night.'

I heard the sound of the door closing again, and soon there were footsteps on the stairs. I opened my eyes and saw Aidyn, carrying a plate with some bread and cheese on it and holding a cup of water in each hand.

'I thought you may need something,' he said, moving closer. 'You might get hungry later.'

'Why are you wearing that?' I asked abruptly as he sat down, handing me the plate and cup. I indicated his balaclava with a nod of the head, 'it's creepy.'

He chuckled, as though remembering a joke but I didn't find it that funny.

'I'm serious,' I said, 'it's *creepy*. Not as bad as the mask you had on before, but I don't understand why you put it back on after taking it off.' I took a sip of the water and realised that I was thirstier than I had expected, draining half of the cup in an instant. As I took a bite of bread and cheese, I shot him a glare, 'do you always watch people when they're trying to eat?'

'No,' he said calmly, 'it's just I still can't quite believe that you're here. I keep expecting to blink and find you gone.'

I took another bite of the cheese, 'why didn't you accept Markus' help?'

It seemed I had finally succeeded in surprising him. 'What?'

'I heard you, before,' I said, 'he stole some salve for your injuries. They looked bad before, so why didn't you accept his help?'

'Because we are not friends,' he said slowly, as if waiting for me to understand something I clearly didn't. 'I don't trust him, and I know he doesn't trust me.'

'Then let me help,' I said, the words slipping out before I could hold them back. There was a short silence which I tried to fill by nonchalantly chewing on some more bread, but deep down I was eager to try anything that might break through the fog that had descended on my memories, and this man seemed to tease essences of memories forward.

'You?' He asked, interrupting my thoughts.

'That's right,' I said with false breeziness, 'from what Erik said you and I are engaged to be married. Apparently.'

'Apparently,' he repeated.

'Then I should be trying to remember things, shouldn't I?' I said, 'and I think helping my future husband when he is wounded might help to jog a few memories.'

'I don't know which ones,' he muttered, but he didn't argue, so I drained the cup and set it down on the plate, looking at him expectantly. 'You're not doing anything now,' he finally said, realising belatedly that I was waiting for him to get the salve. 'I'll wash after everyone else, when they're asleep. Then, if you want to help, you can.'

He took my plate and cup and headed back downstairs, leaving me feeling awkward and confused, wondering if I had done the wrong thing. There was a commotion from downstairs as Stefan and Markus returned with several buckets of water, and I moved to the window again, trying to distract myself from the sounds of them washing below. I opened the grimy glass pane and allowed the noises from outside in the street to enter the room, as the morning drew on.

Erik was the first one to come back upstairs, gripping several blankets that he had found in one of the cupboards downstairs. He had a clean bandage around one hand and no longer looked as grimy or bloody, which was a relief.

'You look tired,' I said, as he yawned and flopped on the bed.

'It's been a long night,' he mumbled, as Stefan came up and lay on the other side of the bed, equally exhausted.

'I'll leave you to rest, then,' I said quietly, 'I'll see you when you wake up.'

'Promise you won't leave,' Erik muttered, reaching out and gripping me as I moved past.

'Sleep well,' I said, squeezing his hand and replacing it. As I reached the stairs I saw Markus, who paused, blocking my way so that I had to brush past him.

'Princess Nina,' he said as I tried to slide around him.

'Markus,' I replied. His arm snaked out and caught me, trapping me between him and the wall and I felt the anxiety begin to grow.

'I cannot believe that you don't remember,' he whispered, 'we were…'

'If you will excuse me,' I said hastily, 'I must join my betrothed.'

It was as though I had slapped him. He froze and then slowly released me, watching with darkened eyes as I passed him and descended the stairs. I heard him move across the room above and settle down, and only then allowed myself to breathe a sigh of relief.

'That was interesting.' Aidyn's voice spoke from the opposite corner of the room. It was strangely dark in here, and I wondered if he was the one making it so.

'What do you mean?' I asked, picking my way across the room towards him. He was bending over a bucket, wringing out one of the rags. He had removed his balaclava and shirt and had clearly been in the middle of washing his face.

'I don't think I've ever seen a meeting between two former lovers end so precipitously,' he said thoughtfully, wincing as he began to wash his arms.

I didn't say anything, but moved closer, noticing how tense he looked, despite his airy tone.

'You don't seem to appreciate someone's privacy, do you Princess?' He asked, starting to sound nettled.

'Not recently, no,' I admitted. 'Besides, out of all the people in this house, you seem to be the one who is most dangerous. I'd rather keep you in sight.'

'Well, that's flattering,' he muttered to himself, turning away from me and the gloom deepened so that he was barely discernible.

'Can you blame me?' I asked. 'Since I woke up, you've attacked me, kidnapped me and stolen my dagger. Hardly what a gentleman would do.'

He scoffed, reached into his boot and withdrew my dagger, tossing it towards the door where it stuck, quivering in the wood.

'There,' he said, 'your dagger returned, Princess.'

It took several hard pulls for me to get it out of the wood, and by the time I had retrieved it he seemed to be nearly finished.

'Alright then,' he grumbled, 'let's get this over and done with.'

He sat down on one of the chairs and held out a small tin of salve. I stalked over to him, placed the dagger down on the table and took the tin from him.

'It would be more helpful if I could *see*,' I said tartly. He snorted and, if anything, the darkness intensified. 'Oh, this is pathetic,' I sniffed, conjuring a flame to hover just above me, providing just enough light to work by. He kept his head turned away, gritting his teeth as I rubbed the salve into the burns that spread across his back. Underneath were other scars, as though someone had taken a whip to him many times before.

'What happened?' I asked as I knelt, trying to keep my touch gentle as I worked.

'The Usurper has a penchant for torture, Princess,' he said tightly. 'For my kind, sunlight is dangerous. If Lady Sybilla had not blessed me, I would not be alive.' My hand stilled for a moment and then carefully, I rested it on his shoulder.

'I'm sorry,' I whispered. 'I didn't know.'

'How could you?' He asked wryly. 'Everything you knew before has been forgotten.'

I continued to rub the salve in, trying to ignore the pain that his words caused. When I finished on his back, I moved around to face him, sitting on the other chair and pulling it closer. When he tried to take the salve from my hands I slapped him away, forcing him to remain still.

'Tell me something that I didn't know from before,' I murmured, wanting to break the silence that was dragging out between us.

'My favourite colour is green,' he said. 'Not like grass but the blue-green from the glow worms back home. I was named after my grandfather, who died in one of the wars between the three Houses.'

'How did you get the scars on your back?' I asked, noticing that he had similar ones around his wrists.

'My father had a particular style of punishment,' he said quietly, 'he would get angry when my brothers and I disobeyed our Elders.'

My hand paused briefly, and then continued rubbing in the salve. It was becoming more difficult to focus, and I avoided his gaze, afraid that he would read more than I wanted him to in my expression. But then I needed to move on to his face, and it was impossible to look away.

'Can you answer some of my questions now, Princess?' He asked, as I leaned closer to focus on the wounds on his face.

'I don't know how useful my answers will be,' I muttered, 'but go ahead.'

'What did you first feel when you woke up?'

That was easy. 'Confused,' I replied automatically, 'lost.'

'And how do you feel here?'

'Still confused,' I said slowly, biting my lip as I dabbed the salve onto his cheek. 'I feel like memories are just out of reach, certain things that I'm told feel familiar, others not so much.'

'And what about now?' His voice was a mere whisper as his hand reached up and held mine still. My eyes met his and I couldn't breathe.

'I don't know,' I managed.

'You're not a good liar, Princess,' he smiled, eyes laughing at me.

I felt myself blush. 'I…' How could I explain the emotions I felt? How to put words to them? I felt terrified and alive at the same time, enticed and anxious about the possibilities that were there in his eyes.

'Help me to remind you what you've forgotten,' he murmured as the flame above us was extinguished, casting us back into darkness. Without the light, I could only feel his breath against mine as he closed the gap between us, until he was inches away from me. 'What do you think, Princess?'

'I think…' The feel of him, the warmth of his hand against mine, was starting to become intoxicating. The space between us was alive, dancing with energy. I swallowed, my mouth suddenly dry. 'I think I would like that.'

He chuckled again and then his hands were framing my face, winding through my hair as he kissed me, gently at first, then with increasing fervour. I gasped, a sliver of a memory returning tantalisingly and I kissed him back, leaning into him as the memory became clearer. He groaned, gripping me harder, pulling me down into his lap, only pausing as a snore came from upstairs, reminding us that we needed to be quiet.

As we sat there, clinging to each other, hearts pounding, I said, 'Erik said that we were in the Underdark for a while, that that was where we signed the betrothal agreement.'

'Yes,' Aidyn replied, resting his head against my shoulder.

'Was there- I think- a waterfall falling into a lake? A grotto with rock pools and glow worms on the ceiling? And you...'

'Yes?' He was looking at me closely now.

'There were white moths,' I said thoughtfully, 'flying around you.'

'Yes,' he repeated.

'Was that real?' I asked, suddenly unsure. He nodded and kissed me again, holding me with such tenderness that I wondered if he thought I would break. The darkness around us faded gradually, replaced with soft daylight so that I could see him clearly again. When we drew apart again, I realised that his cheeks were wet.

'Aidyn,' I whispered, brushing the tears away, 'what's wrong?'

'Dear heart,' he said quietly, 'I thought...'

'Did he tell you about how he murdered his friend yet, Nina?' Markus' voice rang out across the room from the stairway. 'About how he tortured and killed the man who attacked another one of his kind?'

My head jerked up in shock, noting Aidyn's face pale and then go blank. The look in his eyes scared me more than Markus' words had, it was as though a stranger was gazing up at the man on the stairs, one who was completely different to the man I had just kissed.

I turned to Markus, whose rage was emanating from where he stood, fists clenched as he glared at Aidyn.

'Aidyn,' I said quietly, 'what is he talking about?'

'His friend was injured,' Markus growled, 'and your fiancé stabbed them.'

Aidyn's grip on me was so tight it hurt. I gently prised his hands away, trying to figure out how I had clearly gotten into such a mess with two strong-minded men. It was especially awkward not being able to remember anything beyond vague feelings or glimpses of memories.

'Aidyn,' I murmured, 'look at me.' Slowly, his gaze met mine, dragging away from Markus' figure where it looked down at us. 'Tell me if what he says is true,' I said, 'please.'

Something painful flashed in his eyes and then his expression was shuttered again, and I felt the distance between us lengthening despite being so close together.

'He is telling the truth,' he said tightly. 'My friend asked for release, they wanted to go to Erthor's kingdom, and I won't deny that I exacted vengeance for another friend's death. It is Erthor's way.'

Markus snorted from the stairs and I glared at him, furious that he had come and interrupted us, that he had ruined the moment we shared.

'I think you should go, Markus,' I said with forced calm, wanting nothing more than to throw something at him. 'Go and sleep.'

He scowled and strode to the door. 'I'm not going to sleep here with him working his magic on you. Don't trust a word he says, Nina. He just wants to use you for your power, to rule Scardia and escape from the hole under the mountains. He won't be able to keep you happy. He's not even *human.*' His words were bitter and cruel, and I felt his sense of betrayal, of the anger directed at me and the jealousy that was tainting him.

'I think that is my choice to make,' I said firmly. Markus' expression turned bleak and then he stormed out, slamming the door behind him.

I slumped against Aidyn, trembling slightly. 'I don't understand,' I whispered, 'what did I do to cause all of this?'

'Is it so strange that two men would want you?' Aidyn asked quietly, finally relaxing enough after Markus' confrontation to stroke my hair.

'Yes,' I muttered, 'to me it is.'

He bit back a laugh and held me closer.

'I didn't like how you changed when he said those things,' I said, looking at him. 'I felt like you were a different person for a time there. It scared me.'

He sighed, 'We all have different faces and personas, Princess. I can't always be the person I am when it is just you and I, sometimes I'm required to be someone else– a dutiful son, a diplomat, a general.'

'That's different,' I countered gently. 'You disappeared, it was like someone else looking out through your eyes.'

He just held me tighter, rocking me slightly as my trembling subsided.

'Do you think he will be back?' I asked, 'He seemed very angry.'

'He probably just needs to cool down,' Aidyn said, 'It's not easy when you see someone else kissing the person you care about.'

I felt my cheeks go warm again. 'I wish I could remember everything. I wish it wasn't just a blank.'

'Give it time,' Aidyn murmured, pressing a light kiss to my forehead. I relaxed into him, losing myself in the feeling of security in his embrace.

'This feels familiar,' I said softly, 'being with you, like this.' I could sense his smile and closed my eyes, sighing contentedly. Then an errant thought flickered through my mind, as such thoughts are wont to do. 'Aren't you tired?'

He reflected for a moment, then said, 'Yes. And no. I don't know if I could sleep even if I tried. I've dreamed about you being back for so long, a part of me is scared that I'll wake up and you'll be gone again. But this time we won't be able to bring you back.'

'Lie down with me then,' I said, 'I'll be here when you wake up.'

He gave a strangled laugh. 'I think that would raise other problems, Princess.' I ignored him and stood, walking over to the cupboard where some more spare blankets were and then took his hand, leading him up the stairs.

'Come on,' I whispered, 'don't wake the boys.'

Erik and Stefan were fast asleep, curled up in the bed, and there was a rolled-up blanket under the window where Markus had probably tried to sleep. I settled myself down, and Aidyn followed me, sinking down onto the hard floorboards by my side. I tossed the blankets over us and gazed at him, resting my head on my elbow.

'It really is a shame that you wear that mask all the time,' I murmured, tracing his cheek with my free hand. 'I prefer being able to see your face.'

He smiled, lilac eyes sparkling as he caught my hand and brought it to his lips, pressing a kiss to the inside of my palm. I shivered, breath catching in my throat as he watched me closely, gauging my reactions.

'You need to rest,' I whispered, my fingers clasping his, 'we don't know what will happen later.'

'You're right,' he replied, but his eyes didn't close.

'Go to sleep,' I urged, a smile curving my lips. He didn't say anything, just kept watching me hungrily, as though he could never get enough. I felt the harsh beating of my heart in my chest and the pulse through my blood and knew that I had felt the same thing before. But I couldn't forget that Erik and Stefan slept nearby. Or the hard floor. Or Markus' betrayed expression as he left. I didn't want to make a choice that I might regret.

'I want…' I breathed, 'I want to, but not here, not like this.'

He kissed me tenderly, and my resolve almost crumpled at its sweetness. 'Just let me hold you then, Princess,' he murmured, and I settled down against him, feeling him drift off to sleep and then following suit.

Chapter Fifteen

I dreamed again that night. This time I was on a ship, the deck slickened with water, and I was falling. Arms caught and lifted me, but they didn't belong to Aidyn. Markus gazed down at me, eyes flashing as the rain poured down and the boat rocked and there was a loud splash as something dived into the water. He carried me below the deck, Erik following behind, but I was too caught up in him to notice much else. The boat jolted again, and the image faded, leaving me wondering if it had been a dream or a memory, and feeling more confused than I had been before.

It was the screaming in the streets that woke us. The sun was starting to set and outside we could hear people running and crying, the sounds of explosions and shouting in the distance reaching us through the open window.

'Nina,' Erik was shaking me, 'Nina, wake up.'

'He's not downstairs,' Stefan entered the room, looking distressed.

'Who?' Aidyn's sleepy voice mumbled.

'Markus,' Erik said angrily. 'He's gone.'

I sat up, stretching out the pains of several hours spent on the floor. 'I'm sure he's…'

'Don't say he's alright,' Erik snapped. 'Something's happening outside and it's not good.'

'He's right,' Stefan agreed, 'not long ago there was a loud noise from the gates. I think maybe…'

'It's the Winter Solstice,' Aidyn murmured, 'of course.'

'Care to explain?' Erik demanded, as I got to my feet, plaiting my hair back.

'Tonight was when the Usurper was planning to have his coronation,' Aidyn said reasonably, 'Rakael might have brought forward the decision to attack the Capital.'

'We need to find her,' Stefan said, 'she needs to know that Nina's alive.'

'Yes,' Aidyn said softly, 'she does.' I didn't want to ask who Rakael was, but my memory was drawing a blank.

'Who…?'

'But what about Markus?' Erik demanded, cutting me off, 'we can't leave him behind.'

'He's right,' I said, 'the Usurper's guards will be looking for all of us.'

Aidyn shrugged and went downstairs without another word. I followed and retrieved my dagger from the table, watching surreptitiously as Aidyn pulled on his shirt and balaclava.

'Keep your hood up,' he said, 'and stick close.'

Erik and Stefan shut the door behind us as we all exited into the alleyway, into the rush of people who were sprinting up and down the streets, shrieking and covered in grime and blood, heading towards the safety of the palace walls. Children were crying, searching for their parents, and I reached out and gripped onto Erik automatically. He looked at me curiously but I ignored it, focussing on keeping close to Aidyn.

Heavy smoke hung in the air, and as we made our way through the streets, a flaming ball of fire launched past, crashing into houses nearby. There was a shattering of timber and tiles as the roof collapsed, a burst of flame reaching up into the sky. From inside there came a high-pitched keeling cry and I felt something twist inside my chest. I lifted my hand, urging the flames to diminish in size, to lessen the damage, but something was keeping the fire alight, and I watched in horror as it spread to the next house and the next.

'Come on Nina,' Erik urged, tugging on my arm.

'Where would Markus go?' I asked, glancing around in the hope of seeing him in the crowd. Everything was confusion, and we fought against the rush of people racing towards the palace walls. As we moved through the streets, groups of Trackers pushed past, heading towards the roads that entered the Capital, where the sounds of fighting seemed to originate.

'Erik!' Markus' voice reached us from the other side of the street and suddenly there he was, partially hidden behind an abandoned market stall. I changed direction and cut away from the others, leading the way towards him. He watched me approach, arms folded and gaze assessing as I dodged in between the rush of civilians to reach him. It wasn't until I was in front of him that I realised that he wasn't alone. Behind him were shadowy figures in heavy cloaks, who had been shrouded by the narrow street in which he waited. I paused, immediately unsure, until they stepped into the light and lifted their hoods, and I felt a wave of recognition. My chest contracted and I felt a chill spreading from the scar on my stomach. The last words I had heard before I died filled my ears, haunting me.

For Scardia.

'I thought it would be best to bring them to you,' Markus said, pulling me out of the street. 'I know you might not remember…'

'Wait.' I held up a hand to stop him, staring at the group of people, feeling overwhelmed as the floodgates to my memory opened. I gripped onto Markus' arm as I buckled, temporarily losing control of myself. It only took a moment, but it felt like a lifetime passed in those few seconds.

'Nina?' Markus asked, concerned. I felt the others arrive behind me, and Erik touched my shoulder. I looked at Markus' face, and images merged together and formed coherent memories, connecting all the missing pieces that I had lost. A range of sensations ripped through me: relief that he had gotten out of Icevale Keep, tenderness and hurt over our past meeting and then, most predominantly, anger at what I had learned more recently. But now was not the time to argue with him about his lack of honesty and his true relationship with the Usurper.

Instead, I feigned ignorance and said, 'I feel like they are familiar.'

'Nina,' the dark-haired woman said, holding out a shaking hand. 'I'm Jesse.'

I shook her hand and then turned to the other woman, who was staring at me in unflattering shock.

'So, you've lost your memory, Princess?' Rakael asked, and it took everything in me to keep my expression blank and devoid of emotion.

'From what I've heard it should be temporary,' I said calmly, 'but I don't know. Can you remind me who you are?' I held my hand out, proud that it didn't tremble.

'Rakael,' she said, shaking it firmly. 'Leader of the Resistance.'

'We should get off the streets,' one of the guards behind Rakael said. 'The first wave of fighters will be here soon.'

'That reminds me,' Rakael said briskly, turning to Aidyn, 'I need you to take over command of the Dark Elves. They've been refusing to help us for almost a month now. I'll show you where they're based.'

'Once I know that the Princess is safe, I will do so,' Aidyn replied coolly.

Rakael scowled, 'We need those fighters *now*, Lord Aidyn. The Trackers are starting to retaliate with full force and they don't care about hurting the civilians.'

'Aidyn,' I said quietly, 'go, it sounds like you're needed with your people. I will stay with Markus and Erik, they'll make sure that I get somewhere safe.'

Beside me I sense Markus stiffen, and was glad that I couldn't see Aidyn's reaction.

'Are you certain?' His voice was quiet, unsure.

I glanced back at him and said with resolve, 'yes. They need you more than I do right now. I don't want civilians getting hurt in the crossfire, and your men will help make sure that that doesn't happen.' I wanted to hold him, to touch his cheek and tell him that I would be alright and that I remembered everything now, but everyone was watching. So instead, I turned back to Markus and Rakael and said, 'Where can we go? We need to get out of here.'

'I'll lead them to the camp,' Jesse volunteered, and Rakael nodded, watching as we followed Jesse down the alleyway. Erik and Stefan were close behind me, while I stayed at Markus' side, planning what to do next. I was surprised when Jesse knelt, lifting a heavy grille from the ground and dropping down.

'Come on,' she urged, and we jumped down behind her, Markus replacing the grille over the hole in the ground. 'It's easier to move through the sewers than the streets. We'll be outside the city walls in no time.'

The smell was oppressive, forcing me to breathe through my mouth and trying to ignore what I was walking through. Erik's face was screwed up in distaste, while Stefan was covering his nose and mouth with a hand. Markus, like me, looked as though he was trying to ignore the smell and helped me to wade through the muck.

'I wanted to apologise,' he said gruffly, 'about how I acted this morning.'

'Thank you,' I murmured, lowering my voice so that it would be harder for us to be overheard. 'With everything that's been going on, it's confusing to say the least. I don't think it can be easy for anyone.'

His hand gripped my arm, and I noted with surprise that the emotions I had once felt when he held me were still there. Now that I could remember fully what had happened between us, the regret, rage and desire boiled within me, locked in their own private battle.

'I thought I would never see you again,' he said quietly, 'when the Dark Elves got me out of the Keep and I learned it was you who had made them agree to do it, I hoped that you still felt something. But then I learned that you were dead, and Erik had this idea of trying to bring you back. I didn't believe it could happen, yet here you are. It probably serves me right that you don't remember what was between us.' Absentmindedly, he reached up to hold something around his neck, and I caught the flash of copper.

'It sounds like it meant something to you,' I replied, and he smiled briefly.

'The girl I knew wasn't a princess,' he said, 'but when I found out who she really was, all my hopes of us being more were pushed out of reach. Especially considering who my uncle is.'

'And yet,' I said softly, 'you accused her of being dishonest. You said it was her fault for not trusting you with the truth, while not being honest yourself. That sounds very hypocritical to me.'

'What did you say?' He asked, gazing at me with dawning comprehension.

'Leaving out information like that,' I continued, ignoring him, 'has the potential to deepen a rift which cannot be mended. It can cause far too much hurt for my liking. If you wanted forgiveness, you would probably need all the luck in the world.' I moved away from him, striding up to walk alongside Jesse, who smiled at me tentatively.

'How are you feeling, Nina? It's been hard without you the last few months.'

I shrugged, 'I don't feel very different. Just like I was sleeping for a long time and when I woke up the world was slightly off kilter.'

She chuckled, 'that's one way of putting it. I thought when Markus came to find us and explained about you that he'd been given some poison by the Usurper to imagine things.' She touched my shoulder wonderingly, making sure that I was real. 'I can't believe that you're actually here, King Aegis is going to be overjoyed.'

Grandfather.

'I think we will have much to discuss,' I said.

'We shouldn't be too far now,' she said, 'there are several camps set up just beyond the Capital's walls. Once the civilians and Trackers have been pushed back towards the palace, we should be able to move into the city.'

Up ahead there was a patch of light that gradually drew closer, revealing an opening onto one of the lakes which was outside the Capital. The bars on the opening had been filed away, allowing us to slip through quite easily, and we splashed through the shallow water to a collection of nearby tents on the shore. The water was freezing and my teeth started chattering, the relief of the sewage being washed away soon replaced with a numbing cold.

'We should have some spare clothes for you all,' Jesse gasped as she reached the shoreline, 'everyone will be desperate to see you back, Nina.'

At our arrival, a small group had begun to form in front of the tents, curious about who was approaching their small encampment. On seeing me, a cry rang out and they began to clap and shout, sending the message out far and wide that I was alive.

'Nice to keep these things quiet,' I muttered, and Jesse grinned.

'Trust me, Nina, knowing that you're alive will be just what our soldiers will need.'

There was a flurry of motion and I saw people pushed roughly aside as a small, blond woman sprinted towards me. Her face was tearstained and as she reached me she pulled me into a tight hug, crushing the breath out of me.

'Careful Lisette,' I murmured as I hugged her back, 'you don't want to take me down just after I woke up.'

She let out a wordless cry and gripped me harder, shaking with renewed sobs.

'You remember Lisette?' Erik asked curiously, and Markus looked at me with a touch of suspicion.

'Some things are coming back to me,' I mumbled as Lisette began to lead me away towards the tents, wiping her eyes with one hand and keeping a firm grip on me with the other. I glanced back at Erik and Markus, wondering how much they guessed I remembered. I saw Stefan say something to Erik and they began to follow us up the slope. As we passed the group of onlookers, some bowed while others reached out to touch me as I moved, eyes wide with awe.

Lisette pulled me into one of the tents and forced me to sit down on one of the bedrolls. Then she proceeded to check me all over for any signs of injury, until I leaned away with a grumbled,

'I'm fine Lisette.' She frowned at me, and I relented to smile. 'I mean it, I'm fine. I just need to stop smelling like a manure pile and put on some warmer clothes and I'll be as good as new.'

She nodded and indicated for me to stay where I was as she began to pick out some clothing from a nearby bag. It wasn't any of my clothes, but I was pleased to see that it was similar to what I would wear when training– kidskin breeches, a woollen chemise and a thicker leather tunic. I looked down at my boots sadly, they were wet through and still dirty, but they were the only shoes I had.

Lisette made a quick gesture and I handed them over, leaning down to remove my sodden stockings. When I looked back up, Lisette had gone outside, and I was alone. I pulled my cloak closer around me, gaining some comfort from its warmth.

He must have been waiting for Lisette to leave, for not a minute later, Markus was entering the tent, and one look at his expression told me that I couldn't maintain the lie anymore. His mouth was set in a hard line and his arms were folded across his chest.

I felt rather small down on the ground, but waited patiently for him to speak.

'You remember things,' he finally said, one finger tapping against his arm.

I nodded.

'How much?' He demanded.

'Everything.' I kept my tone low, so that it wouldn't carry beyond the walls of the tent.

'Thank the Gods,' he whispered, 'I was right.' He crouched down in front of me, and I watched him solemnly, unsure how to respond. 'I missed you so much,' he said, reaching out and touching my cheek, and then he leaned closer and kissed me.

As his lips pressed against mine I froze, suddenly uncomfortable. I pulled back, breaking away and stopped him from following by raising a hand.

'What are you doing?' I asked quietly, partially to hear his reply and partly to question myself.

'I thought it was obvious,' he said roughly, clearly upset about being rebuffed.

'The last time we spoke,' I said, 'you pushed me away. You hurt me. I was so angry with you.'

'But that's how we are, Nina,' he murmured, cupping my cheek again, 'arguing one minute, making love the next. We are like those flames of yours; that passion forms a bond between us.'

'What about Aidyn?' I forced myself to ask.

He blinked, eyes shadowing for an instant. 'A political alliance. You don't need to stay with him out of some concept of duty. There's another way we can stay together after this.'

There was a moment's pause as I processed what he was saying. 'What do you mean?'

'I spoke to Rakael, on the way back to find you,' he said eagerly, 'she wasn't sure whether you would be up to ruling after being brought back. She said you could abdicate once the Usurper was killed and allow a representative of the people to rule in your place. We could be together, we could sail away and spend the rest of our days as husband and wife. Erik could come with us and you wouldn't have to worry about the Dark Elves or running the kingdom; you can't force yourself to become someone you're not.'

'How do you know that's not who I am?' I tried to keep my tone light and unaffected, but it was difficult. When he had mentioned Rakael I wanted to scream. If we had had this discussion several months ago– before I met Aidyn and Grandfather– what he proposed would have been exactly what I would have wanted.

'Come on, Nina,' he said, laughing, 'you worked at an inn for how many years? You might have helped out in farmsteads and marketplaces, but you didn't spend time learning how to run a kingdom. You know how to do things that are practical and worthwhile, not putting on airs and trying to adhere to unreasonable rules.'

Something tugged in my heart, that long ago yearning, that childhood dream of what freedom could be.

'Markus,' I could barely get the words out. 'I can't keep running anymore.'

There was a cough from the entrance to the tent and I looked up guiltily, wrapping the cloak tighter around me. It was Lisette, with a bucket of water, soap and a scratchy-looking towel– I'd never felt more relieved to see her. Markus stood abruptly and left, not hearing the words that I knew I had to say but couldn't quite bring myself to.

Lisette frowned at me and I blushed. I focussed on stripping and washing myself with the soap, shivering uncontrollably in the frigid air. The towel was rough and it was a relief to pull on the dry clothes, discarding the blue dress that would have been perfect for a summer's day but was far from adequate for winter. Outside the tent the wind picked up, and I pulled on a pair of sheepskin gloves and socks eagerly before tucking my feet into some shoes that were slightly too large for me. My feet slipped around in them, making me feel awkward and ungainly.

Lisette set to work on my hair and soon it was neat and contained in a coronet.

'It wasn't what you thought, Lisette,' I finally said, ignoring her raised eyebrows. 'I'm still trying to come to terms with what's happened. And then there's Aidyn and he…' I broke off awkwardly, unsure how to put what I felt into words. She clicked her tongue disapprovingly and I could sense what she wanted to say.

You made a commitment. Aidyn accomplished what you asked him to, he got Markus out of Icevale Keep just like he promised.

Icevale Keep. The thought of it made me shiver, despite the warm sheepskin and then another thought entered my mind, one that made my heart race.

'Keely,' I whispered, 'where is he? Did he make it out alive?'

Lisette nodded slowly and then gave a small shake of the head. I gripped her hands, suddenly worried.

'What do you mean, Lisette? Do you know where he is?'

She nodded again.

'Is he nearby? Can you take me to him? Please?'

There was so much to say. Apologies to make. My heart was in my throat as Lisette and I left the tent, past the group of celebrating Resistance members and across the campsite to another tent which was significantly larger than all the others. Inside were a range of pallets laid out in rows, and I recognised some of the healers from Grandfather's court moving between them, tending to the wounded. The smell of sickness and death lingered and I felt my stomach seize up.

Lisette led me to the last pallet, not stopping to wait for me as I was noticed by the wounded and the healers. Hands raised to me, I grasped them, murmuring words of comfort to those who were awake and in pain, listening to their prayers and wonder at my being alive. The healers bowed to me before returning to their charges as I moved on, kneeling next to a small girl who clutched onto my cloak. She had been burned down the side of her body and she quivered, one eye staring at me in desperation.

'Can you find my ma?' She asked, her voice ragged. I took her hand in mine, unhooking it from my cloak and holding it tenderly.

'I can try,' I said softly, 'what's your name, child?'

'Lenora,' she whispered, 'Ma and I were at the market when…when…'

'It's alright,' I said, 'I'll do my best to find her for you, I promise.'

'Thank you,' Lenora said, and I laid her hand back down and moved towards one of the healers.

'Do you know what happened to the child's mother?' I asked quietly so that she would not overhear us.

The healer looked at me with sad, tired eyes. 'Most likely she is dead, Princess. That child was brought in with these others from the outer edges of the city where the fighting started. There were so many in that first rush that it was hard to keep track of who everyone was.'

I bowed my head, watching the healer move back to the child and rub a poultice into her wounds. There was a pain in my chest now as I gazed back around the space, the wounded eyeing me as though I would save them from their torment. They needed their princess to be strong, but I was scared that I would crumble. I took a deep breath and continued towards where Lisette sat, checking in with the healers and other victims of the invasion, wondering how many had been hurt by the Resistance or the Trackers.

When I reached Lisette I halted, gazing down at the man in the bed. He looked much better than the other wounded, but as I sat down beside him, I registered the marks across his face, deep lacerations stretching across his eyes and nose that were partially healed. Lisette was holding one of his hands, which looked as though it had been twisted and deformed since I had last seen him. Some of his fingers were missing, and I bit back a sob as I thought of how much pain he must have gone through.

'Keely,' I said, and his face turned in my direction, clearly unable to see me.

'Milady?' He asked, 'Milady Nina? How is this possible? We thought…'

'I'm alive Keely,' I said firmly, reaching out to take his free hand and gripping it tightly. 'I didn't know you survived after you stayed behind, all those months I could've tried to find some way to break you out, but I didn't know. I thought you were dead, and now…' I gulped away another sob that was rising up in my throat, 'I'm so sorry, Keely. It's my fault you're like this; I'm so sorry.' The tears began to fall and I bent over his hand, unable to look at him anymore.

'It's I who should be begging your forgiveness, Milady,' he mumbled, 'I told them where you were headed. I thought I could stay strong but…'

I shook my head, 'They would have found out sooner or later. The Usurper would have suspected where I would go, it's not your fault, Keely. I'm just glad that you're alive.' He gave a rather wobbly smile, and I said, 'it looks like Lisette has been looking after you, at least.'

Lisette shot me a startled glance and Keely's smile widened.

'My songbird,' he whispered, 'I always told you she was a smart one, didn't I Milady? Turns out she was smarter than either of us ever realised. But I miss hearing her sing.'

Lisette rose abruptly and walked away, back rigidly straight.

'I think she finds it as hard as I do,' he murmured, 'I can't see her, and she can't speak to me. Rather unlucky, isn't it?'

'Yes,' I said, realising that he couldn't see my nod of agreement. 'I didn't realise…it seems I've missed out on a lot of things happening while I was…' It felt wrong to say 'dead', so I improvised, 'asleep.'

He shrugged, 'it came as a surprise to me as well.'

'How long will you be here?' I asked, as his voice drifted off.

'There isn't much I can do to help the Resistance,' he said regretfully, 'I can't even help in the infirmary. You need two proper hands for that and the ability to see.' He shifted in the bed and looked away towards the entrance of the tent. 'Sometimes I think I can see faint colours,' he said softly, 'but then I think I'm imagining things. Rakael said that I needed to remain somewhere safe, that I would just be a burden if I tried to help. She's not wrong, either.'

'She doesn't need to be cruel though,' I muttered, and he smiled ruefully.

'She speaks the truth, Milady. I learned long ago that when it comes to Rakael, there's much that is kept hidden and that's the way she likes it. She's not one to share openly with the rest of us.'

'I can understand that,' I said, privately wondering whether if he knew what Rakael had done to me he would be so kindly disposed towards her. I doubted it.

'Nina?' Erik's voice came from the far end of the infirmary tent. I turned to see him waving me over impatiently.

'I have to go, Keely,' I said softly, 'I'm so glad that you're safe. Take care, won't you? I'll be back when I can.'

'Be careful Milady.' His whisper followed me as I moved towards Erik, the wounded patients reaching out again to touch my cloak as I passed.

'Stay safe, Princess Wilhelmina,' they murmured.

'Come on,' Erik muttered as I joined him, 'something's happening.'

'What?' I asked, glancing around the darkened camp, which was lit with several blazing torches now. Night had fallen while I was with Keely and with it the icy chill that set into my bones returned, cutting through my layers of clothing to make my breath catch.

'Something's wrong,' he said, leading me towards a group of Resistance guards who were clustered around someone on the edge of the campsite. I saw Lisette and Jesse standing to one side, looking pale, along with Markus who had his jaw clenched.

'What's happened?' I asked, striding over to them, Erik beside me. 'Tell me.'

'It's King Aegis, Princess Wilhelmina,' one of the guards said cautiously, 'he was leading the attack in the lower section of the city. Trying to get some of the civilians out of the rubble. And then they came.'

'Who?' Erik demanded.

'They looked like women,' the guard whispered in terror, 'but not women. Wings and claws and covered in blood. They were singing, luring people out of the rubble and then slaughtering them. When they saw King Aegis, they took him, carried him to the palace.'

'Sirens,' Jesse said softly, 'it must be.'

'How can I get to the palace?' Numbness was spreading through me, fear creating horrific images in my mind about what was happening to Grandfather. The others stared at me as if I was insane and there was a strained silence.

'You can't go, Princess Wilhelmina,' another one of the guards said finally, 'you're needed back here to rally the troops and assist the wounded. Rakael made it clear that you were to not be near the fighting.'

My fists clenched. It seemed that Rakael had been making far too many assumptions of late; it was time to remind her who I really was. And I would not be staying behind the city walls, hiding out in a tent until the fighting was done, though from the looks on the guards' faces, they wouldn't let me leave willingly.

Slowly, I relaxed my hands and nodded, feigning acceptance. 'Of course, she's right. I just wish there was something more I could do.'

'I'll go back with you,' Jesse said to the guard before turning to me, 'I'll see what we can find out. With the Dark Elves now fighting with us, we should be able to reach the palace sooner rather than later.'

'I'll go too,' Markus said brusquely.

'Take care, Nina,' Jesse said, turning and leaving with and the small group of guards. Erik was staring at Markus, wide eyed.

'You're really going as well?' He asked.

'Seems like the right thing to do,' Markus replied, grasping Erik's shoulder while not looking away from me. 'I need to stop running away from my uncle and what he's done.'

He turned and followed the group, disappearing into the darkness. I hovered for a few moments and then chased after him, not quite knowing what I was going to say, but knowing I couldn't let him leave without saying goodbye.

'Markus,' I cried, and he paused, glancing back at me. I threw my arms around him, holding him tightly. 'Don't do anything stupid,' I whispered against his chest, 'I don't think I could bear it if anything happened.'

'You said you had to stop running, Nina,' he said quietly, 'it seems that I should do that too. There is too much that is unresolved between my uncle and I. There's much you don't understand.' He lifted my chin so that our faces were inches apart, 'I will feel better knowing that you are safe here. Promise me that you'll stay out of harm's way.' He kissed me, not waiting for me to confirm or deny his request.

'Goodbye,' I murmured as he pulled away, watching as he followed the direction of the screams and the smell of smoke.

Chapter Sixteen

I stayed there until he was lost from sight before releasing the breath that I had been holding. Slowly I began to make my way back towards the campsite, allowing the others to catch a glimpse of me before returning to the tent where I had changed. There, I fastened my dagger to my belt, slipped out of the slightly too large shoes I had been given, and tied up my still damp boots that Lisette had returned. Outside, there were quiet voices from the others in the camp and the sound of people going in and out of the infirmary, so it effectively covered the sound of me moving to the back of the tent, carefully lifting the canvas up and squeezing out.

'I thought you might try to slip away.'

I jumped, hand on my dagger as I turned to see Erik casually standing next to me.

'You've gotten better at keeping quiet,' I muttered, relaxing, 'although I thought I asked you to not sneak up on me. How did you know I'd try to get away?'

'It's not like you to just stand back and let other people dive into the action,' he said with a shrug. 'And I thought your memory was still not back yet.'

'Let's get out of here and I'll tell you about it,' I said under my breath, glancing back and forth as I crept between the tents.

'You're not going to try and tell me to stay behind?' He sounded surprised.

'I think you're able to take care of yourself well enough,' I muttered distractedly, 'besides, we're meant to stick together, aren't we? I'm not getting back into the city without my brother at my side.'

'Deal,' he said, as we moved from shadow to shadow. I focussed and summoned the darkness to grow heavier, making it easier for us to sneak away and remain unseen.

'I think it's easiest if we go back the way we came,' I whispered, freezing as some of the guards passed by, holding myself painfully still.

'We don't want to get found,' Erik breathed, as we reached the lake's edge. He was gripping onto the short sword at his waist, his own cloak catching in the wind as he peered behind us, making sure our absence hadn't yet been noticed.

I gritted my teeth as we began to wade through the water, hoping that the noise wouldn't be heard at the camp. The cold deepened but we kept going, reaching the sewer and slipping between the bars. There, I summoned a flame to guide our way, as Midwinter Eve was now well and truly upon us. I tried not to think about what that represented, but pushed ahead, Erik at my side, as we retraced our steps, winding our way beneath the city streets.

'How far do you think we need to go?' I asked finally, when we had turned down several different tunnels and I was starting to feel like we were lost.

'There's an opening,' Erik said, pointing upwards at one of the manholes. I extinguished the flame, and we made our way underneath it, peering upwards. As we had gone through the sewers, the sounds of fighting and muffled cries had become fainter and fainter. Now, from where we stood, I could barely hear a thing, and I wondered where exactly in the Capital we were.

'Boost me up, Nina,' Erik whispered, and I scrunched up my face as I formed a step with my hands, helping to lift him upwards towards the slab that covered the exit. He pushed, straining, and the slab lifted gradually until it had moved to the side. Erik gripped the sides of the manhole and heaved himself out, before reaching down and helping to lift me upwards. He was stronger than I had expected and with a muffled grunt, I was pulled over the edge of the manhole.

We were in a deserted street, the houses around us blackened and smouldering. Smoke filled the air and I covered my mouth with my cloak, eyes watering as I glanced around to get my bearings.

'Where are we?' Erik asked, coughing.

'I think we're in one of the upper districts,' I murmured, squinting through the heat haze and smoke towards the distant towers up on the hilltop, which were lit up with flashes. 'The palace is there,' I pointed, 'come on.'

'What's the plan?' Erik asked as we set off, following my suit as I drew my dagger out from its sheath.

'I don't have one yet,' I replied, 'I'm not leaving Grandfather up there with the Usurper and his Trackers and those sirens. Rakael won't care if he gets hurt, but I *do*. I still need to let him know what I think about being set up like I was in the Underdark, and he needs to explain himself.'

'He might not still be alive, Nina,' Erik said cautiously as we reached the end of the street and entered a square. Here there were even more signs of the fighting, with mangled bodies lying on the cobbles, the blood already starting to congeal. I gripped Erik's arm and led him away, not wanting to look at the faces, some of which I recognised from Grandfather's court. We passed the corpses of Trackers and

Dark Elves and I found myself checking those bodies to see if any of them were Aidyn.

'Nina, come on,' Erik hissed, 'I can hear something.'

I allowed him to lead the way. Slipping behind a low wall in one of the broken buildings, we watched as a number of Resistance fighters came into view, pushing a catapult.

'Load it up,' one of them snapped, and they lifted one of the Tracker's bodies into it, poured some powder over them, and then set it aflame with one of their torches.

'Release!' Another one cried, and the body was thrown high into the air, becoming a burning beacon through the sky to the palace, where it flew over the walls. There were cheers and laughter from the Resistance fighters and they began to do the same thing with the other bodies in the square, not caring about which corpses they loaded and set alight.

'It's awful,' I breathed and Erik nodded, looking sickened. 'We need to try and get away before they find us.' We crept out of the smouldering ruin and stuck to the shadows again, praying that we wouldn't be seen. The soldiers were rifling through the garments of the deceased, taking anything of value before loading the bodies onto the catapult.

'We're nearly out of that powder,' one grunted, 'that damned scholar didn't make enough.'

I stumbled and Erik pushed me on urgently.

'What was that?' Another guard looked up, searchingly, 'did you hear that?'

'Maybe it's a survivor,' one suggested.

'If it's a woman, she's mine,' another laughed, 'once I'm done, you can all have your turn.' I blanched in horror. I'd thought that the Trackers were the only ones to resort to such lengths, how was it that members of the Resistance had similar ideas? It was wrong, so wrong.

'Quick, quick,' Erik muttered, tugging me forwards, sprinting away from the soldiers. Our footsteps rang out along the cobbles and I heard the men behind us cry out and start to follow in pursuit.

'It *is* a girl,' one cried, 'get her.'

'Run, Nina,' Erik gasped, and I tried to keep pace with him, my lungs screaming for a reprieve. We sped upwards, cutting between streets and jumping over bodies, until we burst out into another square and were forced to a stop. Around us blades flashed and struck, as Trackers and the Resistance soldiers fought, caught in a deadly dance. Dark and High Elves were amongst them, some shooting arrows into the fray, whilst others matched the Trackers blow for blow. Other Elves rained arrows down on the fighters from inside nearby buildings, and I realised that- judging from their armour- they must be the Velkranian Wood Elves.

'We have to get through,' I panted, clutching my side as I tried to regain my breath. Erik looked at me, confused for a moment.

'How are you so tired?'

'I've not had the chance to train for quite a while,' I snapped, and then raised my dagger, parrying a strike from one of the Trackers. He grinned crookedly, sizing us up with his eyes.

'What do we have here?' He chuckled, 'A little lost boy and girl?' His gaze rose to my head and then widened as he took in the streak of white in my hair. 'It can't be,' he said hoarsely, 'you're dead.'

'Not anymore,' Erik snapped, striking upwards with his short sword and catching the Tracker unaware, slicing the underside of his chin. The Tracker crumpled, yelping in pain as we dodged around him, fighting our way through the fray towards the palace. The cobblestones were slick with blood, and I slipped as I jumped away from being struck by a heavy mace. Erik ducked, narrowly missing being hit by a stray arrow, and took the opportunity to strike out at the legs of one of our attackers.

By now my hood had fallen back and all of those around us had noticed that the Princess was in their midst. For the Resistance fighters, this caused an upsurge in energy, whereas the Trackers seemed to be disconcerted, with some fleeing back towards the palace walls. At the sight of the Trackers breaking ranks, the Elves pressed on, cutting down the remaining ones ruthlessly. The Resistance fighters laid chase to the Trackers who had fled, their armour bloody and dented, weapons gripped in their hands. There was a keeling whistle and the Elves fell into line, regrouping as one as their commander sheathed his blades and approached us from the other side of the square. His balaclava had been pulled off in the fighting and his face was streaked with dust and grime, blood speckled across his cheeks and pale hair.

'Princess.' Aidyn's voice was curt but unsurprised, as though he had fully expected me to appear in the battlefield and was disappointed that it had taken me so long to do so. 'I suppose it was too much to ask that you remain behind at the camp.'

'We've been training for months,' Erik said hotly, 'we're not going to sit around and wait. Besides, King Aegis has been taken.'

'I am aware,' he said, 'my soldiers and I were nearby when it happened. We were too late to reach his location in time, though.' He stopped in front of us, expression inscrutable, and my heart pounded.

'Aidyn,' I said quietly, 'we need to get to the palace, we have to find my grandfather.'

'I assumed you would want to join the fighting once you knew,' he replied, 'you just need to make sure that Rakael doesn't find you. She is rather insistent about you remaining behind the front lines.'

My jaw clenched as I said tightly, 'she had better keep her distance if she is wise. I've seen what her men are like.' The memory of the soldiers loading the bodies into the catapult and setting them aflame, and the way they had discussed so callously what they would do if they found a female survivor in the rubble, still made my flesh crawl.

'Then we will need to do our best to keep you out of her way,' Aidyn said calmly. 'We will help you get to the palace. Your grandfather's men and the Wood Elves joined my group, it seems they would rather take orders from another like them– even if it's a Dark Elf– than take them from Rakael.' He gave a wry smile, 'come on.'

Erik led the way, heading back towards the assembled Elven soldiers. I walked at Aidyn's side, noting the blazing look in his eyes and feeling my stomach flip in response.

'You're not wearing your mask,' I said quietly, 'I thought you would only remove it when you trusted someone. It seems like a sudden change for you to be alright with it being gone.' It took a moment for him to register my words and then I felt his gloved hand take mine.

'You remember?' I dipped my head in acquiescence, and he held me tighter.

'You haven't answered me,' I pressed, 'about your mask.'

He laughed, 'all this time you wanted me to remove my mask and now when it's gone you want to know why.'

I shrugged, 'pretty much.'

He sighed, 'a Tracker pulled it off. I haven't been able to replace it yet. It feels wrong to be so exposed.' He inclined his head at the Elves before us, 'but the others seem to find it easier to follow someone whose face they can see.'

'Funny that,' I murmured, smiling as Aidyn faced his men, shoulders set with quiet command.

'We're moving out,' he stated, 'our mission has changed slightly. We're getting the Princess into the palace and retrieving King Aegis.'

'The main gates to the palace will be well defended,' one of the Dark Elves said.

'Trackers will be guarding all the entrances,' another one reinforced. 'The other Resistance fighters have gone towards the main gate, surely there's better chances of getting through in numbers.'

'Gawain and Beck are both right,' Aidyn acknowledged, 'which is why we need to rethink our route. I suggest...'

He was cut off by the singing. A low, lilting song that filled the mind with images of warm summer days and absolute bliss. A song that promised to take away one's troubles.

'Prepare yourselves!' Aidyn cried, drawing his swords and turning towards the creatures that were swooping down towards us. I reached for my dagger and then paused, a reckless idea suddenly springing to mind.

'Erik, hold onto me,' I said, gripping him close as I raised a shaky arm into the air.

'Nina, what by the Gods are you doing?' Aidyn demanded, his voice cracking with fear.

I looked at him, calmer than I felt inside, but knowing that I was right. 'They're not here for you, Aidyn. Hide your men and storm the gate. They'll take me where I need to go.'

'No!' He made to move back to me but was blocked by a pair of leathery wings as one of the sirens snatched my arm with their taloned hands, lifting Erik and I up and away.

'I got the Princess,' the siren crowed in jubilation, as several others swooped around us, trying to dislodge Erik, who clung to me tighter. I gritted my teeth as the long nails bit into my arm, staining the sleeves of my chemise red. I held on, determined not to look down, as we were carried across the tops of burning buildings, above groups of fighters and over the palace walls. The sirens were flying towards one of the tallest towers, which, if I remembered correctly, had been a place my father would go to stargaze in happier times.

As we drew closer, I focussed my mind and let the flame rise off my hand, burning the siren that gripped onto me. She shrieked and suddenly we were dropping, falling down onto the hard floor of the tower and rolling to the side with a loud crash. I twisted and hurled a ball of fire at the swooping figures around us, as Erik drew his sword and jumped to his feet, cutting out as they dived, talons extended.

'Come on, Erik,' I gasped, stumbling backwards towards the trapdoor to the lower levels and lifting the iron ring. The trapdoor lifted upwards, and Erik began to climb down the ladder and I followed close behind, a talon narrowly missing my cheek. I pulled the trapdoor closed with a terrified cry and continued to clamber downwards to the winding staircase, joining Erik at the bottom. Both of us were bearing marks from our encounter with the sirens, but we were still standing and that was all that mattered.

'Let's go,' I said, 'they'll find out that we're here soon enough.'

'Where do you think King Aegis is being held?' Erik asked as we began to go down the stairs, keeping an ear out for any approaching soldiers.

I thought for a moment and then said, 'I'm not sure.'

It felt strange to be back in the place of my birth, and memories kept coming back to me. Climbing the stairs with my father to gaze at the Northern Lights flickering across the sky; Lyn chasing me down to bring me back to my lessons and getting puffed on the stairs; sneaking out late at night to watch the heavens and wonder when I would be able to go out and see the world.

When we reached the bottom of the stairs we were in a wide corridor, and I glanced around, looking for one of the familiar alcoves. I spotted one and made my way towards it, finding the old iron torch bracket and pulling it down, hearing the creak of gears as the door opened onto one of the many passageways.

Erik was looking at me, mouth slightly agape.

'How did you know where to find that?' He asked, 'I didn't think the passages went through the whole palace.'

I glanced at him, 'I grew up here, Erik. I'd find it amusing to hide from my tutors for as long as possible. Now come on, we don't want to be in the open for long.'

I heard footsteps and voices coming and I beckoned for him to join me in the passageway, closing the door behind us. It was dusty and narrower than I remembered, maybe that was because I was so much taller now. I held my breath as the guards passed and began to ascend the stairs.

'We need a light,' Erik muttered and in response I summoned a ball of flame, lighting up the passageway. As we began to move, I traced the wall with one hand, searching for the notches that had been cut into the stone many years ago. The passage branched off and I paused, looking left to right.

'The private quarters are in that direction,' I pointed to the right, 'and the throne room is that way,' I indicated left. There was a tugging in my chest, a sense of something greater pulling me in that direction and I followed it automatically.

'Is there a chance he would be in the private chambers?' Erik asked, 'he is a king after all.'

'I'd hazard a guess that the visiting dignitaries are there,' I murmured distractedly, 'the people who the Usurper wants to stay in comfort. He wouldn't want Grandfather to be comfortable, Grandfather was the one who rejected his suit for my mother all those years ago.'

Erik was quiet for a while and then said, 'do you think we'll find him in time?'

I didn't have an answer, only the awareness that at least an hour or more had passed since news had reached us about Grandfather being taken. Who knew what horrors the Usurper had begun to unleash on him?

The passageway had reached another intersection. I could hear voices and rustling of movement nearby and extinguished the ball of fire, shrouding us in darkness. The urge to move onwards was stronger now, calling me towards the throne room, it was becoming impossible to ignore.

'The throne room should be up ahead,' I whispered, 'can you do me a favour?'

'I'm not staying behind.' Erik's tone was firm. 'We're in this together, Nina.'

I smiled faintly, 'this passage has another entrance to the throne room.'

'I know,' he said, 'that was how we got from where we were being kept prisoner to find you. I found it.' His voice rang with pride and my smile grew wider.

'Good. I'll exit here and you go around to the other side. In case anything happens, I want you to watch my back. It sounds like there's people around, so be careful.'

He nodded, 'just don't do anything stupid, Nina.'

'I'll try,' I whispered as he began to walk away. I turned and followed the rest of the passageway, until I had found the indented stone that required just the right amount of pressure to open. I couldn't hear anything from the other side of the wall, so I took my chance, slipping into the room beyond.

There was a statue blocking the entrance to the passageway and I hid behind it, lingering in the shadows on the edge of the room. The stained windows were shattered, and the frigid night air was blowing in, making something sway from the ceiling like a ragdoll. The view outside looked out over the city, full of thick smoke and distant sounds of fighting and explosions.

There was movement from the far side of the room, and I saw a kneeling Dark Elf, his mask flashing silver, and the Usurper reclining on the throne.

'Please let me break him,' a raspy voice said, and I bit back a gasp. The Chief Counsel stood, a curved blade in his hand as he looked upwards at the swinging figure. I followed his gaze and gripped the edge of the statue in dread.

It was Grandfather. Except he didn't look how I remembered him. He looked broken and defeated. Battered. Old. He was strung up, hovering above the points of the throne, clearly unconscious.

'Not yet,' the Usurper said silkily. 'There is still so much more fun to be had, my friend.'

'As you wish,' the Chief Counsel said, moving away. 'Would you like me to command the sirens to retrieve anyone else from the field? It seems that the Princess was lost along the way.'

'She will come,' the Usurper said calmly, 'today is her birthday after all. The Ice Flame will call to her, that is what the stories say. And I will make sure that her blood is spilt over those embers so that they can never rekindle.'

So that explained the sensation I had been feeling.

'Find my nephew,' the Usurper said, 'he will want to be here to watch.'

The Chief Counsel laughed, 'I think it would be wise to bring her betrothed as well. It will bring me great pleasure to make him feel pain. The other Houses will not be interested in him if he dies, they won't question my leadership then.'

'Send the sirens for them then,' the Usurper snapped, 'but tell them to hurry, I want them here when the Princess arrives. And make sure the sirens know not to tarry with them, they will have what's left once we've had our fun.'

'Very good,' the Chief Counsel bowed himself out and the Usurper was left alone on the throne, watching Grandfather swing with a cruel smile. I couldn't stand it a moment longer and squeezed around the statue, summoning the flames into my palm, ready to strike.

'You're in my seat,' I said coolly, my voice ringing off the marble floor. The noises from outside quietened, as if the Gods themselves were watching in anticipation.

The Usurper turned to me slowly, still smiling. 'Welcome back, Princess Wilhelmina. Am I right in assuming that all those precious memories have now been restored? I was so hoping that they would before I had the pleasure of watching you breathe your last.'

'Let my grandfather go,' I snarled, crossing towards him.

'No,' he replied, eyes glinting as I approached. 'I don't think I will. He's been so useful so far, you see. I wouldn't have been able to retrieve you as easily if he hadn't been taken. He proved to be such a wonderful incentive, separating you from your precious Resistance.'

'They aren't mine,' I snapped, gripping my dagger tightly. 'They just want the same things that I do— to rid Scardia of you and your treachery forever.'

He laughed, rocking his head back in mirth. I watched him as he wiped a tear away. 'Oh, my dear Wilhelmina,' he said, 'how naïve you are. Whatever makes you think that they will stop when I am deposed? The Resistance began years ago, long before you were born, you see. It just became more popular for the common folk once I relieved your precious parents of their crowns and you became a figurehead for them. You've seen them, been around them for long enough to know that they won't just settle back into peaceful lives once I am gone. Surely you are smarter than that.'

I thought back to the soldiers I'd seen in the street, to Rakael and her fierce expression as she stabbed me, ranting about a free Scardia. The Usurper was looking at me closely now, at my hand as it involuntarily touched the place where Rakael's blade had pierced my flesh, leaving a lasting mark.

'I think you *do* understand, Princess,' he said softly. 'Once I am gone, you will become the one they hunt down. These anarchists will never be content until they have control of what they think of as theirs.'

'But you will no longer be able to terrorise Scardia,' I replied, lifting the ball of flame higher. 'I remember what you did to my mother, I was there, watching. I'll never forget what happened.'

'Your mother made her choice,' his smile was garish now, 'she and your grandfather decided to reject my suit. Lydia could've had everything. She would still be alive today if she had just listened. But she chose to wed your pathetic father, a man who wanted peace but could barely sit through a political debate.'

'So, you were jealous?' I demanded angrily, 'you killed them because you resented that she didn't pick you?'

'Wouldn't you like to know, Princess?' He taunted, rising off the throne and closing the distance between us. His gaze fell onto the blade in my hand and he lifted his eyebrows. 'How quaint– Lydia's old dagger. It was one that I gave her.'

I struck out angrily, 'Liar.' His arm rose and blocked me, sending a jolt of shock through me.

'You remind me of her, Wilhelmina,' he breathed, deflecting my next blow just as easily. I snarled and urged the fire towards him, the flaming tendrils wrapping around his arm. He laughed again, twisting away and breaking out of its grip, shaking off the sparks with ease. 'Surely you can do better than that,' he crowed.

There was a muffled sound from above us and I glanced upward, seeing Grandfather's eyes open and widen in shock as he looked down at us. The distraction was what the Usurper had been waiting for and he struck out, punching me in the stomach and toppling me so that I sprawled on the marble floor, grunting.

'I thought the Lord of Summer would have had a far more impressive champion,' he said coldly, picking up my dagger from the floor. 'But it seems I am going to be disappointed. I think it will be fitting to spill your blood with your mother's blade,' he said thoughtfully, as he waved a hand and ropes wrapped around my arms and chest, lifting me up to swing alongside Grandfather. I struggled and the ropes pulled tighter, choking the air out of me.

'The more you fight, the harder it will be to break free,' the Usurper called up from down below, laughing at my efforts. 'To think, Lydia would be so ashamed if she could see you now. Her daughter and her father, both such disappointments. Neither of you could stand against me no matter how hard you tried.'

I hung there, glaring down at him as he sank back into the throne, twisting my mother's dagger back and forth in his hands. From time to time, he would glance up at us and smile again, eyes flashing with mirth.

'Grandfather,' I whispered, 'are you alright?'

His face was puffy and swollen, one of the ropes wound around his neck, making it hard for him to reply. I held my breath as he gave a slight nod, and then winced as the ropes pulled tighter. I smiled at him, trying to look reassuring but failing miserably. From my vantage point I scanned the throne room, wondering where Erik had gone. He couldn't be far, but I hoped he was sensible enough to be patient, instead of rushing in like I had.

Chapter Seventeen

We hung there, suspended above the throne and the smouldering embers of the Ice Flame, for what felt like an age. The Usurper remained sprawled across the throne, waiting patiently for something and I dreaded to think what. Grandfather kept silent, watching me disconcertingly, as if he expected me to do something and was waiting for me to figure it out.

There was no sign of Erik, and I could only hope that he was waiting for the right moment. Something cold sliced against my cheek and I blinked, turning to see snowflakes swirling through the throne room, carried in on the chill wind. The snow gave me hope, and I looked towards the dark windows searching for a sign.

'At last,' the Usurper finally said at the sound of footsteps from outside. The Chief Counsel entered the room, with two Trackers dragging Markus and Aidyn close behind. At their appearance the Usurper clapped his hands excitedly, rising slowly to his feet.

'I've missed you, my boy,' he said, clapping Markus on the shoulder as they were held in front of him. 'You really need to stop making a habit of running away.'

'I wish I could say the same, Uncle,' Markus grunted, pulling back against his captor.

'And you brought your Dark Elf friend,' the Usurper said breezily, 'what a pleasure.'

Aidyn barely made a sound in response, and I noticed the Chief Counsel's gaze was fixed on him. I remembered all too well the Chief Counsel's ability to twist the mind, forcing one to experience immense pain or believe illusions to be real.

'But it seems the Chief Counsel is already having his own fun with that one,' the Usurper smiled. 'No matter. He will come around later, just in time for the moment I am crowned King.'

'You will never become King, Uncle,' Markus spat.

'I wouldn't be so sure about that if I were you, boy,' the Usurper replied. 'You see, I've got a special guest who has been eagerly awaiting your arrival.' He gestured upwards and Markus followed his gaze until he saw me. He paled and I could see the angry recriminations in his eyes.

'I understand that you and Wilhelmina have history, Markus,' the Usurper continued softly. 'And I thought it would be so important for her to know the truth about you before she abdicated from her claim to the throne.'

Markus' face became ashen, unable to take his eyes away now from his uncle.

'You see,' the Usurper said sweetly, 'she still doesn't know what happened ten years ago. She was just a child, so it is understandable. You, however, were not, and can enlighten her.'

'You're mad,' Markus said harshly.

'You didn't always think so,' the Usurper chuckled before raising his voice so that I could hear him more clearly, 'you see, Princess, my nephew here adored me while he grew up. I taught him all the things his father wouldn't– how to climb, to shoot and use a sword. I took him out on his first ship, and he was all too eager to follow my lead. He was more like my son than nephew.'

'You bastard,' Markus whispered. 'Don't listen to him, Nina.'

But now I wanted to know more. The Usurper's words cut into me, but I needed to hear what came next. I had to understand what else Markus had kept secret.

'Have you ever wondered how easily my Trackers got into the palace that night, Wilhelmina?' The Usurper asked, teeth glinting in another smile. 'Have you ever wondered why your father was not with your mother? Did the questions ever keep you up at night, haunting your sleep?'

My pulse beat faster, the anger rising like the tide, waiting to be unleashed.

'It was quite simple really,' the Usurper mused, 'your father's men were soft. They let in a poor orphaned boy, one who begged for alms. Little did they know that this particular boy would open the gates for my men. Little did they know that this boy would be the one to distract their king as he rushed to join the fight.' I was staring at Markus, unable to block out the words as a wordless scream filled my mind. 'Innocence can be so deceptive, Wilhelmina,' the Usurper continued softly, 'one should always be unwilling to trust those who look helpless. Their blades are the ones that cut the deepest.'

I couldn't breathe. I couldn't see beyond the haze that was quickly descending, blocking out reason and thought. And it was that moment that Erik chose to strike, sprinting behind the Trackers holding Markus and Aidyn and stabbing upwards, catching them unaware and toppling them. Aidyn crashed underneath one of the Tracker's bodies, while Markus slipped out, grabbing one of their swords and brandishing it.

There was a loud shout of laughter as the Chief Counsel grabbed Erik, twisting his arms behind his back and pulling out his own curved blade. The haze became thicker, and I couldn't control myself, the pent-up scream that had been building inside me finally releasing.

Flames crackled around me, the air was ablaze with heat as I spread my arms and saw wings extend. My breath was hot, coming in thick heaving gasps as I lifted into the air, before plummeting to the ground towards the Chief Counsel, knocking him down and away from Erik. The Usurper stumbled backwards as I landed on the embers, feeling the strength of the ice and fire rush through me.

'Don't touch my brother,' I bit out, my voice ringing off the walls as I hurled a ball of fire towards the Chief Counsel. He ducked away and I could feel him attempt to reach out mind to mind, to force me back into some illusion. I snarled and the flames leapt higher around me, swirling around and around, encasing me in a fiery ball of protective light.

'Nina,' Erik cried, 'look out!'

A hand was reaching through the flames towards me, followed by the Usurper's maniacal grin.

'Your flames don't hurt me, Princess,' he said, 'the Lord of Summer blessed me with gifts long before you. I am invincible.'

'Clever words,' I hissed, dodging away from his blow, 'but you seem to have forgotten one thing.'

'And what is that, Wilhelmina?' He goaded, my mother's knife missing my neck by an inch. I stepped backwards, off the Hoarfrost and he moved forwards, striking out again. This time he caught my shoulder, leaving a deep cut.

'Only a member of the royal family can stand in the Ice Flame and survive,' I whispered, as I raised my hands and the embers at his feet caught alight. The blue flames rose, trapping his legs in their embrace, locking him in place on the Hoarfrost so that he couldn't break free. His eyes widened in horror as he looked down, registering for the first time where I had led him. And then he began to scream, trapped by the circle of ice and fire.

There was a loud commotion from behind me and I turned to see the Chief Counsel crumpling to the ground, Aidyn pressing a blade into his neck. Erik and Markus were locked in a tussle with the Trackers, more of whom had come running at the noises from the throne room. I lifted my arms, summoning the firebird to leave me and swoop upwards to Grandfather, where it cut through his bonds and brought him back down to the ground. The bird released him and soared towards the Trackers, letting out a piercing shriek and diving into the battle with outstretched talons and sharp beak.

I knelt next to his body, noticing the sparks fading back into my skin as the magic became more controlled and I could reach out to touch him.

'Grandfather?' I asked tentatively, shaking his shoulder gently.

'My dear,' he wheezed, coughing, 'how did you do that?'

'It called to me Grandfather,' I whispered, 'the flames… I don't understand it.'

'It recognised you,' he gasped, struggling for breath, 'you've finally come home. I'm so… proud.' He coughed again and I lifted him up until his head was in my lap, suddenly scared.

'Grandfather, don't talk, we need to get you to a healer. Save your strength.'

He let out a cackle, almost a laugh but not quite. 'I'm so glad Erik succeeded. He did well.' I felt tears well up in my eyes and I gripped onto him tighter. 'So much to say, Nina, and I don't have the time.' His voice was getting fainter, his breath coming with more difficulty. 'Marriage contract…should have told you. I'm sorry.'

I nodded, the tears now tracking down my cheeks onto his face.

'My kingdom, you are the next in line. Try to…end prejudice between our peoples.' His wrinkled hand grasped mine, 'marry like your mother did. Love match. I thought it would come.'

'I will do my best, Grandfather,' I whispered, 'but I…'

'Nina,' Aidyn was beside me, 'King Aegis.'

Grandfather turned fading eyes to him and said, 'keep your promise, Aidyn. Don't get too lost in…vengeance. Have a better…brighter life.' He turned back to me and smiled as the light extinguished and he fell limp. Aidyn's arms came around me as I screamed again, the pain in my chest ripping out, lashing out at anyone and everyone.

'Dear heart,' he whispered, 'I'm sorry.'

I could barely hear him through my tears, but his hold grounded me, reigning in emotions that were tumbling out. I couldn't quite believe that he was gone, seeing it in front of my eyes was too much to bear.

'Nina,' Aidyn said, 'we need to help the others.'

I gave a jerky nod and carefully laid Grandfather down, closing his eyes and crossing his arms over his chest. Then I shakily got to my feet and saw that the Ice Flame had simmered down. The Usurper was gone, reduced to fine ash that lifted into the air and merged with the falling snow. I reached into the low flames and withdrew my mother's dagger, which had fallen onto the Hoarfrost. It was cold to touch and I eyed it curiously, wondering whether it really had been a gift from the Usurper to my mother all those years ago, or whether it had just been a lie he had told to cause pain.

'Nina,' Aidyn repeated, 'we can't leave them alone.'

No, we couldn't. I gripped the hilt determinedly and followed him in the direction of the fighting, where Markus and Erik were fending off several Trackers. The firebird continued to circle above, its claws snatching weapons out of their grasp and allowing Erik or Markus to strike them down. On my arrival, the bird returned to my arm and perched there, trilling out a fey song. I looked at it closely and then lifted it higher.

'Clear the way for us,' I ordered, and the bird took off, its wings lighting some of the Trackers aflame as it flew ahead towards the palace gates. As it disappeared, Aidyn and I joined Markus and Erik, parrying the Tracker's blows with our own.

The numbness that filled me helped to clear my mind as I struck and dodged, weaving around the Trackers as they fought back. I couldn't look at Markus as blades clashed, worried that if I did the haze would descend again. All these years I had wondered what had happened to my father. As the Usurper had taunted, it had kept me awake at night, imagining his last moments. Now that I knew– or guessed at least at what had happened– I couldn't lose myself in the anger.

I heard shouting and running footsteps from the end of the corridor, coming from the palace entrance. I glanced up and saw Aidyn's fighters cutting through the Trackers, moving towards us followed closely by Rakael and Jesse, with a group of Resistance soldiers. Markus let out a relieved cheer, and the Trackers turned in horror, watching as their comrades were cut down. The remaining Trackers did not last long, and soon their bodies lay scattered through the corridor, along with several of our own.

'Nina,' Jesse cried, tripping towards us, 'what on earth…'

'You were supposed to be back at the camp, Princess,' Rakael snapped angrily, 'what do you think you're doing here?'

I glared at her as the firebird returned, sweeping down to rest on my wounded shoulder.

'I wasn't going to be left behind,' I said coolly, 'I thought you would figure that out, Rakael. I'm not going to let you insist on making all the decisions from now on; the Usurper is dead and it is time for Scardia to heal.'

'He is dead?' She asked, aghast. 'How?'

'He melted,' Erik muttered, 'in the Ice Flame.'

There was a shocked silence. And then a cheer went up from the soldiers, carrying down the corridor and being shouted out for the city to hear.

The Usurper is dead. Long live Princess Wilhelmina. Long live the Princess.

I watched Rakael's face closely as the call went out, noting the pinched expression and the tautness in her jaw. She was biding her time, clearly angry about the new developments, and I would be ready when she tried to strike.

It took time to lay out the bodies of the wounded and the dead. I insisted that there should not be a difference between them, lying Trackers and Resistance soldiers out side by side. I made an exception with Grandfather's body, watching as several High Elves carried it into an antechamber and laid him on a dais. The palace was a flurry of activity as noblemen and townspeople crowded the space, since those who had been fleeing from the Resistance invasion had taken refuge in the sprawling gardens. Now they approached me nervously, unsure whether I was going to smite them down or smile at them.

I refused to enter the throne room, and instead moved to the wide reception room that was next to the entrance hall. Here the Scardian people began to get reacquainted with their Princess, the nobles a touch uncomfortably, some giving me shifty, defiant looks as I greeted them. I didn't want to reign punishment down on them for supporting the Usurper's rule, aware that in all likelihood they would have had little choice if they wanted to survive. But I made it known that all who had been faithful to my parents and myself, all who were currently imprisoned or enslaved in the Capital, were to be released forthwith. Erik had the honour of taking that missive to the palace aviary, where Resistance soldiers attached documents to multiple carrier pigeons and dispatched them into the night. The news he brought back was that many of the Usurper's troops, such as the sirens and Felshkran mercenaries, had fled, while the Trackers in the palace had been rounded up and marched to the dungeons.

Dawn had well and truly broken by the time I had spoken with the last civilian, grasping their hands and smiling a warm greeting. By then Jesse and several other soldiers had located the envoys from Velkra and Felshkar, who had been hiding in the private suites, including the Velkranian Queen, who dipped into a low curtsey before me, her glittering jewels and ornate headdress flashing in the early morning light. She eyed me up and down, taking in my bedraggled hair, and bloodstained and torn clothing, before meeting my gaze again with a slightly condescending air.

'Princess Wilhelmina,' she cooed, 'a pleasure.' Her voice was sickly sweet like honey, but I forced a polite smile and responded in kind. I might not be as politically savvy as my mother, but I knew better than to provoke one of the neighbouring countries' monarchs. The priority would be rebuilding the Capital and supporting the Scardian people, not waging another war against any of our neighbours.

The visiting dignitaries, whilst thrown off that their original host had been deposed, greeted me tentatively, intrigued to meet the famous lost princess. My cheeks ached from my frozen politeness, and once the last dignitary had been introduced I was ready to collapse. The main thing that they seemed curious about was whether a coronation would be taking place during their visit after all. When faced with this question I refrained from answering, choosing instead to ask them about themselves and their separate roles in their home countries. At this point, I wasn't ready to think about a coronation. My heart was too heavy, and I couldn't bring myself to justify putting on an extravagant show when half of the Capital lay in smouldering ruin.

When Erik offered me his arm, I took it gratefully, eager to escape from the various dignitaries and the piercing gaze of the Velkranian Queen. A pair of Elven guards followed several paces behind us, making sure that the crowd kept a reasonable distance and that I was not disturbed. Although I was bone tired, I knew that it would be a while before I could rest. There were preparations to make for the members of the public whose homes had been destroyed and needed a safe place to stay, and medical care needed to be offered to the wounded.

I guided Erik towards the room where my father had held his councils, although for the most part my mother had been the one to negotiate deals. Sure enough, as I had suspected, the room was not empty. I recognised Elder Haycin, Rakael,

Jesse, several Resistance guards and Aidyn, who were standing around what my father had called the war table. It was a large, round table made of stone, which took up the majority of the space in the room. Sunlight streamed through the high windows and bathed the room in cool light, illuminating the forest scene on one of the thick tapestries. My eyes paused on it for a moment, remembering how I had once tried to hide behind it to overhear a meeting and then was promptly deposited in the hallway.

'Ah, Princess,' Rakael's voice interrupted my thoughts and jolted me back to the present. 'How thoughtful of you to join us.' Her tone dripped with sarcasm and I stiffened slightly, my grip on Erik's arm tightening.

'Princess,' Elder Haycin came over to greet me properly, 'I would like to extend my condolences. King Aegis was a great leader, and we will mourn his passing. Our blades and bows are yours to command.'

I inclined my head. 'Thank you Elder Haycin. I will be in need of your counsel over the coming days.'

'There is still much to do before we can rest easy,' Rakael said brusquely, 'the Usurper's troops have either fled or been captured, it is true, but our primary aim should be to hunt them down before they regroup and launch an attack.'

'We have many wounded, Rakael,' Jesse said quietly, 'and those who wish to mourn the dead. There aren't enough soldiers prepared to go out on a hunt.'

'They will have to,' Rakael said coldly, 'if their Princess wishes it.' Her eyes bored into mine, 'which is what you want, of course, Princess. You cannot let them escape without any punishment, not after everything they have done.'

The room was silent, everyone waiting for my response. Yet I couldn't bring myself to answer right away, for Rakael's words had appealed to the anger that still burned within me, the desire to lash out at my enemies and see them suffer for the pain they had inflicted. I couldn't deny the lure of vengeance. Nevertheless, what Jesse had said was also true.

'Nina?' Erik finally whispered, 'what's your decision?'

My gaze hadn't left Rakael's, and I said, 'we will ask for volunteers to search. Our focus should be on caring for the wounded and rebuilding the city. But we will work to bring justice to those who have fallen and have been impacted by the Usurper's reign.'

She gave a short nod. 'As you command, Your Highness.' With an abrupt bow she left, waving for the other Resistance members to follow. Once she left, I leaned on the war table, the exhaustion from the past twenty-four hours finally catching up with me.

'What would you like us to do, Nina?' Elder Haycin asked gently. 'Our healers are currently tending to the wounded, and we have secured the rest of the palace.'

'Thank you,' I said, 'we should send some men to put out the remaining fires.'

'I think that the Winter Spirit is already seeing to that,' Erik muttered, looking out of the window. I followed his gaze and saw the fine snow falling from the sky, extinguishing the last vestiges of the attack. Although dark smoke still tinged the air over the city, the carpet of white grew thicker, covering up the signs of battle.

'Nina,' Aidyn said, stepping towards me, 'you look like you need to rest. Perhaps…'

'I'm sure Lisette has gone to prepare the Princess' rooms already,' Elder Haycin interrupted smoothly, 'she arrived from the outer camp not too long ago.'

I blinked, surprised. I hadn't seen Lisette pass me by in the hallways, but then I had been so caught up with the dignitaries and the common folk that I had barely noticed what had happened around me. Suddenly all I wanted was to be alone, to have the chance to cry and try to grapple with my conflicting emotions.

'We will send our troops into the city,' Elder Haycin was saying, 'there is still much to be done to clear the streets. Lord Aidyn, if your soldiers and the Wood Elves would join us that would be most helpful.'

Aidyn nodded, 'of course, I'll go and inform them. Then I will see my betrothed safely to her chambers.' His tone brooked no argument and, although I could feel Erik's sudden tension, I couldn't find the energy to disagree with him. Deep down I knew that I would feel safer if he stayed by my side until I was with Lisette. Rakael was still around, and a part of me didn't want to rest until I knew she had left the palace walls. Aidyn departed quickly, his boots clicking on the stone floor. I glanced at Erik, who was watching him leave closely.

'Can you find out what has happened to our other friends, Erik?' I asked cautiously, 'I haven't seen Dylan at all, and Keely…'

'I think I last saw Stefan out by the stables,' Elder Haycin added, noting Erik's sudden attention, 'perhaps he might be able to help you.'

Erik looked at me and I nodded, 'I will rest more easily once I know that the others are safe.' He grinned briefly and followed Aidyn, soon disappearing from view. Once he was gone and I was left with Elder Haycin, I closed the door firmly, checking that the corridor outside was clear.

'I'm glad that we have a moment alone, Elder Haycin,' I said quietly, moving to the head of the table where my father had often stood, and assumed the position I had seen him take many times. Palms down on the stone, I looked up at the captain of my grandfather's men, who had always treated me with kindness and respect. Now his eyes watched me shrewdly as I continued, 'I'm sure that you have been told about how I was brought back from a place that is neither in this world nor the next. How I came back with no memory of my predicament, or who was friend or foe.'

'I have been informed, yes,' Elder Haycin said, 'Rakael has already suggested that a council be formed, and a leader elected in the interim as you come to terms with what has happened. She has volunteered herself as the best candidate.'

Of course she had. I wasn't surprised, nor was I shocked that she had already acted so quickly. The conversation she'd had with Markus had only confirmed that fear.

'Although,' Elder Haycin mused, eyes never leaving mine, 'I sense that there is more to this tale than I had assumed. Seeing you in the aftermath of the fighting only shows how you have taken on the mantle of being Scardia's heir as it should have always been. It makes me wonder what memories have already started to return to you.'

'All of them,' I said honestly. 'I remember everything that happened before I was killed and can interpret what has happened since with greater wisdom than when I awoke.'

'You remember it all?' He repeated, not as though he were expecting an answer but rather as though he needed to process the information himself.

'It seemed that all it would take to restore my memories was to see the person who had sent me to that place between worlds,' I continued, 'and that is why I need to speak with you privately, you served Grandfather faithfully and I trust that you will do the same for me.'

'My sword is yours, Princess,' Elder Haycin had blanched slightly at my words, but his voice was steady. 'I will protect you with my life.'

'I hope it won't come to that,' I gave a wobbly smile, 'I don't want to lose anyone else close to me for a while yet.' I paused and took a breath, forcing the threatening tears away before I kept speaking. 'I wanted to make sure that you knew that the person who struck me down was one who claimed to be a friend, or rather an ally.'

'Ah,' he spoke so softly that I barely heard him, but his understanding was clear.

'As the leader of the Resistance,' I pushed on, 'I would have thought that she would have thought things through more, I wish I could completely understand her motives, I really do. But she was the one who did it.'

A brief, thrumming silence followed. Finally Elder Haycin asked, 'do you think she is aware that you remember?'

I shook my head, 'she might suspect, but I don't think she knows. However, I am loath to be alone around her in the foreseeable future.'

'I will assign guards to you immediately, Your Highness,' he said calmly, 'and I will make sure that she is supervised discretely until you decide how you would like to proceed.'

'Thank you, Elder Haycin,' I said gratefully, relieved that I had made the right choice. There was a knock at the door and I opened it, seeing Aidyn on the other side.

'Lord Aidyn will watch over you while I see to what we discussed, Your Highness,' Elder Haycin bowed low, 'your instructions will be fulfilled.' He strode out, leaving Aidyn and I alone. I was struck suddenly that this was the first time we had been alone together since the night before, and I felt a warm blush spread across my cheeks as I glanced away, overcome with awkward shyness.

'Come, dear heart,' Aidyn said softly, offering me his arm which I took automatically, wondering why I couldn't come up with some kind of witty remark or something to fill the silence that now stretched between us. We passed many people in the hallway, but I didn't take note of their names or faces, too lost in thought and tiredness to care.

'What is on your mind?' Aidyn asked as we began to ascend the grand winding staircase, nodding briefly to some other Elves who were preparing to depart. His gaze returned to me and again I couldn't think of what to say. 'If you're worried about any of the Usurper's men, I can assure you that they have all been dealt with,' he continued, 'they are in the dungeons and under guard.'

'I wasn't afraid of that,' I said, 'it's not the Usurper's men who I'm worried about.'

'I won't let anything happen to you, Nina,' he said firmly, 'I've already organised a watch. No one will enter your chambers while you are resting, I swear.'

'You know,' my quiet voice turned reflective as I thought back, 'that night when I was attacked– when the Trackers infiltrated the Underdark– I saw things when I was dying. Just like when I was in the Trial and needed help. You were watching over me then, weren't you?'

His face had gone ashen and he nodded slowly. 'I saw it.'

'Then you know who I need to be wary of,' I said carefully. He nodded again. We were walking along a carpeted hallway now, having climbed up several floors and down another long hallway lined with narrow alcoves with flickering braziers. Despite the flames, the palace was chilly and I pressed closer to him, partially for warmth and partially because of a different need.

'I'll make sure no one gets too close,' he promised under his breath.

I knew he would. It eased the anxiety that had begun to form whenever I thought about Rakael and what she would do.

We arrived in front of two familiar ornate doors that were designed with golden vines. I didn't recognise these as the doors to my former chambers, but for a different reason.

'No,' I said automatically, 'no, these aren't my rooms—they're my mother's.'

'I was told that these rooms were being prepared for you,' Aidyn sounded confused, 'You are going to be Queen, Nina. These rooms are yours now.'

He was right, but I didn't want to admit it openly. It felt wrong to claim my mother's rooms as my own. I held his arm tighter as he knocked, and Lisette opened the doors.

'Don't leave yet,' I whispered to him, 'please.'

'I'll get cleaned up and return to check on you,' he said, 'I've been placed in one of the chambers nearby.' I nodded and allowed Lisette to lead me inside, shutting the doors behind me. She pulled me into a hug almost immediately and then clicked her tongue disapprovingly as she surveyed the state I was in. Her gaze was reprimand enough and I felt a slight stirring of shame as I sat down on the padded chaise lounge next to a roaring fire.

'I couldn't tell you about what I was planning to do, Lisette,' I said, 'you would have tried to stop me, admit it.'

She shrugged and began to strip my clothes off, cleaning my wounds with a damp cloth. I winced, nails biting into my palms as the wounds stung, some beginning to bleed anew.

Lisette rubbed in a poultice and began to wind gauze around them, tying them securely with deft knots. She helped me into a soft lawn nightgown and began to brush out my hair as I pulled a robe over me. I didn't want to think about the memories that the robe brought up, recognising it as one my mother had used many times. It struck me as odd that it was still here in her rooms and I looked around, noting how, little had in fact changed in ten years.

My mother's rooms were large and had tapestries on the walls, detailing the Eastern Lands and the High Elf court. Now that I had been there myself, I could recognise the distant town of Lowton, the silver birches, the staircases and vines. As a child I hadn't realised that the place or people depicted in the fabric were real. There were glass doors that led out onto her balcony, which still seemed to have a set of chairs looking out over the gardens, the Capital and the Hoarfrost Glacier. The four-poster bed was grand and had mystical creatures carved into the posts. I couldn't remember my mother ever actually sleeping there though, she had usually spent the night with my father in his adjacent room. Her writing desk and high-backed chair were still in the same corner, while the nearby door led into her dressing room, where her clothes, shoes and jewels had been. There had been so many times that I had slipped in there, desperate to grow up faster to wear similar finery.

'It feels wrong to be in Mama's room, Lisette,' I said finally as she began to plait my hair. 'And it's strange that nothing seems to have changed.'

She glanced around and nodded, tying my plait with a blue ribbon. She hovered for a moment, as though unwilling to leave, and I gave her a small smile.

'I'll be alright, Lisette,' I said softly, 'Aidyn will be back soon.' Her eyes became suspicious and I quickly added, 'he won't be staying for long and I won't do anything stupid, I promise.'

In all honesty, I was too tired to have the energy for much more than talking, so I was relieved when Lisette seemed to accept my answer and headed out, the bloodied clothing over one arm, the washbasin in her hands. As the door shut behind her, I stood and began to inspect the room more closely. The thick carpet underfoot was gentle under my aching feet as I moved closer to the tapestry depicting the Eastern Lands. Before, I had been able to distinguish figures amongst the trees, but now I could see the Elves running, fighting and laughing through the court. In a central tree, seated on a throne, was a tall man with a woven crown around his forehead. His eyes shone blue, like those of his daughter who sat beside him. Both had blond hair that fell down their shoulders as they stared out from the scene. I reached out to touch them, tears pricking my eyes, as I wondered how long it had taken my mother to create the scene, stitch after stitch. Had she felt the same tearing in her heart as she plied her needle, the same sad yearning for a home and family she would never see again?

'Mama,' I whispered, 'Grandfather.' There was heat rising in my throat, cutting off the air and pushing the tears to the surface. I bent my head and allowed them to fall, as the emptiness that had been threatening to engulf me for the past hours finally took control.

I didn't hear the door open and by the time I sensed the presence behind me, it was too late to react. Strong arms pulled me into an embrace, and I froze, taking a moment to register who was holding me and realising that my dagger was on the writing table, out of reach.

'It's alright, Nina.' His voice was gravelly and hoarse. 'It's over now.'

'Markus.' I was shaken, torn between the desire to be held and the urge to lash out, to hurt him how I had been hurt. 'What are you doing?'

'What does it look like I'm doing?' He retorted gruffly, pulling back to look down at me, brow creased. 'I'm trying to comfort you.'

I stared at him mutely and stepped away, moving over towards the fire and clasping my robe more securely around me. 'I wasn't expecting you.' I spoke remotely, with a chilly distance. He hovered for a moment and then followed.

'I thought you would be swarmed with people needing you,' he said, 'once you were alone, I thought it would be the perfect time to talk about what we discussed, about going away together and your abdication.'

A buzzing filled my head, and it took everything in me not to snap right there and then and release some of the magic that was starting to pulse through me. Instead, I kept my tone neutral as I queried, 'oh?'

'We discussed it, Nina.' He stepped closer, annoyance starting to enter his voice. 'You, me and Erik, sailing away to far off lands. Remember?'

I pursed my lips. 'I remember *you* talking about such a thing. I don't remember agreeing to it, though.'

'You know it's something you want,' he said mulishly, and I met his dark gaze, wondering how interesting it was that some memories remained ingrained which were merely holding grains of truth.

'I can't, Markus.' I said bluntly. 'I thought I made that clear to you. My people need me; Scardia needs me. I can't leave it behind, I'm not the same person I was when we crossed the Meridian together.' He opened his mouth to interject and I held up a hand, silencing him. 'Also,' I continued, my voice becoming like the ice that had encased my heart, 'I need to know whether what your uncle said was true. Did you help his men to break into the palace that night? Were you the one responsible for my father's death?'

All the colour drained from his face, and he looked like I'd struck him. 'You can't believe what he said,' he bit out, 'he was a compulsive liar, a manipulator. He only wanted to hurt you, to hurt *us.*'

'I think we were already hurt, Markus,' I said quietly, noting that he had neither confirmed nor denied my fears. 'Now answer my question.'

There was a long silence. It dragged out, filling the room with unspoken anger and pain, and the weight of his betrayal cut deeper than I had thought I could bear. Finally, he bowed his head and said, 'I was a boy, not much older than Erik. My uncle was my idol, he told me what to do and how to do it, and I obeyed. It's a decision that has haunted me ever since. I knew as soon as I thrust the knife in that I had done the unthinkable and that I would be damned for what happened. And when I found my uncle standing over your mother's body, I couldn't bear it; I ran. I fled that night, just like you, and found work as a deckhand on the first ship out of the harbour.'

I turned away from him, leaning my head against the mantle over the fire, unable to look at him a moment longer. My temples were pounding as I tried to calm my breathing, anger pulsing through me.

'And now, it seems,' Markus said quietly, 'the only one who made me think I could have redemption has decided against granting it.'

His words seared into my heart and I bit my lip, trying to hold back the new tears that had risen to my eyes. 'I think,' I managed to say, 'that you need to go. I can't talk to you now.'

His hands gripped my shoulders and turned me, pulling me into another embrace and I struggled, wanting nothing more than to be alone. However, Markus had always been stronger than I, and he held me firm as he kissed me, pinning me between him and the fire. When he pulled back my hand flashed out, slapping his cheek with a loud smack.

'Don't forget what you would turn your back on,' he said as he stepped away. 'I made a mistake when I was young. I have changed since then, I've become a better person and I want to share my life with you.'

'Get. Out.' I was shaking with anger now, barely able to control the flames that were sparking from my fingertips. He obeyed, pushing past a figure in the doorway as he left, one hand to his cheek.

'How long were you standing there?' I asked brutally, the fury lashing out as I crossed my arms and sank onto the chaise. My knees felt wobbly, and I couldn't meet the lilac eyes that watched me from across the room.

'Long enough,' Aidyn said coolly, closing the door as he approached. 'I came in when there was mention of you two running away together.'

I cringed. 'I'm surprised you didn't leave immediately.'

'So am I,' he admitted, 'but your response piqued my curiosity. And since you were both so engrossed, I didn't think you would take too kindly to being interrupted.'

I glared at him. 'You *stood* there and watched him kiss me?'

'You made it clear that you didn't want him to continue,' Aidyn's tone was detached now. 'If he had, it wouldn't have been for long.'

I cast a dark look his way before glaring at the fire. As if I wasn't already feeling disturbed from Markus' admission, now I also felt embarrassed that Aidyn had seen the whole thing.

'Nina,' he sat down beside me, 'did you mean what you said? About not wanting to run away with your captain?'

I rolled my eyes and grumbled, 'why do I keep getting asked whether or not I'm sure about things? I'm needed here. Even if I wanted to, I couldn't go away. And now…' I broke off, cursing the tears that threatened to fall again, 'After Papa, I don't think Markus is "my" captain anymore. I don't know if I can forgive that.'

'I'm sorry.' I looked at him, shocked, until he added, 'About your father. It wasn't right for you to find it out like that.'

'You knew?' I demanded, suddenly angry again.

'I suspected he had done something on the Usurper's orders,' he admitted, 'I didn't know the gravity of it though.' His hand reached out and grasped mine gently. 'I wasn't going to be the one to poison your mind with accusations which may have been false. I can understand why Markus would want to hide his past from you, for you to see the man he has become and not the man he used to be. With you I've always tried to be truthful. I wanted you to know the real me, not the son my father created.'

I looked at him and his steady gaze helped the anger and hurt to dissolve into a dull ache. 'I always tried to be honest with you too,' I said quietly. 'I didn't try to hide behind one of my pseudonyms. I'd stopped running by the time you met me, but the person I'm expected to be is someone I don't know I'll be able to live up to.'

He smiled and his other hand cupped my cheek. 'I know she will be,' he said, 'because you are already her.'

Wetness stung my cheeks as the tears fell, and as his thumb brushed them away, I closed the distance between us and kissed him. I wrapped my arms around his neck, my hands in his hair as warmth spread through me from the tips of my fingers down to my toes. The kiss deepened and I moaned, gripping him tighter as we fell on the chaise. His eyes danced with mirth at the expression on my face and he chuckled, pulling me up.

'I thought you were tired, Princess,' he teased, 'don't you want to sleep?'

'Oh,' I stood, distancing myself from him and glanced at the bed. 'I suppose I did. I mean, I *do*.'

'You don't sound convinced,' he said, smiling.

'Well,' I searched for something to say, my brain sluggish. 'It is quite light in here, I don't know how well I can sleep in daylight.'

It was a poor excuse and I could tell from his raised eyebrows that he knew it.

'I can help with that,' he murmured as he stood and made to move towards the door. With a gesture of his hand, the light in the room dimmed, heavy curtains pulled across the windows and darkness fell. The fire had become smouldering embers, and I followed him, reaching out and grasping his hand as he reached out to open the door to leave.

'Aidyn,' I couldn't quite get the pleading note out of my voice and hated myself for it. 'Stay with me, please.'

He went very still. 'You ask a lot, Princess,' he sounded strained.

'I *am* tired,' I said quietly, 'but I'll feel better if you stay with me. I'm not ready to be alone in this room yet.'

'Only until you fall asleep,' he said grudgingly, 'then I will go outside.'

I smiled and tugged on his hand, ignoring his muffled chuckle as I led him towards the bed. I was grateful for the dimmed light, as I slipped out of the robe and got under the heavy blankets, hearing the thuds as his boots hit the floor. He lay on top of the covers, and I snuggled closer, resting my hand on his chest.

'Aidyn,' I finally said.

'Mm?' He clearly thought that I had already fallen asleep.

'I *am* tired,' I repeated softly, 'but…'

'But?' He asked, and I could hear his wry smile.

'But I'm not ready to sleep yet,' I whispered, gazing up at his dark profile.

'You really are incorrigible, Princess,' he murmured before he bent and kissed me, showing me just how much could be done to ensure someone slept well.

Chapter Eighteen

Aidyn was gone when I awoke. Lisette, however, was there, pottering around the room and opening the curtains. Early morning sunlight shone through the glass and I realised that I had slept longer than I had expected. Hastily, I got out of bed, shivering as my bare feet hit the floor. Lisette bustled over and led me into the dressing room to prepare me for the day ahead. When her hand hovered over one of my mother's gowns I shook my head.

'No, Lisette,' I said, 'I want to wear something to pay my respects to the fallen.' She looked at me and nodded. There was a knock on the door and she paused in the process of brushing out my hair to answer it. She returned almost immediately, Jesse behind her.

'Good morning,' she said brightly, 'I was hoping to catch you before you got too caught up in discussions with the others.'

I smiled, then winced as Lisette began to pull and twist my hair up into one of her more severe styles. 'Have the guards started to help repair the damage from the fight?'

'Some,' Jesse replied, leaning against the doorframe and looking with interest at the racks of clothes and shoes in the room. 'The snow helped to douse the remaining fires. The bodies in the streets have been taken to the morgues, to prepare for burial. Most of the townsfolk are still in the palace, although some have left to go back to their homes.'

'That's promising,' I said as Lisette began to fasten on one of my mother's black dresses, pulling on the stays and attaching the overskirt, which glistened with silver thread- I was surprised that it fit. Lastly, she clasped a dark fur cape around my neck.

'Rakael wanted you to know that she has complied with your wishes about the prisoners,' Jesse continued, 'she said it has been taken care of.'

I glanced up at her, my boot laces half tied. 'What do you mean?' A creeping sense of dread was grasping at my chest and I felt a wave of foreboding.

She looked confused, 'the prisoners– you said that you wanted justice for the fallen. So Rakael followed your orders.'

'I gave no orders,' I bit the words out as Lisette took the laces from my rigid fingers and quickly tied them. 'What did she do?'

Once Lisette's hands were out of the way, I was striding out of the dressing room, Jesse on my heels as I left the bedroom. Outside, two Elves stood to attention and fell into step behind me.

'She gave the order for them to be made an example of,' Jesse said quietly, 'for justice to be served.'

'She had no right,' I was furious now, knowing that I would be too late to stop it.

'They're outside,' Jesse said, 'Rakael felt that a public display would send an effective message to those who might think about disagreeing with our regime.'

So, it was a regime now?

I walked faster, muttering greetings to the people we passed, heading towards the wide doors that opened onto the gardens. As we made our way through the halls, I couldn't help but notice the hush that seemed to have fallen over the palace; the sense of uncertainty, the cold presence of death. Those we saw may have whispered greetings, but they avoided eye contact, their faces were pale and stricken, and those who did look at me either had fear or distrust simmering in their eyes.

'It's not pleasant, Nina,' Jesse tried to pull on my arm; to slow me down as we approached the doors. 'You don't want…'

'I never gave the order to exact vengeance,' I snarled, roughly jerking my arm out of her grip and striding outside into the biting cold. Snow crunched under my feet and I paused, taking in the bodies hanging from the palace walls. There were more than I had realised, and they hung like grotesque decorations, swaying in the wind. I forced myself to move forward, noting the groups of women and children who huddled underneath some of the bodies, wailing and crying.

'Why are there so many?' I asked Jesse.

'These are only some,' she replied, mouth scrunched up in distaste. 'More were paraded through the town, to the city walls. She made an example of everyone who supported the Usurper: guards, Trackers, mercenaries.'

'It was horrible,' a small voice added, and I looked down to see Erik, who had his hands shoved in the pockets of his fur coat. 'She said it was on your orders. That the townsfolk needed to watch, to see what would happen if they spoke out against the Resistance and its leadership.'

'You were here?' I asked, horrified. 'Didn't anyone try to stop her?'

'She had too many guards,' Erik said, 'The Elves were either in the city, or sleeping.'

'Rakael has lost her reason,' Jesse said softly, 'I fear that her thirst for revenge has taken over.'

'You don't say,' I said sarcastically, glaring at her. 'I thought she would at least listen to you though, Jesse. Why didn't you try to stop her?'

She looked at me sadly. 'I did, Nina. But she claimed to have your support, and once she said that we couldn't argue unless we wanted to have the same fate.'

I blanched and gripped Erik's hand. 'Where's Elder Haycin? He must be aware of this.'

'He's been in the city,' Erik said, 'I don't think he's returned yet.'

I stared at the hanging corpses, at the Resistance guards standing alert along the wall, ensuring that none of the common folk could cut down their victims. On seeing my approach, one of the children who had been huddled next to her mother stumbled towards me, her hands chapped and shaking in the cold, and dropped at my feet, grasping at my skirt.

'Please Your Highness,' she cried, 'please tell them to let my Da down, he hasn't done anything wrong. He won't hurt you or the Resistance, he's never done anyone harm. Oh please.' Her shoulders were racking with uncontrollable sobs and her voice cracked, making her next words indecipherable. On noticing her daughter's absence, the girl's mother looked up and let out a cry, hurrying forward to drag her child away.

'Come, Felice, come away.' Instead of going with her mother, Felice's grip on my skirt only tightened.

'She has to let Da go,' she sobbed, 'she's the Princess, it's her job to look after us. Da always said…'

'Hush Felice,' her mother admonished, casting a terrified glance at me, her eyes darting away from making contact with mine. 'Forgive us, Your Highness. Please don't take my child away.'

I opened my mouth to reply that I would never do that, but Erik beat me to it.

'She's not like that,' he said kindly. The woman shot him a suspicious, frightened look and then glanced from me to the swinging bodies along the wall. A shadow descended over her features and she shook her head, pulling Felice away with renewed vigour.

'Please, Majesty,' Felice implored as her mother finally succeeded and dragged her back, 'please let him come home.' She pointed a shaky finger up at one of the bodies, a wasted figure of a man who in my heart I knew was already in the realm beyond.

'This isn't right,' I said curtly, striding towards the guards purposefully.

'Are you sure this is a good idea?' Jesse asked cautiously. I spun to face her, glaring.

'What do you mean, Jesse?' She took a step back hesitantly, and I pushed on. 'I am not going to stand idly by and allow my people to think that I condoned this.'

'But what about Rakael?'

I pursed my lips tightly, the memory of Rakael's expression as she thrust the sword into my stomach flashing across my mind. She wanted a Scardia free from the monarchy, from both my lineage and the Usurper's tyranny. Turning my people against me was clearly part of that plan and it sickened me.

'Rakael will need to watch her back,' I snarled, 'and you will need to choose which side you will support Jesse. I may not want to but if I am forced to deal with traitors in my court then I will do what is necessary.'

Her eyes widened and she said quietly, 'and what– pray– is necessary?'

Erik was also looking at me strangely, like he didn't recognise me. I didn't reply but turned away, shaking not from the cold, but from anger. When I stopped in front of the guards at the base of the wall, they stood to attention, gripping their halberds and striking them to the icy ground.

'Your Highness,' one said, 'have you come to inspect the prisoners?' He sounded proud, excited even. The way they were looking at me expectantly made me realise that they anticipated praise for their efforts, and I felt sickened.

'I want the bodies to be cut down,' I said, and the guards glanced at each other, confused.

'Cut them down, Your Highness?'

'Yes.' My tone was commanding now, irritated that they were hesitating. 'Cut them down immediately.'

'But they have not all been strung up, Your Highness,' one of the guards said, confused. 'We received clear instructions that none were to be cut down until all traitors had been made an example of.'

'Oh, I think an example has clearly been made already,' I said angrily, pointing with a quivering finger at the men who hung above us, swaying eerily in the morning breeze. The guards shuffled uneasily, glancing from my stern expression to the hanging figures.

'Take them down.' I repeated forcefully. 'Now.'

'Right away, Your Highness,' they said quickly, stepping backwards hastily.

'And you,' I pointed to the one on the right, 'go and send word to the other guards to cut down the rest of the prisoners.'

'Yes, Your Highness,' he stuttered.

'Go.' I waved my hand and he departed at a run, while his companion went to the narrow stairway leading up the wall to the ramparts. Once there, I watched as he began to cut down the hanging corpses, before turning away, unable to bear the sight.

'Come on, Nina,' Erik muttered as he pulled on my arm, 'let's go inside. It's freezing out here.'

I nodded mutely, the light pressure leading me away, back towards the palace. I allowed myself to be taken past guards and courtiers who had noticed what was happening by the walls and were now whispering to each other. The soft chatter followed me as we made our way to one of the receiving rooms, where some servants hastily set about lighting a fire in the grate and fetching refreshments, before fading into the background, watching me in avid curiosity. I hadn't realised that I was trembling, and the cup of tea shook as I lifted it to my lips, taking a restorative sip.

'Jesse,' I said once I had placed the cup back onto its saucer, 'go and make sure that the guards are doing as I instructed. When I next go outside, I don't want to see any evidence of what happened this morning. The bodies should be taken to the morgues along with the other corpses, no matter who they were. Then the families will need to be informed.'

Jesse inclined her head, dark hair swinging across her shoulders. 'I'll do that right away, Nina.' She turned and departed, boot heels clicking on the stone floor. I watched her leave, thoughtful for a moment.

'Erik,' I said, quietly enough so that none of the servants or courtiers hovering around the doorway or edges of the room would easily hear. 'Sit with me.'

Erik had been standing at my back, and now he perched next to me on one of the embroidered settees. 'What is it, Nina?' He asked, concerned.

'Where is Rakael?' It took everything in me to keep my tone calm and composed, but I could see the flash of concern in his eyes. I gripped my hands together and forced myself to remain in control, to not let loose the fury which threatened to overwhelm me.

'I'm not sure,' he said awkwardly, 'when I last saw her she was heading into the town, following the prisoners towards the outer walls of the city.'

I nodded slowly, breathing deeply and recalling the sense of calm that Grandfather had tried on many occasions to instil in me. With a commanding gesture, I summoned one of the guards hovering in the doorway to my side.

'Your Highness?' He asked cautiously, 'what do you require?'

'I want Rakael found and brought to me,' I said simply, 'as soon as possible. I am not overly patient this morning.'

He bowed low and departed, the clank of his sword hitting his armour fading away into silence. I stared into the flames in the grate, ignoring Erik's worried gaze until he spoke and the moment of quiet was broken.

'What are you intending to do, Nina?' His gaze was intent on my face, and despite the worry in his expression, his voice didn't waver or tremble. I met his eyes steadily, feeling the sense of tiredness descend once more, even though it was still morning and I hadn't been awake too long. 'Nina?' He pressed.

'Hm?'

'What are you going to do?' He repeated, eyebrows drawn together. I didn't like seeing him look so, it still struck me that he was young– barely an adolescent– and he shouldn't have such burdens on his shoulders. But it seemed that the Gods had different thoughts, they had chosen him to live a life of hardship, like me, and to test him to prove his worth. Who knew what they would require from him once he had reached manhood?

I took a breath and finally said, 'I'm not sure. We need to tread carefully with Rakael, but she needs to recognise that she cannot give orders on my behalf, not unless I have given her leave to do so. She needs to be reminded that she is not in charge of running Scardia, no matter how much she may wish otherwise.'

Erik nodded slowly. 'I don't think she'll take that well.'

'Nor do I,' I admitted with a heavy sigh. I looked back into the flames, lifted my hand and focussed, twisting them back and forth. Erik didn't say anything, just watched as the fire began to spiral and reform, until small creatures were prancing back and forth in the flames and then fading up the chimney in a flurry of sparks. Using magic helped to calm me, and by the time I heard the guard returning with another, sharper pair of footsteps, I was ready to face Rakael.

She didn't stand on ceremony when she entered, halting just inside the doorway and staring at me directly, unblinking. 'Princess.' She sounded annoyed, as though I had interrupted something important.

'Rakael.' I lowered my hands and rose to my feet, so that I wouldn't be looking up at her. I wasn't going to be made to feel inferior. Not after what she had done.

'You requested to see me?' Her tone was slightly aggressive now, expression distasteful. I wondered for a brief moment what I had ever done to cause her to dislike me so, what the monarchy had done to push her to hate us so much.

241

'I understand you've been busy,' I said, trying to keep my expression neutral, knowing that she would see emotion as a sign of weakness. 'I had no idea you would take my words so quickly to heart and be so prompt in your distribution of justice.'

Her mouth twisted into a smile that looked like a grimace. 'I'm glad you approve.'

'I didn't say that,' I said coldly. 'Quite the opposite in fact. You need to recognise that I am not going to be like the Usurper. I will not condone such measures which aim to frighten and suppress the Scardian people.'

Her mouth tightened imperceptibly, and a pulse began to twitch in her temple. 'They were enemies, Princess. They were people who kept the Usurper in power, who obeyed his orders and sought to keep you from regaining the throne.'

'There are many who fall into those categories who were not strung up along the walls,' I said, 'what right did you have to choose who was made a spectacle of? You know me Rakael. You know that I would never support such actions.'

'Forgive me, Princess.' It sounded as though the words were sandpaper in her throat. 'I simply wanted the Usurper's followers to get the message that you were not a weak or indecisive ruler. You've got to make a strong impression to avoid any repercussions.'

Her words pricked my temper but, by some miracle, I kept it contained. Instead, I smiled, albeit coolly. 'I appreciate your consideration of such matters, Rakael. However, in future, I will be the one to give such orders. You need to trust my judgement.'

She bowed low. 'Yes, Princess.' She turned to leave, face turned away so I couldn't see her reaction to my words.

'Oh and Rakael,' I began, and she paused in the doorway, 'I will not be as lenient if you give such orders again. Those who seek to undermine the crown will not be treated with compassion. I do not forget those who betray me so easily.'

'Of course, Your Majesty.' Rakael's tone was muted now, as though she were struggling to contain her anger. Without another word she left, and I felt relief spread through me.

'Erik,' I said, 'let's find Elder Haycin. He needs to be informed about what has happened, although I'm sure he will have already heard about it.'

'You're sure you want to leave the palace? Will it be safe?' Erik asked doubtfully and I gave a short, decisive nod.

'I need to go into the Capital, to help however I can. Besides, even if someone tries to harm me, I'll have my protector close by.'

Erik grinned and stuck to my side as we departed, walking briskly back out of the palace and across the gardens towards the gates. I noted the hanging posts with ropes swaying eerily in the wind, but thankfully the corpses had been taken down. I gripped my cloak tighter around me and moved on, stepping deliberately across the frozen ground. As we passed through the gate, I ignored the guards' looks of concern and gazed ahead.

The fires had been doused from the battle, but the charred remains of houses contrasted starkly against the snow, which lay in drifts around them. The snow was stained from dirt, blood and ash making me feel slightly ill. Despite this, I could see evidence of the streets having been cleared of bodies and debris, with groups of Elves and men still working together to pull heavily loaded carts. We moved closer to them, careful to not slip on the icy cobbles, and I realised that Markus and Aidyn were amongst them.

It was strange to see them together, now that I could remember everything I had done with both of them. Watching them wrenched my stomach into tight knots making it difficult to breathe properly.

'Markus,' Erik called out, 'Aidyn.' In a flash he had left my side and gone over to them, reaching out to assist in lifting some rubble into the cart. Both paused and glanced over, realising at the same time that Erik was not alone.

'Princess,' Aidyn said solemnly, nodding. Markus just stared at me, dark eyes burning intensely. I found myself shivering, but not from the wintry chill.

'Don't let me disturb you,' I said as I drew closer. 'I came to see if there was anything I could do.' I looked away from them, casting my eyes over the square up ahead to avoid meeting their gazes. 'Your men have done well.'

'Thank you, Your Highness,' one of the workers grunted, as he deposited a broken segment of a beam in the cart. 'We'll have the city cleaned up in no time.'

I smiled, a snowflake landed on the tip of my nose and I blinked at the sudden burst of cold.

'Your Majesty.' I looked up and saw Elder Haycin striding towards me from the square, his thick cloak flapping around him. I felt myself relax for the first time in hours and excused myself from the group of workers, hastening towards my advisor.

'Elder Haycin,' I cried, 'I've been looking for you.'

His expression was guarded and he said grimly, 'there are things we must discuss, Your Majesty. Come with me.'

'You can stay if you like, Erik,' I said over my shoulder, 'I'll be safe with Elder Haycin.'

Erik nodded, gritting his teeth in concentration as he carried some of the broken wall to the cart. Aidyn and Markus watched me leave, and I was grateful that Elder Haycin had arrived so soon. I fell into step beside him as we moved back towards the square, passing more groups of workers helping to repair the damage.

'I just heard about the prisoners,' Elder Haycin said under his breath, keeping his tone lowered so that we would not be overheard. 'The guards were saying it was on your orders. Tell me this isn't true.'

'Of course not,' I said quickly. 'Rakael claimed to misinterpret my words. I have already spoken to her about it, but I think it's only a matter of time before she tries something else to undermine me. She might guess that I remember what she did. I'm not sure how she will react if she does, but I'm sure it won't be good.' Elder Haycin nodded as I continued, 'I asked Jesse to spread the word about taking down the prisoners. Those who are still living are to be taken into the dungeons until I have time to decide their sentence. I want you to take charge of seeing that happen, Elder Haycin, and to ensure that Elven guards are stationed in the dungeons. I don't want to rely on the Resistance fighters anymore, not when their leader is unstable.'

'As you command, Your Majesty.' Elder Haycin said. 'I think you will be pleased to hear that the Elves have been working well together. Lord Aidyn and his companions have been key in assisting with that endeavour. With any luck, our peoples will be able to collaborate more in the future, without fear or distrust about the other's motives. Of course,' he eyed me shrewdly, 'an alliance between the two courts is something highly anticipated.'

I didn't respond but halted for a moment, gazing across the square at one of the temples in the city. This one was mainly untouched from the carnage, its spires rising high into the air, the walls decorated with intricate stonework. I knew that Elder Haycin expected the proposed alliance to go ahead, for me to accept the marriage and potentially begin planning a grand wedding. Perhaps it would be in this very temple that Dark and High Elves would be joined, but I wasn't quite ready to take that step yet. There was still much to be done, and I couldn't disregard my conflicted feelings. I also didn't feel safe making such a decision until I knew what would happen with Rakael.

I changed the subject and asked, 'how long do you think it will take to restore the Capital?'

If Elder Haycin was disconcerted by my change of topic, he didn't show it. 'Our efforts today have been going well, as you have noticed. By sundown most of the streets will be clear, although the morgues are over-full. I suggest a state funeral for the fallen. In the Eastern Lands, when one passes they were either returned to the earth or cremated to be one with the four winds. Considering the time of year, I would suggest arranging funeral pyres.'

'The ground will be half frozen by now,' I mused, 'it'll be hard to dig mass graves. If the morgues are close to overflowing then we'll want to act sooner rather than later.' I paused as I watched a child pull his mother's arm, leading her towards the temple where a procession of mourners was congregating. 'Do you think we can arrange for several funerals to be held throughout the city, so that the families and priests are made aware? I'm sure we will be able to organise for some woodsmen to source lumber for the pyres. I want the fallen to be given all due honours.'

Elder Haycin nodded. 'I will take care of organising that for you, my lady.'

I moved on again, 'Come. I must pay my respects.'

He followed me as I led the way to the temple steps and ascended them, stopping from time to time to grasp a mourner's hand or express my sympathy. Under Elder Haycin's watchful gaze I finally reached the doorway and entered, heading towards the altars at the far end. Inside was peacefully quiet, save for the soft whispers of muffled prayers from the mourners, who sat in the pews and laid offerings by the various shrines. As I passed them, some raised their eyes and stared, transfixed. I approached the furthest altar and knelt on the stone floor, not caring about my skirts getting dirty as I bent my head in prayer.

I asked Erthor for guidance and wisdom as I sought justice, from Sybilla I requested clarity. I prayed for the fallen— for Lionus, Lord of the Dead, to see them safely on their journey to the land beyond. I thanked Helebor for his gifts of magic, for entrusting the spirits to bestow power on me. I asked him for strength, for I was sure that my gifts would be needed again soon. I sent out a prayer to the Winter Spirit, seeking counsel for the next part of my journey.

I don't know how long I knelt there, but when I was done, I lit a candle and placed it by one of the shrines. The mourners and priests had been watching me and now they felt comfortable approaching, either to ask for alms, blessings or, in the case of the priest, to thank me for returning to the Capital at last. Elder Haycin remained at my shoulder so I didn't get overwhelmed, and for that I was grateful. At last, I gave him a nod and he led me out and back to the palace.

When we reached the formal gardens, it was almost nightfall and my body was numb. Elder Haycin stopped and said, 'Your Highness, I thought you would want to know that King Aegis has been placed in the Royal Crypt. The High Elves will want to pay respects to him before he is cremated.

He was both a benevolent and wise king. He will be sorely missed by those of us in his court.'

I bowed my head. 'Thank you, Elder Haycin.' As we entered the palace, the sounds of laughter, loud discussion and music met our ears, coming from the dining hall. It seemed as though people's spirits were high after the fall of the Usurper and his Trackers. I came to a halt, suddenly unwilling to go and join them, despite my hunger.

'You go ahead, Elder Haycin,' I said quietly. 'You've been working hard all day, please rest awhile.'

'What about you, Your Highness?' He asked.

'I want to be alone with Grandfather.' Now that I was certain where he had been taken, I needed to see him.

'I'll have some guards keep watch outside the crypt, my lady.' Elder Haycin bowed low and then waved over an Elven soldier, who saluted and followed as I made my way past the dining hall and down the stairs towards the depths of the palace.

The Royal Crypt had always scared me as a child. It was cold, dark and musty, and candelabras dripped wax, flickering with pale light. The stone tombs of my predecessors stretched along the walls, built into alcoves. In the centre of the room was an altar made of Hoarfrost, glistening white. On a dais in front of the altar lay Grandfather's body.

He had been cleaned up since I had last seen him, someone had washed him and changed his clothes. His expression was peaceful, eyes closed and hands clasped across his chest. I felt my breath catch as I stared at him, desperately wishing that he would open his eyes and awaken. There were so many things I had wanted to say, so many questions and answers I still needed. But he was gone– gone to the place which I had glimpsed before the Winter Spirit saved me– and now I would never hear his voice again.

'We had so little time, Grandfather,' I whispered, as I knelt next to him. My legs ached in protest but I persevered, ignoring the pain. I reached out and touched his hand with my own, shivering at its pallid coldness. 'I had so many things I wanted to tell you. I needed to hear why you kept the proposal from me. I never got to hear your explanation.' Hot tears burned my eyes and fell down my cheeks. 'I was determined that you would explain yourself but then…then…' I let out a choking sob, 'I'm not ready for you to go yet. I don't want to say goodbye.'

It was like losing Mama and Papa all over again. The tearing sensation in my chest intensified and I bent over him, sobs racking my frame as I clutched his chest, mourning the last remaining member of my family. After being alone for so long, finding him had been a godsend. It was cruel to lose him so soon, to have only had a few short months to know him and begin to feel whole again. Now he was gone like so many others whom I had loved.

'I love you,' I whispered, 'I don't want to be alone. I don't want to be the last one. I need you to guide me, you knew what was best, even when I thought it wasn't.'

The shadows lengthened on the walls and the candles burned lower, but I didn't move. I stayed there, clutching onto Grandfather and shedding the tears I had kept in. I didn't hear the footsteps behind me until a hand reached out and touched my shoulder.

'Nina.' It was Aidyn, Erik beside him looking worried. 'Come away now. You've been down here for hours, it's late. You need to rest and eat.'

I looked at them, eyes red and aching. I was cold all the way through and didn't think that I could move. A part of me recognised their concern, but another part wanted to stay, to mourn and grieve in peace.

'In the old tales, women would mourn for three days and nights when their loved ones passed on,' I murmured through numb lips, 'they would tear their hair and beat their breasts, weeping over the dead. It was what the Gods decreed should be done.'

'The Gods know that you mourn your grandfather,' Aidyn said softly. 'You don't need to re-enact some old tale to prove that.'

'You don't need to stay down here all night, Nina,' Erik added, 'you can't closet yourself away. You're needed to make decisions and continue to help the living.'

His words, although true, cut deep. I pulled away from Aidyn's hand and laid my head back down on Grandfather's chest, over the place where his heart should have been beating. Nothing but silence met my ears and new tears pooled in the corners of my eyes.

'Nina, you must rest.' Aidyn knelt beside me, carefully enfolding me in his arms. 'You don't want to get sick. You're frozen, come dear heart.' He was warm and I allowed him to help me as I rose unsteadily to my feet.

'Come on, Nina,' Erik said, reaching out and taking one of my hands, leading me out of the crypt. 'Lisette has prepared a tray of food in your rooms for you.' I allowed him to pull me along, but with my spare hand I held tight to Aidyn's gloved one, forcing him to follow and making us look like a strange human chain.

My rooms were warm, the fire crackling in the fireplace and Lisette waiting anxiously, a tray of food on the writing desk. Once I had been guided down into the chaise, the tray was placed over my lap and I began to spoon soup into my mouth. Erik and Aidyn stayed nearby, Aidyn choosing a leatherbound book from one of the shelves to peruse while Erik watched me, both he and Lisette ensuring that I swallowed every bite. As I ate, I began to feel better, slowly thawing out from the cold that seemed to have embedded itself into the very marrow of my bones.

Lisette ducked into the dressing room and I heard the sounds of a bath being drawn. Once the food tray was empty, she re-entered and led me away, shutting the door to the dressing room and leading me into a small alcove where a bath was hidden behind a screen. The water wasn't too warm but I didn't mind, I wasn't in the mood to rest in a bath for too long. I washed myself quickly, wincing as my wounds were rinsed. Lisette helped me to wrap myself in a towel and then began to reapply the same poultice from the night before, wrapping fresh bandages around the cuts. My hair was brushed and tied back, and I was dressed in another soft lawn nightgown, my mother's robe providing extra modesty. Lisette clicked her tongue in approval and led the way back into the bedchamber, before giving me a brief hug and leaving, shooting Aidyn a sharp look as she departed.

Erik had gone in the time I was bathing, and Aidyn was stretched out on one of the chairs, boots crossed in front of the fire and the open book in his hands. It was such a domestic scene that I was struck dumb for a moment, unnerved by it.

'Erik was getting tired,' Aidyn said, glancing up at me briefly from his book, 'he wanted you to know that he would be back in the morning to make sure that you slept well.'

I tried to smile but whatever I managed was wobblier than I wanted. 'I don't need him to be checking up on me.'

'You had us worried,' Aidyn continued as he returned to his page. 'Elder Haycin let us know where you'd gone but it had been ages. We weren't sure if something had happened to you. Erik told me about Rakael.' There was something else in his tone now, and I couldn't quite decipher what it was. 'He told me about what happened this morning too.'

I shuddered, the warmth I felt by the fire suddenly receding as the memory of the swinging corpses came into my mind. I pushed it away, sitting down on the chaise and curling my legs into my chest.

'It was awful.' I swallowed, 'and I was too late to stop them, so many were already…' I broke off, determined not to let any more tears fall. I had wept so much today I wasn't sure that I would have any tears left. Something in my voice made him look up and then he had put the book down and was sitting next to me, holding me again.

'It's alright,' he said, 'you did what you could. That's what matters.'

'I was too late,' I whispered. 'With Grandfather, with the prisoners…there were children there, watching, begging me to help their fathers.' I remembered Felice, her innocent gaze, her faith that I would help and my eyes welled up again.

'I wish you had told me before I heard about it from Erik,' Aidyn said quietly. I looked up at him, confused.

'But I just did,' I said.

'After Erik told me,' Aidyn reminded me before smiling, abashed. 'I guess I must be a bit jealous, I'd rather be the first person you tell about these things.'

'But you weren't there this morning,' I said slowly, 'I barely saw you all day.'

He shook his head, chuckling slightly. 'It doesn't necessarily have to make sense. I just…I like to know how you're feeling first.' He shrugged, 'this isn't something I'm used to, Nina. It's not a nice feeling, being jealous.'

My heart had started beating fast and I didn't trust myself to speak in case the wrong words came out. His hand traced my cheek, wiping away the faint tears that had begun to fall.

'Don't cry, dear heart,' he murmured, 'you'll make everything right. I know you will.'

'How are you so sure?' I asked, mesmerised by the look in his eyes. They twinkled with a soft glow and his smile deepened to reveal something that I had been trying to avoid seeing for a long time.

'Because I love you.'

I bit my tongue to stop myself from replying. I just stared, finally confronted with the truth that I had ignored. I wanted to respond- to say that I loved him back- but I wasn't sure. I'd rushed into that feeling with Markus and now I was scared; terrified even.

The silence dragged out and then the moment for me to answer was gone. Aidyn's expression didn't obviously change but there seemed to be a tightening in his mouth and I saw the shutter come down over his eyes, cutting me off. Perhaps my not replying hadn't been the best idea.

'Aidyn…'

'It's alright, Nina,' he cut me off, 'you don't have to say anything.'

But it wasn't. Not really.

He made to stand up and go but I clung onto his arm, anchoring him to me. He glanced down, surprised, waiting. My mind was spinning, awash with emotions which railed at me for anything and everything – for not speaking up about my feelings for him sooner, for still being confused about Markus and what we had shared, for leading Aidyn on with a marriage contract that may or may not be broken.

'It's been a long day, Nina,' Aidyn said finally, 'it's late.'

'Aidyn…'

'Goodnight Princess.' He spoke formally and extricated himself from my grasp, bowing as he left, closing the door with a sharp click behind him. I rose and moved over towards the bed, before crawling under the covers, wondering why I felt so sad and alone.

Chapter Nineteen

It was as if the dream had been waiting to play the minute I closed my eyes.

Grandfather was strung up next to me in the ropes, high over the throne room. He was battered and bruised, his skin rubbed raw from the tight bindings. He was unresponsive as I called out and begged him to look and see me nearby. Instead, he hung there, eyes glazed and defeated as he vaguely took in the scene below us.

The Usurper's golden hair glinted and he bared a grin up at us, looking like a feral beast. I struggled harder, fighting as the ropes twined even closer around me, suffocating me. One covered my mouth, cutting off my cries and I began to gag while desperately trying to breathe.

'You didn't really think that you could beat me, did you, little girl?' The Usurper called up to us, laughing. 'Did you honestly think that you– a poor excuse for a leader– had the skills to beat me at my own game? I'm not so easily beaten, Wilhelmina. You'll live in fear, looking over your shoulder for me. I will dog your footsteps and make sure you don't find peace. No one will think you fit for the throne, you'll never be able to rid yourself of living in my shadow. Everywhere you go, I'll be there, reminding you of what you ran away from.'

I beat against the restraints, trying desperately to break free.

'You won't have any friends to help you, little princess,' the Usurper crowed, 'just look around you.'

I twisted my head as best I could. The ropes around Grandfather had moved while I had focussed on the Usurper, wrapping themselves around his neck until he swung in the air, like a broken marionette. Beside him were other bodies– Erik, Aidyn, Lisette, Jesse, Dylan, Markus, Keely…They hung lifeless, eyes open and blank, seeing nothing but the world beyond. I fought harder, reaching out towards Erik and Lisette, screaming into the gag which began to dig deeper into my mouth and down my throat.

I awoke then with a cry and retched, rushing to the balcony and coughing up the contents of my stomach over the balustrade. It was still dark and the air was frigid, freezing my bare feet within moments. I gasped, clutching onto the icy stone and hiccupping as the remnants of the nightmare faded and I could remind myself that my friends were not dead, that the Usurper had been incinerated in the Ice Flame. I was safe, for the moment.

I stepped inside shivering, and moved over to the embers of the fire, summoning the flames back to life. Uncontrollable shudders racked my body as I curled next to the fire, wishing that I wasn't alone. I longed for comfort, for someone to hold me and remind me that it had only been a dream. Yet no one came, and so I stayed there, afraid to sleep again in case the nightmare returned. As dawn broke, I forced myself to rise and wash, slipping into one of my mother's gowns of deep burgundy, which was easy enough to do up on my own. Over the top of my dress, I pulled a cloak lined with soft fur which helped to keep the cold at bay. I brushed my hair back and pinned it up, before leaving the room, grateful that few people had risen.

A guard stood to attention outside my chambers, and I inclined my head to him as I passed, moving towards the dining hall. Despite the early hour, some of the guardsmen were already awake and the servants had laid out platters of food on the long tables. I took a few morsels and then sat down at the high table alone. It wasn't long before Erik joined me, looking rather disgruntled.

'I thought you would be in your rooms,' he said as a greeting, 'I was going to walk with you to breakfast.'

'I woke early,' I said, not wanting to linger on thoughts of the nightmare.

'Your Highness.' Elder Haycin paused before my seat and bowed. 'There are members of the court and the Capital who wish to have an audience with you. Perhaps after breakfast you might spend some time in the throne room?'

I nodded, remembering how my father had dedicated time each week to holding audiences with members of the public. It had been something that even as a young child I admired, for he made sure to listen to his people and assisted in solving any issues they had. I wanted to reinstate a similar practice, one where the people would feel comfortable to approach me with their problems, no matter how small, and know that I would listen with an open mind.

'Of course, Elder Haycin,' I said. 'Please spread the word that I will make such audiences a regular occurrence, as my father and grandfather did before me.'

He bowed and moved away, speaking rapidly with a contingent of Elven guards by the doorway. Erik, who had been shovelling food into his mouth while we spoke, glanced up from his heavily laden plate.

'Would you like me to stay with you, Nina?'

I shook my head.

'I'd feel better knowing that you can help with restoring the city to its former glory. The people need more help rebuilding and that is something I cannot easily do.'

He nodded, looking slightly relieved. I smiled, recognising that he would rather be doing physical labour instead of standing to attention, listening to endless requests. To be perfectly honest, I felt a bit of trepidation about it, but was determined to try my best. It was what my parents and Grandfather would have expected me to do.

I noticed Aidyn enter the dining hall, yet he sat at a distant table with a group of Dark Elf companions, leaning towards them and laughing at their discussion. His companions still wore their masks, but Aidyn's face remained uncovered, and I watched him keenly, wondering if he would turn to see me, but he didn't. My chest tightened and I looked down at my plate, suddenly no longer hungry. Erik didn't notice my sudden change of demeanour but remained intent on his own food, rapidly demolishing his breakfast.

Markus and Rakael were seated close together on another table, and I felt Markus' gaze burning into the side of my face. I kept my eyes averted and rose hastily, leaving my plate mostly untouched.

'If you want to finish my food, you can Erik,' I said, and his face lit up. He never had been one to reject second helpings. I kept my back straight as I left the dining hall, making a beeline for the throne room.

I hadn't been there since the Usurper and Grandfather died. Thankfully, when I entered, I was alone. I strode across the marble floor, towards the throne and the Ice Flame. The embers still glowed with pale light, and I could feel the flames lying dormant, waiting for the moment I was crowned to rise again. The familiar pull of magic drew me closer, and I knelt beside the embers, raising a palm over them. Sparks flickered and spiralled up my arm, but my clothing didn't catch alight. I felt my mouth twist into a smile and then raised my eyes to the ceiling, the memory of my nightmare suddenly returning.

The ropes that had been there were gone, cut down after the events of that night. Now I could see the domed ceiling, the paintwork detailing the heavens stretching out. The morning sunlight streamed in through the open windows along the edges of the room, showing a remarkable panoramic vista of the Hoarfrost Glacier and the Capital. It would be a while before the stained glass could be replaced, and so chilly air filled the room. I was grateful for my cloak, pulling it closer around me.

In the city I saw workmen already beginning the reconstruction of houses, the distant sound of hammering rising up to me from down below. I turned away and moved over to the throne, suddenly uncertain. Was I really ready for this?

I shook away the thought and seated myself, arranging my skirts around me. Although the throne was made of finely carved Hoarfrost, strangely it was not uncomfortable. It was cool to the touch, but not numbingly so, and I sat there patiently, waiting as the first of those seeking an audience began to trickle through the doors and line up to speak with me.

I gestured for the first one to come forward, a well garbed gentleman who had a pointy chin and steely eyes. As he neared me, he bowed.

'Your Majesty, I am Lord Tyfe.' I inclined my head politely and held out a hand which he took and pressed to his lips.

'A pleasure, my lord,' I said. 'What brings you here today?'

And so began a long morning of requests, apologies and grievances, some of which were petty, while others more serious. For some like Lord Tyfe, there were issues with land holdings and borders with neighbouring estates, which required a follow up audience with the other party. In contrast, others came to speak of poor crop yields and weak livestock. Only a few came to complain about members of the court– a lady who had stolen another's fan, one who had lured another's chef to work in her own kitchen. With these issues I had little patience but tried to control my temper. By the end of the morning, my head was splitting and I felt inundated with problems, many of which were out of my control to fix. Yet one constant idea remained, each plaintiff expected me to solve whatever issues they had, whether it was possible or not.

When a maid informed me that the luncheon had been served, I ended the audience for the day, thanking those who had come to see me and asking those remaining to return another day. If I had hoped that I would have some respite during luncheon, I was wrong. As soon as I sat down to eat, Dylan came to my side, looking distracted. I smiled at him, not having seen him in what felt like an age.

'Dylan,' I said, 'where have you been?'

'I was helping outside the city,' he said as he began to fill his plate. 'Rakael had me in one of the camps outside the walls overseeing the distribution of the black powder.'

I looked at questioningly. 'Black powder?'

'Do you remember in King Aegis' court when I was struggling with a particular Karshkan formula?' Dylan asked, and I frowned as I thought.

'You said it was something that would rival the Gods' power?'

He nodded. 'I figured out the correct quantities while you were…well, I got the quantities right and it created a black powder. When it is lit it explodes, and Rakael had the Resistance soldiers use it in the attack. I didn't realise how much devastation it would cause, I guess I got caught up in the discovery, in the moment of success when I got the quantities right. And when I walked through the city and saw what happened…'

'You felt responsible?' I prompted as his voice trailed off and he dipped his head.

'I know I wasn't the one who made it happen, but I was the one who showed the Resistance how to make it.'

'I guess that when there's a war going on, many people do and create things that they probably wouldn't during times of peace.' I said slowly, 'it seems to me as though when people fight with each other, they change into different creatures, who are more inclined to be ruthless.'

'I'd always been happy amongst my books,' Dylan said, his eyes still averted from mine, 'until King Aegis and Rakael enlisted my services for their fight, now I feel as though I can't even face people in the street. It's like they know I'm the one who created the source of this destruction…'

'You weren't,' I said firmly, placing a hand over his and stopping him. 'If you spend time blaming yourself for what has happened and what others have done with your work, then you will never be able to stop feeling guilty. You're not the one who began this fight; the Usurper did that when he took power. He was the one who inflicted unspeakable horrors on these people long before the Resistance stormed the Capital. Besides, don't forget that it was Rakael who pushed you to identify and locate those formulas.'

He acknowledged my words with a sigh. 'I know you're right, but that doesn't stop me from feeling guilty.'

I nodded, understanding. 'Well, if you found anything that might help with restoring the city to its former glory in those tomes of yours, then please let me know. Were there any designs or blueprints for anything that could help us?'

He thought for a while, brow creased in thought. 'I remember coming across something. With your permission, I'll set myself up in the library and see what I can find from my notes.' He paused and then added, 'it would be good to feel as though I was contributing something worthwhile instead of something destructive.'

I smiled. 'It would be nice to hear about different concoctions which could help the healers instead of a range of poisons.' I thought about the many wounded, about Keely who had lost his sight and still bore the marks of long months of torture. If Dylan could find something that might ease their suffering it would be a step in the right direction.

He chuckled and wiped his monocle, before replacing it over his eye. 'I'll do my best, Your Majesty.'

'Consider it a royal command,' I grinned, relieved that his morose expression had faded.

'I was also wanting to check on you,' he said in an undertone. 'I understood from Erik that since you came back you had some trouble with your memory. I've got the recipe for a potion which I transcribed from the Karshkan alchemists that could help restore what was lost.'

I silenced him by raising a hand, checking around us to see who was nearby. I didn't want this conversation to be overheard. If Rakael caught wind of what Dylan had found out, neither of us would be safe. Already I was treading on thin ice with her, and I couldn't risk her finding out that Dylan had a way of restoring my memory, even if it had already come back.

'Come with me,' I said, rising and pulling on Dylan's arm, leading him out of the dining hall and towards one of my receiving rooms. As we left, one of the Elven guards rose from his table and followed behind us. Once we reached the receiving room, I closed the door behind us, quietly asking the guard to stand watch outside and to make sure that we would not be disturbed. He gave a silent nod in acknowledgement and stood to attention, one hand resting on the pommel of his sword as he watched the empty corridor.

I turned to Dylan who was watching me, slightly confused at my behaviour, and stated, 'It's not safe at the moment to make statements like that in public, Dylan. There are people around who do not want me to remember what happened in the Underdark.'

He frowned. 'Like who?'

'The person who killed me.'

He eyed me closely and then said, 'you already remember, don't you?'

I nodded. 'But I think that I would like you to make me some of that potion anyway, just in case.'

'Why?' He queried, 'if you remember, you don't need to have the potion.'

I sat down, head in my hands. 'I *think* that I remember everything, but I cannot be sure. Perhaps my memory really hasn't all come back properly, I don't know.'

'I see.'

'I can't allow anyone else to know about this though, Dylan.' I reinforced, 'please don't tell anyone else that you know how to brew this potion. I couldn't bear it if...'

'I'll be discreet, Nina,' he said quietly. 'I'll send word with Elder Haycin when it is prepared. I should have it ready by tomorrow.'

'Thank you, Dylan.' I stood belatedly as he opened the door and departed, leaving me alone. I chose not to remain there however, and followed him out, the guard behind me as I headed out to the gardens. As I descended the steps, I noticed some of the foreign dignitaries- including the Velkranian queen- strolling through the snow-dusted grounds. On seeing me, they paused in their walk and I felt obliged to close the gap between us, realising that the majority of those present were members of the Velkranian court and some of their guards.

Their queen was decked out in finery, her hooped skirts wide and catching on the shrubbery. Her cape was made of ermine fur and matched her muff. Her hair was pulled up into a tight style, interlaced with beads and feathers. I noted the heavy make up on her face, which the female members of her retinue had mimicked. Her eyebrows had been plucked away to almost nothing, her mouth painted red, her face powdered white and eyes lined with charcoal. It was too much for my tastes, but all the same I felt a bit uncomfortable in my simpler clothing compared to the cohort of finely dressed people around me.

'Princess Wilhelmina,' the queen said sweetly, 'please join us. We were just taking a turn around these quaint gardens.'

I forced a polite smile and inclined my head, 'thank you, Queen Wonkila. I would be delighted.'

Oh, thank the Gods that I had spent so many years lying through my teeth until it came easily.

Queen Wonkila smiled back and indicated for her retainers to move away, allowing me a place next to her as we walked. 'It has been such a difficult time these past days, my dear,' she said, once we were several paces ahead of her group. 'I would never have guessed when we left Velkra that there would be such violence within days of our arrival in Scardia. Not that I am displeased that you are back in the court where you belong,' she added conspiratorially, 'but it has been *hard*. We shall of course stay for your coronation.'

I wished she wouldn't.

'But we really must return to Velkra soon,' Queen Wonkila continued blithely, 'this land is far too cold for my liking. It's so … rough. Although,' her eyes lit on a group of Dark Elves heading back to the palace, Aidyn in the lead, 'I suppose there are some advantages.'

I forced my face to remain impassive as her gaze met mine. I wouldn't let her see the reaction her words had provoked in me, the automatic whip of jealousy that had curled around my heart.

'Those Dark Elves,' Queen Wonkila mused, turning back to watch Aidyn and his men disappear into the palace. 'There's something primal about them, isn't there?'

I didn't reply. Primal wasn't the word I would have used to describe them, but the tone of desire in her voice made me uneasy.

'I would very much like to meet their leader,' she continued, 'perhaps he would like to visit the Velkranian court.'

'You could always ask him,' I said, carefully focussing on the path ahead, reminding myself to breathe deeply. I had thought that the fact of my betrothal would be well known by now, although maybe that wasn't the case. It was however, with a bit of extra force that I added, 'but don't be too disappointed if he refuses. We are betrothed.'

Instead of accepting the information and backing off, Queen Wonkila raised her eyebrows in surprise. 'A betrothal? Really?'

'Indeed.' It was getting harder to keep my tone even.

She laughed shrilly and her eyes flashed, amused. 'Oh, my dear, why should that matter? Marriages of convenience are done everywhere. But once you have wed, well, who's to stop you from finding pleasure elsewhere?'

An image of Markus filled my mind before I could push it away and I felt myself blush. Queen Wonkila gave me a knowing smile. 'I would be all too happy to assist you in any way, as you start your reign, my dear. I love to host visitors from foreign lands for many months at a time. Velkra is a lovely country to visit and my court is very welcoming.'

Oh, I could bet it was.

'That is very considerate of you,' I said. 'You must get exhausted from having so many visitors for so long.'

She giggled. 'Hardly. There's something so invigorating about having banquets and parties, isn't there?'

'I'm afraid I wouldn't know,' I said coolly. 'I haven't had the opportunity to host many parties.'

'You have a lot of catching up to do, my dear,' Queen Wonkila said, 'that must be the first thing on your agenda once you are crowned.'

I gave her a small smile, forcing the edges of my mouth upward to avoid seeming rude. Deep down I knew that hosting a large, month-long party would definitely not be first on my list after the coronation. We had almost completed a full turn of the gardens now, and I was unbearably glad.

'Thank you for keeping us company, my dear,' Queen Wonkila said sweetly, 'don't forget to think about my offer. I am *so* very happy to help you in any way.'

'You are most thoughtful, Queen Wonkila.' The words felt like acid in my mouth, but I spoke them anyway, painfully aware that I couldn't risk offending my political neighbours. 'I believe that the coronation will be happening soon, so you will not be inconvenienced much longer.'

'How gracious of you, Princess Wilhelmina,' she cooed, deigning to grasp one of my gloved hands with the tips of her fingers. 'Until then, my dear.'

'Yes,' I managed, 'until then.'

With that and a rather nauseating smile, Queen Wonkila and her Velkranian retinue left me, heading back towards their rooms. I watched them leave, still schooling my expression in case anyone saw me. As I was about to follow them inside, I noticed a flicker out of the corner of my eye. A flash of skirts and long dark hair disappeared behind one of the hedges. I followed, intrigued.

I reached the point where the figure had vanished and looked around curiously. 'Hello?'

She was pressed so tightly against the hedge, standing deathly still that I almost walked past her. Her eyes were squeezed shut and it looked as though she was holding her breath, waiting for me to pass and leave her be.

'Jesse?' I'd never seen her like this before and it worried me.

Her green eyes opened and blinked, registering my presence. 'Oh, Nina, it's you.' She sounded strained, unlike her usual self. 'I was just…I mean, laundry. Yes, I was going to collect the laundry for the soldiers. The maids really need help with…'

'Jesse.' I interrupted her babbling, 'what are you doing here?'

'Here?' She looked confused and I widened my eyes in surprise.

'In the hedge?'

'Oh, yes,' she glanced around distractedly. 'The gardeners wanted some help, I thought I'd do some pruning.'

I stared at her, concerned. It wasn't like her to lie and she was terrible at it. 'Jesse,' I said, 'tell me the truth; what's going on?'

She wilted under my gaze and whispered, 'have they gone?'

'Who?'

'The…' She bit her lip, swallowed and said, 'the Velkranians.'

I peered around the hedge. Most of Queen Wonkila's retainers had entered the palace, although a few guards were dawdling in their wake.

'Pretty much.'

She moved from her hiding spot and peeked around. 'No, no, I think I'll just stay here a while longer.'

'Then I'll stay with you.' I stood beside her, taking in the fear that she couldn't quite hide in her expression. 'What is it about the Velkranians that has you so scared?'

Her eyes flicked to mine and then away again, resting on one of the guards. Her mouth trembled and then stilled. 'Do you remember when I told you I knew what it felt like to try to forget someone?' Jesse's voice was low, almost too low to hear. Before I could reply she said, 'of course, you can't. Sorry, sometimes I forget you don't remember what happened before you were brought back.'

I half shrugged, unwilling to admit that I could remember all too well how Jesse had mentioned it in Markus' ship, in an attempt to make me feel better.

'Why don't you tell me about it?' I said gently, 'whatever it is, it's clearly upsetting you.'

She let out a tremulous laugh. 'There was someone, back in Velkra.' Her gaze remained on the last of Queen Wonkila's guards, who had halted on the top step back into the palace. I looked at him, noting from afar little except for his tall stature and dark hair. Yet Jesse's eyes drank him in as though he were the rain after a long drought. As he disappeared, she pulled back, hiding once more. 'He saved me, many years ago. Like you I lost my parents young. I was raised by a family friend, Barnaby, my mentor and guardian. He relocated to the Deep last year to study the mer-people. But this man, *that* man,' she indicated the palace with her finger, 'he took me to Barnaby. He became a friend– a confidante– as I grew up, and we fell in love. When I was fifteen, he proposed and I accepted, intending to wed after I turned sixteen.' Her mouth twisted and I realised that she was holding back tears. 'There were things I didn't know about him though. He did things, terrible things and I couldn't forgive it. The man he was and the man I thought I knew were two different people. On our wedding day he never showed up. I lost my temper and left. But everywhere I have gone since, he has followed.'

'What's his name?' I asked, 'Perhaps I can request that he be sent back to Velkra?'

She shook her head. 'I haven't spoken his name since I left. I made a vow to myself, to become strong and independent and able to live by myself without needing a man to take care of me. My life changed since I left him, but it has become so much more. Yet he still finds ways to follow where I go. Even if you tried to help, it would only make things worse.'

'Once the coronation is over, the Velkranians should be leaving anyway,' I said. 'Until then, we can make sure that you avoid them. He won't find you.'

Jesse smiled and nodded, faint traces of colour starting to bloom in her cheeks again. 'Thanks Nina, but I won't stay for too much longer. If he's here, it'll only be a matter of time before he finds me. He's persistent.'

It sounded like he couldn't take a hint, but I refrained from saying so. 'Would it help if I had him locked up for something?'

'No.' Her eyes widened with horror as she added, 'that would reflect badly on you and damage your relationship with Queen Wonkila. You can't afford that.'

I had known this, but her initial response still surprised me. I watched her closely and then said, 'you still have feelings for him, don't you?'

'Of course not.' She spoke too fast for me to believe it. 'That would be preposterous.' She glanced back around the hedge. 'It looks like the coast is clear. Thanks for listening, Nina. I think I'll head into the city for a while, I can help with arranging the funeral pyres. I'll see you later.' She didn't wait for a reply but strode off, moving quickly through the snow towards the city gates and I watched her leave, wondering if she regretted telling me so much.

The afternoon passed quickly and as night fell, I found myself seated again in the dining hall, Erik on one side of me and Elder Haycin on the other. I had spent most of the afternoon in the palace discussing key priorities with a scrawny man named Balthasar, the steward. I listened to his advice about the servants, those who were essential and those who still needed to be employed over the coming weeks. I nodded and made notes, instructing him to go ahead with his recommendations. It was blatantly clear that the palace was understaffed, especially with so many people staying there.

As dinner was served, I registered Aidyn sit down with his fellow Dark Elves, and Markus with the Resistance members. There was a hush as the Velkranians came into the hall to join us and out of the corner of my eye I noticed Jesse slip out. Queen Wonkila paused beside Aidyn to speak to him behind her fan, and I heard a high-pitched giggle travel across the room. I felt my cheeks redden as I looked away, anger pulsing through me.

'Nina,' Erik muttered, 'control yourself.'

I clenched my fists in my lap, stifling the sparks which had flown upward.

'Keep calm, Your Highness,' Elder Haycin said softly. 'She's coming over.'

Of course Queen Wonkila would seat herself at my table, it was only polite. However I didn't feel particularly kindly towards her after what I had just seen. Yet I schooled my expression and hoped that no one apart from Erik and Elder Haycin had noticed my slip of temper.

'I couldn't resist coming to join you this evening, Princess,' she said coyly as she reached my table. Her eyes narrowed at Erik, who blinked, frowned and then stood, moving to the other side of Elder Haycin. I missed his presence immediately as Queen Wonkila took his spot, the smell of her perfume assaulting my nostrils. 'I can't believe you allow children to eat at your table, my dear,' she said in a loud whisper. 'I really need to teach you how things are done before I return to Velkra. We can't have the Princess of Scardia associating herself with waifs.' She let out a tinkling laugh and prodded at her food, taking miniscule, dainty bites.

'Erik is my brother,' I said coolly, 'he is always welcome at my table.'

'Don't be ridiculous, Nina,' Queen Wonkila trilled, 'I may call you that, may I not? Seeing as we are to be such dear, bosom friends.'

I almost choked on my wine. Bosom friends? With her? Never in a million years.

'I mean,' she continued bluntly, 'taking care of the poor child is one thing, but letting him eat with you? Is he even of the same class?'

I didn't know how to respond. Queen Wonkila interpreted my silence as confirmation of her own thoughts. 'Of course you cannot allow such a habit to continue, Nina, only your most trusted advisors and royalty may sit at your table. You can't begin your reign getting confused with the class system, it is in place to ensure that the kingdoms run smoothly. You cannot give peasants and servants hope to aspire to something better than what they were born into.'

There was silence on my other side and I could feel the tension radiating off from Erik. I didn't turn to look at him but was surprised that he had managed to hold his tongue, I was finding it hard to hold onto mine. The woman was insufferable.

'I believe in running the kingdom as my parents did,' I said, trying to keep my tone level, 'and as my grandfather did in the Eastern Lands. All are welcome and all have a place here. There are different classes, of course, but I will listen to each person's requests equally. And,' I took another sip of wine, 'if– perchance– a "waif" wanted to aspire to greater things, I would want to create a kingdom where that would be possible.'

Queen Wonkila laughed as though I had said something incredibly witty, but her eyes did not. 'You are amusing, Nina. Why, next thing you'll be pushing for something radical, like allowing women to attend universities. But then we are all naive when we start out in our positions of power, it takes time to truly understand the responsibilities of the crown.'

'In fact, I think women having the option to attend university is an excellent idea,' I said sincerely. 'Although Scardia is not yet in the position to make such changes. Our priority will firstly be on reviving our farmland. We have not had many bountiful harvests in recent years.'

Queen Wonkila wrinkled her nose in distaste. 'I hope, my dear, that you won't become a radical thinker or– even worse– an agriculturalist. Farming is hardly a topic of interest for a young lady of nobility.'

I raised my eyebrows despite my best efforts to keep my features emotionless. 'I want to help my people as best I can.'

'And you will, my dear,' Queen Wonkila patted my hand with her own, which twinkled with heavy jewelled rings. 'Trust your advisors to take care of such matters for you. It's what those men are for. No one wants to have a ruler who gets their hands dirty in the fields.'

I twisted my face into a smile. 'How insightful of you, Queen Wonkila.'

She tittered and eyed me over her fan. 'But of course my dear, it is my pleasure to assist. On another note,' she leaned closer, 'That Dark Elf gentleman we discussed seemed quite intrigued by my offer. Perhaps he will be coming to Velkra sooner than expected.'

Something inside me plummeted to the pit of my stomach. Unconsciously, I glanced away from Queen Wonkila's avid gaze and sought out Aidyn. He was laughing with his companions, much as he had been at the midday meal. If he sensed my gaze, he ignored me.

'He was so enchanting,' Queen Wonkila continued, 'although I understand why you might feel apprehensive about entering into such an alliance. It takes a strong woman to tame one of their kind.' The food I ate no longer had any flavour, feeling instead more like ash. My wine goblet was already empty and I poured some more, trying to block out her poisonous words. 'Not that you aren't sweet, my dear, but you do lack experience. Powerful, compelling men are drawn to like-minded souls. Besides,' she pointed towards Markus who sat by Rakael, 'that one hasn't taken his eyes off you. Although unsuitable for a husband, he would make a suitable companion, if you catch my meaning.' She winked and I rose abruptly to my feet.

'I'm afraid I am weary,' I managed, 'pray, excuse me Queen Wonkila.'

'But of course, Nina,' she said sweetly. 'You need to rest before the funeral services tomorrow, and your coronation, of course.'

'Of course.' I nodded and departed, forcing myself to slow down and not stride out of the room. Once I was outside the dining hall, however, I sped up, leaving my guard trailing behind as I hurried to my chambers. Lisette was still at dinner and I shut the door behind me, panting and shaking from suppressed emotions.

I felt like I was suffocating. I went to my dressing room and pulled off my dress, throwing it onto the ground and untying my corset. Everything was just getting to be too much – the expectations from the courtiers, the people, my advisors and Queen Wonkila. In my mind I saw Erik's face, watching me bright-eyed and hopeful, certain that I would deliver the country from the long years of famine, hardship and strife. My heart panged as I contemplated just how much effort and dedication that would take. I remembered Queen Wonkila's shrill laughter and harsh words, how she had emphasised that I should leave such things to the men to sort out.

But it wasn't just the expectations which were causing me distress. The rampant confusion inside me continued to plague my thoughts, the conflict between two men who were as different as night and day, yet both wanting to provide me with what they thought was best. Now, with Wonkila's words echoing in my mind, I was faced with a new opportunity which seemed highly distasteful. But since she had suggested it, the concept trailed through my mind, tempting me.

It threw me how each time Markus did or said something which pushed me away, he then found a way to pull me back and appeal to that original flutter that would go through me when we met. His approval of Rakael's tactics and aims disagreed with mine, as did the knowledge about his true identity. It didn't go unnoticed that he had been all too eager to throw accusations at me when he discovered who I was, and how he had been hiding the truth about his connection to the Usurper that whole time. If it hadn't come to light when they were captured, would he have ever told me the truth about what happened that fateful night? Would I have ever learned the identity of my father's killer?

And then there was Aidyn. While Markus and I were, as he said, two flames which burned bright, Aidyn was the slow burning ember. He was the kind of man to watch and think before acting, countering my often-blunt directness with smoothness. Yet I wasn't sure how much of what he felt for me was true. I knew that Grandfather and King Lysander had struck an agreement and that I had signed it before my death, but surely it could be argued to be void now. He had said that he loved me, but he himself had told me about the situation in the Underdark, how rare it was for Dark Elves to leave and marry outside of their society, and how the breeders were kept separate. Was I merely a means to an end? A way for him to escape that fate? However, I couldn't deny the anger and the jealousy that had reared its head when Queen Wonkila spoke of him like a potential lover.

I cursed and threw the corset down to join the discarded dress. Dragging my nightgown over my head and tying my robe securely around me, I moved towards the fire and urged the flames to climb higher. Yet I still felt stifled, desperate to escape and be alone, completely alone. Outside, the faint lights from the Capital and distant stars were glimmering, the light from my chambers illuminating the snowy balcony. I opened the doors and stepped outside, ignoring the biting cold and drawing in deep, ragged breaths.

And then another thought cut through the others; was it really necessary that I choose one of the two? Who was to say that I had to rule with someone at my side? Thanks to the Elves in Grandfather's court, I was a virgin again and therefore would be considered pure by the realm. As they had said, all those months ago, there was more power in ascending the throne as a maiden. Why couldn't I begin my rule alone and determine the needs of my people based on my own experience and counsel? The concept both terrified and excited me. But then, if I chose to lead independently, what would happen to Markus or Aidyn? I knew neither would like that option, but would they wait? Would they be patient? My mouth twisted, recognising that– Aidyn at least– had already been so for many months.

'You seem pensive, Nina.' The soft, low voice pierced the air, and I gripped the icy railing tightly for a moment, my fingers going numb. Turning, I took in her pale features, the fine hair and cool eyes, gazing into mine intently.

'My lady,' I said, grateful despite my surprise that she was here. Since the passing of Grandfather, I was in dire need of advice. I had prayed that she would appear, that she would return to help me see clearly.

'It is a cold night for you to be out, child,' she said simply, even though she herself was barefoot and wore only a simple gown. I smiled and shrugged.

'I needed to get away for a while, I hadn't realised how exhausting or confronting leadership would be.'

She nodded sagely, 'it will be at first, Nina. Do not forget that you were not raised like your parents were, with years of training and instruction on how to rule and take care of a kingdom.'

Gods, wasn't I aware of it. Queen Wonkila had emphasised that knowledge even more.

'There is much work to do to help restore Scardia to the way it was before the Usurper began his reign,' the Winter Spirit continued, 'you are aware that the land suffered under his rule. There are some simple steps you can take to help restore balance across Scardia and to assist with the regrowth and rejuvenation of the land.'

'How can I do that, my lady?' I asked desperately, 'I want to help, but I don't know what to do first.'

No one wants a ruler who gets their hands dirty in the fields. Queen Wonkila's voice filled my mind and I pushed them away, resenting them.

'You have already begun to make reparations through rebuilding the Capital and choosing a merciful approach to how you deal with your enemies. The removal of the deceased who were strung up around the palace walls was a key step in forging the trust that your people have in you.' The Winter Spirit smiled at me approvingly and I felt a rush of gratitude, the discussion with Rakael and her insinuations still rankled within me, so it was a comfort to hear that the Gods approved of my actions. 'To answer your question,' she continued, flicking some snowflakes out across the gardens below with a wave of her hand, 'you will need to tap into the natural magics that you learned about in your grandfather's court. You can call on the natural forces to assist in rejuvenating the land, you will need to travel around the country to do so, as this will be a large undertaking. I recommend incorporating it into your Royal Tour, which you will need to do after the coronation.'

I blinked, considering her words and realising how this task would drain my powers, would I be able to cope with it?

'This endeavour will not necessarily yield immediate results,' she said gently, 'it will take time for the land to heal. You will simply be giving it a push in the right direction.'

I nodded slowly, it made sense.

'But I gather that there is more that is weighing on your mind, my child,' she smiled, her hand lifting my chin so that I was looking at her. 'You are conflicted. There is one who has caused you great distress.'

That was one way of putting it.

'I don't know what to do,' I sighed, 'or more specifically, who to choose. They both want me to decide, and I keep second guessing myself and what I feel.'

'Ah, human emotions,' the Winter Spirit smiled, 'over the years I have seen my fair share of them.'

'But you were human once,' I cut in, 'you experienced love yourself, did you not?'

There was a long pause and I looked into her eyes, suddenly wondering if I had overstepped my bounds. Her eyes were clouded, and the snow began to come down around us in thick flurries.

'I was. Once,' she said slowly, as if the memory were both painful and distant. 'Or at least I believed it was. However, I learned that some promises made are not always true.'

I remembered the tale all too well, it was one of my favourites in Scardian lore. After giving her heart to a traveller, the Winter Spirit had been sold out to angry townspeople who had sought to bring her down, the man she loved leaving her behind with a pocketful of coins. However, the story said that he had returned to her, pleaded forgiveness and together they had ventured into the realm beyond, following the Northern Lights towards the heavens. Yet, from the Winter Spirit's expression, I began to wonder if the ending of the tale had been merely that– a tale, a fiction created to appease children's thirst for happy endings.

'Did he not return to you, my lady?' I asked quietly, watching her closely. She smiled sadly, her expression bleak and resigned.

'The man who claimed to love me took the coin he was promised,' she clarified, 'leaving me to the mercy of angry peasants. If it wasn't for my powers, I would have died then, yet the Gods came to my aid, inspiring me with strength. I escaped to my refuge, cloaking my disappearance with a snowstorm which I hoped would stop the townsfolk from following me. To my chagrin, they soon were at my door, the one who was said to love me leading them, torch in hand, sword in the other.' She lifted one of her long sleeves to reveal her arms, which from the elbows up were crisscrossed with white scars, as though someone had sliced them back and forth with a blade. 'He led the assault. My power had only incited the people's fear and his own, and they were not gentle. I came to when they had gone, my home around me was falling apart, and I crawled to the window of my tower and watched as they began to torch the land nearby. I begged the Gods to assist me. My mother and father– Erthor and Fionne– heard my pleas and they showed me the way to the heavens through the Northern Lights. They had been watching over me since I had escaped their home, noting as my powers grew and I began to demonstrate skills they considered useful for being a seasonal spirit. When my father ascended me to that role, I was provided with a way to assist those in need and punish the ones who deserved it.'

'Did you ever learn what happened to the townspeople who went after you?' I asked quietly, caught up in the sad reality of her tale.

'Many lived the remainder of their days in that town, unable to decipher why killing the Ice Queen did not stop the eternal winter.' Her tone was cold and emotionless now. 'The traveller left the far north, travelled throughout the world until he one day settled down in a Velkranian town with a woman who was meek and suffered under his fists.' She glanced down, pulling the sleeves of her gown down, covering the scars carefully. 'When his wife was with child, I could stand back and watch no more. It was no coincidence that he did not make it home late one winter's night from the tavern. They found him the next morning, frozen and alone. It was a kindness I could grant to his widow and their unborn child, and justice for the girl I had once been.'

Her story came to a close and we stood in silence. I was unsure how to break it, uncertain about what to say. In all the times the Winter Spirit had visited me, this was the first time that she had shared something so personal, and I didn't know how to respond.

'But you can learn from my mistakes, my child,' she said gently, 'when words and actions do not align, be on your guard. I told you once to trust your instincts and I would remind you of that now.'

My only problem was that my instincts were sending conflicting messages and it was too hard to understand what they were trying to tell me.

The Winter Spirit smiled and added, 'perhaps you would appreciate it if I could give you a gift. A glimpse of what I see in store for you.'

I gazed at her, shocked. 'Do you mean…'

Her smile widened and she moved her hands in a concise, sharp motion, causing shards of ice to whirl together and condense into a mirror, floating before us.

'I can only show you a moment of what lies ahead, but remember that this is neither confirmed nor certain, it will depend on your choices.'

I nodded, staring eagerly into the reflective ice. The Winter Spirit murmured words in a strange language, making the hairs on the back of my neck stand up. As she spoke, icy runes appeared on the mirror, and I recognised them as the Ancient Tongue, the language of the Gods. The runes vanished before I could decipher their meaning and then my attention was commanded by the image that was starting to appear on the icy surface. I leaned closer, barely breathing as a painful grip tightened around my chest, sending an ache through me.

The image solidified, and I recognised the palace fountain, the spot where the Lord of Summer had visited me all those years ago. But in this vision, he was nowhere to be seen, although warm sunlight was reflecting off the water. Two small figures were laughing, one jumping in and out of the fountain, the other balancing along the edge, arms sticking out to the sides, tongue between his teeth in concentration. I was so focussed on his expression that I almost didn't notice the white melding almost seamlessly in his hair. I felt a tug in my heart and peered closer, hardly able to breath.

'Be careful Gael,' the girl who was splashing in the water cried, her green eyes crinkled with worry as the boy wavered and began to lose his balance. She reached out to help but instead they both tumbled into the fountain, spluttering and coughing.

'Seline,' Gael grumbled, 'I was fine. Just because you're two minutes older doesn't mean you can just…'

'I thought you needed help,' Seline retorted, eyes flashing as she flicked her damp, red hair out of her face. I noted the white streak that stretched through it and my breath caught in my throat. Her brother snorted and splashed her, before leaping away and out of the fountain as she tried to catch him again.

I noted that, unlike his sister, he seemed paler, his wet spiky hair plastered to his forehead. Then his eyes lit up and he cried out, 'Papa! Uncle Erik!'

I followed his gaze and saw two men dressed in dark leather approaching, one who was holding a bundle in his arms, the other who had clubbed back hair and a scar stretching down his face. I stared, as Erik laughed and tossed Gael up into the air, the boy whooping in delight. Seline had struggled out of the fountain after her brother and raced over to join him, pulling on Erik's arm to have a turn as well.

'My goodness,' Erik chuckled, 'you have both grown so much.'

'We're seven now,' Gael said proudly. 'I'm almost old enough to be a page.'

Simultaneously Seline pouted, 'You've been gone for an age. Last time we saw you it was midwinter. Will you stay for a while?' She leaned closer, 'Mama misses you when you're away too long.'

Erik grinned and shrugged, 'I can never stay away too long, you know that. But there are others who need to be helped and your mother is often the one to send me to help them.'

'Like when you helped Auntie Jess?' Gael piped up, eyes wide.

'Indeed,' Erik nodded.

'Gael, Seline,' the children's father chided gently, 'you'll wake your brother. Come now, your mother is waiting, we'll need to get you both cleaned up before dinner.' He stretched out a hand and Seline gripped it, her smile wide as she gazed from her father to the wrapped bundle in the crook of his other arm. I peered closer, making out a small face, eyelids closed in peaceful slumber and a tiny fist that had somehow gotten out of the blanket, gripping tightly to his father's sleeve. I drank in the sight, the sense of rightness that filled my heart as I watched them paused for a moment in a perfect tableau. Then together, the group of four headed back towards the palace and the image vanished as though it had never been.

The icy mirror disintegrated and separated in the wind, and I turned to the Winter Spirit, who smiled at me before saying, 'as I said, what you saw is only a glimpse of what could be. Depending on your choices, this may never happen.'

Something stung my eyes, and I scrubbed at them, embarrassed that tears had risen to the surface so quickly.

'Do you have any more advice for me, my lady?' I asked instead, trying desperately to not let her see my sudden weakness.

Her eyes crinkled at the corners and she lifted my chin upwards, forcing me to meet her gaze. 'I do not need to advise you more, my child,' she said calmly, 'if I remember correctly, you know who your family chose as your suitor. That was a decision long in the making, longer perhaps than you had realised. Some things are fated, and it seems that you yourself understand that.'

I stared at her, suddenly confused. 'What do you mean? My grandfather arranged the proposed alliance with the Dark Elves, didn't he?'

She inclined her head slightly, 'Partially. But the original arrangement was suggested in discussions with your parents as well. When your grandfather rejected a Dark Elf as one of your mother's suitors, it caused resentment to fester between the two courts. On your birth, there was a possibility of building bridges between the two kingdoms and mending the rift that had been formed. Of course, it was not confirmed who your potential groom would be, the Dark Elves were too dysfunctional, too intent on fighting amongst themselves for a clear prospect to be chosen.'

I clutched tighter to the railing as the world around me spun, the surprise of this new revelation making me realise how much more planning had gone into the proposed alliance than I had realised.

'I didn't know.' Was all I could manage to say. 'I had no idea.'

'How were you to know?' The Winter Spirit said kindly, 'your grandfather did not tell you as he believed there was no need. Your parents had no intention of letting you know about their proposal until you were older. And now, you have the chance to form that connection, to help the Dark Elves work their way back to the light.'

I stared at her, slowly processing what she had said. The words that she spoke made me tremble with a premonition of things to come, the sensation that what she foresaw would not affect myself, but the children I had seen in the vision. It made me feel both foreboding and concern for them, along with a desire to protect them, to nurture them so that they would be strong enough to face whatever came their way.

The Winter Spirit released my chin from her cool grasp and stepped back, preparing to leave. 'Whatever you decide, Wilhelmina Fiordlasher, know that I will be watching over you, no matter the outcome of your choice.'

Before I could form a response, she turned with a flick of her skirts and vanished in a flurry of snowflakes. I was left alone on the balcony, with more questions than I had had before her arrival.

Chapter Twenty

The next day passed in a blur. I felt like I witnessed things from outside myself, so caught up was I in my thoughts that the previous day had caused. Seeing Queen Wonkila and Aidyn walking together around the gardens only made things worse.

For the funerals, I wore a black gown, dark cloak and heavy veil, which covered my face from the curious gazes of my people. Elder Haycin and Erik stayed near me, leading me from one funeral pyre to the next, as I summoned the flames to life in each one. Smoke curled upwards into the sky, and the cries of mourners, wailing children and wives penetrated my ears, forming a backdrop to my confused misery.

I spoke formally, impersonally, at each pyre, recognising the fallen and pledging to bring a new time of peace to the land. By the end of the day, my voice was hoarse and I was exhausted, having had to exert a greater amount of magic than I anticipated due to the snow that kept falling from the heavens. Elder Haycin had ended up supporting me on his arm as we returned to the palace, telling me about the preparations for my coronation which would take place two days later. I nodded and agreed to his suggestions, barely registering much beyond the basic details. Instead, the Winter Spirit's words stuck in my mind, contrasting with Queen Wonkila's sweetened barbs from yesterday. Additionally, the image of the twins and their baby brother haunted me and had entered my dreams, allowing me little sleep yet again. When I thought of them, I was filled with a yearning I had never experienced before, one that gripped my heart and encompassed my senses, obliterating all else.

That night I asked Lisette to bring a tray to my chamber and stood by my mother's tapestry, contemplating the two seated figures on the carved thrones. My mother and Grandfather stared out at me, and I wondered what they would tell me.

You know who your family chose as your suitor. The Winter Spirit's voice filled my mind. *That was a decision long in the making.*

Strong, powerful men are drawn to like-minded souls. Queen Wonkila's voice intruded, *you are sweet – but you lack experience.*

I sank down into the chaise, twisting the flames back and forth in my hands before sending them back into the fireplace. The vision the Winter Spirit had shown me had highlighted one thing, a future where those children were a reality.

'Seline,' I murmured to myself, testing the word out on my tongue. 'Gael.' Unconsciously, I summoned the flames back into my palm and I saw them again, two young figures chasing each other around a fountain. I found myself smiling, eyes filling with tears of longing as I watched them greedily.

The knock at the door was so quiet that I didn't hear it, too focussed was I on the figures in the flames. I jumped when a deep voice said, 'Lisette wanted me to bring you this.'

In an instant the figures flared up into sparks, merging with the flames in the fireplace. I held myself still for a moment, calming my heart back down and trying to regulate my emotions.

'Thank you.' I turned as Aidyn placed the tray down on the writing desk. It was the first time we had been alone together since he had told me that he loved me, and the awkwardness was palpable. He nodded and began to head back towards the door, and I felt a sudden panic.

'Aidyn, wait.' He paused, hovering in the doorway, regarding me emotionlessly.

'Princess?'

'Stay a while,' I said tentatively, 'please.'

'The Velkranian Queen has requested my immediate assistance, Princess.' His tone was shuttered, and I felt my anger flare. What game was she playing? She had no right to just sweep in and commandeer him like this. As though what I felt didn't matter, as though I didn't…

I stood abruptly, unable to hide the irritation his words caused. 'I'm sure she will be able to find someone in her own retinue to assist her.' He raised his eyebrows and I scowled, glaring towards the fire, as the flames spun higher, spurred on by my emotions.

'She was most insistent that *my* presence was required, Princess.'

Gods, I wanted to storm right up to Queen Wonkila and slap her insipid face.

Strong, powerful men are drawn to like-minded souls.

Could it be that he actually wanted to go to her instead of staying with me? The thought slipped its way into my mind, making me doubt the certainty I had had in his feelings for me.

'Well, if you want to go to her, then by all means don't let me hold you up.' The words were harsh and bitter, tearing out of me before I could stop them. He was silent, watching as I moved over to the tray on the dressing table where I picked up the goblet and took a shaky sip of wine.

'She seemed to be of the belief that you *wanted* me to visit her.' His tone was cool and hard. 'She was adamant of the fact. Was she correct?'

'If you wish to go to assist her then I cannot stop you.' I said curtly, as I took another gulp. The wine tasted strange, slightly off, but I ignored it. 'You are your own person, Aidyn. I'm not going to control you.'

'You haven't answered my question, Princess.' Aidyn pressed as I drained the goblet and poured another. I didn't respond, unsure what to say or how to say it. 'You should eat as well,' he chided, moving away from the door towards me and taking the goblet out of my hands. 'You shouldn't drink on an empty stomach.'

I glared at the plate but acquiesced, prodding a potato with my fork and taking a small bite. My hunger from earlier had vanished into queasiness, and I blamed him for it. Aidyn watched me closely, brow furrowed as I took a second bite, forcing myself to swallow. Grudgingly I took the plate over to the chaise and sat down, prodding the remaining food with my fork. It was somewhat gratifying when he sat down nearby, still holding the goblet out of my reach. A part of me wanted him to break the silence that now spread between us, but I also wanted the moment to remain timeless, unbroken. For a few moments I could delude myself into believing that nothing was wrong, that there wasn't some invisible barrier between us which I had inadvertently put there.

'Nina.' He was all seriousness and my heart ached, remembering how just a few days ago he had held me, kissed me and his eyes had whispered sweet truths. Now one would never guess that he had admitted to loving me. I allowed myself to meet his gaze, wondering why my stomach wouldn't stop churning.

'Yes?'

'Did you tell the Velkranian queen that you wanted me to visit her court?'

My brain was starting to go fuzzy, and my words seemed to slur as I spoke, 'I didn't argue with her.' His gaze hardened slightly and I blinked, why was it becoming harder to focus on his expression? How much wine had I drunk? Suddenly a laugh bubbled up and escaped before I could stop it.

'Do you find it amusing?' His tone was frostier than I had heard it previously. I wanted to say that I didn't, that I wasn't sure why my brain and mouth were no longer working cohesively, but instead I said,

'She said you were *primal.*' I laughed harder, my body convulsing with mirth.

'Primal?' It seemed as though I had stumped him. He looked confused for a moment, before the emotion faded once more. My laughter turned into coughs and I doubled over, covering my mouth to muffle them and struggling to breathe. When the coughing fit partially subsided, I looked up, lightheaded.

'Sorry,' I wheezed, 'I don't know what's wrong with me tonight.' My hand was damp and I looked down, surprised to see blood in my palm. Aidyn's gaze followed mine, dawning horror in his eyes. 'Oh,' I murmured faintly, 'that doesn't look good.'

I fell back against the chaise, and my plate of food slipped to the ground with a clatter as I collapsed, my throat swelling to cut off my breath.

'Nina?' Aidyn asked, placing the goblet down and gripping my arms. 'Nina?!'

I wanted to ask him what was happening, but I couldn't get the words out. Instead, I made some rather unattractive gurgling sounds which, had I been in my right mind, would have made me want to dig a hole in the floor and disappear. My body shuddered and I knew no more, falling into a dead faint.

Something was flashing above my head, catching the firelight and shining into my eyes. I ached all over, my mouth was dry and scratchy, and my stomach felt as though it had been stabbed from the inside. What had happened?

'She's awake,' a voice said, relieved. 'Your Majesty?'

The world began to slowly come into focus, and I registered Dylan's monocle on its chain peering down at me. His eyes were shadowed, as though he hadn't slept. I opened my mouth to speak but couldn't get any words out, only a soft, strangled noise.

'She needs water,' Dylan said brusquely, and another hand placed a glass to my lips, lifting my head so that I could drink. I realised that it was Markus and allowed my eyes to travel around the room, searching for Aidyn.

'Lord Aidyn has gone to ground,' Markus said curtly, 'your guards are looking for him as we speak.'

I widened my eyes in surprise, confused. Dylan kept quiet, bending over a mortar and pestle nearby and crushing various herbs together. Lisette hovered into view, carrying a pot of hot water over to him, her cheeks pale and eyes red. Had she been crying?

'He poisoned your wine, Nina,' Markus said gently as he urged me to drink some more water. 'If I hadn't been passing the corridor and seen him rush off then who knows what would have happened.'

It didn't sound possible, I couldn't believe that Aidyn would do such a thing. But my head was fuzzy and it hurt to think, so I closed my eyes, raising a hand to my temple.

'Captain,' Dylan said, 'I think perhaps you should go and join the search. Princess Nina needs to rest.'

Markus' expression clouded over and he touched my cheek, the sensation startling me. I pulled back and saw his mouth tighten. 'I'll make sure we find him and lock him up.' With that, Markus left, and I allowed myself to relax slightly. Lisette came over to take his spot next to me, stroking my hair back and arranging a blanket around me.

Dylan met my perplexed gaze and explained quietly, 'I was on my way to give you the potion we discussed when I heard what was happening. There was a loud commotion, Markus was shouting about attempted murder and Aidyn had vanished. I came to help and found you, well…'

Lisette clicked her tongue and he paused, glancing at her. She frowned distastefully as he placed the mixture he had been crushing together into the nearby pot, allowing it to infuse.

'Your body had already tried to purge the poison from your system when I got here. If you hadn't been sick, then I don't know if we would have been able to save you.'

Lisette nodded, biting her lip. Her fingers trembled as she brought the water back. I drank again and swallowed painfully, before croaking, 'I don't believe that Aidyn would do this.'

'It does seem unlikely,' Dylan acknowledged, 'But Markus and your guards are on the hunt for him. I hope for his sake that he can keep out of sight until this situation is resolved. He was the one to bring you your tray, so some will argue that it was easy for him to poison the wine.'

'It could have been equally easy for someone else to poison it before it left the kitchens,' I pressed, turning to Lisette. 'Did you see anything, Lisette? You prepared the tray after all.' Her eyes widened and I realised that my tone might have been interpreted as accusatory. 'I don't believe you would poison me either,' I hastily added, 'but I can't believe Aidyn is responsible. Did you leave the tray alone for any period?'

She thought for a moment and then nodded, making some quick gestures.

'You left it alone for five minutes?' Dylan queried and she ducked her head in agreement.

'Then we need to find out who could have accessed the wine at that moment,' I said, trying and failing to get up, 'We should…'

'You need to rest, Your Majesty,' Dylan interrupted, both he and Lisette pushing me back down onto the chaise. 'You are in no condition to go traipsing around the palace on the hunt for a poisoner.'

'I'll do it.' Another voice piped up from near the doorway and I craned my head around to see Erik, his hand resting on his short sword.

'Erik,' I whispered, and he stepped closer.

'I'll find out what happened, Nina,' he said determinedly, 'I know how to be discreet. Just make sure you don't leave this room. Whoever did this will know that they failed in their attempt and might try again.'

I managed to nod, although privately I wanted Erik to stay as far away from the poisoner as possible too. Erik gave me a small smile, as though he could read my thoughts. 'I'll be careful, Nina,' he said quietly, 'I promise.' And then he was gone, darting out of the door without another word.

'Here.' Dylan was pouring out the steaming concoction into a cup now, 'drink this. It'll help to purge the ill humours from your system and restore balance.'

I obeyed like a child, too weak to argue. The potion was slightly acrid in flavour and I almost spat it out, but Lisette watched me grimly, making sure that I drank all of it.

'That is disgusting,' I finally managed to say. 'What's in it?'

'Well,' Dylan glanced down at the various bottles and jars he had spread out on the ground. 'There are a few dried newts, some calamint and sage, some frost-spider eggs…'

'Actually,' I interrupted, my stomach churning again, 'don't tell me. I don't want to know.'

Lisette smiled and handed me the water, allowing me to rinse my mouth out.

'I also have the memory potion, Nina,' Dylan said, holding out a small, stoppered bottle. 'I cannot guarantee that it will work but…'

'Thank you, Dylan.' I took it from him and then had Lisette open it when I struggled to unfasten the lid. With her help, I sat up and drained the bottle in one, noting that this potion tasted significantly better than the previous one. It was sweet, like honey, with a spicy aftertaste. Dylan and Lisette watched me curiously for a while until I said, 'I don't feel any different. But I think that's a good thing.' I felt relief flow through me, it eased my mind to know that my memories were still there, that I didn't have anything blocked out. I noticed something flutter on one of the hanging curtains, a flicker of pale wings disappearing into the folds.

'I think I would like to rest, Lisette.' I said as she helped me to my feet and over to the dressing room. 'And Dylan,' I turned back and smiled at him as he began to pack up his ingredients into a bag. 'Thank you. If not for you, I probably wouldn't be here. I won't forget it.'

He bowed. 'It's just lucky that I had ingredients on hand that could help, Your Majesty.'

'All the same,' I said softly, 'I won't forget it.' Lisette tugged me into the dressing room and began to change my clothes, preparing me for bed. It took a lot of effort to remain standing, when all I really wanted to do was crumple down in a heap. 'Make sure that there are guards outside when you leave, Lisette.' I murmured, as she led me to the bed and helped me under the covers. 'I won't try to go anywhere.' I chuckled dryly, 'I doubt I have the strength to move far on my own.' Lisette made a motion, gesturing that she would stay with me but I shook my head. 'No, go and rest in your chambers, Lisette. I'd like to be alone.'

Her eyes were worried and she shook her head adamantly. I took her hands and said, 'with the guards outside no one will be able to come in to hurt me, Lisette. Please, go and rest.'

She huffed and I could tell that she disapproved of my request. I hugged her and she gripped me tightly before moving away. She looked back at me from the doorway and then left, leaving me alone. I waited for a moment and then sat up against the pillows, glancing over at the curtains.

'Come here, little one.' My voice was soft and still scratchy from my ordeal. I opened my palm, waiting patiently for the creature to flutter down onto it. The lunar moth's wings flicked back and forth, pulsing with pale light. I cradled it in my hands, careful not to scare it off. 'Is he alright?' The moth sat silently, its antennae quivering. I sighed, 'he needs to stay hidden until we sort out what's happening.'

Aidyn would be good at hiding. I knew that he would use the shadows to his advantage, fading into obscurity until it was safe to return.

'Tell him that there are places he can go,' I whispered, 'the palace is full of secret passageways in the walls. He can use them to keep ahead of the guards and Markus.' The moth regarded me, dark eyes unblinking. 'He has to stay safe.' I reinforced, 'until we can prove that he had nothing to do with the poisoning. Make sure he knows that…I couldn't bear…' I cut myself off, taking a shaky breath before lifting my hands and urging the moth to fly. 'Go and find him,' I said, 'please.'

The moth flicked its wings, the pale glow travelling across the room and then up the chimney, disappearing from view. I lay down, staring up at the ceiling and the canopy above my bed, reflecting on everything that had transpired in the past hours. It was getting harder to keep my eyelids open and so I succumbed to the lure of sleep, hoping that by the time I awoke, everything would be resolved.

I dreamed that I was hiding in the walls, crouched to a hole in the stone, holding my breath and listening intently. Around me the ground was dusty and cobwebs caught in my hair, but I ignored their eight-legged occupants, focussing on the raised voices coming through my peephole.

'I can't believe it.' My father's voice was cracking with fury. 'He's gone too far.'

'My liege,' I recognised the voice as that of Jekyll, my father's Master of Arms. 'There is news from the coast. Lord Niall has sent a fleet of warships flying his colours. They have attacked the shipyards.'

My father cursed, slamming a fist down on the table.

'Vincent,' my mother said, 'be calm. We won't achieve anything if we are guided by anger.'

'He has sent a direct threat to us, Lydia,' Father stormed, 'I should have cut him down when I had the chance but I thought a merciful approach was best.' He laughed brittlely, 'I won't make the same mistake again.'

'Dearest,' my mother caught his arm, her touch soothing him. 'We will gather our troops and counterattack.'

'I can organise the army immediately, Your Majesty,' Jekyll nodded. 'We can be ready to march at dawn.'

'Then do so,' my mother said, 'we must show Lord Niall that we are not easily intimidated and do not take threats lightly.'

Jekyll bowed and departed, closing the door behind him, leaving my parents alone. My father broke the silence, moving over to Mama and enfolding her in his arms. 'The time has come sooner than we expected, Lydia,' he said quietly, his words barely reaching me in my hiding place. 'You have to escape with Nina; go across the Meridian to your father. He will keep you safe there. Scardia is no longer safe for you or our child.'

'I will not leave you,' Mama whispered, her voice catching, 'don't ask that of me, Vincent.'

'You must,' Papa urged. 'When it is safe, when Lord Niall is defeated, then…'

My mother was crying now. 'We are to have another child, Vincent. I don't want to go through childbirth alone.'

Her words made my father pause and then cling her tighter. 'That is all the more reason for you to go to safety, Lydia. Your father will protect you all until you can come home.'

'Promise me that you will stay safe,' Mama whispered, 'promise me, Vincent.'

'I swear,' Papa replied, 'I'll be here when you return.'

In the tunnel between the walls, I crawled away, pondering what my parents had discussed. I didn't quite understand what they had meant, but one thing had clicked in my mind, wiping away most of their words. When I snuck into my room, elation began to course through me and let out a whoop of excitement.

I was going to be a sister, I was going to have a sibling to play with and look after. I wasn't going to be alone anymore.

I awoke with a jolt and a groan, the aches in my body returning with a vengeance. I lay there for a moment, remembering the dream, which I now recognised as a memory that I had pushed away to the dark recesses of my mind many years ago. Perhaps that potion Dylan had given me had indeed worked and was helping me to recall events from my childhood and the dark times which I had tried to keep buried. I had always wanted company, a sibling or friend to ease the loneliness in the palace. It had been cruel that, when my parents were expecting another child, their lives had been brutally cut short. Perhaps that had been why I had adopted Erik, made him my brother so readily. If my mother had borne her baby, my sibling would have been close to Erik's age. The thought made me swallow back tears, understanding why I had repressed the memory for so long.

I sat up and reached for a glass of water, wincing slightly as I drank. My throat was still tender, but my mind felt clearer than it had the night before. The door opened and Lisette entered, carrying a bowl of porridge and a pot of tea on a tray.

She was followed by Jesse, who said, 'it's safe, Nina. We've had the food and drink tested.'

Lisette nodded seriously and placed the tray over my lap, pouring the tea out into the cup. I picked up the spoon and began to eat the porridge, grateful to have a reason not to speak.

'The coronation preparations have been temporarily postponed until you are better.' Jesse continued, watching me carefully. 'Markus is still searching for Aidyn. The Dark Elves are in an uproar, there's talk that they'll fight back if the accusations aren't dropped.'

I could understand why, I was surprised that they hadn't already retaliated.

'Rakael has started organising the Resistance soldiers in case they try something,' Jesse continued. 'I just find it so surreal, in one night everyone is turning on each other.'

I did too.

'He didn't really poison you, did he, Nina?' Jesse asked gravely. 'It's hard to believe the rumours.'

I met her gaze levelly and said, 'I don't believe it. Aidyn wouldn't do that.'

'Of course he wouldn't.' Another voice spoke from the doorway and I looked up, seeing a Dark Elf I hadn't met before. He was shadowed by two High Elves, who watched him warily, hands on their blades in case he tried something.

'Who are you?' Jesse asked, standing in front of me, reaching for her own weapon. 'You are not permitted in the Princess' chambers.'

'We are currently not permitted to go anywhere,' the Dark Elf snapped impatiently, mask glinting. 'I require an audience with Princess Wilhelmina.'

'What is your name?' I asked quietly, gesturing to Jesse to stand down. 'I'm afraid we haven't been introduced.'

'I am Beck, Princess.' The Dark Elf bowed low, raising his fingers to his masked forehead. 'Aidyn is my younger brother. He has been falsely accused. We will not accept such injustice and mistrust from the Scardian people.'

'I know,' I said, hand shaking as I placed the spoon down on the tray. 'I don't believe Aidyn is responsible. I think someone is trying to cause a rift between us and use it to their advantage.'

'We do not take kindly to accusations of murder, Princess,' Beck said calmly, 'my people are much angered by these statements, especially after we lent you our swords in your fight. Aidyn made a vow to protect you and you signed a betrothal contract before the Gods; he would not jeopardise that promise.'

'Please let the Dark Elves know that I do not believe these accusations,' I said quickly, 'I want this manhunt to stop as much as you do. I want Aidyn to be safe.' I paused for a moment, breathing heavily and Lisette helped me to drink some of the tea.

'I will try to assuage their anger, Princess,' Beck said grimly, 'but I cannot confirm that their anger will remain in check. Your people need to find the person responsible soon, otherwise there will be another fight on your hands.' With that he bowed again and left, the High Elf guards stepping hastily aside so that he could pass. I turned to Jesse and said,

'I need you to report to Elder Haycin and send the word that I want this search to be stopped immediately. The Dark Elves are right, we need to get this sorted out.'

'I won't let you down,' Jesse said, and she strode out of the room.

'Lisette,' I spoke quietly to avoid being overheard, 'has Erik found out anything? Have you seen him?'

She shook her head and I sighed, taking another mouthful of porridge. It was infuriating that I had so little energy and it was taking all of my concentration to keep my hands steady. Lisette bustled around the room, finding things to tidy and rearrange. She opened the curtains and I gazed out of the windows, at the heavy grey clouds and swirling snow. There was a crackle as Lisette tossed some more logs onto the fire. She noticed that I had stopped eating and hurried to my bedside, fussing over me.

'Thank you for taking care of me, Lisette,' I said softly. 'I don't know where I would be without you.'

She blushed and lifted the tray away, noting approvingly that I had finished my breakfast. Before I could lie down again, she had returned and lifted me up, supporting me to the bathing chamber and depositing me in the waiting bath. The short walk across the room had tired me and I allowed her to wash my hair, rubbing in scented oils. When she was done, I was bundled into a towel and propped in front of the fire, where she began to brush and dry my hair. I felt myself relax, sinking into a state between waking and sleeping, almost as though I were meditating. The sensation made me pause for a moment and I asked Lisette to bring a bowl of water over. She obeyed, placing it in front of me before continuing with her ministrations. I gazed into the water, my eyes glazing over as I found that state of peace once more, breathing deeply.

Show him to me, I urged. *Show me where he is.*

An image began to reveal itself on the surface of the water, a shifting mass of darkness and shadow. But something was wrong, the image refused to focus, instead a presence pushed back against mine, forcing me backwards.

No. I pressed harder, urging the image to appear and show me what I sought. Yet the darkness wouldn't budge, pulsing across the water, and I began to realise what was happening.

When you have practised magic for a long time, Aidyn had said once, *you can shield yourself.*

Was that the reason why I couldn't see him? Was he protecting himself from being found?

Aidyn, I thought, sending out a silent plea, *don't hide from me. Please. Let me know that you're safe.*

The water rippled and for a moment I thought it would reveal its secrets to me, but then the door crashed open and the sudden noise made me jump, breaking the trance.

'You cannot honestly expect us to just stop the search.' Markus' voice was incensed. I took a steadying breath, closed my eyes briefly and then looked up at him. Lisette had a hand on my shoulder, keeping me seated and giving me a source of strength.

'I do,' I said. 'You've allowed your judgement to be clouded by anger. Aidyn wouldn't hurt me.'

His face twisted and I felt a moment of fear; he was no longer the man I had loved all those months ago. He stepped closer, fists clenched.

'Markus?'

His expression was unrecognisable. 'You didn't see him, Nina. I did. If he wasn't guilty, he wouldn't run away. He's just as bad as those who followed the Usurper, except he tried to worm his way into your affections first. He deserves the same treatment as those other traitors. Rakael was right.'

'What are you talking about?' I demanded, shocked. 'What do you mean, Markus?'

He gazed at me, unsmiling and cold. 'I don't think you understand, Nina,' he said, 'With the agitators gone, you and Rakael will be able to get more done more quickly. You'll be able to step down without fear of another uprising, now that the Usurper's main supporters have been dealt with. If Aidyn wants to cause a rift between Scardia and the Dark Elves, then he should be treated with the same swift justice when he is caught.'

I watched him, feeling myself go pale. It was as if he had begun to speak a different language, I couldn't understand him. 'How can you say that?' I asked, 'I thought that you would see the similarities from when your uncle took over and what has happened here. I don't want to start my rule the same way; I want to forgive, not exact vengeance.'

'And yet I remain unforgiven,' he said bitterly. I stared, astonished that he could expect me to forgive him and move on from what I had discovered so quickly. Lisette gripped my shoulder, and I realised that she was unaware of what had passed between Markus and I.

'You did something heinous,' I said slowly, 'it isn't something that I can forget. I told you that I needed time.' His glare shook me, and I continued, 'I don't want the distrust between humans and Elves to carry on. You need to stop hunting Aidyn down so we can figure out what really happened.'

My words only incited his anger further and he stepped forward, fists clenched until the knuckles were white. It was as though he were preparing to strike me. 'I am trying to keep you safe, Nina,' he snapped, 'how can you not see that?'

'He wouldn't hurt me, Markus.' I repeated, eyeing his fists as they drew closer. 'And neither would you.' I could feel Lisette's body radiating with tension, her grip was painful and

I sensed that if Markus took another step towards us, she would rush at him.

Markus stopped, looked from me to his hands and then left as abruptly as he'd entered, leaving us trembling in shock.

'Help me get dressed, Lisette,' I finally managed to say, and she helped me to my feet. 'I'd rather not be wearing a towel if we have any other unexpected visitors.'

Markus' appearance had shaken me more than I would have guessed, and the image of his clenched fists as he approached lingered in my mind's eye. I didn't want to dwell on what might have happened if he hadn't stopped, if his anger had continued to control him. It was enough to turn my blood cold.

Chapter Twenty-One

By nightfall, I was feeling much better. Lisette hadn't left my side all day, except to get me more food and restorative brews. Elder Haycin and Dylan had checked on me during the late morning, but there had been no sign of Erik and I couldn't help but start to feel worried about his delayed absence. When the evening meal had been cleared away, I couldn't hide my concern any longer. It wasn't like Erik to disappear, something wasn't right.

I was distracted from my thoughts by a soft knock at the door. Lisette opened it to reveal Stefan, who eyed me nervously.

'What's wrong, Stefan?' I asked, wondering what had brought him to my rooms. He had always been awkward around me and so I smiled at him, hoping to make him feel more at ease. If anything, my smile made him cringe away.

'I came to get you, Your Majesty.' His voice was low and trembled slightly. 'Erik is…he needs you to come to join him. Alone.' He shot Lisette a look as she made to tie her cloak around her shoulders. She raised her eyebrows, shaking her head in flat refusal.

'Did Erik send you to me with this message?' I asked calmly, my mind working quickly. His breathing hitched and he gave a jerky nod, but his eyes glanced downwards and away, unable to make contact with mine.

'Lisette, stay here.' I instructed, 'wait for me outside, Stefan. I will join you shortly.'

He nodded and ducked out of the door, and I turned to Lisette, motioning for her to come closer. 'I will need my outdoor things. And my dagger.' Lisette frowned but obeyed, her mouth pursed in disapproval. 'I need you to let Elder Haycin know about this, Lisette.' I whispered, 'Stefan's clearly lying through his teeth, but I think Erik might be in trouble. If I must go alone to ensure his safety, then I will.'

She nodded and handed me my dagger to strap to my thigh. I gripped the handle, feeling a sense of comfort from its well-worn leather, and allowed her to fasten my cloak. 'Let him know as soon as the coast is clear.' Lisette gave another short nod and then I left, following Stefan as he led me down the corridor. The Elven guards made to join us, but I indicated for them to remain, ignoring their confused glances.

Stefan walked fast and I couldn't keep up, my strength was still not back to normal. When he realised that I wasn't keeping pace with him, he glanced back impatiently.

'Where are we going?' I asked carefully, as we began to ascend one of the winding staircases.

'He's at the top of the highest tower,' Stefan said miserably. I didn't bother to ask him why.

'And who is with him?'

Stefan's eyes widened but he didn't answer, I didn't expect him to. Whoever it was clearly scared the boy and I was starting to suspect who. We continued up the stairs, needing to pause more often as I ran out of breath quickly. Eventually we reached the ladder which would lead up to the top of the tower. Once there, Stefan glanced at me worriedly, then began to climb without a word. Sighing in resignation, I followed on his heels, thinking that this would be the perfect opportunity for someone to strike me down. I held my breath as Stefan disappeared through the trap door, and prepared myself for an ambush.

To my surprise, the blow to my head never came. But I felt the tension in the air and I turned, hand hovering over my dagger. There was a muffled cry, and I saw Erik on the far edge of the tower, struggling to break loose from the tight ropes which strung him up to the eaves. Stefan stood beside me, frozen, staring from Erik to the figure who was sitting in a chair, watching us.

'I was wondering when you would get here,' Rakael said coldly, 'you took your time.'

'Let Erik go,' Stefan said, 'you said if I brought the Princess alone then you would release him.'

Rakael watched him, unsmiling. Her expression reminded me of how she seemed before she stabbed me in the Underdark, and I gripped my dagger.

'I could,' she mused, twisting something long and shiny in her hands. 'Or I could just get rid of the witnesses.' She lifted the strange device and a loud explosion echoed around us, making the ground tremble. I covered my ears and screamed as Stefan slumped beside me, shuddering as he clutched his side, where a pool of dark blood was starting to spread.

'Rakael,' I said when the ringing in my ears had stopped, 'what are you doing? This is madness.' I knelt beside Stefan, who moaned in pain, and pushed his hands down over the wound.

'How fascinating,' Rakael was examining the device in her hands and I heard the awe in her voice. 'This will herald a new age for Scardia. We will be unstoppable.' She laughed, 'who could have guessed that that idiotic scholar would locate the blueprints for something so useful?'

Oh, by the Gods. What had Dylan done?

'What do you want, Rakael?' I asked, forcing my voice to remain steady. 'You've already tried to kill me once without success.'

'Twice, actually,' she said casually. 'How was I to know that Lord Aidyn would force you to vomit most of the poison? Luckily Markus saw him and jumped to conclusions, so that provided a good distraction.' She eyed me shrewdly, 'I thought you remembered more than you were letting on. But when I heard Dylan mention a memory potion, I thought it was best to act sooner rather than later. I don't like to take chances.'

'You must have been disappointed when that failed too,' I said through gritted teeth, my eyes not leaving the strange contraption she held, which now was pointed at me.

'I will endeavour to not fail a third time,' she said.

The question burst out of me before I could stop it. 'Why, Rakael? What have I done to you? Why are you doing this?'

Her eyes blazed. 'Because Scardia will be better off without a weak monarch. The country should be led by the people, for the people. Everyone will be equal, there won't be a class system to keep us segregated. Your family continued that tradition, of overlooking the poor and the weak and supporting the wealthy. The Usurper made it worse. Scardia should be free. My husband, bless his soul, was part of a group who promoted a Scardia of equality and strength, without a corrupted leader having sole power.'

I blinked, shocked at her radical ideas; what she was saying didn't sound like how I remembered my parents at all.

'But that's only part of it, Princess,' she snarled. 'You've not had to work for leadership. You expect everything to be given to you— respect, wealth, power. You spent most of your life running away, too cowardly to fight back. You're not worthy to lead Scardia. In time the people will understand that.'

'I have worked hard.' The injustice of her words struck me and I felt my control on my temper slipping and sparks flew up from me. Rakael laughed.

'Don't think a fire show will scare me, Princess. I've been burnt before and I came out stronger.' She indicated her scars, 'these remind me every day of what I lost, but also what I have achieved. And if you think that you– an insignificant girl– can stop me now, then you are mistaken.'

There was a crash as the trapdoor opened behind me and two figures crawled out, startling me. They seemed to be equally surprised to see us, so intent had they been on chasing and evading each other. I jumped to the side and rolled away as the device in Rakael's hand exploded again. Part of the stonework shattered behind me, and I cried out.

'Just in time,' Rakael smiled. 'I was wondering when you two would show up. The Princess' two swains can never be too far behind her.'

'Rakael,' Markus gasped, 'what are you doing?'

'Isn't it obvious?' Aidyn retorted angrily.

'You said that you wouldn't hurt her.' Markus stepped closer and I felt my heart drop. 'You promised me, Rakael.'

'Markus,' I began, 'you didn't...'

'He has been most helpful, Princess,' Rakael said sweetly. 'It's incredible what people are willing to do when they care about another.' Her gaze went from Markus, to me to Stefan. 'But it does get quite tedious watching you try to decide who to choose, so I'll make it easier for you.' She looked at Aidyn, 'I never liked you, Lord Aidyn but your men were necessary. And now you've fulfilled your purpose.'

Before he could move, there was another explosion and Aidyn crumpled to the ground. I screamed again and rushed to him, falling onto the stone floor and cradling his head. His breath was coming out in shallow gasps and his face was scrunched up with pain as he held the wound in his chest.

'Markus,' I cried, 'help me.' I glanced up and froze when I saw the device aimed at me again. Rakael's smile was wider now, teeth bared, and I shivered.

'It really is incredible what that black powder can do,' she mused, 'I wonder if it will grant you a quick death or a slow one.'

'You said that we would be able to leave Scardia,' Markus said doggedly, moving between us and raising his blade. 'You don't have to do this Rakael.'

Rakael watched him with a strange curiosity, almost as though he were a scrawny dog that kept coming back for scraps after being kicked away. 'Oh, but I *want* to, Captain. And I would have thought that an expert liar like yourself would be able to sense when someone wasn't being truthful with you. Such a shame.'

There was another blast and it was Markus' turn to fall.

'What a waste,' Rakael said dispassionately as she stood and looked down at him. I leapt to my feet, anger lending me strength, and hurled a ball of fire towards her. She dodged, chuckling and drew a curved blade from her belt. 'Remember this, Princess?' She crowed as we began to circle each other around the edges of the tower. 'I thought it only fitting that you be killed a second time with this sword.'

'You're insane,' I gasped as I evaded a wide swipe of the blade. 'I knew you were ruthless, Rakael, but I never thought you were crazy.'

She laughed again and our blades clashed, the force jarring my arm and making me wince. Sensing my weakness, she pushed harder, twisting the blade and almost dislodging it from my grip.

I was reminded of when we would train in Grandfather's court, but this time she fought with deadly intent, eyes boring into mine and mouth contorted in a horrific smile. This time I fought back with desperation, aware that one wrong move would result in my death. Out of the corner of my eye I saw Erik struggling to break free of his bonds, and those who had fallen lay still, clutching their wounds.

I blinked and my dagger was flying out of my grip, landing under Erik's dangling feet. In another moment, the curved sword was pressed to my throat and I felt a trickle of blood drip down onto the blade.

'Never let your guard down, Princess,' Rakael hissed, 'you always were too easily distracted. You never learn, do you?'

'Neither, it seems, do you,' I whispered. I let flames envelop my body, spreading along my arms and legs, until they passed from me to her, catching onto her clothing and wrapping their tendrils around her neck.

Rakael let out a harsh cry and staggered backwards, the sword dropping to the ground. She stared at me through the flames as they rose higher, accusing me of all the wrongs she had suffered, and a small part of me felt a pang of mercy— a desire to douse the flames and help her to heal. But then she lifted the strange contraption and fired, although this time it wasn't aimed at me.

Time seemed to slow down as I watched the round metal ball fly through the air, cutting through the rope holding Erik to the rafters. The wind was picking up and he fell, out and over the side of the tower.

I didn't stop to think. I didn't hear Rakael's final laugh as I pushed her aside, not caring as she toppled after Erik, the fire encasing her body. I didn't even look back at Markus or Aidyn or Stefan.

I didn't think. I just jumped.

Chapter Twenty-Two

I heard stories later about what happened that night; about how the Ice Flame lit up the sky, burning through the snowstorm that had blown in from the mountains. Some spoke of a creature with wide, fiery wings which dived down from the tallest tower, catching one of the figures plummeting to the ground. Others said that an angel came from the heavens to save him, catching the undercurrent just in time to avoid both of them hitting the earth. The same could not be said for the other one who fell, the Resistance Leader who had been responsible for plotting to overthrow the crown and to cause a new war with the Dark Elves.

For me, however, I knew the truth. Just like before when the Ice Flame had imbued me with its power, once again it came to my aid. My mind focussed only on Erik as I leapt over the edge of the tower, ignoring the frigid air and howling wind. I reached out, time fading into an age as my fingertips scrambled to catch hold of him. After two attempts I succeeded in gripping his arms, pulling him to me as I let out a loud cry, feeling the fiery wings rip out of my back, lifting us up towards safety. His eyes were squeezed shut in terror, but as he felt the change in momentum they opened, and he stared at me, tears of relief and shock mingling together.

'It's alright, Erik,' I said, the wind tearing my words away. 'I've got you.'

I held on tightly as we began to sweep back up to the tower, noting the cries and shouts from the guards on watch as we passed them. We landed beside Stefan, who picked up my knife and began to cut through Erik's bonds. The adrenaline was fading and I sensed the Ice Flame retreating back into me, the magic fizzling out until I was no longer encased in the fiery glow. When his gag was removed, Erik got shakily to his feet and rushed at me, hugging me until I thought the breath would leave my body.

'You saved me, Nina,' he whispered into my neck, and I was suddenly struck with how much he had grown in the last months. How was I only noticing it now? 'I thought…'

'It's alright,' I soothed, stroking his hair with one hand. 'You didn't expect me to let my favourite protector leave me all alone, did you? You said it yourself, we have to stick together. No matter what.'

I didn't want to dwell on how close the ground had been, on how close I had come to losing him, and myself. I had lost one sibling before they were born, I was not going to lose another.

The sound of the trapdoor being opened made me glance up, and I saw Elder Haycin, Lisette and several guards spill out, weapons in hand. Elder Haycin took in the bodies and immediately began barking orders, ensuring that the guards carried the men and Stefan downstairs to the infirmary. Lisette hurried over to Erik and I, enfolding us both in her arms and crying silent tears.

'Lisette, we're fine,' Erik grumbled, trying and failing to pull away from her. Then she saw the cut along my throat and began to make gestures which were too fast to interpret.

'Your Highness,' Elder Haycin came over, 'are you alright? What happened?'

I bent to pick up my dagger and returned it to my thigh, saying, 'Rakael was behind the poisoning. She pushed for us to distrust the Dark Elves and attacked us.'

'And where is she?' He asked tentatively. I pointed to the side of the tower and began to shake, the shock setting in.

'She fell.' I didn't want to admit to pushing her, albeit by accident.

Elder Haycin gave me a shrewd look and then nodded, choosing against asking anymore questions. 'Let's get you both back to your chambers, you need to be tended to by a healer and then you must rest.'

I acquiesced and allowed him to lead the way down the ladder to the twisting staircase, wondering if I would ever be able to climb up the tallest tower again without being haunted by Rakael's maniacal smile.

It took close to an hour before Lisette was satisfied that Erik and I were safe and adequately looked after. She hovered over us as the healer tended to our injuries, forcing us to stay seated and drink cup after cup of mint tisane.

'How are the others?' I asked the healer, 'will they be alright?'

The healer was silent for a while and my stomach clenched with anxiety. 'The wounds were unlike what we have seen before,' he finally said, 'I understand Elder Haycin sent some men to retrieve the weapon that was used. We will want to examine it.'

'But will they survive?' I pressed, gripping Lisette's hand until my knuckles were white.

'Lord Aidyn and Captain Markus both lost a lot of blood, Your Highness,' the healer said gently. 'They haven't woken up yet, but I am confident that they will, in time.' He took in my expression and added, 'you will need to rest as well, Your Highness. You have gone through a lot in the past twenty-four hours, you need peace and quiet.'

I didn't think that I would get any peace when the image of Markus and Aidyn's bodies were still imprinted in my memory. Lisette squeezed my hand reassuringly and I met her gaze, finding strength in it. Erik sat on my other side, not speaking, but he reached out to take my other hand in solidarity.

'I must leave you, Your Highness,' the healer said. 'I must tend to the other patients. Pray, excuse me.'

'Of course,' I said automatically as he bowed, 'thank you for all of your help.'

When he had departed, I pulled my robe tighter around myself, shivering. Erik knelt by the fire, gazing into the flames with a shuttered expression, his mind elsewhere. Lisette drew out a ball of wool and began knitting, the needles clicking back and forth in the silence. We stayed like that for a while, and I didn't want to be the first one to speak. I was grateful for having them both there, but a part of me thought that if I started to voice aloud what had happened that night then my grip on my emotions would splinter and break apart, like a shard of ice.

I thought about what Rakael had said, about how she had played us for fools. I wondered how Markus had believed her promises and how Stefan had fallen victim to her game. His presence raised a question and so I finally broke the silence and asked,

'Erik, how did Rakael capture you? How did Stefan get involved?'

Erik blushed and glanced down at his hands, which clasped his knees tighter to his chest. 'I was reckless. I followed her, a part of me suspected that she might know who was responsible. But she knew that I was there and caught me off guard. Stefan saw me and came to see what I was doing and then he got caught too. If he hadn't been there then I could have fought her but she…'

'She knew how to play on your weaknesses?' I was starting to understand, albeit a bit late. I wondered whether Erik was aware of the secrets his expression was revealing.

Erik blushed again and glared at his knees. 'I'm not weak.'

'No,' I said softly, 'I know you're not. But when we care about others it's harder to be single minded when you fight. The need to protect is strong and can be used against you. Once someone knows the desires of your heart they might use it as a weakness.' He stilled, as though my words had some deeper meaning that only he understood.

'So, it's better not to care?' His voice was harsh and I shook my head.

'Erik, love doesn't make you weak. It just changes your perspective on what is important.' I glanced at Lisette, wishing that she could speak up and support me. Instead, she put her knitting down and drew Erik into her arms, holding him like a mother would a child. 'I'm just grateful that she didn't hurt you,' I said gently.

'She said that I was bait,' Erik muttered into Lisette's shoulder, 'like a bloody worm on a hook. I could've fought her, but she disarmed me and used my blade on Stefan. It was just like that time with the Tracker all over again.'

'She was very skilled, Erik,' I said carefully. 'There was a reason why she led the Resistance and was in charge of the training drills. She could have helped us make the country better, but something in her snapped. She was insane.'

Lisette nodded and pulled me into the hug with one arm, so that she held us together by the fireplace, almost as though we were a family. It struck me then that we had become one over the past months. I might have lost my parents and unborn brother or sister, but with these two beside me, I realised that I had gained another family. One that wouldn't fall to the Usurper and his minions.

'I was scared that I'd lose you,' I continued, 'when you fell, I...' His eyes were staring into mine and I knew that he understood what I wanted to say. 'If I can, I will always try to help you.' I whispered, 'because I know you would do the same for me.'

He gave a jerk of his head in assent, and I caught a glimpse of the man I knew he would grow to be. It gave me hope.

'Lisette,' I murmured, 'do you think you could let us go now?'

Erik's mouth stretched in a grin as Lisette frowned and then released us. 'I should probably go to bed. Elder Haycin mentioned that he wanted me to report to the barracks tomorrow morning.'

'Goodnight then,' I said, wondering how many hours remained before dawn. I was certain that sleep would evade me should I try to rest. Erik stood and headed out, pausing briefly in the door to say,

'Thanks Nina, for, well, you know.' He blushed again and then strode away, leaving me unsure about what he'd been thanking me for. Meanwhile, Lisette seemed to take his departure as a sign that I too needed to get into bed and so began to hustle me over to it. I clambered under the covers and watched her hang my robe over the chair and bank up the fire. When she saw that I was still awake, she came over and sat beside me, stroking my hair until I drifted off to sleep.

Two days passed and I wasn't allowed to go and check on Markus or Aidyn. The healers were tight-lipped about their condition, and I began to fear the worst. To take my mind off it, I spent time with Dylan, who had taken it upon himself to break apart the strange contraption Rakael had used and then rebuild it, finding the blueprints amongst her belongings. The Resistance was leaderless, and I was pleased when two men named Ryan and John proposed disbanding it so that those who had homesteads could return to them. I offered those who had fought a place in the barracks, for I would need to have soldiers. By the end of the second day, almost half of the Resistance had moved out of the palace, preferring to stay in the outer camps and Capital, still assisting with rebuilding efforts in the meantime, but wanting to leave for their own homes after my coronation.

I avoided Queen Wonkila and her retinue, finding my time taken up with preparations for the coronation with assistance from Elder Haycin and the Temple's High Priest. I had been seen to by a range of seamstresses, who had worked day and night on preparing a new gown for the event, a decadence which I did not want but was flatly told was an expectation. Throughout all these events, Lisette stayed nearby, and Erik popped in and out as he was tasked with assisting more frequently in the barracks. Although I found myself missing his presence, I was pleased that he was being treated more like a page, helping to carry, clean and prepare armour and weapons for the palace knights. It seemed, at least from afar, as though having these tasks was helping him to keep his mind off what happened with Rakael. At mealtimes when he sat beside me, he spoke only of his new duties, much like he had back when we had been in Grandfather's court, as though nothing troubled him. But deep down I wondered if he really was as sanguine as he appeared and hoped that if he felt the need to talk then he would know that I would be there. I noted that he and Stefan seemed to remain separate, Stefan remaining with the Elven guards while Erik ingratiated himself with the palace ones. Elder Haycin had mentioned to me that once the coronation happened, the majority of the Elves would return to the Eastern Lands, save for those who chose to remain to help reinstate peace across Scardia. He explained that the Wood Elves had already departed, the cold climate and large crowds being too much for them. Apparently, they preferred to live a solitary life in their forests, and there was tension between themselves and the Velkranian queen. It made me wonder if Velkra really was as secure and perfect as Queen Wonkila made out, or if there were other troubles hiding under the surface.

This news, although not unexpected, brought a pang of remorse. I trusted the Elves more than the disbanded Resistance members but knowing that Elder Haycin would stay until I had chosen my own council brought some relief.

'I will remain with you until you no longer require my services, Your Majesty,' Elder Haycin reinforced, 'but we also must have a steward in the Eastern Lands, watching over the High Elves, since you will be based here.'

I bowed my head, recognising that I would trust him to act in that role, but I was not ready yet for him to return across the Meridian. A part of me wondered if I ever would cross it again, and see the Elven court and the bustling streets of Lowton in the distance.

'Thank you, Elder Haycin,' I murmured.

'My men also brought word that the camps around the city are being disbanded,' he continued, 'I understand that one of the infirmary patients was requesting to speak to you. I had one of the guards escort him to your salon where you would be less likely to be disturbed.'

I smiled and nodded again, 'I'll go and check on him.'

'Be gentle with him, Your Majesty,' Elder Haycin added as I made to depart, 'he has been through much at the Usurper's hands.'

I strode away, heading towards the salon where Erik and I had taken shelter a few short days before. As I opened the door, the waiting guard stood to attention and bowed.

'Your Majesty,' he said politely, 'thank you for answering the summons so promptly.'

'Milady?' The man sitting on one of the chairs looked around eagerly.

'Keely,' I said gently, moving next to him and taking one of his outstretched damaged hands in my own. 'Thank you for coming. How are you faring?'

As soon as the question left my mouth I regretted it. His smile faltered slightly and then turned wry as, with his free hand, he indicated the bandage over his eyes.

'It's taken a while to get used to not being able to see what's going on around me, it has,' he said. 'But the healers have done what they can to heal some of my injuries.'

He definitely looked better than he had when I last saw him. His cheeks were less hollowed, the wounds faded away to pale scars and he had been dressed in new clothes. His hair was clean and pulled back, and I felt a pang as I remembered how he had been in Little Fleming all those moons ago, someone who inspired fear and respect. Now, whilst certainly a wraith of that man, he did appear to be imbued with a new strength, one that was unbroken despite the torture he had suffered.

'Lisette has come to see me from time to time,' he continued, oblivious to my thoughts. 'At least, I have been told that it's her. Every time I try to speak to her, she cannot answer.'

'Yes,' I said softly, 'she's mute.'

He nodded sadly. 'Do you remember how she would sing? When I heard she wasn't a budgerigar anymore, but an Elf, I thought that she must have such a beautiful voice. Ah well.'

I gripped his hand and said, 'she can communicate, just without words. Lisette finds ways to be understood.'

'Whereas I cannot see.' He sounded bitter now.

'You need to learn how to see without your eyes, my friend,' I said gently. 'I remember that you had that ability to see beyond what the average person could in Little Fleming. I know that you will be able to do it again.'

'Perhaps, but without my sight I don't know how I can be useful to you, Milady.' He looked downward, embarrassed at his new weakness. 'I was thinking that maybe I should leave, go someplace where I won't be a burden.'

'Oh Keely, you will be one of my guards of course,' I smiled, tilting his head towards mine. 'You always were the best bouncer in Little Fleming. It will be hard at the beginning but I'm sure that you will be able to develop your other senses to compensate for your sight. The Gods saved you for a reason, Keely. I have faith in you, just like you had faith in me.'

'Milady…'

'I don't want you to argue, Keely,' I said firmly. 'Besides, I doubt Lisette would let me live in peace if I allowed you to creep away in the night.' I reflected on Lisette's expression as she sat beside Keely in the infirmary, her reaction in the Underdark when I told her that he was alive and knew that I was right. It wasn't my place to tell Keely about Lisette's feelings, but they were as clear to me as daylight. If I permitted him to leave then she would not forgive me, and I valued both Lisette and Keely too much to let that happen.

'Promise me that you will remain here,' I said, 'give palace life a chance.'

He gave a lopsided smile, shrugged and nodded. 'If that is your command, Milady. I'll do my best.'

'Good,' I sighed, 'and I expect you at the coronation tomorrow. It will mean a lot to me.'

He inclined his head and then rose to his feet, reaching out to grip onto a walking cane for balance. I watched as he left with the guard's assistance, thinking that my suggestion was indeed a strong possibility. In time, I was sure that he would recover in spirit as well and gain confidence. I refused to believe that, just because he had been blinded, he was no longer able to live a full life. Even if Keely didn't become a guard, I knew that he could assist with mediating issues with a calm and steady approach. I wouldn't allow him to run away, as I had done for so long. Following him, I allowed my feet to guide me towards the crypt where I knelt beside Grandfather.

The stones under my knees were slightly damp from the cold and I shivered, my breath forming around my face in a pale mist. I allowed myself to relax into my prayers, murmuring them so that the soft hum of my voice reverberated off the walls. Grandfather's body was exactly as it had been when I had last visited, although I could see that some items had been placed beside him, trinkets and flowers mainly. It seemed that the Elves had begun to pay their respects to him, so I would need to arrange his funeral soon. The prospect of him being well and truly gone made the ache in my chest intensify and the tears fall again. I longed to delay giving the instruction to organise the event, knowing that once I did it heralded a new time, one which my grandfather would not be part of.

'Watch over me, Grandfather,' I whispered, 'guide me to do what's right, and give me strength for the coronation tomorrow.' With that I rose to my feet and departed, wiping my cheeks on the edge of my trailing sleeve so that no one outside of the crypt would see that I had been crying.

I retired to my rooms, finding the seamstresses and Lisette waiting for me to have one final fitting before the ceremony the next day. By the time they had finished the alterations and ensured that each layer of fabric was draped just right, I was exhausted. When the seamstresses closed the door, I let out a moan and collapsed on the chaise, and Lisette rolled her eyes.

'I'm not being dramatic, Lisette,' I groaned, 'I'm tired. In the past two weeks, I have come back from the dead, killed the Usurper and a mad Resistance leader, been poisoned and had my throat cut. Oh, and I'm still not allowed to see either Aidyn or Markus in the infirmary. I don't know if they're alright or…' The thought was too much to bear, so I just said, 'I think I'm allowed to want some peace and quiet after being poked and prodded with needles and choked in that corset.'

Lisette raised her eyebrows as though I were overstepping my bounds, and bustled next door to prepare my bath. I closed my eyes and lay back against the cushions, wondering how many people would attend the coronation the next day. The last thing I wanted was to fall over in my long skirts in front of a large crowd and make a fool of myself. Particularly— my face scrunched up at the thought— the Velkranian queen and her painted court. I couldn't imagine her ever stepping wrong at such an event or doing anything to disrupt her coiffure. Whereas I...

The sound of Lisette returning made me open my eyes and blink away the thoughts. I didn't mean to compare myself with Queen Wonkila, Gods, I didn't want to. She was everything that I was determined not to be– insipid, petty and self-absorbed. But she was beautiful and knew how to carry herself like a royal. It still felt as though I were pretending when I acted thus, and a small, self-deprecating part of me recognised that it probably always would.

Chapter Twenty-Three

The day of my coronation dawned bright and clear, the whirling snow that had fallen the past days taking a brief respite, as though the Winter Spirit was watching and ensuring that the day would pass without incident. The weather was only one challenge overcome, however. The dress was another one altogether.

'Just hold still, Your Majesty,' one of the seamstresses grunted as she yanked on the bindings of my corset. 'Breathe in for me now.'

If I had had any breath left, I would have told her that I didn't see the need for such a contraption. Lisette seemed to read my thoughts and shot me a warning look, letting me know that today of all days was not the time to argue.

There was another sharp tug and then the corset was tied, effectively stopping any possibility of me breathing properly until it was undone. Next thing I knew the other layers were attached one by one, so that by the end I was draped in a multilayered gown, trimmed with lace and glinting with jewels sewn into the bodice and skirts. Lisette took to my hair with speedy efficiency, until it was twisted and coiled up high, pinned with matching gemstones. An ornate necklace of gold and rubies was placed around my neck, its weight making me pause for a moment as I got used to it. Lisette waved the seamstresses away and they left, allowing her to clip earbobs onto my ears and layer my hands with rings and bracelets.

There was a knock on the door and Lisette opened it to reveal Erik, who was dressed in his own finery. I was pleased to see that it also looked like he had bathed. His hair was neat and clean, his face showing no sign of the ordeal he had been through on the highest tower.

'It's time, Nina,' he said, his tone serious. 'Elder Haycin told me to let you know that everyone is ready, and the High Priest is waiting.'

'Thank you, Erik,' I replied, suddenly nervous. The long-ago sensation of wanting to flee was there for a moment and then faded as I took a deep, calming breath. A year ago, I would have followed that instinct and run away. Now though, I couldn't afford to follow such desires. Not anymore.

Lisette paused in front of me and lifted a hand to my cheek, her eyes glowing with pride. I understood what she meant and inclined my head. 'Thank you, Lisette. For everything.' Her eyes filled with tears, which she brushed away as I turned to Erik, 'would you mind if I took your arm, Erik? Just for a while.'

He nodded and I accepted his offered elbow, linking my hand through it as we made our way down the corridor. Lisette followed us, holding my train.

'It's hard to believe that today has arrived,' I said quietly, our footsteps echoing off the stone walls. 'If you had told me a year ago that I would be here, walking these halls again, I would have been certain that you were mad.'

'I could say the same thing,' Erik replied. 'If you hadn't come to Mister MacMillan's Inn then I would probably still be there. In my craziest dreams I never thought that I would end up somewhere like this, that I would have seen the places I have. Who knew that you would turn out to be the long-lost princess when you came into that kitchen.'

His eyes were shadowed with memories and I recalled the moment, opening the door and seeing a scrawny waif in the filth. Who would have guessed that he would become as dear to me as my own flesh and blood?

'I guess it was a surprise to find that out,' I smiled, and he shot me a grin. 'And now we're here,' I murmured as I paused in the hallway, the doors to the throne room up ahead. I gripped his arm tightly, the nerves resurfacing as the doors beckoned me, the low murmuring of many people coming from the other side.

'You'll be alright, Nina.' Erik said gently.

'I think I'm going to faint,' I whispered, going pale.

'It's okay,' he reinforced. 'This is what you've been waiting for all your life, remember?'

I forced myself to nod, because right then all I wanted to do was remain frozen to the spot, unable to progress another step.

'Your people need you, Nina,' Erik pressed. 'Come on, it's time.'

I allowed him to lead me to the doors, and it felt as though the corridor had stretched so that each step felt like a lifetime. When we reached them, Erik untangled my hand from his arm and gave me a quick smile, before ducking inside, slipping through the doors before they fully opened.

There was a hush on the other side, and I felt Lisette behind me, making some final adjustments to the fall of my skirts and train. A fanfare of trumpets began to play and I saw the doors swing wide, revealing what must have been close to a hundred people waiting.

Breathe, in and out, take slow, deep breaths. I heard Grandfather's voice in my head, calming me. With his words in my mind, I began the long walk towards the Ice Throne and the High Priest, who stood waiting in front of it. I kept my eyes fixed ahead of me, but in my peripheral vision I saw many of my friends, guards and visitors. I also noted that most of the Scardian nobility were present, decked out in their best finery. There were two faces however which I did not see, and I shoved the momentary rush of disappointment away as I approached the High Priest. When I reached him, I knelt to the ground and bowed my head, listening as he began to intone the roles and responsibilities for a ruler of the Ice Flame.

His voice was deep and booming, rebounding off the walls and travelling through the open windows to the grounds below. My knees were numb by the time he had called on the Gods to bless my ascension to the Ice Throne. I made sure to answer when he called on me to speak, vowing to protect Scardia and her people, to watch over their interests and to bring lasting peace. I sensed his movement and then felt him lower the crown onto my head.

'May all who stand here bear witness,' he declared, 'today the Heir to the Ice Flame– Wilhelmina Constantina Fiordlasher– has made the solemn vow to guide Scardia and its people into a new age. She kneels before you, a humble supplicant to the Gods for their favour, and may she now rise as your Queen.'

I lifted myself up, balancing the crown on my head, and took from the High Priest the sceptre and orb of Hoarfrost. I took it, and the orb glowed with a fiery light which filled the room as the Ice Flame burned high above the throne, smouldering embers no more. Distantly, I was aware of the trumpets playing, cheering from those in the throne room and voices coming from below in the Capital. I turned carefully and then sat on the throne, making sure to give Queen

Wonkila and her court an inclination of the head before I sought out those dearest to me.

Dylan, Erik and Jesse were side by side, cheering with wide smiles, while Lisette and Keely stood to the side, each with an arm around the other. Elder Haycin and his guards saluted me, along with the Dark Elves in their masks. And then my eyes fell on the two whom I had thought were not there, standing just inside the doorway. I smiled, relieved that they were alive and safe; my eyes fixed on one and I felt the familiar rush that I associated with magic. I saw his expression falter for a moment and then soften as he met my gaze, and it was as though no one else was there.

I remained seated on the Ice Throne for several minutes before handing the orb and sceptre back to the High Priest, who placed them on a pair of cushions, proffered by two pages.

'Your Majesty,' Elder Haycin said, 'come. Your people await.' He led the way through the crowd towards a wide balcony which overlooked the city. As I passed those in the throne room, the men bowed reverently, the women dropped down into low curtsies and the guards opened the doors onto the balcony, where I stepped outside.

The air was frigid, and the untouched snow crunched underfoot as I halted at the banister. Below I saw hundreds more people, stretching out through the palace gardens and down the streets into the Capital. As I emerged from the throne room, a loud cry rose up and any fears that I may have harboured about being rejected by the public faded away. I smiled and waved to them, seeing banners and flags wave back as the people began to celebrate, their voices raised in unison as they cried, 'Long live Queen Wilhelmina! Blessed be the Chosen of the Ice Flame!'

I remained on the balcony for a while, responding to the cheering masses until the cold became too much. While my dress was beautiful, it did not provide protection from the elements and my feet had already gone numb. I lifted my skirts and turned to go inside where the courtiers and visitors were congregated, yet Elder Haycin was no longer in the doorway to escort me. Instead, I took another proffered hand and re-entered the room, gazing at the man who waited for me.

'Your Majesty,' Aidyn bowed over my fingers, much as he had done when we first met, except this time I could read the expression in his eyes.

'My lord.' Gods my heart was pounding, I was sure that he would be able to tell. 'I didn't know if you would be here. I've not been given any updates from the healers on how you both were faring.'

'Neither the captain nor I would have missed this,' Aidyn said gravely. 'And do I detect a hint of worry in your tone, Majesty?'

'Not at all,' I replied, smiling as I wound my hand through his arm. 'You must be mistaken, my lord.' He dipped his head, biting back a smile of his own.

'My apologies then, are needed,' he said with false seriousness, 'for making such an assumption of you, Majesty.'

I condescended him with a nod and lifted my chin, allowing him to lead me through the throngs of courtiers who tried to attract my attention. As we passed them, the Dark Elves bowed, while the members of the aristocracy cut us off, forcing us to pause and for me to speak with them for a few moments. Queen Wonkila wormed her way over, eyes lingering on Aidyn as she curtsied to me, congratulating me in a condescending tone on maintaining my poise throughout the ceremony. It took a supreme effort not to give her the cut direct, but I reminded myself that I couldn't allow my temper to interfere with diplomacy. When she raised her gaze to Aidyn and smiled coquettishly however, I couldn't help myself from tightening my grip on his arm, anchoring him to my side. She didn't notice the movement, although Aidyn was aware, casting me a sideways glance that did little to ease my discontent.

'I'm afraid we really must continue on,' I finally said through a forced smile. 'Perhaps we might talk more later, during the banquet.'

Queen Wonkila inclined her head, 'but of course, my dear. You must greet your subjects as Queen. It's very important to make a good impression on the right people, especially considering all that has happened since you came of age.'

Her words dripped honey, although there was a coolness in her eyes as she looked from me to Aidyn, and I began to wonder if she had in fact noticed my reaction. I nodded to her and was then stopped by Lord Tyfe, who requested leave to speak with me about his estate once the celebrations were over. Before I could say more than a few words, another noble was calling for my attention and then another. Through the masses, I could just make out my friends leaving the room, heads bent together in discussion. I felt a momentary pang that I couldn't join them, until I saw Lisette waiting for me inside the doorway. Keely had departed with Erik, Dylan and Jesse, while Markus had disappeared. Where did he go?

'Are you ready to leave, Majesty?' A dry voice asked, and I glanced at Aidyn, realising that he had noticed my lack of attention and perhaps guessed where my thoughts had travelled to.

'That would be most welcome,' I said gratefully. He made surprisingly quick progress through the court, not caring about pushing some of the more enthusiastic nobles aside as they tried to stop me.

'I understand that there is to be a banquet and dancing,' he said thoughtfully. 'My kin said that the kitchens had been busy since before dawn to prepare it.'

'It seems extravagant,' I muttered as we exited the throne room, Lisette following behind us. 'We could easily feed half of the Capital with that food. I can't help but feel like it's a waste.'

'There will be time to make changes,' he said quietly, and I was surprised that he had heard me. 'But the people want this celebration, it is said that there are to be parties across Scardia tonight to commemorate your coronation.'

'Winter is never kind in Scardia,' I replied, 'many of those who are celebrating will be using up large portions of their winter stocks. How will they last the next few months?'

'You will find a solution,' Aidyn said firmly. 'For tonight, Majesty, you have to enjoy yourself.'

I was struck at his words, pondering why it hurt that he had said 'you' instead of 'we'. Could it be that he wanted to accompany Queen Wonkila to Velkra? Was he no longer thinking of staying here at my side?

'I hope, though,' he continued, oblivious to the direction of my thoughts, 'that you will grant me a dance this evening.'

'Only one?' The question escaped me before I could stop it and I felt my cheeks redden as he looked at me. 'I mean, of course. I am sure that it will be most pleasant.'

Deep down I cringed, and I sensed Lisette wince behind me. Thankfully, Aidyn didn't reply, but I was sure that he was offended. His face became shuttered again and he didn't speak the rest of the way to my rooms. Once there he bowed and left, giving me the opportunity to groan and slump on the bed, the crown tumbling off my coiffure onto the sheets.

Lisette shut the door and pulled me up with a surprisingly strong grip. She gave me a pitying look and then lifted the crown carefully onto the dressing table. I was relieved when she began to strip the coronation dress off me, replacing it with another, which thankfully did not require the corset to be strung so tight. The new dress was a square cut in sapphire blue velvet, decorated with silver thread. I removed the jewellery and laid it beside the crown, while Lisette tweaked my hair, replacing the jewelled pins with silver ones. On my forehead she placed a twisted diadem, encrusted with diamonds and sapphires. When she lifted the necklace for me to wear, my heart skipped a beat, memories returning in a flood.

I remembered the last time I had worn this necklace, feeling the heavy, cool weight of the strings of diamonds against my skin. I remembered my mother's calm voice, cajoling me into removing it, explaining how I would wear it at my first ball. It seemed that she had been right, I would indeed wear her diamond necklace at my first Scardian ball.

Lisette, oblivious to my melancholy, lifted the necklace up and around my neck, fastening it securely. She stepped back, content with her handiwork and I took a breath, steadying myself.

'I guess we should head downstairs to the banquet, Lisette,' I said finally. 'Stay with me?' She nodded and gave my hand a reassuring squeeze. 'I wish Grandfather could be here,' I sighed as we left my chambers.

Lisette caught my eye and gave a small smile, her expression answering my unspoken questions. Yes, she seemed to say, he would be proud of you today.

When we entered the dining hall, the banquet was just beginning. The tables were heavily laden with food and goblets of wine, courtiers clustered around them, laughing and talking as they drank. At my table I saw Erik, Aidyn, Elder Haycin and, to my dismay, Queen Wonkila waiting for me. As we entered the room, Lisette slid away to join Keely and Dylan at their table, leaving me to make my way alone. Voices hushed and the court rose to its feet as I passed, hoping that they couldn't see my shaking hands. When I reached my seat, Erik pulled it out for me and I sank down gratefully.

'Raise your glasses to our Queen,' Elder Haycin boomed, startling me so that I almost jumped out of my seat. 'To Queen Wilhelmina Constantina Fiordlasher. May she live a long, bountiful life and guide Scardia with an open heart and steady hand.'

'To the Queen!' The court intoned, goblets raised in unison.

'To Nina,' Erik said from beside me, winking at me.

'To the Queen,' Aidyn repeated, his gaze watching me steadily. All of a sudden I couldn't breathe, I lifted my own glass to my lips, sipping the wine but tasting nothing.

The next courses seemed to drag, my plate was filled again and again, even though I was not very hungry. Aidyn and I did not speak, yet we spoke to others, leaving an awkward silence between us. I wanted to break it but lost my nerve each time, unable to think of something to say that would distract him from Queen Wonkila on his other side. I was all too aware of his proximity to me, his movements and the soft chuckle of his laughter at something Queen Wonkila said.

Every time I felt my hackles rise, and I had to control my breathing so as to not lose control and set something ablaze. Instead, I drank more wine and tried to swallow my food. It was supposed to be a happy occasion, so why did I just want to cry?

While we ate, a band of musicians played in the gallery above us, and I tried to focus on the music to avoid hearing the murmured conversation to my left. Finally, the food was cleared away and the strains of the first dance began to play. The court turned to face me, waiting for me to give the order for the dancing to start. I smiled and waved my hand, gesturing for the couples to join the floor.

My smile froze though when I heard Queen Wonkila say, 'may I have this dance, Lord Aidyn?'

Something spasmed in my chest but I forced myself to stare straight ahead, the smile plastered across my face as they stood and moved out onto the floor. They started to waltz and a small part of me observed that they looked good together, moving with ease around the floor. That thought only made me want to cry even more.

'Nina?' Erik asked, frowning, 'are you alright?'

'Perfectly.' I replied, 'shall we?' I didn't wait for him to argue but stood and gripped his hand, pulling him out onto the floor and beginning to waltz.

Erik winced as he stepped on my foot, 'sorry.'

'It's fine.' I looked at him, desperately trying to avoid following Queen Wonkila and Aidyn with my eyes. Gods, what was wrong with me?

'I don't think I'll ever get this dance,' Erik mumbled.

'It'll get easier,' I said gently, 'I promise. Besides,' I twirled out and back, 'you've improved a lot since the first time we danced together. I can't think of someone else who I'd rather have partnered with me through my first dance as Queen.'

In truth, I could, but I wouldn't admit it. The hurt was still too raw.

'You're not as good a liar as you think you are,' Erik said honestly, and I felt myself blush. He grinned and I rolled my eyes, biting back a smile of my own. I didn't speak again until the dance finished, and I curtsied.

'Thank you, Erik.' He bowed and then was tapped on the shoulder by Jesse, who was wearing a veil to cover her features.

'Dance with me, Erik?' She asked gaily, and then catching my eye, she whispered, 'I'm trying to remain incognito.' I raised my eyebrows, hoping for her sake that the Velkranian man she was trying to avoid wouldn't see her.

'Nina?'

I turned and looked up into Markus' eyes. He had been hovering in one of the alcoves on the fringes of the room, and now he was offering me a hand to lead me through the next dance. I wavered for a moment, and then remembered that Aidyn was still dancing with Queen Wonkila, and accepted. Markus led me onto the floor and we began to step through the measure. I wondered if he was remembering the other time we had danced, in the galley of his ship all those moons ago, back when I had been Karliah and he was a ship's captain, back before both of our true identities were revealed and everything changed.

'I suppose congratulations are in order,' Markus said, 'for your coronation. You must be happy.'

'Thank you,' I replied awkwardly. 'I was glad to see you there, I was worried after that night on the tower. You were badly hurt.'

'The Elves used their magic to heal me,' Markus said stiffly. 'But I will keep a scar. Much like Aidyn.' He jerked his head in Aidyn's direction, and I followed it, glimpsing Queen Wonkila let out a peal of laughter. 'I need to apologise to you, Nina.' Markus continued, 'I believed that Rakael was right. That if Scardia was ruled by the people then you and I could be together. She made it sound possible, I was wrong to trust her. I'm sorry.'

I nodded, not trusting myself to speak, realising that he had more to say.

'Even today, I hoped that you would turn it down,' Markus said softly. 'That you would reject the crown and come back. But I realise now what you've been trying to tell me since you got your memories back. You belong here, you are needed here.' His tone turned bleak. 'This palace, the Capital, they are a part of you, this land is your home.' I nodded. 'It's not mine, Nina. It hasn't been for a long, long time. I need to return to the place where I can be who I want to be, where I belong.'

'You're going back to the sea?' I phrased it as a question, but deep down knew that he had made his decision.

'Yes.' He led me off the floor, not caring that the dance was not yet finished, and we stopped by the alcove where he had been before. 'I will leave tomorrow, on the morning tide.'

'Where will you go?' I asked.

'Anywhere,' he replied, mouth lifting in a faraway smile.

'I will miss you,' I said softly, 'and I'm sorry too for the hurt and pain I have caused. For what it's worth, if things had been different, if I had really been a farm girl when we met, I would have stayed forever.'

'I wouldn't have let you go,' he said simply, lifting my hand to his lips as he pressed a kiss to my knuckles.

'If you ever return to Scardia, I'll be in need of an admiral.' I smiled, half joking, half serious. 'I hope you find happiness, Markus.'

'Thank you, Nina,' he said, 'I won't forget that. Goodbye.'

With that he bowed, turned and left, and deep down I knew that it would probably be the last time I saw him. I turned away in the alcove, facing the wall, biting back the tears that rose treacherously to my eyes. The last thing I needed was to be seen crying at my coronation ball.

'Majesty?'

I scrubbed my cheeks with my palm and glanced around to see Aidyn who was, thankfully, alone.

'Are you alright?' He asked, watching me shrewdly. I took a deep breath and exhaled.

'No.' I froze, shocked that I had spoken honestly and instantly regretted it. 'Excuse me.'

I moved past him, cutting around the edges of the dancers and exited the hall, heading outside to the gardens. I needed to be away from people, somewhere quiet where I could regain control of my emotions. Sparks were starting to flicker up from my palms and I gripped them together, trying to force the magic to stop.

The night was dark, with stars glistening across the sky, reminiscent of the glow worms by the Lake of Tears. I tried not to remember the times spent in the grotto behind the waterfall there, and sped on, stamping through the snow as I made my way to my destination.

The fountain was frozen solid, the stone encased in ice, and I leaned against it, ignoring the cold and damp seeping into my skirts. Alone, I let my tears fall silently, lifting my face towards the heavens and squeezing my eyes shut. The silence was mine for a moment, and then it was broken by a muffled curse and heavy footsteps.

'By Erthor, what do you think you're doing out here?' Aidyn's voice was exasperated, and I opened my eyes, anger rising as quickly as the sparks to my fingertips.

'I wanted some peace and quiet.' I snapped, 'I wanted to be *alone.*'

'I don't believe you,' he retorted. 'It looks more to me as though you are actively pushing people away again.'

'You're one to talk,' I cried, bitterness and jealousy almost choking me. 'Can you blame me when you've been cosying up to Queen Wonkila all night?'

'While you have been dancing with your lover?'

'Former lover.' I corrected sharply. 'And besides, he's leaving tomorrow. I probably won't see him again.'

'So that is why you're crying.' His tone was accusatory now and I glared at him.

'Not entirely,' I retaliated.

'Then why?' He pressed, stepping closer, hands on hips.

'If you have to ask then you really are obtuse,' I scowled, crossing my arms and turning away. A part of me felt like a petulant child, but by now I was so angry and hurt that I didn't care.

'Fine.' He snapped, and then he reached out and pulled me up into his arms.

I cried out and struggled, 'what do you think you're doing?'

His mouth tightened. 'Claiming my dance.'

I was speechless for a moment, and he used my silence to his advantage, turning me around and around in the darkness, our feet moving in unison. I followed his lead automatically, unable to look away from his eyes. The moon shone down on us, bathing us in Erthor's light as we danced, gradually increasing our pace, twisting and turning back and forth, hands touching and releasing only to meet again. No matter how fast we moved, we were never apart for long and soon my heart was pounding, not just with exertion, but also desire.

'Can you hear it?' Aidyn murmured, 'the music?'

When I focussed, I could. It drifted through the garden from the open palace doors and up from the streets of the Capital. Yet I didn't feel like we needed music, save for the beating rhythm of our hearts.

Eventually we returned to where we had started, by the fountain, foreheads pressed together, breathing deeply. I didn't want the moment to end, to return to the party and act as though nothing was wrong.

Aidyn made to pull away, but I gripped him tighter. 'Don't.' He looked at me, confused. 'Don't go,' I whispered, 'please.'

'If that is what you wish,' he said and I shook my head, struggling to verbalise my thoughts coherently.

'No,' I said, 'I don't want you to stay because *I* want you to. I want you to stay because *you* want to.'

'Nina…'

'Are you going to join Queen Wonkila in Velkra?' I spoke so quietly that I thought for a moment that he hadn't heard me, yet he tensed and stood unmoving. 'Are you going to leave?' I asked, suddenly terrified to look into his eyes and so, coward that I was, I stared down at our feet in the snow.

'I was under the impression that you had entertained the idea,' he replied, the low timbre of his voice making me shiver. 'The Velkranian queen is persistent.' With gentle pressure, he lifted my chin so that I was meeting his gaze. 'I need you to be honest with me, Nina. One moment you say you want me here, the next you don't care if I leave. I am not a saint, my patience has its limits. I can't stay in this strange limbo that we seem to have fallen into.'

'The thought of you leaving with Queen Wonkila...' I swallowed, my throat suddenly dry. 'I can't bear it.' His face was shrouded in the night, and I began to wonder if he was manipulating the darkness to remain hidden, so that I couldn't read his expression. 'I don't want you to leave me.' My pulse was racing now, nerves vibrating with the things I wanted to say but was scared to speak aloud.

'Why?'

He was determined for me to admit to my feelings it seemed– like he had.

'I love you.' The words were soft, yet in the stillness of the night they were clearly audible. The gardens around us hushed, the music dimming as though the world was waiting for Aidyn's reply.

'I rather hoped you did,' he said, as his arms came around me and pulled me close. Before I could retort, his lips were on mine, kissing me insistently, and I allowed myself to be swept up in the moment. In his arms I felt secure, and I clung to him, determined to not run the risk of losing him again. When we broke apart, the darkness that had been shrouding his features was gone and I could distinguish his smile in the moonlight. 'I have loved you for a long time, Princess.'

'I'm not a princess anymore,' I chided, the anxiety that I had felt melting away into giddy exhilaration. 'I happen to be a queen.'

'My apologies, Majesty,' he said with teasing chagrin, 'I won't make the mistake again.'

'You'd better not,' I smiled, raising my hand to trace his cheek. 'I've been known to possess an unruly temper.'

'I'll have to watch my step,' he said, 'or just find other ways to distract you.'

I opened my mouth to reply and then he kissed me again, effectively cutting off any rejoinder I might have made. When we broke apart this time, he said, 'now tell me, Majesty, was that *pleasant* enough for you?'

I laughed and he joined me. 'Indeed, my lord, it was.' I leaned into his embrace and his arms tightened around me, warming me all the way through. When he stepped back, I glanced up, surprised as he then knelt in the snow.

'I thought that I should probably try this again,' he said, 'seeing as the first time, you were under slight duress.' I watched him, surprise mounting as he reached into his pocket and withdrew something small that sparkled in the moonlight. 'Wilhelmina Constantina Fiordlasher, will you marry me?'

Happy tears filled my eyes and I nodded, half laughing, half crying. 'Yes, yes, I will.' I watched as he pushed the silver ring onto my left hand, and I gazed at it admiringly.

'It used to be a Dark Elf tradition to give a symbol of Erthor to their chosen partner,' Aidyn said, 'I thought it might be time to reinstate that tradition.'

'I love it,' I whispered, the moonstone on the band glowing with ethereal light. I was reminded of the Underdark and the grotto by the Lake of Tears. The silver band was twisted like vines, and I remembered the High Elven court amongst the treetops near Lowton. He had combined the two realms into one and it was perfect.

'I hoped that you would,' he murmured, and then he kissed me again, this time however we couldn't halt our hands from exploring each other, teasing and caressing as our lips met again and again. My blood became heated and I wanted more, pressing closer and gasping as he began to kiss my neck at the point beneath my ear. I moaned, trembling, desperate for him to continue, but then became aware of distant voices coming from the palace.

The sounds intruded on our privacy and we broke apart, both breathless, both caught up in the same mad yearning. When we regained our composure he said, 'should we return to the ballroom?'

Honestly, I wanted to remain where we were and kiss him again, but the cold air of the night was starting to finally hit me and so I nodded. As we walked back inside, I remained anchored to his side, hands clasped, neither wanting to relinquish the other.

Our return to the ballroom was noticed by some, but it seemed that the majority of the court had been so caught up in their wine and merriment that they hadn't registered our departure. I saw Erik and Elder Haycin share a conspiratorial smile as we entered together, while Queen Wonkila put her wine goblet down abruptly, eyes flashing with annoyance.

'Dance with me, dear heart?'

'Always,' I replied, warmth spreading through me as he led me onto the floor and we joined in the waltz, twirling along with the other couples. As that dance flowed into another, I held his gaze, allowing the feelings in my heart to shine through my eyes and be reciprocated in his. The world around us disappeared and all that mattered was the man in front of me. I smiled, knowing that, with him by my side, our children would know all the love and affection that we had both missed, all their lives.

Epilogue

The wedding had been all I could have wanted and more. The gown was inlaid with pearls with a train almost as long as the one I had had for the coronation, one month before. I held a bouquet of snowdrops, the climate too cold for the white orchids that Aidyn had once given me. I made the slow walk down the aisle of the Temple, focussing only on he who waited for me at the end, and the High Priest behind him.

Aidyn didn't show any sign of nerves but smiled, his face lighting up as I drew nearer. He had smiled a lot more of late and I liked it, relishing the few moments we were able to spend together. As soon as our betrothal was reaffirmed publicly, there had been a million things to organise and prepare, leaving Aidyn and I little time to ourselves. Within a few hours though, we would have as much time as we wanted together. I was sure that he was anticipating it as much as I did, as those rare times we had been given a few moments of privacy over the past month had only increased our desire for each other.

There had been a period of mourning though, we had held funerals for those dear to us who had fallen in the battle, the Elves standing sentinel as Grandfather and Alex were finally laid to rest. Aidyn had asked that Alex's ashes be returned to the Underdark and scattered there, and his brothers would see that task through after our wedding. Yet during those moments of grief we had been there for each other, and I was able to glimpse how our future could be.

I halted in front of him, and we held hands. The High Priest tied them together, his words fading into the background as I held Aidyn's gaze. I managed to speak the correct words and repeat the statements when prompted, vowing to love, honour and protect the man before me. Aidyn responded in kind, promising to work in partnership through good times and bad.

'The Gods have assessed both of your hearts and found you worthy,' the High Priest declared, 'may your vows to each other be witnessed by them and all of those present today. From now on, you will face each day as partners in marriage, may you both remember the solemnity of the vows you have spoken today, and your love burn as constant as the Ice Flame. You may now exchange a symbol of your devotion and promise to protect each other.' He looked over at Lisette who approached with two rings, each wrought in silver, in a similar design to the ring Aidyn had given me. I then turned to Elder Haycin, who handed me a newly crafted sword, with a decorated blade and an ornate handle. Carefully, I placed the ring over the pommel of the sword and handed it to Aidyn. He accepted it and in return withdrew the sheathed sword at his side. This one was older, battle-worn, and made of obsidian, glinting black in the candlelight. On its handle he placed my ring and offered it to me, and I took it, removing the ring and placing it on my finger.

As the High Priest finished speaking, the watching crowd began to cheer, and Aidyn bridged the distance between us and kissed me. I felt the familiar rush of heat and saw the answering fire in his eyes as we broke apart. We turned together to face the crowd and began to make our way out of the temple, to the waiting sled which would carry us through the snow, which was now lying in heavy drifts all over the Capital. As we passed, the Dark and High Elves drew their swords to form a guard of honour, although I noted that Erik had worked his way into their numbers, a proud grin on his face. He winked at me and then gave Aidyn a respectful nod. For a moment I wondered when his attitude towards Aidyn had changed, but then realised that I was just glad that it had.

It took a while to pile my long skirts into the sled, but eventually we were able to depart, waving at those who had followed us out. Snow was falling in thick flurries, and I reached down to grasp the heavy furs that had been placed in the sled to keep us warm.

'We're finally alone,' Aidyn said quietly.

'It won't take too long to reach the palace,' I replied, wrapping one of the furs around his shoulders. As I leaned in, his arms reached up and held me firm against him, so that we were cocooned together, inches apart. I looked at him, snowflakes catching in my lashes.

'Then we should take advantage of every moment we have.' His eyes glinted and then he was kissing me in the way that ignited the blood and banished reason. It was the kind of kiss that demanded more, that hinted at what was to come and left me breathless. Despite the falling snow, we found a way to keep the cold at bay, and by the time we reached the palace I could barely think straight, let alone string a few words together. Aidyn however seemed very pleased with himself and chuckled at my reaction, one hand gripping mine as we entered the palace for the wedding feast.

I preferred the celebrations for my wedding significantly more than those for my coronation. Primarily because the Velkranian court had long departed, but also since this time everyone was celebrating. I saw Lisette and Keely off to the side of the festivities, arms around each other and swaying to the music. Jesse moved from partner to partner, her laugh loud and expression vibrant and carefree now that her former lover had left. I danced with Erik and Dylan, even with Elder Haycin and Aidyn's brothers. Yet primarily, I danced with my husband, smiling into his lilac eyes and feeling a sense of rightness in the world.

That was before my head turned and I inhaled a faint scent of spices, a warm breeze brushing against my cheek. I glanced up and saw at the far end of the room a man in robes of gold and crimson, his dark eyes sparkling with amusement. As our eyes met he smiled, and I heard his voice echo in my mind.

Are you content, my chosen? Did you think that I would stop watching over you? Your wish has come full circle, it seems, and you have found the freedom you sought. I will see you again, Wilhelmina Fiordlasher, for my chosen still has a role to play in my plans.

In an instant he was gone, as though he had never been there, and I was left to ponder his words, shivering slightly at their implication. I didn't want to see the Lord of Summer again, I didn't understand his reasoning or games, but perhaps the next time we met I would be better prepared. I only hoped that I wouldn't end up like his previous chosen human champion.

'Nina?' Aidyn had noticed my distraction, and I shook my head.

'It's nothing, don't worry.'

'It's time.' I nodded my understanding, my nerves thrumming with anticipation. He held out a hand and I took it as we made our departure, our guests waving us off. We headed towards my rooms, neither speaking another word to the other but our hands clasped tightly, refusing to let go.

A servant had left out a decanter of honey mead and two goblets for us to share, and Aidyn poured it out smoothly. I watched the firelight play across his features and wondered if he was as nervous as I suddenly felt. The last time I had been intimate with someone I had been caught up in the moment; there hadn't been months of waiting and teasing, being offered glimpses of what would happen but never actually making love.

'Here, dear heart,' Aidyn said, handing me one of the goblets. I accepted it silently and we clinked them together before we drank, the sweet mead giving me liquid courage to say,

'I'm nervous.'

He regarded me levelly, absorbing what I said and then he reached out and took my hand in his, suddenly concerned. 'Nina, if you want to wait longer, we don't have to do anything tonight.' He looked deeply into my eyes and added, 'I can wait, if that is what you want. I don't want you to do anything you're not ready for.'

My eyes widened and I knew that he meant it. He wouldn't try to force himself on me, to seek pleasure elsewhere or try to pressure me. That made all the difference.

I shook my head, 'I'm not saying that. I just…I want everything to be perfect and I'm worried that I'll do something wrong.'

He laughed and pulled me into his arms, ignoring the mead that splashed over his tunic at the spontaneous momentum. 'By the Gods, that doesn't matter to me, Nina. We have all the time in the world to work out how to make things perfect. I just want to be with you.'

I smiled and rested my head against his shoulder, 'that's a relief.' He led me over to the chaise and we sat down by the fire, taking more sips of mead. With a wave of my left hand, I urged the flames higher, so that the room was filled with a rosy warmth. As my hand was lifted, my engagement band flashed with fiery light and I peered closer, noting how the colours within the moonstone seemed to shift and twist.

'It looks like the Ice Flame,' I murmured, 'when the light catches it just right.'

'That was one of the reasons why I chose that particular stone,' Aidyn said quietly. 'I thought it encapsulated all three realms in one– the two closest to your heart and the one I was raised in.'

'The Underdark isn't close to your heart?' I queried, still gazing at the ring.

'It wasn't the kindest place to be raised,' Aidyn said wryly. 'The best times were when I was outside or secluded by the Lake of Tears.'

'You don't want to return there, then?'

He was silent for a while, pondering the question. 'Perhaps one day,' he finally said, 'but I have no real desire to go back. I'm not sure who will be in power now, whether the sects will work together or fall into disarray again. Our union has just ensured that the Dark Elves will not attack the Scardians or High Elves. Amongst themselves though…'

'We don't have to go back if you do not wish it,' I interrupted gently. 'I just thought that you might.'

'All those I care about are dead, those living I can see in the scrying bowl.' His voice turned sorrowful and I squeezed his hand.

'I'm sorry about Alex.'

He bowed his head and took a shaky breath. 'They would be happy to know that we succeeded in the end. They wanted the best for us, they trusted that everything would work out.'

He fell silent, and I reached out to touch his arm comfortingly, resting my head on his shoulder. After a few minutes, Aidyn recovered himself and then placed his goblet down, before reaching down and taking mine away.

'Aidyn?' I followed his lead, his touch insistent as I was pulled up and led towards the bed. Without a word, his lips met mine and I surrendered, melting against him as he held me tight. I barely registered his hands start to move, to begin unbuttoning my gown. When we broke apart, my cheeks were flushed and I was breathless, watching with fascination as he began to remove his own clothing. The scar across his chest was still new, a permanent reminder of that night on the tallest tower. Yet, even with that, in my eyes he was everything I wanted.

I untied my shoes and stepped out of my gown, still partly shy as he moved behind me to undo my corset. My hair fell down my back, cloaking my nakedness as the clothing fell away, and I was struck with an unwillingness to turn around. As if he could sense my thoughts, Aidyn began to kiss across the back of my shoulders and neck, each touch sending a shard of heat through me. I gasped, sinking back against him, and his arms came around me again, anchoring me.

'I love you,' he whispered in my ear, and I looked back, catching his gaze.

'And I love you,' I replied softly. His mouth crinkled in a smile and I knew that everything was going to be alright.

That first night we shared as husband and wife was so much more than I could have expected. Together we explored each other with hands and lips, laughing away any awkwardness and finding new ways to experience pleasure. This time there was no pain, only a slight pressure, and then mounting tension before blissful release. I didn't care about staying quiet this time, but cried out as the intensity grew stronger. Afterwards we lay, spent, in each other's arms, the bedsheets somehow twisted at the bottom of the bed.

'You know,' I sighed as he pulled the blankets back up over us and I settled down to rest against his side, 'I think if you can manage to do this every night, then I will thoroughly enjoy being married to you.'

He chuckled, 'I think we have a lot of time to catch up on. I still haven't quite forgiven you for letting me believe that you wanted me to become part of the Velkranian court.'

I shuddered and rested my head on his shoulder, one arm across his chest pinning him to the bed. 'If I have anything to say about it, you will be staying right here.' I paused for a moment, contemplating his words, and then a sly smile stretched across my face. 'How exactly were you wanting me to make it up to you, husband dearest?'

There was a twinkle in his eyes as he replied, 'lots of ways, Majesty.'

My grin spread wider as I rolled over him. Who was to say that we had to wait? Besides, tomorrow we would begin our tour of Scardia, as the Winter Spirit had recommended. It might be a while before we would have such privacy again.

'Tell me.'

'As you wish, my Queen.'

In answer, I leaned down and pressed my lips to his, feeling safe in the knowledge that, no matter what troubles would threaten us, we would face and overcome them together.

The End

Acknowledgements

'Fire on the Ice' would not have been possible without the support and advice from so many people. First of all, I would like to thank Ian, Natalie and Brittany, along with the team at the Book Reality Experience for their help with cover designs, editing and the publication process. I am so grateful to have their support and expertise assisting me with my novels.

Secondly, to my husband, Jordan, for being there to breakdown ideas and provide feedback, not to mention making the endless cups of tea I need to have in order to write. I am incredibly lucky that you support me in my creative endeavours and am thankful to have you at my side.

For my family and extended family, thank you for understanding when I leave events early, do not answer messages or have a tendency to lose focus on conversations when in a writing flow. Unfortunately, that will never stop – it's one of the joys of being a writer.

Finally, to the readers who have followed Nina's journey from the beginning. Without you, this ending would not have been half as much fun to write, because if not for your requests for the final instalment in the trilogy, it may have taken twice as long to arrive. I am already working on returning to Scardia, for there are many tales still to tell, so that everyone can achieve their heart's desire.

About the Author

A booklover from an early age, Rose began writing stories from the age of seven and this passion continued into a life-long dream of becoming a writer.

When she is not reading a new book, jotting down ideas in a notebook or pottering around in her veggie garden under her cats' supervision, she can be found either on the stage in her other passion – amateur theatre – or teaching English and French to high school students.